PRAISE FOR TH[illegible] OF JO GOODMAN

"One of the premier Western romance writers, Goodman delivers a solid plot with engaging characters. There's plenty of sexual tension, and from its rousing beginning to the powerful climax, there's enough adventure to satisfy fans."

—*RT Book Reviews*

"This first-rate tale easily measures up to its predecessors and will make readers eager for their next visit to Bitter Springs."

—*Publishers Weekly* (starred review)

"A tender, engaging romance and a dash of risk in a totally compelling read . . . Gritty, realistic, and laced with humor."

—*Library Journal* (starred review)

"Jo Goodman is a master storyteller and one of the reasons I love historical romance so much."

—The Romance Dish

"Fans of Western romance will be thrilled with this delightful addition to Goodman's strong list."

—*Booklist*

"A wonderfully intense romance . . . A captivating read."

—Romance Junkies

"An exciting American romance starring two likable protagonists and an overall wonderful cast."

—Genre Go Round Reviews

"Exquisitely written. Rich in detail, the characters are passionately drawn . . . An excellent read."

—*The Oakland Press*

"For the pure joy of reading a romance, this book comes close to being some kind of perfection."

—Dear Author

Berkley Sensation titles by Jo Goodman

KISSING COMFORT
THE LAST RENEGADE
TRUE TO THE LAW
IN WANT OF A WIFE
THIS GUN FOR HIRE
THE DEVIL YOU KNOW

The Devil You Know

JO GOODMAN

BERKLEY SENSATION, NEW YORK

An imprint of Penguin Random House LLC
375 Hudson Street, New York, New York 10014

THE DEVIL YOU KNOW

A Berkley Sensation Book / published by arrangement with the author

ISBN: 978-0-425-27744-7

PUBLISHING HISTORY
Berkley Sensation mass-market edition / May 2016

PRINTED IN THE UNITED STATES OF AMERICA

10 9 8 7 6 5 4 3 2 1

Cover photo credit Claudio Marinesco.
Cover design by Rita Frangie.

For the Logan Road growing up gang.
You are the devils I know, especially you, Davy.

Prologue

Pancake Valley, Colorado
October 1891

"You reckon he's dead, John Henry?"

When Annalea Pancake received no reply to this inquiry, she did two things simultaneously: She poked at the inert body with a forked stick that she was certain would be her finest divining rod ever (if touching it to the pale gray flesh at the man's temple did not relieve it of its fantastical powers), and she looked over her shoulder at John Henry.

John Henry, for all that he was her boon companion, gave no sign that he was interested in her latest discovery. Indeed, he found the stick far worthier of contemplation, especially when she waved it in front of him as if she might finally throw it.

"You think this is for fetching, don't you?" Annalea lightly dragged the stick through the grass and watched John Henry follow the movement. His dark brown eyes shifted from one prong to the other as she wiggled the stick, but he did not pounce. He raised one eyebrow, which had the effect of wrinkling his entire forehead, and regarded her solemnly. Apparently there was no dignity in pouncing, and John Henry, with his short legs, improbably long ears, and doleful expression, had reason to embrace dignity where he could find it.

"I'm not tossing it, so put that out of your mind. Could be I'll find an underground spring. Wouldn't that be something?" She used the stick to point to the supine stranger. "Come here and have a look. C'mon. Better yet, have a sniff." To demonstrate, Annalea made a show of sniffing the air. She breathed in the familiar fresh scent of the tall grass, had a hint of cool, clean snow from the mountaintops, and caught the faint, sweet smell of pine sap that always lingered on the back of the wind.

The man, though, had no particular odor save for a certain earthiness, but then he looked to have been dragged a ways over the hard ground, through the grass, and probably through Potrock Run, judging by the condition of his clothes, torn, green-stained, *and* wet.

He was not wearing a coat, which was neither here nor there, except for the fact that cold weather had been settling in Pancake Valley and this man was not dressed for it, even when he had been in one piece. In fact, his clothes, once fine enough for a Saturday night dance in Old Man McKenney's barn or even a Sunday service if it was Christmas or Easter, were now tattered in so many places that it was easier to see what he *wasn't* wearing. Small bits of gravel dust were embedded in his black woolen jacket. The sleeve was torn and the seam at the shoulder was split so she could glimpse a deep gray vest embroidered with silver threads. One of his legs was cocked sideways, not broken, she didn't think, but wrenched at an unfortunate angle that was going to trouble him if he came to his senses. His trousers were torn beyond any seamstress's ability to properly mend, and the knee she could see was scraped raw and dotted mostly with drying blood. The punishing trail that had been forced upon him had cost him a shoe. And the one he had left was by no account a shoe for a man working the land. This shoe, a black and short-heeled, low-cut boot, belonged to someone who made his living from town business. A merchant, she thought. Maybe a government man or a lawyer. Either of those occupations would go a long way to explain what happened.

Annalea was not encouraged that during her assessment and contemplation, the man never stirred.

"I don't suppose you're of a temperament to help me turn him over," she said to John Henry. The hound kept his distance. Annalea sighed. "That's what I thought. You are a disappointment to your kind." She pitched the divining rod and shook her head when John Henry barked his approval and hurried after it. "Surely a disappointment," she said under her breath.

Annalea dropped to her knees from her hunkered position and placed one hand on the unconscious fellow's shoulder and the other at his hip. She steeled herself, counted down from three, and gave him a mighty push. For all the effort she put into it, she only managed to move him sideways a few inches, not turn him over. She studied the problem, tried to think what her sister would do (because Willa said there were no problems, only situations), and came to the conclusion that this situation could be managed with a bit of leverage and momentum.

"Bring that stick back here, John Henry!" The words were no sooner out than she felt the dog nuzzling her skirt. "Oh. So you have."

After a short, playful skirmish, Annalea had the stick in her possession. She shoved the forked end under the man's belly and started to rise. Her intention was to rock him back and forth with her foot and use the stick to lever him up and over, and in principle, it should have worked, *would* have worked, if the man had only continued to lie there, but it seemed he objected to being gutted by a divining rod with prongs nearly as sharp as the very devil's horns.

With a mighty groan, he pulled out the stick, tossed it sideways, and flopped hard onto his back.

John Henry followed the arc of the stick and trotted off.

Annalea fell on her backside, legs splayed in front, arms braced slightly behind. She stared openmouthed for a full five count before she said, "Well, I figure this means you ain't dead."

The man not only did not open his eyes, but slowly raised one forearm to cover them. For a long time, he merely sipped the air, and Annalea supposed the act of drawing a breath pained him. It surprised her when he spoke.

"I might be dead," he said. "It feels like I might be dead."

"Probably feels like you *want* to be dead. You're in a bad way, mister."

He said nothing.

"What happened?" asked Annalea. When he remained silent, she drew her legs together, folded them tailor fashion, and then leaned forward and rested her elbows on her knees. She stared at the man's profile, wished he would remove his forearm so she could judge the shape of his face better, and said, "It'd be proper for you to tell me on account of you needing help and me needing to decide if I'm going to fetch it. Can't really help you on my own now, can I? Too scrawny. Ain't grown into my proper size yet, Willa says. And you can't count on John Henry to fetch anything save a stick."

As if on cue, John Henry arrived to drop the stick in Annalea's lap. She picked it up, poked the man in the ribs with it, and although he grunted softly, he made no move to snatch it from her. Shrugging, she sent it flying.

"Most people reckon me to be a good girl. Leastways them that don't know I once stepped over my pa when he was passed out drunk and blocking the doorway instead of helping Willa get him into bed. I mention this because you should know that it can go either way, depending on you. I like to think I'm predisposed to helping a stranger. The Good Samaritan comes to mind, you see, and that's a powerful story in favor of offering you suckle. On the other—"

"Succor," he said.

"How's that?"

"Succor, not suckle."

"Mister, there's a bigger calf to rope here. As I was saying, judging by the rope burns on your wrists and the marked trail your sorry self left across this hillside, I am concluding you were dragged to Kingdom Come and then left for carrion. That's the kind of evidence that makes me wonder if you are a bad man, and maybe you deserved what you got. You have to admit it appears that someone thought you deserved it. After I hear from you, I'll make up my own mind."

Following this speech, Annalea clamped her mouth closed and waited. Now that he knew what she was capable of, she thought she might be rewarded. She was, at least partially. He raised his forearm a fraction, looked at her askance, groaned softly, and then covered his eyes again.

"How *old* are you?"

"Ten. Nearly ten. That is to say that in eight days I will be ten. I am to have a new dress if Willa finishes it by then.

Willa's my sister. It is supposed to be a surprise, but I spied her sewing late one evening, and the fabric was the very one I pointed out as a favorite of mine at the mercantile. I didn't mean to catch her out. I wasn't trying. I was thirsty is all, and when I got up to get a glass of water, I saw her, and I went right back to bed so she wouldn't know. It no longer mattered that I was thirsty." She drew a deep breath and let it out slowly. She frowned, puzzled. "I don't really see that my age accounts for anything."

"I wondered if I might be in expectation of you expiring anytime soon," he said dryly. "Apparently not."

Now it was she who remained silent, this time to good effect.

"I am a bad man," he said. "A villain, if you must know. Unworthy of your concern or your assistance. There. Go away."

Annalea did not move but regarded him more curiously than before. "What sort of villain? Thief? Murderer? Defiler of womenfolk?"

"Jesus," he said softly.

"Ah, blasphemer." Quickly, before he could ask where she came by every other notion, she added, "I read. All sorts of things, if you must know."

"Seems like you should stop."

She ignored the suggestion. "Well?"

"Well what?"

"You have not yet informed me as to the precise nature of your villainy."

"Ah. That." He gingerly lowered his forearm and opened his eyes enough to squint at a patchwork of bright blue sky and thick cloud castles. Twin creases appeared between his dark eyebrows as the corners of his mouth slowly turned down. "I don't know," he said finally. "But as you said, there is evidence to suggest someone thought I deserved this treatment, so you should proceed cautiously. Better to believe I am a bad man because that seems the most likely truth."

"Do you really not know, or are you perhaps trying to protect me from learning of your heinous crime?"

His frown deepened and he turned his head a few degrees in her direction. "I really don't know."

Annalea watched with interest as he tentatively flexed his hands. His thumbs and fingers all worked, but when he dug the heels of his hands into the ground and tried to push upright, it seemed that something as hot and jagged as a lightning strike shot through his left arm and shoulder. A spasm stiffened the muscles in his neck, and he strained to catch his breath.

"Maybe you don't remember me telling you that you're in a bad way, mister. The way your left shoulder's all droopy, I'd say something's out of joint. Hard to tell for sure until we get you out of your jacket, but I figure that shoulder's the least of what's ailing you. You're a bloody mess, but I don't think you've been shot. You'd know if you'd been shot, wouldn't you?"

Annalea fell quiet while he took inventory. She fingered one of the long, cocoa-colored braids that had fallen over her shoulder and raised the feathered tip to brush it back and forth under her jaw.

"If you live, you're going to need some new clothes. God's truth, though, if you die, we'd be a sorry lot to let you meet your maker in what you got on. Either way, you're going to get a new suit out of this."

"That's a comfort."

She smiled and nodded guilelessly, as if she had no comprehension of the sarcasm in his tone.

"You gotta name, mister? Or you forgot that, too, along with the heinous nature of your crime?"

He turned away, stared directly at the sky, and made no attempt to shield his eyes from the sun glancing off distant, snow-covered peaks. After several long moments, he said, "It'll come to me."

While Annalea was considering that, John Henry sidled up to the stranger and sniffed. "*Now* you do what I asked," she said, shaking her head as the hound kept his nose to the ground and walked the perimeter of the wounded man. "I already figured him for alive so you sniffing around is of no account. Go find a rabbit."

Annalea was still trying to sort out what to do. This was not a situation, no matter what Willa said about such things. This was a problem. Could be that helping this man would bring down trouble on their heads. Could be that letting him die was a sin so grievous that she would never atone for it. It did not ease her conscience that the villain was not asking for her help. His stoic acceptance of his circumstances struck her as rather noble, and that spoke to a more virtuous nature than a criminal one.

She was not one for sitting on a fence and found the position uncomfortable in the extreme. At some point she knew her indecision would become intolerable, and she would have to choose with no sense of whether she was being reckless or wise.

It did not come to that, however, because John Henry did a surprising thing after he stopped sniffing and lowered himself beside the stranger's awkwardly angled shoulder. Without giving the slightest indication of what he meant to do, John Henry tipped his head toward the man's roughly abraded cheek and licked.

As a sign, it was good enough for Annalea. Satisfied that John Henry had knowledge of truths that she could not yet fully appreciate, she trusted his judgment. Willa might see it differently, but telling Willa would relieve Annalea of her burden.

"John Henry likes you, so I am going to be a Good Samaritan and do what I can for you." She uncrossed her legs, rose to her knees, and unfastened her woolen coat. He made a weak protest, which she ignored, and placed the coat across his chest. She raised the collar so it protected his neck and the lower half of his face from the cold and gently tucked it in around his shoulders and upper arms. "You probably should try to stay awake. I don't know why exactly, but Willa always says that when a ranch hand takes a spill and knocks himself senseless. If Willa says it, it's probably important. She doesn't much waste her breath."

"Unlike you."

Annalea grinned toothily, revealing a space where the cusp of an incisor was starting to push through. "I take after Pa."

The stranger had nothing to say to that.

Annalea looked him over, wondering what else she could do for him before she made her way back home. "It's two miles or so that I have to cover to reach the house, and there's no telling if Willa will be there, but I'll do my best to hurry and find her. John Henry will stay with you." She pointed a finger at John Henry and gave him a stern look and a sterner order. He flattened himself beside the stranger and offered up his most sorrowful expression. "Pitiful dog," she whispered, bending to knuckle him between his ears.

She was struck by an urge to knuckle the crown of the man's head in the same manner, but he tucked his chin more deeply under her coat and she knew she had given herself away. It was just as well. He might be pitiful, too, but even a bad man had his pride.

Chapter One

Pancake Valley was seventy-five square miles of prime grazing land, fit for raising beef cattle for the Chicago stockyards and smart, surefooted horses for cutting herds, mountain tracking, or outfitting an Army troop. The lay of the land bore no resemblance to any sort of pancake, flapjack, or johnnycake, nor was it properly a valley. But upon claiming the land in 1839, Obadiah Pancake declared its peculiar saddle shape to be a valley and so it was known from that day forward.

Wilhelmina Pancake had known her Grandpa Obie, remembered quite clearly sitting on his lap in the rocker he brought all the way from Philadelphia because he promised Granny that he would. She remembered that Granny complained, mostly good-naturedly, that excepting for the years she was nursing her sons, Obie and Willa got more use out of that rocker than she ever did.

Grandpa Obie was gone almost a score of years now, having taken a spill from a fiercely bucking mare that he was trying to break. Instead, the mare broke him, snapping his neck like a frozen twig. Willa had known he was gone before she reached him, and she had wanted to put the mare down, but Granny had stopped her, taking the gun out of her hands and holding her so tightly that Willa thought she might suffocate in that musky bosom. She hadn't, though, and was glad for those moments because it was only a few years later that Granny passed.

Some days Willa missed that bosom, missed the comfort of it the way she missed her grandpa's lap. From time to time, she sat in the rocker, but it wasn't the same, and unless Annalea crawled into her lap—and really, Annalea was getting too big to be an easy fit—Willa found sitting there to be a bittersweet experience that was best avoided.

Willa lifted her face to the halcyon sky, tipping back her pearl gray Stetson, and let sunlight wash over her. She remained in that posture, one gloved hand resting on the top rail of the corral and the other keeping her hat in place, and waited for sunlight and the cool, gentle breeze to press color into her cheeks and sweep away the melancholy.

"Use your knees!" she called to Cutter Hamill as she pulled herself up to stand on the bottom rail. "Get your hand up! She's going to throw you!" No sooner had the words left her mouth than the cinnamon mare with the white star on her nose—named Miss Dolly for no reason except that Annalea declared it should be so—changed tactics and crow-hopped hard and high, unseating her rider and forcing him to take a graceless, humiliating fall.

Miss Dolly settled, shaking off the lingering presence of her rider even though she could see his face was planted in the dirt. She nudged him once with her nose as if to prove there were no hard feelings, and then she walked toward Willa, her temperament once again serene.

Willa threw one leg over the top rail, and then the other. She sat perfectly balanced, her boot heels hooked on the middle rail, and braced herself for Miss Dolly's approach and inevitable nuzzling.

"You all right, Cutter?" she asked as she held the mare's head steady and stroked her nose. "This little lady has no use for you climbing on her back."

Cutter lifted himself enough to swivel his head in Willa's direction. "She's no lady, no matter what Annalea says." He laid his cheek flat to the dirt again. "Anyone else see me fall?"

Willa looked around. Except for animals of the four-legged kind, the area was deserted. "Happy's inside the house, making dinner if you can take him at his word, and Zach must be in the barn, leastways I don't see him out and about. Seems like I'm the only witness, and you know I don't carry tales."

"I don't know that," he said. "I don't know that at all."

She chuckled. "Go on. Get up and shake if off." Willa

could not repress a sympathetic smile as Cutter groaned softly and pushed to his knees. He rolled his shoulders to test the waters, and upon discovering he was still connected bone to bone, scrambled to his feet.

Unfolding to his full height, he shook himself out with the unconscious ease and energy of a wet, playful pup. At nineteen, Cutter still had a lot of pup in him, though Willa knew he thought of himself as full grown into manhood. She had suspected for a time that he favored her in a moony, romantic sort of way in spite of the fact she was five years his senior and his boss, at least in practice, and she was careful to treat him as fairly as she did the other hand and not encourage any nonsense.

Annalea, though, did encourage nonsense, and took every opportunity to make faces behind Cutter's back but with Willa in her open line of sight. Annalea would pucker her lips and make a parody of kissing. She also liked to hug herself and pretend to engage in what she imagined to be a passionate embrace. In the first instance, she looked like a fish trying to capture a wriggling worm; in the second, she looked like the wriggling worm. Thus far, Cutter had not caught her out, but odds were that he would eventually, so Willa saved the scold that Annalea was certainly due and waited for the more enduring lesson of natural consequence.

Cutter removed his sweat-banded hat and ran one hand through a thatch of wheat-colored hair before he settled it on his head again. He grinned at Willa. "You want me to give it another try?" he asked.

"Give what another try? Getting thrown?"

He flushed but held his ground. "I thought I'd—"

"I know what you meant. Lead her around, let her walk off the jitters, and then take her to the barn and wipe her down. And talk to her while you're doing it. You don't talk to the animals nearly enough, Cutter. Miss Dolly will respond to your voice if you sweeten it a bit."

Cutter regarded her skeptically but kept his questions to himself. He dusted off his pants and shirt and dutifully started walking toward Miss Dolly.

Willa chuckled under her breath when the mare sidled

just outside of Cutter's reach as he approached. "Sweet talk, Cutter," she called to him.

"Is that what you want, girl? Sweet talk?"

At the sound of the smooth, tenor tones of her father's voice at her back, Willa shifted so sharply on the fence rail that she nearly unseated herself. "I thought you were making supper."

"I *am* making supper. Just stirred the pot. No harm leaving it alone for a minute. I saw Cutter take a fall and thought maybe I should check on the boy myself."

"He's fine, Happy."

Simultaneous to Willa's pronouncement, Cutter yelled over. "I'm fine, Happy."

Willa returned her attention to Cutter but spoke to her father. "See? You have it twice over. Better go check on that pot because it won't stir itself."

Happy shrugged, and except to reach for a flask inside his scarred leather vest, he didn't move. "Feeling a chill," he said by way of explanation, although Willa had given no indication she knew he had his flask in his hand. "So what about that sweet talk? You lookin' for some of that from Mr. Cutter Hamill?"

Willa pretended she hadn't heard him.

He'd been christened Shadrach Ebenezer Pancake at birth, but family lore had it that he carried on with so much chortling gusto that it was only right and natural that he should be called Happy. Since he had answered to the name all of his life, most folks did not know he had another, which suited Shadrach Ebenezer just fine when he was a youngster, and later, when he was a husband and then a father. But now that he was a widower, barely a father, and usually a drunk, he wore the name like a hair shirt, and that, too, suited him in a dark, humorless fashion.

Happy sipped from the flask, capped it, and returned it to his vest. He folded his arms and set them on the top rail a short distance from where Willa sat.

"You should have a hat on," said Willa without glancing down. "Wind's picking up."

He nodded. "Going back in directly." Still, he didn't move.

Willa sighed. "You already burned supper, didn't you?"

"I might've scorched the biscuits."

"Stew?"

"I expect most of it will be good if we don't draw the ladle from the bottom of the pot."

Willa said nothing.

Happy grimaced in response to her silence. "I swear no one speaks as loudly as you do when you hold your tongue. Wouldn't hurt at all for you to let it out. Might even feel good uncorking that bottle of mad dog temper once in a while."

"I doubt it," she said, and her words were carried away on the wind. She called to Cutter before he disappeared into the barn. "Take your time. Supper's going to be—"

She stopped as a movement a hundred yards distant caught her eye. She tipped her hat forward to shade the winking sunlight and squinted at the tree line as a figure burst into the opening and continued racing toward them. "Now what is she up to? And where is John Henry?"

Happy scratched his head. "Damned if I know."

"I wasn't talking to you."

"Well, there's no one else around, is there?" Happy was forced to move when Willa swung her legs back over the fence and jumped down. He was perhaps all of two inches taller than his daughter, and when they were eye to eye, she looked right through him. He shivered. "I swear that cold shoulder you like to give me is a damn sight frostier than any wind coming off the mountains. I got ice splinters prickling my skin."

"Another reason you should have worn a hat."

"Maybe so. But I got this." He patted his vest to indicate his flask.

Without comment, Willa turned smartly on her heels and started off toward Annalea. Cutter, she noted, had also observed Annalea coming at them at a flat-out run, and she motioned to him to secure Miss Dolly and follow her. Her father stayed where he was, which to Willa's way of thinking was a point in his favor.

In spite of Willa's head start, Cutter's long legs carried him farther and faster, and he reached Annalea a few strides before she did. Willa wondered if he regretted it when

Annalea launched herself at him. He staggered backward but managed to stay upright, sweeping Annalea into his arms before she caused his second spill of the day.

"Whoa! Whoa there, Annalea." Cutter set her down, unwound her arms from around his neck, and looked her over. Her cheeks were deeply flushed, and she was breathing hard. Her pigtails had mostly come undone. She inhaled loose, flyaway strands of dark hair and her fingers scrabbled at them to keep them out of her mouth. He simply shook his head. "Ain't no one called you for supper that I recollect, so what's chasing you?"

Willa caught up to the pair in time to hear Cutter's question. "Answer him," she said, her eyes focused once again on the tree line.

"She can't talk yet," said Cutter. "Near as I can tell, she's not hurt, but she's run a ways."

Willa gave her full attention to Annalea when she observed no disturbance in trees. Nothing was chasing Annalea except perhaps her own imagination. "Is he right? You're unhurt? Just nod your head."

Annalea sucked in a deep breath and nodded hard so there could be no mistaking the matter.

"Where's John Henry?"

Annalea pointed behind her.

"So he's following you?"

"No," Annalea said on a thread of sound. "Told him to stay."

One of Willa's expressive, arching eyebrows lifted a fraction. John Henry was devoted to Annalea. That the dog would stay anywhere without her was extraordinary, if it were true. "And he listened to you? That seems . . ." She paused, looking Annalea over again. "Where's your coat?"

"Left it with John Henry."

"That's no kind of answer."

"No kind of good answer," said Cutter.

Annalea shot him a withering look. "There's a man," she told Willa, using her thumb to point over her shoulder. "I found him a ways back close to Potrock Run, and I left John

Henry with him to stand guard. He's hurt, Willa. Bad hurt. The man, not John Henry. I figure we should help him, Good Samaritan–like. That'd be the Christian thing to do."

"Maybe," said Willa. "And maybe not."

Annalea nodded gravely. "I already entertained that argument, but you go on ahead and have it out with yourself."

Willa gave a small start, blinked once, and then surrendered in the face of Annalea's clear and righteous expectations. "Very well. Cutter, sounds as if we'll need a wagon." Out of the corner of her eye, she saw Annalea nod. "Go on. Take care of that while I find out what else we need." She put her arm around Annalea's shoulders and gently urged her in the direction of the house. "C'mon. You're shivering."

"He was worse cold than me. That's why I gave him my coat."

"Well, I suppose that was a kindness as long as you don't take ill. If that happens, I might say it was foolish."

Without breaking stride, Willa shrugged out of her jacket and tucked it around Annalea. "Could be I'm foolish as well." She bathed in the warmth of Annalea's radiant and knowing smile all the way back to the house.

Happy wanted to come along and see the trespasser for himself, but Willa told him plainly that was not going to happen. She left Zach in charge of making certain her father did not attempt to follow. Happy was just tipsy enough to trip over his own feet. On horseback, he was a sure danger to himself and the animal, and there was still the matter of supper. Zach, at least, could be counted on to put something on the table they could actually eat.

Cutter and Willa rode on the wooden bench seat with a shotgun resting between them while Annalea huddled under two woolen blankets in the bed of the wagon and offered directions and commentary as necessity or her mood dictated.

"I don't think there will be any call to shoot him," said Annalea. "He is not likely to give you a reason."

Willa patted the Colt strapped to her right leg. The last

thing she did before she left the house was put on her gun belt. Annalea had not commented at the time, but clearly she had been thinking about it ever since.

"We don't know anything about this man, and we don't know what to expect when we reach him. It's a certainty he didn't drag himself all over creation, so it could be that whoever did that to him is still around. Better to be prepared than not. Don't make me regret not tossing you out of the wagon and leaving you with Pa and Zach."

Willa looked back at Annalea, her eyebrows raised. "You understand?"

Turtle-like, Annalea poked her head outside the shell of her blankets. She nodded once. "I think the guns are an abundance of caution."

"Nothing wrong with that," said Cutter.

Annalea harrumphed too softly for Cutter to hear, but Willa caught it and quickly averted her head before Annalea saw her lips twitch.

Cutter pointed to a split in the pine trees up ahead. The parting made a natural fork in the trail. "Which way, Annalea? Right or left?"

Annalea mumbled under her blanket and Willa interpreted. "She says left."

Cutter gave the reins an expert tug and guided the mare to the left. Under his breath, he said, "You reckon he'll still be alive?"

Willa shrugged. How could she possibly answer? For Annalea's sake, she hoped he was, so she said that.

Annalea rose to her knees and inched toward the bench seat. She leaned forward, poked clear of the blankets, and inserted her head between Cutter and Willa. "Did I tell you he wanted me to leave him where he lay?"

"No," said Willa. "You did *not* tell us that."

"I figured he was talking out of his head so what he said he wanted was of no account." She nudged the shotgun a little to one side to make more room for her head. "John Henry licked his face. It was kinda sweet, him showing partiality like that, and I judged it to be a good sign."

Willa smiled wryly. "Of course you did."

Annalea suddenly thrust an arm between the pair to motion toward the bend up ahead. "Just around there. Look, you can see the grass is trampled coming off the hillside. He was dragged that way. Probably over that patch of rocks, too, and then across Potrock because he's on this side of it. Someone sure had it in for him."

"More like some*ones*," said Cutter, following the trail that emerged from the trees and took a meandering route toward the run.

Willa nodded. She was more interested in where the trail began than in where it ended. She looked as deeply as she could into the cluster of limber and lodgepole pines. The thick, scaly trunks made it difficult to see what might be hiding behind them, and the canopy of boughs cast a shadow across the area that the lowering sun could not penetrate. The surest way to learn if someone was watching with the intention to harm was to find Annalea's stranger and tend to him.

"There!" said Annalea, waving her hand up and down. "I see John Henry! Over there." She stopped waving and grabbed Cutter by the elbow to guide him as he was guiding the horse. "Do you see him?"

Cutter did. "You stay down in the back, Miss Annalea. Under the blankets would be better than out of them."

Annalea made a face with every intention that he should see it.

Willa clamped her hand over Annalea's head and firmly pushed her down. "Do what Cutter says. We will let you know when you can get out of the wagon." Willa noted that Annalea complied, albeit with little grace. And as compliance was all she cared about at the moment, she said nothing.

Cutter had not brought the wagon to a full stop before Willa hopped down. She left the shotgun with him and walked straightaway for the circle of trampled grass, opening her jacket and resting her hand lightly on the butt of her Colt. It was only when she reached John Henry and the stranger that her hand fell away.

It was clear at first glance that the man posed no threat. What required further investigation was whether or not he was breathing. Willa snapped her fingers to move John

Henry out of the way, but he remained steadfastly obedient to the orders of his mistress and stayed nestled in the crook of the man's arm.

"Call your dog!"

Willa winced as Annalea's shrill whistle split the air around her, but John Henry leaped to the extent that his short legs would permit and hurried off toward the wagon. Shaking her head, Willa hunkered beside the stranger and bent her ear toward his mouth.

"You must be the help."

Startled as much by the warmth of his breath on her cheek as she was by his speech, Willa jerked back and stared into a pair of plainly pained and singularly colored blue-gray eyes.

"Wilhelmina Pancake. Willa."

"Ah."

He closed his eyes, and Willa was tempted to check for breathing again. She motioned for Cutter instead. "Bring the bandages and blankets. We can tend to some of these wounds before we put him in the wagon." She began to lift Annalea's coat but paused when the man shivered mightily. "It's got to be done," she said. "Hurry up, Cutter." She handed off the coat and took the bandages and blankets when Cutter arrived.

Cutter tossed Annalea her coat and then bent to help Willa. He whistled softly. "It's like she said. He's in a bad way."

"He can hear you," Willa told him. "Dip a couple of bandages in the run and wring them out. I'll clean the scrapes. How do you feel about putting the shoulder back in place?"

"Squeamish."

Willa and Cutter stared at the stranger because the response had come from him, and even though his eyes remained closed, it was as if he knew they were regarding him with equal parts astonishment and wariness because he said in a voice as abraded as his flesh, "I have a say, don't I?"

Willa glanced at Cutter, who she saw was looking a bit squeamish now that the stranger had spoken, and said, "I'll figure it out."

Cutter nodded and was off to do her bidding before she changed her mind. The stranger said nothing.

"There's really no choice," said Willa. "Not if you hope

to have full use of your arm again. I can help you sit up if you can't do it on your own. I promise you the ride back to the house will be easier if I fix your shoulder now."

He made a small movement that might have been a shrug or a pathetic attempt to rise. Willa took it as the latter and slipped one arm under his back. He was not much in the way of help as she began to lift, and she could have used Cutter just then to lend some strength, but she heaved and he groaned with her effort and his own, and between them he came to a sitting position.

Willa could now see more evidence of his injuries. His jacket, vest, and shirt were shredded, and beads of dried blood, like so many black pearls, dotted the length of the abrasions. Under her examination, the lean muscles of his back jumped once and then were still. She tore her eyes away and said, "Tell me what happened."

"Do you need the distraction for what you're about to do or is it for my benefit?"

"Can't it be for both those things? Besides, you are going to do most of the work."

"I am?"

Willa nodded as she studied his legs. Annalea had said one of them was turned at an awkward angle, but that was not the case now. They were lying straight in front of him, the feet slightly turned out. "Start with what happened to your left shoe."

"I don't know where my shoe is."

"Which is not quite the same as telling me how you came to lose it."

He said nothing.

"Can you draw your knees toward your chest?" He grunted softly as he showed her that he could. "Wrap your arms around your knees. Palms over your kneecaps." Because his movements were slow and cautious, and she could hear the short, stuttered breaths he took, Willa thought Annalea was right about him having some cracked ribs. She lent him assistance, making sure his fingers were laced and the thumbs were up before she released him. "Grip tightly."

He frowned in anticipation of what was coming.

Willa looked up as Cutter returned. "Find a place to stand so Annalea can't see. I don't need eyes in the back of my head to know she's watching."

Cutter's eyes darted in the direction of the wagon. "That's a fact." He stepped sideways and blocked Annalea's view. "Does he have a name?"

"Imagine so. He hasn't offered it, and I haven't asked."

"She was more interested in what happened to my shoe."

Cutter's mouth twisted to one side in a look of perfect puzzlement. He scratched behind his ear. "Is that right, Willa?"

"It is."

"I guess you have your reasons."

"That's right." She saw that the stranger's grip had loosened, and she pressed his hands together. "In a moment I want you to lean back. Not far, not fast. I'll tell you when. Cutter, stay where you are. I'm going to move behind him to cushion him if his grip fails and he falls backward." Willa dropped to her knees and then into position. She laid her hands lightly on the stranger's shoulders. "All right. Lean back now."

The first movement was tentative, testing, and Willa put some strength into her fingers so he could feel the weight of them. "More," she said. "Lean back more. I've got you."

He did, this time with more confidence. His knuckles were bloodless, but the grip remained firm.

"You can shout," Cutter said.

Willa added, "Curse if you have a mind to."

"That's right," said Annalea, stepping out from behind Cutter. John Henry appeared from under her skirt and between her legs. "There's no ears here that haven't heard the like before, and that includes Mr. John Henry. As I recall, I heard you blaspheme on earlier acquaintance."

"Jesus," he said under his breath.

Annalea nodded sagely. "That's what I recall, too."

Willa looked sharply at Annalea. "I told you to stay in the wagon. Cutter, how did she get around you?"

He flushed but held his ground. "Sneaky as a sidewinder."

"I am," said Annalea, clearly proud.

"Then bring your sneaky self over here and hold his

knees." She tapped her patient on his uninjured shoulder when Annalea was in place. "You don't have to hug him that hard."

"Oh." Annalea offered the stranger a rueful smile. "Sorry."

Willa thought she heard him curse under his breath again, but it might have been intended as a prayer this time. "Keep leaning back," she told him. "That's it. Stretch. More. More."

There was an audible popping sound when the shoulder joint realigned. Willa, Annalea, and Cutter all blinked. The stranger groaned once and then was silent. A heartbeat later his laced fingers unwound, his hands dropped away from his knees, and he collapsed against Willa.

"I didn't expect him to faint," Willa said, carefully lowering him to the ground. "But maybe that's better all the way around. It will ease the ride back for him *and* us." She shooed John Henry out of the way as the dog came forward to sniff the stranger. "Annalea, put John Henry in the wagon and fetch me a cloth large enough to make a sling." She stretched out an arm toward Cutter. "The damp cloths, please."

While Willa tended to the stranger's cuts and scrapes, the rope burns around his wrists, Cutter walked off with the shotgun to explore the clearly marked trail made by dragging the man onto Pancake land. Annalea stayed with Willa, assisting now and again, but mostly she sat cross-legged at their patient's feet, still and contemplative.

Willa tied off the sling and critically eyed her work. She looked to Annalea to invite comment. When none was forthcoming, Willa made a small adjustment to the knot and padded it with a cloth she folded into quarters.

"You are uncharacteristically quiet," she said. When Annalea had no response to that, she added, "And apparently deep in thought."

"Hmm." Annalea's eyes did not stray from the stranger. She was leaning forward, chin cupped in her palms, her elbows resting on her knees. "Do you figure him for a criminal?"

"Hard to make a judgment there. Is that what you're trying to do?"

"Uh-huh. I am wondering about the nature of his activities. It's a sure thing you don't get dragged behind a horse and left for dead if somebody ain't pissed at you."

One of Willa's dark eyebrows kicked up. "Language."

"Sorry. If somebody *isn't* pissed at you."

Willa's lips twitched, but the raised eyebrow stayed in place a moment longer. "Have you considered that Happy might know him?"

Annalea's head lifted a fraction as she frowned deeply. "Why would Pa know him?"

"Because he spends considerably more time in Jupiter than any of the rest of us."

"Yes, but mostly he's in the Liberty Saloon or the jailhouse." Her frown faded, replaced by a lopsided grin as she comprehended her sister's point. "Oh. I see. Liberty or the jail."

"Happy could have made his acquaintance in either place," said Willa. "But if it happened, I'm inclined to think it was probably the jail."

"He and Pa might have shared a cell. Wouldn't that be something?"

Willa did not hear any condemnation in Annalea's tone. In fact, she seemed unreasonably intrigued by the notion. "I was not suggesting that they shared a cell. I was thinking of the posters hanging in the sheriff's office. Happy might have seen this man's likeness on one of those." Shrugging, Willa returned her regard to the man's countenance. Where the skin wasn't scraped, it was bruised, and where it wasn't colored red and purple, it was ash. Sometime during her ministrations, the left side of his face had begun to swell. If he tried to open his eyes, he would only be able to see out of one. That struck Willa as a damn shame, although not, she reflected, for the same reasons it would strike him. She was remembering the exceptional clarity and color of his blue-gray eyes. "Right now I am hard put to believe his mother would recognize him."

Annalea nodded in agreement. "He seems worse off than when I found him. I didn't think that was possible."

Willa started to explain how that had come to pass, but her attention was caught by Cutter's shout from two hundred yards up the hillside. "What's he saying?" she asked Annalea. "And what has he got in his hand?"

Annalea had already jumped to her feet. "It's the shoe. He found the shoe."

"Lot of fussing for a shoe, though I expect this fellow will be glad of it. Wave Cutter back here. We need to go."

Annalea cupped her hands around her mouth and shouted for Cutter.

"Not what I asked," Willa said dryly. "And here comes John Henry. I'm not sure the dog knows his name yet, but he does recognize that come-to-me cry of yours. Go on, Annalea. Walk him out to meet Cutter." After Annalea and the dog hurried off, Willa spread one of the blankets on the wagon bed and another beside her patient.

"What about your name? It's the least of what we need to know, but we have to call you something." She did not really expect a response, but she did not think she imagined a shift in his breathing. Could he hear her? She pressed on, regarding him more keenly. "On the other hand, Dr. Frankenstein's monster never had a name, and truth be told, you put me a little in mind of him."

Willa waited for a twitch and was rewarded when she glimpsed his long fingers curling the merest fraction. It was something at least, although if she were being strictly honest, she had hoped that it would be his mouth that twitched. Because all things considered, it was rather a nice mouth. Not particularly amused by the odd thought, Willa reined herself in as she gathered the soiled cloths and went down to the run's gently sloping bank to rinse them. She had just finished wringing them out when Cutter and Annalea returned, John Henry quite literally dogging their footsteps.

Willa slung the damp cloths around her neck and stood. She absently brushed herself off as she approached the trio. "Did you find anything besides that shoe?"

"Bits and pieces of clothing. Evidence that there were four horses, but I think only three other men. Best as I could figure out, he rode with them for a ways, probably from town, before things took a turn. Could've been planned from the outset, and they surprised him, or maybe he had his suspicions and no choice in the matter. Plenty of good hanging trees back there, and we know they had a rope, but I can't say if that was their intention and they had a change of mind."

Willa nodded. "Lots of ways to kill a man, but if his death is less important than his suffering . . ." Her voice drifted off.

"Yep."

Cutter's laconic response prompted Willa's rueful smile. "You think you can put that shoe on him without twisting the foot overmuch?"

"Sure." Cutter immediately bent to the task.

"We are going to move him onto the blanket and carry him to the wagon. We will have to lift him over the side."

"What can I do?" asked Annalea.

Willa did not have to think about it. "You have the naming of him. Choose carefully. It's his until he decides it isn't."

Annalea straightened her shoulders and nodded gravely. She crooked a finger at John Henry and he dutifully followed her back to the wagon. She set him on the bed and climbed in, and the pair of them sat beside the stranger for the whole of the journey back. John Henry occasionally sniffed the man's privates as if they might hold the secret to his identity while Annalea teased out his name in more conventional ways, testing them one by one on the tip of her tongue. By the time they reach the ranch, she had it.

"He is Augustus Horatio Roundbottom," she announced when the wagon stopped.

Cutter asked, "Are you certain?"

"I am. I reckon he won't cotton to being addressed with any variation of Augustus or the more formal Mr. Roundbottom, and we will have the truth out of him soon enough."

Willa's smile was perfectly serene. She nudged Cutter with her elbow and whispered, "That's my girl."

Chapter Two

Willa directed Annalea to get help, which she once again did by using her lungs, not her feet. Zach came on a loping run, while Happy followed much less steadily, and the newly named Mr. Roundbottom was taken to the bunkhouse to be tended, which involved stripping away his tattered clothes, assessing the extent of his injuries, and then giving him a thorough scouring.

"Is he going to live?" Annalea asked from her position in the open doorway. She stood on tiptoes and craned her neck to see over her sister's bent shoulder, and when that gave her no view, she ducked her head to try to peek between Willa's elbow and Cutter's hip. Cutter stepped sideways, closed the gap, and Annalea's exasperation was audible.

Willa's attention to her task never wavered. "What were you told, Annalea?"

The thread of impatience in Willa's voice was not something one could miss; therefore, Annalea was simply ignoring it. "I want to see," she said stubbornly. "I found him."

"That doesn't make him yours."

"I named him."

Happy set his shoulder against the bunkhouse's log wall and crossed his arms in front of him. He almost accomplished the stance casually, but at the last moment, he lost his equilibrium and more or less tipped sideways.

"Annalea," Willa said. "Escort your pa to the house."

"But—"

"Go on. And mind that if he stumbles, you don't go down with him. I've got my hands full."

Zach knuckled the underside of his salt-and-pepper chin

stubble and looked over at Happy. "How about we finish supper?" He cocked his head toward the door, where Annalea continued to hover. "She can set the table."

Willa smiled to herself, appreciative of Zach quietly stepping into the breach.

Zachary Englewood had been a young man, not much older than Cutter was now, when he came to work for the Pancakes. With his preternatural gift for knowing good horseflesh, he proved his worth to Obadiah early on. When the patriarch died, there was no question in anyone's mind that he would stay, even though times had turned hard with bad weather and plunging cattle prices. He was a good wrangler, a better than middlin' cook, and had a steady hand with the horses, but his real value to Willa had always been his ability to manage her father. He was not a peacekeeper or a confidant to either of them, but he had a way of knowing what needed to be done, and he did it.

Happy pursed his lips, moved them side to side as he thought. "I'm cogitating. Can't say that I care for the name 'Roundbottom.'"

Annalea gave him a narrow-eyed look, one that she had seen Willa use to great effect. "Then you tell us his true name."

"Can't say I know it, 'cause I don't."

"You sure?" Annalea's gaze remained fixed. "Willa says you might have made his acquaintance in the saloon or maybe saw a poster of him hanging in the jail. Did you?"

Happy slowly scratched the back of his head as if the answer could be uncovered there. "No," he said finally, lowering his hand. "Don't recollect that I've ever seen him, but you have to allow that he's not at his best."

Cutter spoke under his breath. "He's not the only one."

Happy frowned deeply, the totality of his expression aimed at Willa. "And, Miss Wilhelmina Pancake, you go on poisoning Annalea's mind against me with your talk about saloons and jail, and just see if you and I don't have words one day. Real words. You understand me?"

"All right," said Zach. "That's enough." Taking Happy by the arm, he tugged lightly and lent support when Happy listed heavily to one side. At the open door, Zach put a large hand around the back of Annalea's neck and turned her around to face the yard. He ignored her protesting whimper and John Henry's low growl and set them all on a course for the supper table.

"Close the door," Willa told Cutter. "I don't trust Annalea not to sneak back here. And then I need you to take down the lantern and hold it just here." She pointed to a spot above Mr. Roundbottom's right thigh.

Cutter did as instructed. After several long moments in which the only sounds were the stranger's labored breathing and the crackle of the fire in the woodstove, he said, "Sure got quiet."

Willa paused long enough to cut him a sharp look. For good measure, she added, "It *was*."

"Oh."

Cutter remained silent after that, and even later, when Willa straightened and studied the whole of her work, he did not offer a comment.

"You can put the lantern back," she said, stretching her shoulders. She slowly twisted at the waist until her spine cracked and the relief she felt made her sigh.

Cutter held out his hand. "Give me the tweezers." She did, and he returned them to the small box of rolled bandages and other sundries they had brought from the house. Mr. Roundbottom's extensive abrasions were liberally swabbed coppery red with Parson's Restorative, a medicinal tincture, which, according to the label, was efficacious on burns, blisters, cuts, scrapes, and punctures. It was Willa's opinion that there was enough alcohol in the bottle to tempt Happy when his stores were low, which was why she kept it hidden behind three books he never touched: Homer's *Odyssey*, *Pride and Prejudice*, and the *Holy Bible*.

"He's going to need a couple of blankets," she said. "And tonight, you and Zach will have to keep the fire up."

"That won't be a hardship," Cutter said. "Cold's setting in. Zach gets stiff with it."

Willa nodded. She'd noticed the same but never mentioned it. Zach might show off his swollen knuckles to get out of doing fine work, but that was on his terms. For Willa to bring it up in conjunction with his regular duties would have been humiliating for him.

"How about some blankets?" asked Willa. "And what are we going to do for clothes?"

Cutter pulled woolen blankets from two empty bunks and snapped them over Mr. Roundbottom. "I guess if you're thinking about clothes, that means you're thinking he's going to live."

"I don't know about that, but I know it doesn't set right if we have to plant him naked. I would also never hear the end of it from Annalea. Apparently she's already thought about it and says it wouldn't be Christian."

"I suppose she has a point, but it seems wasteful of a good suit."

Willa looked Cutter over, sizing him up. "Well, it wouldn't be your suit even if you had one. Best I can tell, what you and our guest have in common is height. He's filled it out while you have a ways to go. Happy's too short."

"And Zach," said Cutter, "is more suited to the Roundbottom name than this fellow."

Willa's lips twitched. "Best if you keep that to yourself."

"Don't I know it." He returned his attention to Mr. Roundbottom. "We've got a trunk in here with some clothes, all of it left behind because someone didn't think it was worth mending or because it didn't fit any longer. I suppose there might be something for him."

"Look through it after we eat. You're going into Jupiter tomorrow morning, and you can get whatever else he'll need there, but mostly you're going to find out what you can about him. No one needs to know he's here. You just need to listen to what folks are saying because it's a certainty someone is saying something."

"I reckon that's true."

Willa waved him off. "Go on to the house. Eat your supper. I want to sit with him awhile."

It was also true that she did not want to sit with Happy, but it was not the sort of thing she could say to Cutter, even if he was thinking it. She always felt a little cowardly when she purposely set about avoiding her father, especially when she did not give Annalea the same option, but right now cowardice seemed a better course than confrontation.

"You sure?" asked Cutter. "I don't mind sitting a spell." He placed a hand over his abdomen when his insides rumbled.

"Your stomach disagrees." She tilted her head toward the door. "Go. And shut the door on your way out."

As soon as Cutter was gone, Willa pulled up a stool and sat. "Perhaps a more appropriate name for you would be Mr. Possum. Would you prefer that to Augustus Horatio Roundbottom?" Her question was followed by a long silence, so long that Willa began to wonder if she was in the wrong, but as she reasoned that she was not all that often in the wrong, it seemed there was nothing to lose by holding out longer. So she did.

His sigh was short but clearly communicated his annoyance.

"You are not the only one annoyed here," Willa said. "And I have considerably more cause to feel that way."

"I don't doubt that you think so."

She ignored that. "I'm not sure that you were ever unconscious, at least not as long as you pretended to be, but I am reasonably sure that you won't give me a straight answer. I am going to assume that you heard that Cutter will be going to Jupiter tomorrow. I can't say what he will learn, but if your trouble started in or around there, he will hear about it. If you heard that, then you know about the clothes in the trunk, and you are probably thinking about getting dressed and getting on. I stayed behind to make sure you know that I am not prepared to allow you to leave. Pancake Valley is not a sanctuary, but I won't turn you over to the sheriff without knowing your story. I'd like to hear what you have to say if you're up to it. That's your way out. You can always say you're not."

He opened the only eye he could and stared at her. "Why do you care?"

Willa's brow creased as she frowned. "I don't care. I'm curious."

"Well, so am I. I think I'd like to hear what the good citizens of Jupiter are saying."

"That's it? You still want me to believe you don't remember any of the particulars that landed you here?"

"I remember particulars," he said. "Just not the ones you want to hear. What I recall happened after that girl and her dog found me."

"Annalea and John Henry."

He nodded, winced, but did not lift a hand to cradle his head. The blistering pain reminded him he was alive. "Your sister?"

"Depends if you're referring to Annalea or John Henry." Willa spied the faintest of dimples crease the right corner of his mouth. It faded quickly, but she knew she had not imagined it. That he could raise even the slightest smile in these circumstances was interesting, but she acknowledged the fleeting dimple intrigued her more. "What about your name, Mr. Roundbottom? Any recollection there?"

"Roundbottom. That was diabolical."

"Only if it works. Will it?"

"Israel McKenna."

"Middle name?"

"Court. My mother's maiden name."

Although he had answered without hesitation, Willa wondered if she could believe him.

"You don't know if you can trust my answer."

Willa supposed he only needed one good eye to read her doubt. "If it's your name, why keep it to yourself for so long? We asked you before."

"I didn't recall it before. I told the girl that I'd come to it directly."

"Annalea. Her name is Annalea."

"It doesn't matter if you believe me."

"I suppose not, not from your side of things. But from where I'm sitting, it matters to me that I *can* believe you. I could have left you lying by Potrock Run, where you would have been carrion in a day or so and picked clean a day or so after that, but instead I brought you to the valley, invited you into the midst of my family, and I would rather not regret what I've done. Tell me more."

Israel Court McKenna shifted under the blankets and

drew them up around his shoulders. His bare feet were exposed. He shivered.

Willa did not wait for him to ask for another blanket. She took one from Cutter's bed and tucked it around Mr. Roundbottom's feet. He was not Israel McKenna yet, not to her. She returned to the stool and said nothing. He knew what she wanted, and he had to know that she would sit there until she heard it from him.

He spoke carefully, as if every word required effort and pain was the consequence of saying any one of them. "Herring, Illinois. Outside Chicago. Father was—is—a minister. Mother is a minister's daughter and a minister's wife. Little brother is a saint. I am not."

Willa's eyebrows lifted. "That's all? Father is a minister and you are not a saint?"

"Believe it?"

She did. "As a matter of fact, I do, but I would like to hear more. The name of the first girl you asked to dance."

"Beatrice Winslow."

"Why is your brother a saint?"

"He does the right thing. Always."

"You?"

"Hardly ever."

She believed that, too. He had been trussed tight and dragged over hard ground. That probably was not something that happened to his brother. It was difficult to imagine that he did not bear some responsibility for what was done to him. "All right, Mr. McKenna, why were you in Jupiter?"

"I never said I was."

"But you were."

"I expect so."

Willa snorted. "Something else you'll remember directly?"

"Can't say."

"Convenient."

"Not really."

Suspicion made her eyes narrow. She regarded him darkly. "What do you do?"

"Do?"

"How do you make your living?"

A hand snaked out from under the blanket. There was a slight but observable tremor in his fingers as he plowed them through his hair.

The gesture drew Willa's gaze to silver threads at his temple. There were only a few, but his sifting fingers had exposed them, and the contrast was startling, slender filaments of light against the sooty blackness of his hair. She wondered how old he was but did not ask. She still needed an answer to her more important questions.

"We searched your pockets," she said. "You had no money."

"I believe I was fortunate to have pockets." When she continued to stare at him, he said, "You're wondering if I was broke or robbed."

"And?"

"I don't know."

Willa said nothing.

"Would you prefer one over the other?" he asked.

She shook her head. "Just thinking how it could have played out and which side of right you might have been on."

"More likely which side of wrong."

"I was giving you the benefit of the doubt." She stood suddenly, scooped up a clean, dry cloth from the basket, and headed for the door. "I won't be but a minute."

She did not caution him to remain where he was because she really didn't believe he could go anywhere. She left the door open in the event he called for her.

Willa made straight for the pump, where she soaked the cloth with fresh, icy cold water. She wrung most of the water out while she walked back to the bunkhouse and folded the cloth into quarters. When she reached the threshold, she was greeted by two things simultaneously: an empty bunk, and her uncooperative guest standing at the piss pot trying to manage the sheet hitched around his waist with one hand and his cock with the other. To aid in the endeavor, he had removed his sling.

Shaking her head, Willa stepped back out of the doorway and to the side, electing to give him privacy and some measure of dignity. She knew he could have used her help, but she could not imagine that he would accept it without an argument and be the worse off for it. She leaned against the rough log wall of the bunkhouse, closed her eyes, and allowed herself this brief respite. She could hear cattle lowing in the distance and the muffled snuffling of horses coming from the barn. Annalea's laughter drifted across the yard from inside the house, each staccato note of it bright and clear, and it was easy for Willa to imagine that John Henry was the source of her delight, as he often was at supper time.

A smile tugged at the corners of Willa's mouth. Annalea was certainly feeding John Henry under the table, and Happy, Cutter, and Zach were all pretending not to notice. Good manners were taking a pass tonight, but Willa was philosophical about it. It was not as if there wouldn't be future opportunities to practice them.

Willa roused herself from her reverie and pushed away from the wall. She had purposely not listened for sounds from inside the bunkhouse, so she had to step up to the threshold again to see if her patient had pissed or fallen. It was also quite possible that he had done both.

He was gingerly easing himself onto the bunk when she entered. The sheet was still hitched around him, although set precariously low on his hips and tangled around his legs. He looked up as she was coming toward him, but she couldn't say whether he was relieved or annoyed to see her.

"Here," she said, holding out the damp, cool cloth. "Put it over your eye and hold it there. She yanked on the blankets that were trapped under him and might have dislodged the sheet entirely if he had not had a firm grip on it. "Go on. You can lie down now."

He started to lean back slowly but couldn't manage the strain and simply collapsed instead.

Willa winced. "I should have put an arm under you."

He grunted softly but otherwise remained quiet.

Willa tapped the fist that was still only clutching the damp cloth, and when he unfolded his fingers, she took it from him and laid it over his swollen eye. When he closed the other one, Willa repositioned the sling on his arm and shoulder. She could actually see tension leaching out of him.

His head rested more heavily against the pillow as his chin came up. The muscles in his neck and shoulders relaxed. His breathing came steady and evenly, but she did not mistake this for a sign that he was sleeping or unconscious. She had the sense that he was withdrawing, insulating himself, and that notion both puzzled and intrigued her. She settled both blankets over him, tucking the lower one around his feet and the one on top around his arms.

The stove was in need of attention so Willa poked at the fire and added wood. She stayed close, warming her hands first and then her backside. When she turned around, she saw that he was watching her. He did not even try to pretend that he wasn't.

Willa stared back. "Well?"

"Wishing I had two good eyes."

Willa's right eyebrow rose in a perfect arch. "Is that so?"

"Mm."

"Have a care. I could easily give that black eye a twin."

"Oddly enough, I have no difficulty believing you."

"As it should be." Without a word regarding her intention, she rounded the bunk and retrieved the piss pot. She angled it into the lantern light and observed the quantity and color of the urine. "No blood," she told him, tucking the pot under her arm. "You're a lucky man."

When he did not comment, she glanced at him over her shoulder. He had placed his forearm across his eyes and was slowly, almost imperceptibly, shaking his head. "Having trouble believing me now, are you?"

"Just trouble believing," he said under his breath.

Chuckling, Willa carried the pot outside and emptied it. She fell in step beside Cutter on the way back. He was carrying a supper tray, and the acrid, smoky aroma of charred stew wafted up from the bowls. Her stomach rumbled, and she hoped it tasted at least a tad better than it smelled.

"How's Mr. Roundbottom?" asked Cutter.

"He says his name is McKenna." Willa stopped at the pump to wash up and then traded Cutter the pot for the tray. "Israel McKenna. I think he's telling the truth about that. If he remembers what happened out there today, he's not saying."

"If?"

"I'm not sure he knows. He says he doesn't. You'll have to be careful asking around tomorrow. There's no good reason to give him up yet. He's not going to hurt anyone here."

"Not today," said Cutter. "And maybe not tomorrow or the day after that, but you can't be sure it will always be that way."

"I'm aware."

Cutter merely nodded and stepped aside to allow Willa to enter the bunkhouse first. He followed, dropped the pot beside McKenna's bed, and toed it under the bunk. Willa was pushing the round table he and the other hands used occasionally for meals, and more often for cards, closer to McKenna, and he helped her situate it at the bedside.

"Can he sit up on his own?" asked Cutter.

"Ask him," said Willa.

"He's sleeping."

She looked over at McKenna. "He's not sleeping. He's listening. I think he's genuinely curious about what we know."

"Well, damn. That's not much."

Willa pushed the stool at Cutter and dragged a chair to the table for herself. She sat. "Tap him on the shoulder—the injured one." The suggestion was enough to encourage Israel McKenna to open his eye. "See?" she said to Cutter. "Possum."

He nodded. "Do you need help sitting up, Mr. Roundbottom?"

The eye narrowed, first on Willa, then on Cutter. "The name's McKenna. Israel McKenna."

"She told me, but I like Roundbottom. So, are you hungry? It's stew. A little on the blackened side but still edible. Zach brewed some white willow tea to ease your pain. You should drink up. Now what about that help? Can you feed yourself?"

Willa tapped the bowl of her spoon against the table to get the ranch hand's attention. When he looked over, she gave him an eyeful of reprimand.

"I saw that," said Israel. "I can stand up for myself."

"Sit up first," she said. "Then we'll see about the other." Mr. McKenna was not amused, she noted, but Cutter chuckled. Willa decided to ignore them both and concentrate on her dinner. They worked it out before she finished sopping up the last of her stew with a warm crust of bread.

"Tell Cutter your middle name," she said, leaning back in her chair.

"Court," he said. "Are you testing me?"

"Yes."

He shrugged, winced, and then massaged his injured shoulder. "I have to stop doing that."

"For now."

"How long before it's better?"

Cutter broke in. "This a first for you?"

"I think so."

"Wouldn't have thought you could forget something like that."

"Here we go," Willa told Cutter. She stopped short of rolling her eyes. Her stomach was full and just now eye rolling seemed like too much effort. "The convenient inconvenient memory." She turned to her dinner companion and saw he had chosen the white willow tea over the stew. Except for grimacing and the occasional smothered groan, he had been stoic about the pain. But whether it was silence born of experience and expectation or some need to keep it from her, she didn't know. "Or is inconveniently convenient?" she asked him. "No matter. You'll be out of the sling in a few days, and you will notice improvement in a couple of weeks, a month at the outside. If you don't care for it, though, the muscles will tighten and you'll have problems there for the rest of your life."

"It's true, Roundbottom," said Cutter.

Willa tapped the table again, this time with the flat of her hand. "Careful, Cutter. If he listens to me, he won't always be in a sling, and he might be a credible shot."

Israel shook his head. "I'm not."

"Are you sure?" asked Willa.

"I am. Did you find a gun or a gun belt?"

"No, but as I told you, we didn't find any money either."

Cutter asked, "Did you have money?"

"I don't know."

Willa closed her eyes briefly and rubbed the lids with a thumb and forefinger. "How did you get to Jupiter?"

"I don't know." He put his spoon down and pushed the bowl away. "You're the one who thinks that's where I was."

"You agreed with me."

"Because it seems likely, but I don't know it for a fact." He plowed his fingers through his hair again. "How does anyone get to Jupiter?"

When Willa didn't answer, Cutter did. "Mostly train these days. There's a U.P. spur from Denver. You know what the U.P. is, don't you?"

"The Union Pacific."

"That's right. Do you think you might have taken the train, Mr. McKenna?"

"Israel. And I don't know." He ignored Willa's sigh. "Did I hear you say back where you found me that I might have ridden out with some others?"

Cutter's eyebrows laddered his forehead as they rose. He looked at Willa.

"I told you," she said. "He was listening even back then."

"I'll be darned." Cutter massaged the back of his neck. "Yeah, I said it could have been like that. I thought there might be three, maybe four horses. Stands to figure one of them was yours. I didn't take a lot of time to look around on account of we needed to get you here, but I can do that tomorrow."

Willa shook her head. "Jupiter tomorrow. I'll go back. It's Pancake land. It's my responsibility."

"Is that why you rode out to find me?" Israel asked. "Your land? Your responsibility?"

"I rode out because Annalea asked me to. I brought you back because it was necessary."

"The right thing to do?"

"Yes."

"My brother would approve."

There was no mistaking the derisive smile on that battered face, and Willa remembered that he'd said his brother always did the right thing. His brother, the saint. Well, she was not that, and she doubted it could be said of the other Mr. McKenna. "What is your brother's name?"

"Quill."

"Quill," she repeated. "I've never heard it before."

"It means cub. That's what he is. The cub. My little brother."

"And is Quill in Indiana with your parents?"

His lips twisted briefly in a scornful smile that further distorted his features. "Illinois. You know my parents are in Illinois."

She did not pretend that she had made a mistake, and she did not apologize for trying to challenge his story. Instead, she turned to Cutter and directed him to take the tray to the house. "And tell Zach to make a poultice for Mr. McKenna's eye and bring it here."

Cutter darted a sideways look at Israel and then leaned over, picked up the damp eye pad lying on the bed beside him, and pressed it into Israel's hand. "You can put that back over your eye now that you're done eating. Swelling's about the size of an egg, and the color's the same purple shade of sky just as night's creeping in. It'll be full-on black in the morning."

"The tray?" Willa said, pushing it in Cutter's direction. "Now?"

"Yes, ma'am," he said solemnly, too solemnly. He practically telegraphed his wink and nod. "Right away."

Willa waited until he was gone before she sighed. "He's not wrong, you know. About the size of the swelling or the color."

Israel placed the pad over his eye and held it there. "He took some pleasure in telling me."

"I know." She stood, pushed the table back, and then helped him lie down.

"He did it because he likes you."

"I know."

"I mean that he's sweet on you."

"I knew what you meant." She adjusted the sling, tucked the blankets, and then looked him over. "Odd for you to say, though."

He shrugged then clenched his jaw against the pain. After several long seconds, he slowly released the breath he was holding and closed his eye. His lips parted around a curse but he did not give it sound.

"Hurts some, does it?"

His breath hitched on a short, almost inaudible laugh, and he grimaced. "Some. Yes."

Willa wagered he had never paid much attention to his ribs. He would be a fool not to now. She pulled the chair closer to the bunk so that when she sat, her knees touched the thin mattress. She leaned forward, resting her folded forearms on her thighs. "I can't say this easy," she said quietly, "but it needs to be said. You were sorely abused today, and I don't know how it will end for you. I'm not a doctor, and it never occurred to me that you would want me to send for one, but if you—"

"No."

"All right. I don't pretend to know the extent of your injuries. I know what I can see, and I know what can be done about that, but there's things I can't see and wouldn't know what to do about if I could. You took some hard knocks to your head, and you have a couple of knots under your scalp that might be something or nothing. You have not said anything about your head, so maybe it doesn't hurt as much, or at least any worse, than your shoulder or your ribs or your eye or—"

"Or my knee," he said. "My knee's wrenched."

"Or your knee," she repeated quietly. "Or any other part of you that's scraped, cut, or peeled away. Some injuries are going to pain you worse before they get better, so you have to be prepared for that. I think—"

"If I live," he said. "I have to be prepared for it, if I live."

"That's right."

He turned his head a fraction toward her and opened his eye. "But you're more worried about my head."

Now that he could see her, she nodded. "I don't know how to judge the state of your faculties without asking you questions and hearing your answers."

"So annoying me with them was intentional."

"Yes."

"But the number of questions you asked . . ."

"To keep you awake."

"And the kind of questions . . ."

"To learn as much as I could as quickly as possible."

"So you will know where to send the body."

"Do not flatter yourself that I would go to the trouble or spend the money. I am only sending notification. You'll go in the ground here."

He stared at her with his one good eye, and then a chuckle began to vibrate his chest. Wincing, he pressed the arm in the sling against his injured ribs to hold them steady.

Willa smirked. "About the only thing you have not strained, sprained, or swollen is your funny bone, but you keep laughing like that and it's going to kill you."

He caught his breath and waited until the pain in his side passed before he spoke. "I take your point."

"Good." She sat up. "Now tell me about your brother. Does he still live in Illinois?" Willa was not certain he meant to answer her, but it turned out that the reply was only a long time coming.

"Whatever happens, you don't involve him."

"But—"

"I mean it."

She did not understand, but she acquiesced. "All right."

"Ever," he said.

"All *right*." When he continued to eye her, she said, "I am not taking a blood oath."

"Hmm." He blinked once and then turned his head to stare at the roof.

She said, "When Cutter gets here with the poultice, you can rest. Sleep if you like, at least for a while. Zach will know how often to wake you."

He nodded, said nothing.

"Do you want more white willow tea?" The cup had been empty when Cutter took it away. "Zach can brew more."

"No. It was enough."

"I am going up to the house to see what's taking so long. Don't let Cutter rile you when he comes back with the poultice. Rest. I'll look in on you tomorrow morning."

"Elm Street," he said suddenly. "Twenty-two Elm Street. Herring, Illinois. The Reverend and Mrs. James McKenna."

Willa's lips parted. She stared at him while he continued to stare at the rafters.

"My parents' address," he said. "In the event you need it."

"I don't think I will. I've changed my mind. You're too ornery to die on us."

Chapter Three

Israel Court McKenna did wake the next morning and had to sort through several simultaneous thoughts to make sense of any one of them.

First and foremost, there was the fact that he was awake and wished that he was not. For the time it took to draw a full breath, he wished he were dead and meant it. There was no part of him that did not hurt. His hair hurt, for God's sake. Every strand.

He grasped at another thought, scrabbling the sheet with his fingers as though the thought had real weight and texture and substance. The woman—Willa—had said he was too ornery to die, and she might have been right. Probably was. He had been cursed all his life for his disobedience, his willfulness, and he had never been in a position to claim he stood opposed to things as a matter of principle. Mostly he did it out of sheer perverseness.

Now he wondered what perverse thing he had done this time. It was not a thought he wanted to dwell on. Not at all. It pained him more than his hair, but he had to consider it. He'd been honest with the girl. The young one. Annalea. He had been truthful about the kind of man he was. A bad one. And he had also been honest with her sister. He did not know what happened to bring about this mean justice. He had no memory of Jupiter, although when Cutter suggested that he might have arrived by train, it resonated.

Why would he have gone to Jupiter when his destination was a ranch outside Temptation?

Cutter said Jupiter was a spur that started in Denver, which meant the town was on a dead-end route. It made no sense that he would have boarded a train to nowhere when there was somewhere he particularly wanted to be. But then again, he had done foolish things before, so there was precedence for this.

He had meant to change, had really believed he could, even thought he had begun, but here he was without ways or means, clearly past redemption. Was it an irony that he had actually, finally resisted Temptation, or only egregious wordplay? That errant thought made him chuckle, wince, and then recall that Willa had warned that his funny bone would kill him.

Israel removed the poultice from his eye and gently explored the puffy skin around it. If there was any change, he couldn't tell. He searched for the cloth Willa had put over his eye before the poultice arrived, but he could not find it. He used a corner of the sheet instead to try to clear the crusty matter that filled the seam between his upper and lower lids. He did the best he could, but he needed a damp cloth and stopped before he did more injury.

"Good," Annalea said. "You're awake. I brought you breakfast." She set a tray on the table. "Oatmeal and more tea. Oatmeal on account of Willa thinking you should have soft food and tea for your pain. I guess you had some trouble chewing the meat in the stew last night. Could be you have a couple of loose teeth. Better to keep them in your mouth."

"Where is your sister?"

"That's all you have to say?"

"It's a start."

"So is 'good morning.'"

"Good morning. Where is your sister?"

"She rode out to the place where we found you."

"Already? She said she was going to look in on me." He wondered if he sounded disappointed. He was. A little.

"She did that earlier. You were sleeping and you were fine and she has chores. Cutter's gone to Jupiter, and Zach is in the barn putting fresh hay into the troughs. Pa's snoring. He's the only one here who sleeps in. Willa says things go better if we let him."

Israel cast his eye past Annalea to the doorway. "I don't see your dog."

"John Henry sniffed out a rabbit. He'll come back eventually."

"With the rabbit?"

"Probably not. He doesn't have the bloodlust. I do, though. That's what Pa says makes me so good with my slingshot. Your eye looks awful, by the way. Do you need help sitting up? Willa said you might but that you probably wouldn't ask. Was she right?"

"I need you to leave."

Her face crumpled and she thrust out her lower lip. "Why?"

"Because."

"But I'm supposed to make sure you eat your breakfast."

"And you can do that, but first you need to leave."

Annalea's lower lip began to quiver.

He was unmoved. "Can you also cry at will?"

She blew out a breath hard enough to make her lips vibrate and then gave him a saucy grin. "I can, you know."

"I figured. It's a gift. Now go."

Annalea rolled her shoulders so her twin braids fell forward. She tugged on them as she backed out of the bunkhouse, her gaze never straying from his. "I reckon I got it in my head now why you need privacy. Holler when you're done. I'll be right outside."

"Wonderful," he muttered. Lord, he would be grateful when he could walk to the outhouse.

Willa made a striking figure on horseback. She sat tall and straight in the saddle, relieving her mare of the full burden of her slight weight. She was a skillful rider and learned most of what she knew from her father before he became a slave to the bottle. He had her in the saddle before she could properly walk; at least that's what she had been told. It might even have been true because she felt the most at ease while she was riding, whether she was flying with the wind or resilient in the face of it.

It was another cool morning, the fourth they'd had in a row, and Willa stopped once to pull a black woolen scarf out of her coat pocket and wrap it around her neck and the lower half of her face. In the east, the sun was climbing in a cerulean sky but not offering much in the way of heat, and to the north there was a front approaching, an endless gray cloud carpet unrolling in her direction.

Willa's mount was a sleek, cinnamon-colored mare with an ebony mane and dark brown eyes as expressive as those of a heroine in a dime novel. Willa named her after her personal favorite, Miss Felicity Ravenwood.

Willa guided Felicity along Potrock Run until she came to the place where Annalea had found Israel McKenna. She dismounted, searched the area for what they might have missed the day before, and found a short length of rope, still knotted in the middle, with blood on it. She guessed that it was what had bound his wrists. There was nothing extraordinary about the rope itself—she had coils of the same back at the ranch—but the knot intrigued her because she hadn't seen one like it used by cattlemen.

Deciding that it was worth studying later, she stuffed it in the pocket where she had kept the scarf and remounted to cross the run. Felicity picked her way across the shallow stream with the same delicate care for her hooves that her namesake might have shown for a new pair of kid shoes.

"You have the sensibility of an Eastern debutante, don't you, girl?" Willa gave her a light pat on the neck as Felicity climbed out of the run. "And the heart of Joan of Arc. Let's go."

Willa followed alongside the trail of crushed grass and scattered rock. Twice she saw narrow strips of material torn from Israel's jacket and trousers, and both times she left them where they lay. The trail divided in the midst of a stretch of old boxelders, and Willa reasoned the riders did not follow the same trail through the trees on their return trip. She found evidence of Israel's passing in the heavily furrowed bark of several boxelders, threads of fabric snagged by the gray-brown trunks, and she kept Felicity moving slowly in that direction.

When she reached the clearing on the other side, she saw

what Cutter had observed in the multiple hoofprints, the movement of restless horses, and the damp outline of shoes that did not belong to any four-legged animal. She did not pause there long but kept going, taking the route the riders had used when they fled in hopes of finding where they had come from and where they had gone.

She was crossing the meandering run a second time when she saw two riders approaching from the northeast. Willa urged Felicity forward until they were on the other side of the run and then held her up. She recognized the men as much from their mounts as she did from the manner they rode them. As a precaution, she opened her coat to put her Colt in easy reach and unstrapped the holster. She also had a rifle in the tooled leather scabbard if there was need for it, although she reckoned that if she were serious about using it, she would be taking aim right now.

The lead rider was a large man, not heavy, but heavily built, broad and big-boned. He held himself erect, although not stiffly. It was the natural posture of a man always at attention, but the effect was that he drew attention. He had a presence beyond what could be accounted for by his physical size. When she was a child, Willa had imagined that he could suck the air out of a room. As an adult, she knew it to be a fact.

Willa steadied Felicity as the riders drew closer. They had slowed once they recognized her. The follower in the pair was wearing a thick leather coat with a lamb's wool collar turned up to his ears. The coat added bulk to his lean, compact frame, but he still did not approach the size of his companion. Willa wondered if that had been the intent when he purchased it. Eli Barber had never really tried to step out of his father's shadow, and whatever space he had created for himself, the shadow he cast was in Malcolm Barber's image.

They wore identical hats, silver-banded black Stetsons that bore none of the sweat stains and grit of the hats worn by the men who worked for them. They shared the same coloring, fair skinned, sandy hair, and green eyes, but for all of that, they were not peas in a pod. Eli's features were better defined, not like his father's, whose were broad and flat. He had a narrow face with a clean jawline, full lips, and faint hollows under high cheekbones. Eli's hair brushed his forehead while his father wore his swept back under his hat, and although Malcolm's face was carved by a less deft hand, he was as handsome as his son in a roughhewn way.

Willa tugged on her scarf, lowering to just under her chin so she could greet them. It was her practice to never give either of the Barbers the first opportunity to speak, and if she could have the last word as well, so much the better.

"Morning, Mal. Eli. What are you doing on my land?"

"Now, Willa," Malcolm said patiently. "Is that really how you want to begin? A debate over whose land this is?"

"I said 'Morning' first."

"So you did."

"And there's no debating it," she said. "The only person questioning the survey, the government land office, and the judge's ruling is you." When Willa saw Eli casually raise his hand, she added, "And your son. So I'm asking again, what are you doing on my land?"

"Looking for rustlers, or at least trespassers. Haven't determined if there are missing cattle, but my fence has been cut, so it seems likely. My men are counting head now. Trail led us here."

"Huh. Rustlers. As it happens, I'm looking for a couple of cows that wandered off from the north pasture. I didn't consider rustlers. It's been a while since we had that kind of trouble."

"Well, it's never not a possibility."

"True." She jerked a thumb over her shoulder to indicate the ground she had already covered. "There's no point in the two of your troubling yourself any further, especially seeing as how you are three miles deep onto my land and how I've been where you're heading and saw no evidence of rustlers or your cattle. I don't suppose you've seen my cows?"

Malcolm Barber's expression turned regretful. "Sorry, Willa, but no. No sign of them."

"But you'd send them this way if you did see them."

"Of course. I'll deliver them to your front door if you like."

She shook her head. "You get within forty yards of the front porch and Happy will shoot you. You know that."

"Your father could give lessons on how to hold a grudge."

Willa said nothing. She looked pointedly to the ridge where they had first appeared and waited for them to leave. It was only when they brought their horses around that she spoke. "Always nice chatting with you, Eli."

Yes, she reflected, as they rode away. She'd had the first word and the last. All in all, a satisfactory encounter.

Israel had alternated once between lukewarm white willow tea and cold oatmeal and was set to take his second sip of tea when he remembered that Annalea was still waiting outside. She had been quiet so he considered there was at least some chance that she had wandered off to find her dog. The hope that this was true decided him in favor of calling for her, although he hedged his bet by not calling very loudly.

He was not inclined to favor children, although he had nothing specific against them. True, they tended to be sticky and inquisitive and unruly and more often than not they got underfoot, but any of those traits, whether alone or in combination, was not enough to put him off them entirely. His awareness of his unsuitability as a parent did that. It made him a careful partner in bed, even with women who assured him that they were past their childbearing years.

He wondered again what he might have done in Jupiter, if indeed he had been there. Bedded the mayor's wife? The preacher's daughter? The sheriff's niece? Had he been so foolish or desperate or both that he had abandoned precaution for a tumble?

He was following this line of reasoning when Annalea burst in the door, throwing it open so wide that it slammed against the wall. That thud brought his head up and effectively put a period to his thoughts.

She was wearing an apple green gingham dress with a full apron stamped with tiny blue flowers. Those flowers fairly danced until she ground to a halt in front of him. Without preamble, she said, "What did you do with it?"

It took him a moment to realize she was asking about the piss pot. "No," he said firmly. "Leave it."

She took her hands out of her deep apron pockets and set them akimbo. Her chin came up in a manner he was beginning to think was a family trait.

The pot was under the foot of his bunk, and Israel realized he must have slanted his eyes in that direction because she was on it like a beggar on a penny. She had it halfway to the door before he thought of anything to say, and by that time it hardly seemed worth saying. In short order, she returned it empty, pushed it under the bunk, and joined him at the table. She rested her elbows on top and her chin in her palms and regarded him openly.

"Don't you have chores to do?" he asked, resuming his meal.

"Done. Or mostly done. I have things to do when you finish your breakfast. I already made my bed, washed the morning dishes, blackened the stove, swept the kitchen and front room, collected eggs and fed the chickens, and took out your pot. Now I'm keeping you company."

"That's a chore?"

"Today it is."

"Hmm." He swallowed a spoonful of congealed oatmeal made slightly more palatable by the dollop of strawberry preserves that had been stirred into it. "I already guessed you blackened something this morning. I thought it might have been your shoes, but they could still use a good polishing."

Annalea pressed her lips together, thinking. "Do I have a smut on my nose?"

"Those are freckles. You have a smut on your cheek." He shook his head when she knuckled her right cheek. "Other one. You got it."

"You have the kind of smuts that don't come off when you rub them."

"I'm sure. Do you suppose you can find a mirror for me? I'd like to look."

"Not while you're eating."

"That bad?"

"Worse."

He nodded. "It feels worse."

"I am supposed to ask about your knee."

Israel flexed it under the table. It hurt, but he had been

able to put weight on it when he answered nature's call and when he dressed. The clothes that had been left for him were well-worn but clean, and they fit reasonably well. The faded chambray shirt was loose and the trousers rested low on his hips, but he had no cause for complaint.

"The knee's better than it was yesterday," he told her.

"What about your head?"

"Let's say that I know it's there and leave it at that."

"All right. I'm supposed to get you to walk outside. Not far, Willa says, just enough for you to stretch. She says you'll seize up otherwise."

"Willa says a lot, doesn't she?"

"Not really." Her mien turned thoughtful. "Not as much as me."

"I think that's probably true." He finished off the tea and set the cup back on the tray. "I didn't thank you yesterday. So thank you."

She snorted. "You told me to go away yesterday."

"I did, and you didn't listen."

"That's right, and here you are." She waggled her pursed lips back and forth as if she were swishing water in her mouth. When she stopped, she asked, "What should I call you? Mr. McKenna? Israel? Augustus Horatio Roundbottom?"

"Don't you dare, brat. Call me Israel."

She grinned at him and dropped her hands away from her face. She folded her forearms on the table. "You can call me Annalea. I should probably address you as Mr. McKenna when Willa is around. She is one for manners, mostly because our mama's gone and she thinks it's her duty to raise me not to be a heathen. Plus, she went to an academy in Saint Louis for young women when she wasn't much older than I am, so she learned some things that she feels compelled to pass on. I have to take it all in or she says she'll send me there."

"You believe her?"

"I do."

He nodded solemnly. "Then you better call me Mr. McKenna, though I can't promise that I'll always answer to it. Now about that mirror? I bet Cutter or Zach have one in their shaving kits."

Annalea went to Cutter's bunk because it was the closest. She rummaged around the small trunk at the foot of his bed and found a framed mirror about the size of man's palm. She held it behind her back while she gave him the benefit of her thinking. "You should sit back on the bunk in case you faint. I won't be able to get you up off the floor on my own."

"Noted." He scooted back a few inches and held out his hand. She presented the mirror to him with the kind of gravity usually reserved for conferring a diploma or a knighthood. He took it and held it up to his face, and then he blanched. Or at least he thought he did. It was difficult to see any change in his pallor given the artist's palette of color that was now his complexion. "You did warn me."

"I did."

His features were so distorted by swelling that he was unrecognizable to himself. It was not only that the left eye was closed, but also that it resembled a pig's bladder—if the pig had drunk from a trough of port wine and absinthe. He gave his head a quarter turn and surveyed the line of his nose. It appeared to be unbroken with the familiar bump on the bridge exactly where he remembered it and not slanted to one side the way the rest of his face seemed to be.

His mouth was dominated by an upper lip that rested like an overstuffed bolster pillow on the lower one. He tried to smile. The effect was grotesque. He should be living under a bridge in a child's fairy tale, collecting tolls from billy goats. He thrust his chin forward and examined it from all sides. It was scraped so raw that he might as well have plowed the lower forty with it, and then again, that was a fair description of what had happened. There were also abrasions on both cheeks and across his brow and quite possibly more silver threads at his temples. The short version of what he saw was that he was a mess.

He turned the mirror over, set it down on the table, and pushed it toward Annalea. "You can put it back."

She took it but did not leave her chair. She tilted her head to one side and studied him, a small crease appearing between her brows.

"What?" he asked. "Something I missed? Am I growing another lump?"

She shook her head. "I've been wondering what you will look like when all the clutter is gone. I asked Willa if she thought you might be handsome, but she said she didn't know and that it was not important."

"It's a little bit important."

"That's what I thought. No one wants to be ugly, although if it turns out that you are, I am sorry for saying so. I do like your eye. The color, I mean."

"This one?" He pointed to the pig bladder.

Annalea curled her lip. "No. The one you can see out of."

"Huh." He envied her the shrug she gave him. Thus far this morning, he had managed to avoid that response. Thinking about it made him adjust his sling.

Annalea's chair scraped the floor when she pushed back from the table. She hopped up and returned the mirror to Cutter's kit. "I'm going to take the tray to the house and then I'll be back for you."

"Back for me? For what?"

"Our walk. So you don't seize up, remember?"

"Oh, that walk." He looked around at the floor. "I don't see my shoes anywhere."

"Willa told Zach to put them outside last night so it'd give you pause in case you wanted to leave."

"Leave? I don't even know where I am."

"Guess Willa didn't think of that." She retrieved the shoes from just outside the door and gave them to him. "I could help you put them on."

"I can manage."

"I'll clean them up tonight."

Israel supposed that meant the plan was to put them out of his reach again. It was a wholly unnecessary precaution, but it seemed Willa was going to have to come to that conclusion on her own. He might have brought her around to believing he was Israel McKenna, but here was proof that she did not trust him.

Well, good for her. He did not trust himself either.

* * *

Willa waited until Mal and Eli Barber were over the ridge before she set Felicity on their path. She did not put it past them to circle back so they could watch her. If they were out of her sight when she reached the rise, she would know that's what they were up to. If they were headed back to Big Bar by a direct route, she would still be able to see them.

She dismounted just before she reached the crest and left Felicity behind a rocky alcove while she carefully climbed to the top of it. She stretched out flat and pulled herself by the elbows to the edge. When she was reasonably confident that she could see and not be seen, she raised her head and shoulders to look down the other side of the ridge.

It seemed that Mal and Eli were in no particular hurry to return to Big Bar. Not only were they still visible, but they had traveled only a little more than half the distance that she had estimated. She swore softly. Malcolm Barber wanted to make sure she saw them. He was deliberately provoking her, taking his time leaving her land. She would not have been surprised if he had taken a piss somewhere to mark the territory he thought was his.

The dispute over the land had originated between her grandfather and Malcolm's father, Ezra Barber. When it was open range and ranchers were driving cattle long distances to market, property boundaries were more of a gentlemen's agreement than a hard line. The railroad, barbed wire, and an influx of homesteaders changed that. Ezra put up his fence first, claiming the herds were mingling and he was tired of cutting out his branded cattle from Obie's. Since Obie was of the opinion that Ezra had never done much in the way of separating the two herds, and that he was essentially a rustler posing as a respectable rancher, Obie was initially in favor of the fence. That lasted until he learned Ezra was not going to let him through to take his cattle to market, and as the route was the most direct, Obie could either pay for the right to travel over Ezra's land or he could go around. It was never a real choice for her grandfather.

He went around Ezra's land, and then he went around Ezra.

The plan for the Union Pacific spur from Denver had been to lay track to Wheaton. That would have been another advantage to Ezra, but Obie got to the surveyors first and made a convincing case for Jupiter. They accepted his proposal—in no small part because it came with a substantial bribe—and set the rails to Jupiter. It was then that Ezra tried to move his fence line, though the attempt was made more out of sheer cussedness than for any substantial benefit.

The government surveyors sided with Obadiah. The ones that Ezra hired studied the same land grants and had an opposing view. They determined that when Ezra set his fence, he created a boundary that was well inside the property he owned. Whether it had occurred because Ezra did not know how to properly read a map or because of his need for expediency did not matter. It had no bearing on the result. The law did not recognize ignorance as an excuse and looked on expediency as proof of greed. In effect, Ezra had turned over acres of grazing land, and Obie's subsequent use of it year after year made it Pancake land in the eyes of the law, if not in Ezra's.

By Willa's reckoning, it was two years ago in August that Ezra Barber died. She did not precisely regret that she had not visited Big Bar for the viewing and burial, but it would have made it more settled in her mind that he was dead. Perhaps if the dispute had died with him, it would be different, but Ezra made sure it lived on in Malcolm, and Malcolm stoked the fires in Eli.

These days it was about the water. She had the source for this area of land, and they did not. She had seen evidence that someone was trying to divert the flow from the mountain lake, but she had no proof that the Barbers were responsible. Several years before Ezra died, after two unusually warm winters were followed by drought and the lake receded, Willa proposed temporarily sharing access to the water. She did this over Happy's strenuous objections and his prediction that her grandfather would rise from his grave to throttle her.

It did not come to that because Ezra turned down her offer. The old man was convinced that she must have poisoned the lake and meant to kill off the herd that grazed in his southwest pasture. Malcolm finally convinced him otherwise, but then he balked again, demanding to know why *he* should share what rightfully belonged to him. That put them at an impasse but apparently saved her from a throttling.

Willa had been satisfied with the outcome because there was no Christian charity in her heart when she made the offer, no nobility of reason. She did it because she needed to prove that she was better. Better than the Barbers. Better than she had hoped she could be. Just better.

Willa shivered, as much from the cold as the tenor of her thinking, but she stayed where she was until Eli and his father disappeared into a knot of limber pine, and waited another ten minutes to be certain they would not show themselves elsewhere.

When they did not, she mounted Felicity again and took her down the slope by an alternate route. She reconnected with the wider trail Israel McKenna's tormentors had taken before they tied him up and followed it until she couldn't. If the men had come from Big Bar, she was not going to be able to prove it. It looked as if Malcolm and Eli had tramped around and through the same area, although she had no way of knowing if they were trying to hide evidence or uncover it.

Reluctantly she halted her search, but since she was out, and the lake was not a hard ride for Felicity, she made the decision to go there and satisfy herself that Malcolm and Eli had not gone before her.

Israel had Annalea's shoulder for a crutch but was careful not to rest too much weight on it. He ignored her encouragement to do otherwise and used her primarily for balance when they paused.

So far, they had stopped at the chicken coop, where he politely admired the mottled, single-combed Java hens as Annalea named them one by one. The Leghorns were particularly spritely, shaking their wattles so they snapped like small red flags in a brisk wind.

Zach was bringing Miss Dolly out of the barn when Israel and Annalea were going in. He touched his forefinger to the brim of his hat in greeting. "So she got you up."

"Was it ever a question?" Israel asked dryly. He looked down at Annalea and saw she appeared affronted that the outcome might have been in doubt.

Zach chuckled and tapped Annalea on the head. "No, it wasn't. You hear, Annalea? I don't bet against you. Ever."

That raised her broad smile, and she nodded, satisfied. "I was bringing him to see the horses, but most especially Miss Dolly. You have them all out."

"Just taking her to the corral to mingle with her friends. Why don't you follow me?"

Annalea showed Israel where to stand. He folded his arms across the corral's top rail, leaned into it, and almost sighed aloud with the relief it provided for his knee. Relaxing, he watched Zach lead Miss Dolly around the perimeter of the corral while Annalea chattered.

When Zach's circling brought him abreast of Israel again, the ranch hand slowed and regarded him with a gimlet eye. "You look like . . . well, I can't properly say because I've never seen the like before. You could scare crows. We keep a good-sized garden in the summer. Mostly squash is all that's left, but varmints and scavengers are always a problem no matter when they show up."

Israel got the message. He wanted to ask questions about the ranch, about the location, even about what Zach did in the course of his day, but decided that inquiries would be treated with suspicion and likely misinterpreted. Zach moved along before he could change his mind.

Annalea climbed the rail with the agility of a monkey. She sat down at his elbow and pointed to Miss Dolly. "Isn't she beautiful? I wish we did not have to sell her, but that's what we do. Breed, raise, and sell them."

"Do you ride?"

She regarded him from under raised eyebrows. "Of course." She indicated a bay mare on the smallish side at the far end of the corral. "That's Ophelia. She's mine, and she's jealous because I have not spent any time with her today, and also because I said Miss Dolly was beautiful. She is very sensitive, is Ophelia."

"I see."

"And obedient." Without warning, Annalea put two fingers to her lips and whistled shrilly. That sound drew the attention of every horse in the corral except Ophelia. It also brought John Henry running. "Mostly obedient," Annalea said. "Would you like to meet her?"

Israel's ears were still ringing, and he felt a wave of nausea that probably had nothing at all to do with that jarring whistle. His head hurt, suddenly and abominably. "Another time. I'd like to go back to the bunkhouse."

"But you've hardly seen anything."

Zach was coming around again. "Annalea, escort him back. He's fair on his way to collapsing. I'd rather not carry him, and you can't."

She hopped down, apologies spilling from her lips like bees fleeing the hive.

"It's all right," Israel said. "I'm fine. We should save something for tomorrow, shouldn't we? The outhouse, for instance."

Giggling, Annalea took him by the arm and led him on a slow, measured trek to the bunkhouse while John Henry circled them like a dervish.

Willa sought Zach out as soon as she returned to the ranch. He was splitting wood by the back porch, but he put down the axe when she came abreast of him.

"Is Cutter back?" she asked.

Zach shook his head. "Didn't expect either one of you to be gone this long, especially not you. I thought about riding out, but I didn't want to leave Annalea here with McKenna, and I didn't want to leave McKenna here with Happy."

"Good thinking."

"Did you learn anything?"

"Nothing I'd hoped for. How is our patient?"

Zach reported on the morning's doings. "Annalea's been looking in on him off and on. She says he's always sleeping. She's in the barn taking care of Ophelia if you want to hear more."

"I'm sure she'll bend my ear." She threw a leg over the

saddle and swung down. "I'm concerned about Cutter. You could go and see what's happened to him now that I'm back."

"You sure?"

She nodded and then held up a finger when Zach took a step toward the barn. "First, tell me what Happy's been up to."

Zach pointed to the half cord of wood beside the porch. "Well, he was stacking for me, but I guess he got tired of that. The house or the barn would be my guess. Sorry, Willa, I can't keep an eye on him and get my work done."

"I know. He's not your responsibility. Go on." She handed him Felicity's reins. "Take her. I'll be along to care for her after I check the house for Happy."

Israel held his breath as Happy tipped his chair back on two legs and set his heels on the bunk frame. The man had an uncanny balance when he was not drinking, or maybe it was not so much a natural talent as a habit that came from enjoying a slightly skewed view of his surroundings. Last night Happy's flask had been visible as a rectangular outline against his vest, but as far as Israel could tell this afternoon, he was not carrying it anywhere on his person.

And that, Israel thought, was a damn shame. A drink might have quieted the dull throbbing in his head. He released the breath he was holding and waited for Happy to come to the point of his visit. He had to suffer the older man's squinty-eyed scrutiny first.

Happy folded his arms across his chest. "Willa said you'd look worse today than you did when she brought you here, and by God, she was right."

"I have the sense that she usually is."

"Well, then, all the sense wasn't knocked out of you, 'cause it's true. Might be her most annoying trait, although I would have to think on that some. There are choices, you understand."

Israel said nothing. He recalled that his father also had a list to choose from, but characterizing his flaws as annoying would have been a compliment, and being right would never have been among them.

"You were lucky our little Annalea found you."

"Yes."

"You figure out who's responsible for your predicament?"

"Mostly I figure I am."

"Do you? Now why do you think so? You remember something you maybe want to get off your chest?"

He shook his head. "Is that why you dropped in? To hear my confession?"

"Dropping in is neighborly, and I don't hold with confession. Damn papist nonsense if you ask me. As it happens, you're the only person on my land that I don't know as well as I know my own hairy ass. I was of a mind to change that."

Israel resigned himself to another interrogation. Resignation came with a deep sigh and an unfortunate vision of Happy's hairy ass. "What do you want to know?"

"Your intentions."

"My intentions?"

"Uh-huh. If you live."

"If?"

"Jury's still out now, isn't it? What I heard from Annalea is that you hobbled around this morning and then came back here and slept. Every time she looked in on you, you were sleeping. Always in the same position. Never moved. She held a mirror under your nose to make sure you were breathing."

"Clever girl." Israel could have said he was playing possum again, that he hadn't wanted to be bothered by Annalea, but what good reason did he have for lying except custom? The truth was that he had never once heard Annalea either coming or going, and he should have felt her presence if she had been holding a mirror under his nose.

"Your head hurt?" asked Happy. "Looks like there's a lot of pain behind that eye."

"It's not so bad."

"Sure. You toss your breakfast?"

"Thought I might, but no." Annalea had managed to get him back to the bunkhouse before he embarrassed himself in front of her. The nausea passed once he was lying down and able to close his good eye.

"Not a doubt in my mind that you're concussed. Are you dizzy now?"

"No. It's passed."

"I noticed you didn't shake your head."

Israel smiled weakly. "It's probably better if I don't."

"I've been concussed myself a couple of times."

"So it doesn't kill you."

"No, not unless something bursts under your skull. You feel like anything's going to burst?"

"No."

"That's probably good, but I can't say for sure that you would feel it until it happens, then you'll drop dead. I've seen it. Happened to a friend of mine and the doc explained it to me." He unfolded his arms and knuckled the underside of his chin thoughtfully. "Better to be optimistic about your chances, I think, and that brings me back to your intentions. You're not from around here. I'd know you if you were, even with that face. Seems like everyone wants to know where you were, but I'm wondering where you were going."

"Can't say."

"Because you can't remember or because you don't want to say?"

Israel realized that Happy Pancake was not to be underestimated when he was sober. The lie came easily to his lips. "I can't remember."

"Huh. It's early days yet. It could still come to you."

"Why is it important?"

"Well, if you recollect where you were going, you might move on. You might move on regardless, but it could be that you're already finding reasons to stay."

"What reasons?"

"Your safety for one. No one's going to hurt you here."

Israel's experience told him otherwise. "Willa said what happened to me happened on Pancake land, and we know she's always right."

"It didn't start there, that's for damn sure, and that's why

I'm proposing another reason you might have for staying. Revenge. When you know who did this to you, you are going to want to get some of your own back."

"Am I? Maybe I will take a page from scripture. Turn the other cheek."

"Son, it looks like you already done that. Several times. Revenge ought to be your calling now."

"Hmm."

"There'd be work for you here if you stuck around while you sorted things out. You had no money on you."

"So I keep hearing."

"Annalea sure as hell didn't empty your pockets."

"I didn't mean . . . never mind."

Happy nodded, accepting an apology that was never quite given for a slight that was never intended. "You'll need a horse, tack, decent clothes, better boots, and food and sundries. Unless you mean to steal all that, in which case you'll be caught and hanged before you get out of the valley, you'll need money. You won't get credit unless you're settled somewhere and you can't get settled if you don't stay."

Israel clamped a forearm over his eyes. "I'm dizzy now."

Happy chuckled. "I bet. You can earn fair wages here."

The bunkhouse had beds for eight. Only two others were being used. "If that's the case, why aren't there more men?"

"Just keep a few on this time of year. Zach's a fixture, but Cutter came in the spring and Willa kept him when she paid out last wages to the others. There was a fellow who was supposed to stay through the winter, Dave Huggins, but he took ill with a lung infection and decided to leave for warm climes. The others were already gone, and Willa said she'd make do. Now that you're here, I figure she doesn't have to."

Israel lowered his arm. He flexed his fingers, making a loose fist that he eventually left that way. An infant had a better grip than he did. "What makes you think I know anything about ranching?"

Happy's wiry eyebrows climbed his forehead. "Jesus, Mary, and Joseph. What makes you think I do? I had a look at your clothes and your shoes, and I got you figured for a whiskey drummer or some other kind of peddler. Hair tonic. Ladies' necessaries. Curiosities from China or maybe Europe. Medical elixirs. Hell, your experience on a ranch isn't what matters. Once you're healed, you'll have two hands and two legs strong enough to use. We can put those to work."

"You've been thinking on this pretty hard."

"Some last night when I was holdin' up the wall over there, and some more this morning while I was still abed. But you haven't heard the best part."

"I haven't? You mean there's something better than safety, revenge, and hard labor?"

"Hell, yes. There's my daughter. Willa's a looker, ain't she?"

Israel frowned as deeply as his swollen mouth and rigid brow would permit. "Pardon?"

"She's pretty."

"Uh-huh." Pretty hardly described her. She was damn near beautiful, probably would be once he could see her clearly. He had no difficulty recalling the features that were set in her oval face or how they were framed by loosely braided hair as dark as coffee. She had widely spaced eyes the same color as her hair and a slim nose placed dead center between them. The perfect symmetry ended at her wide mouth, which was canted slightly to one side. It was more noticeable when she spoke or smiled or, really, when she just breathed. The angled lift of that corner commanded attention, or at least it commanded his attention. That faint upward slant to her lips gave the impression that she was either harboring a secret or chronically skeptical. Both ideas intrigued him.

She had a long neck and slender shoulders and a willow-like suppleness to her long-legged frame that belied her strength. She dressed like a man but carried herself like a woman, and Israel imagined she did the work of both.

He continued to regard Happy with a wary eye. Nothing about Willa's looks or her demeanor gave him a clue as to the direction of Happy's thoughts because surely it could *not* be that the man was proposing a match.

"She's not married," Happy said.

"I'm not sure I understand." Actually, he was sure he didn't.

"That's it. She's not married."

"Not for lack of offers, I suspect."

"No, that's right, and I admit there were some proposals that she showed real good sense turning down. Trouble is, she's turned them *all* down, and now she's staring at spinsterhood."

"How old is she?"

"Twenty-goddamn-four."

"An old maid, then."

Happy grunted, nodding.

Israel decided he might as well ask the question outright. "Why are you telling me?"

"The girl's got to marry someone sometime, don't she? Trying to motivate her, that's my aim. No harm giving you something to think about."

Israel wondered at Happy's game. Any overtures he made to Willa would surely result in her running in the opposite direction, most likely into someone else's arms. Was that it? Was that what Happy meant by motivating his daughter? Israel wasn't certain what he should say to that so he said nothing.

Happy stretched his arms wide and rolled his neck. His bones creaked and crackled. He let the chair drop to all four legs and got to his feet. Behind him the door opened. He looked over his shoulder and grinned.

"Willa, you're back. Good. We were just talking about you."

Chapter Four

Willa unwound the scarf around her neck and unbuttoned her coat. She ignored Happy's overture. If they truly had been talking about her, she didn't want to know what had passed for conversation.

"What are you doing here, Happy? I'm not sure Mr. McKenna is fit enough for your company."

"He ain't thrown me out. I was leaving on my own."

She stood aside, cocked an eyebrow expectantly at him, and made an ushering gesture toward the door. He grinned back at Israel, and gave him a what-can-you-do shrug that made Willa think that maybe she *should* know what they had said about her. As Happy sauntered past, she breathed in deeply but not loudly. The air immediately around her father was fragrant with soap and hair tonic, not alcohol. That was interesting.

"He hasn't been drinking," Israel said when Happy was gone.

Willa's chin lifted a notch. "What do you know about it?"

Israel raised the hand that was partially trapped by the sling in an apologetic, surrendering fashion. "I don't know anything."

"That's what I thought." She walked over to the chair Happy had pulled up to the bedside, but she did not sit down. Instead she stood behind it, bracing her arms against the back of it. "How is your head?"

"Foggy." He paused, thoughtful. "Although your father's visit might account for it."

Willa did not smile. She held up three fingers. "How many?"

"Three."

"First girl you asked to dance."

"Bea Winslow."

"Middle name."

"Court."

"Do you know where you are?"

"Other than in a bunkhouse on Pancake land, I haven't a blessed clue."

Willa nodded, satisfied. "I guess you needed that sleep. Doesn't seem as if it did you any harm. Annalea says you didn't puke, but she thought you might. Is she right?"

"You can check the pot yourself."

It was not an answer to her question, but she let it go. He was a tad touchy about bodily functions, regardless of the reason she had to know about them. "I hear you walked as far as the corral. What about your knee? Is it any worse for wear?"

He stretched his injured leg under the blankets and moved his foot side to side to test the range of motion in his knee. "No worse," he said. "Still twinges."

"Do you think you can get up, walk around some? Annalea's brewing a pot of white willow tea for you. I'll take you up to the house and you can have a cup there. It will make the walk back more tolerable." Before he gave her a proper answer, she pulled away the chair to make room for him to sit up.

"You're a bully," Israel said.

"Mm-hmm."

He sighed. "Looks as if I'm going." He grasped one edge of the bunk with the hand he could properly use and pulled himself to a sitting position. He pressed the arm in the sling against his ribs and took a couple of shallow breaths before he shifted in place and brought his legs over the side. Willa had his shoes waiting for him and hunkered down to put them on. "I can do that," he said stiffly.

"I know." She slipped the ankle boots on him anyway. "But it's no slight on your manhood to let me help you." She stood and offered him her arm. When he took it, she steadied him to his feet.

"Afraid something will burst in my brain?" he asked.

"What?"

"Happy said because I took so many knocks to my head that something could still burst inside it. That's why you helped me. You didn't want me to bend over."

"It's as good a reason as any, but mostly I just wanted to move us along."

"Is what Happy said true?"

"You should really have a coat," she said. "It is considerably colder than it was this morning, but I don't suppose that anyone's ever left a coat behind. We'll wrap a—"

"Is it true?"

Willa blinked at the interruption. She turned her head to look at him, and when she did, his blue-gray eye bored into her. She had the odd moment to wonder what it would be like when he could fix her with two eyes before he repeated his question.

"Yes, it's true. It happened to Denzel Suggs a few days after he got kicked in the head by a stallion he had no business trying to break. I guess Happy didn't tell you that Denzel never recovered his right mind after that. He was glassy-eyed, couldn't walk a straight line, and only answered to his own name about half the time after my grandfather pulled him out of the corral. He improved some, and then he didn't. Denzel dropped dead at Happy's side, so I suppose he remembers it right." She pointed a finger at Israel. "And I don't believe any of it is relevant to your situation. Happy should have kept what he knew to himself." She had the sense that that was probably true about a number things.

Willa lowered her hand but continued to face him. "There's no question that you were concussed, but it seems to me that most of what bothers a person after it happens is fading for you or already gone. If you have a hankering to worry about something, you might want to worry about whether you'll ever get another girl to dance with you. You are *not* looking pretty."

"I was not worried. I was curious."

"Uh-huh." With her free hand, she yanked a blanket off the bed and helped him get it around his shoulders. "Let's go."

Israel did not move when she did. He held her back until

she looked at him again, and then he said, "I guess you're wondering if there is any pretty under this clutter."

"I wasn't," she said. "It's not important."

"It's a little bit important."

Willa's chuckle tickled the back of her throat. "So I heard."

"Annalea," he said under his breath.

"Of course." She tugged and this time he fell into step beside her. "Don't ever think you can say something in front of her that she won't commit to memory. She can't help herself."

Zach and Cutter returned at suppertime, but as they had already taken a meal in Jupiter's only restaurant inside Jupiter's only hotel, Zach offered to carry Israel's food out to the bunkhouse while Cutter cared for their animals. Willa would have liked to hear right then what they'd learned, but she saw Annalea had her ears perked. Happy looked as if he might ask a question so Willa tapped his foot under the table. Only John Henry was uninterested, but then, he had a steak bone to occupy him.

When supper was over and the dishes were washed, Willa marched Annalea off to bed. There were more protests than usual, but the outcome was the same, and Annalea was tucked in tight, just the way she liked. Willa read to her from Uncle Remus until her eyelids fluttered and her pink, bow-shaped lips moved sleepily around unintelligible words. She kissed Annalea on her perfectly smooth brow and whispered a prayer for pleasant dreams. Annalea did not stir when Willa turned down the lamp, or when she backed out of the room and every board creaked under her boots.

Happy was not in the front room, but his flask was. He had left it behind, lying on its side next to the book he had been reading, or pretending to read, when she took Annalea to bed. Willa picked up the flask, shook it, and realized it was full. Returning it to its place, she made straightaway for the bunkhouse, wondering if he was sharing a bottle instead.

They were all there sitting around the table when she

arrived. Someone had thought to move it closer to the stove. Happy and Cutter were perched on stools, Zach reclined in a chair, and Israel sat at the foot of his bunk, his long legs stretched under the table, one elbow resting on top, the other in the sling resting protectively against his ribs.

Relieved to see that there was no bottle on the table and none at Happy's feet, she removed her coat and dropped it on the closest bed. "You haven't started, have you?"

"Waiting," said Zach. He dragged the empty chair beside him away from the table. "Saved it for you."

She thanked him, thanked them all, and sat. She looked directly at Cutter. "I didn't think I'd have to send Zach after you. What happened? What did you hear?" Out of the corner of her eye, she saw Israel McKenna lean forward. The wait for him must have seemed interminable. She raised an eyebrow when she saw the predominant Adam's apple in Cutter's neck bob once as he swallowed. "Well?"

"I stopped at my ma's first 'cause it'd strike her odd if she heard I was in town and didn't take the time to see her. She's sewing dresses for Mrs. Hardesty and her daughter and doing the smocking on a christening gown for Tabby Meredith's new baby, and naturally I had to hear about that."

"Naturally," Willa said dryly.

"I gave Ma some money I've been saving to help her along, and then I asked, real casual like, if she heard about any new arrivals in town. I told her you were lookin' to hire a man since Dave Huggins took ill and left."

"Impressive," she said, and she meant it. She also was suspicious. "Did you come up with that on your own?"

If Cutter contemplated lying, even for a moment, it wasn't clear. Everyone saw his eyes dart in Happy's direction.

Unconcerned, Happy shrugged. "The boy needed guidance. I stopped him before he rode out this morning and then I went back to bed."

Willa stared at her father, openmouthed, and then looked around the table and saw a similarly slack-jawed expression on Zach's face. That made her clamp her lips closed.

Cutter went on. "But Ma said that except for Mr. and Mrs. Cuttlewhite returning from Denver, she hadn't heard anything.

She told me to check with Mrs. Abernathy because she had rooms to let and it seemed a cowman would go there to board instead of the Viceroy, the hotel being pricier and all."

Willa leaned into the table and stared hard into Cutter's guileless eyes. "I swear, Cutter Hamill, you move your story along or I am going to put my foot so far up your behind that you'll be able to chew on my toenails for breakfast."

The threat seemed reasonable to everyone at the table. They nodded, Cutter hardest of all.

"Mrs. Abernathy didn't have any new boarders so I checked at the Viceroy just in case. There was a fellow that came by to inquire about a room not long after the train arrived, but Mr. Stafford said the hotel was full up. He said the man didn't leave a name and suggested I try the boardinghouse or the saloon. I asked him how I would recognize the man if he was hanging around the saloon because I sure was interested in making his acquaintance since you were looking to hire. Mr. Stafford sorta chuckled at that and told me he didn't think the man would know one end of a horse from the other. That gave me some hope that it might be our man here." He stole a look at Israel and said, "No offense."

"None taken."

"Stafford described a city fellow to me, someone wearing black except for a gray vest with silver threads. For some reason the vest made an impression, which was good because I remembered Mr. Roundbottom was wearing one like it."

"Now I'm offended," said Israel.

No one cared.

Willa prompted Cutter. "So you went to the saloon."

"I did, but not until after I talked to the Cuttlewhites. Sure enough, Ma was right about them just returning from Denver, but they didn't have a recollection of who got off at the station because they were the last to leave their car. The platform was deserted by then."

Willa sighed. "And the saloon?"

"Right. Found out the man had been there. Had a drink. Was invited to sit for cards to make a fourth at poker but declined. Buster Rawlins was there, and he wanted to know why I was asking, so I told him what I told everyone else, namely that you were looking to hire. 'Course he wasn't interested because he's been with the Barbers for years and makes decent money, but he said he'd inquire around on your behalf."

Willa asked, "So there wasn't any trouble in the saloon?"

"No, ma'am. Best I can tell, the man just up and disappeared. Sheriff Brandywine said Jupiter's been real quiet. He had his feet up on his desk when I walked in, and we had a cup of coffee together, which gave me time to look over the posters tacked behind his desk. I didn't see Mr. McKenna's name among them, and I had no expectation that I would recognize his picture from the face we're looking at now." He slipped another sidelong look at Israel. "No offense."

"Mm-hmm."

"The sheriff offered to let folks know that you're hiring, same as Buster, but he was not hopeful. He thought everyone was pretty settled with their situations. He never saw the fellow I was asking after, but then he had not been called out on account of any ruckus. He figured the man left on the late train."

"Except I didn't," Israel said.

Willa shook her head. "Don't get ahead of yourself. We can't be sure the man in the gray vest was you. You were wearing a jacket but no coat."

Cutter nodded. "And no hat. Stafford said the man was wearing a hat. A brand spanking new one that hadn't been properly broken in. I guess that's why he figured the man for a city fellow and not fit for ranch work." The words had barely left his mouth and his expressive blue eyes were already clouding over with another thought. "Oh, and maybe because the man was carrying two bags."

Happy's eyebrows lifted at this intelligence and he grinned at Israel. "Told you I had you pegged as a peddler."

Israel's grunted, and the sound stayed deep in the back of his throat.

Willa was compelled to point out: "There were no bags, no evidence of any contents that might have come from those bags, and therefore no reason to peg Mr. McKenna as any one particular thing yet."

"Whiskey drummer," Happy said. "I had it in my mind that he's a whiskey drummer."

Willa's mouth took a wry twist. "Wishful thinking."

He shrugged. "Where there's hope . . ."

"Is there anything else?" Willa asked Cutter. "Anything you're only now remembering." She held up her hand when he opened his mouth to speak. "Just what's relevant. It has to be relevant."

"Then no." He ducked his head a fraction and lowered his eyes. Everything about his demeanor from his hunched shoulders to the way he was biting the inside of his cheek was a study in sheepishness. "I got nothing."

"Zach? There is a lot of time to fill in. Suppose you do that for us."

"Cutter did not give all his money to his ma. He had enough for a few drinks in the saloon and a roll with Louisa Keys upstairs. That's where I found him. I'd say more but a pup needs a scold not a beating."

Cutter groaned softly and blushed to the roots of his wheat-colored hair.

Zach was unsympathetic. "If you didn't want anyone to know, you shouldn't have stayed so long at the fair."

"I was asking Louisa questions same as I asked everyone else," he said defensively.

"Uh-huh. Did she know anything?"

"No."

"That's what I thought." Zach turned back to Willa. "He needed some sobering up so I took him to the hotel for supper." Here his gaze rolled over to Cutter again. "Which you will pay me for because there wasn't a damn thing about it that was my treat."

Willa pressed her lips together, but it was only to smother her laughter.

Happy slapped his thigh.

Israel put three fingers to the side of his head and closed his eyes.

There was silence, and then Willa's gaze darted between Cutter and Zach. "Did one or both of you recall that you were supposed to bring back clothing for Mr. McKenna?"

"Israel," he said, although there was no real insistence behind it.

Willa's focus never wavered from her ranch hands, but she spoke to Israel. "Why don't you lie down?"

He removed his hand from his temple. "Can't. Might miss something."

Happy snickered. "Then if you're not going to puke, you should probably open your eyes. At least the one you can see out of."

Israel needed just one open eye to slide a jaundiced look at Happy. That look was only slightly less cutting than he intended because he was white-knuckling the edge of the table at the same time.

Willa continued to regard Cutter and Zach expectantly. "The clothes?"

"In my saddlebag," Cutter said. He added in a much smaller voice, "Which I left in the barn after I tended to the horses."

Zach put up his hands, palms out in a gesture that was meant to communicate no responsibility in the matter. "He said he had everything when I found him. I asked."

"Got everything at the mercantile," said Cutter. "Mr. Christie had his hands full with Mrs. Hardesty and her daughter choosing china patterns so he was distracted when he was adding up the purchases. He had it right to the penny, of course, but he didn't seem to notice that the clothes couldn't have all been for me. I did not put it on your credit. Paid cash like you said, and I got out of there."

"And *then*," said Zach, "he went to Liberty Saloon."

They all nodded as one, even fair-haired Cutter, who was flushing to the roots of his hair again.

Willa asked the table at large, "So what do we know?"

This was followed by a lengthy silence.

She swiveled her head in Israel's direction. "Anything you heard sound familiar? Like it might have happened to you?"

He was a long time answering. "No," he said finally. "None of it."

"You're sure?"

"I went through it all again. The train, the hotel, the bags, the saloon. Nothing. I *want* to remember."

"If it was you," said Happy, "what do you think you were carrying in those bags?"

"Clothes? Look, Happy, I am not a peddler. I never sold hair tonic or miracle cures or ladies' necessaries."

"Shame."

Willa's eyes narrowed sharply. "So you *do* remember how you made your living."

"I told you it would come to me directly."

"And?"

"It did. I'm a writer. A reporter for the Chicago *Evening Journal*. Or I was. I think I must have quit."

This declaration was received with more silence.

"A reporter," Willa repeated. Her head titled slightly as she continued to eye him with considerable skepticism. "You know that's something that can be verified."

"I will give you the name of my editor." He corrected himself. "Former editor."

Zach asked, "Why do think you must have quit?"

"Because I'm here. I can't think of a story that I would have chased this far."

"Because you got no grit?" asked Cutter.

"Because the paper wouldn't have paid."

Cutter sat back on his stool. "Oh."

"Hmm."

"All right," Willa cut in. "So if it wasn't a story that brought you here, what did?"

"Don't know."

"What's the last thing you remember clearly?" asked Zach.

"Walking down Wabash Avenue on my way to the paper. I was coming from the bank. Jones and Prescott."

Happy scratched his chin. "Did you have bags with you?"

"Why? Do you think I robbed the bank?"

"Hadn't exactly occurred to me, but now that you mention it."

"Did you?" Cutter asked.

"Did I rob a bank?"

"Well, yeah." Cutter said this in a perfectly reasonable tone. He looked around the table for support. "Why not?"

"Because it's against the law?" Sarcasm had crept into Israel's voice. "I'm only hypothesizing, you understand."

Zach put his large hand over Cutter's leaner one and patted it gently. "He's not likely to admit it just because you asked."

Cutter was forced to agree this was true, although it was clearly not a vote of confidence in Israel's favor.

"For the record," said Israel. "I did not rob the bank. I withdrew money; hardly enough to paper the bottom of one bag, let alone fill two. I also believe I said I was walking, not running, down Wabash."

Under her breath, Willa said, "Jesus and Jehoshaphat." In spite of how softly she spoke, or perhaps because of it, she garnered everyone's attention. "What we know is that a man wearing a gray vest embroidered with silver thread, sporting a new hat, and carrying two bags arrived in Jupiter and did not stay long enough to make much of an impression on anyone, or really, any impression at all."

"Don't know that to be strictly true," Happy said, ruminating aloud. "Let's say for argument's sake that our man here is the same one who tried to register at the Viceroy. Take a look at him. That's right, Israel, don't turn away. Give them an eyeful." After a moment, he continued. "Seems to me that to come by that pretty face he must have made an impression on someone. I'm reasonably certain it was not a good one." He winked at Israel. "I'm only hypothesizing, you understand."

Israel nodded. "Sounds about right, though."

No one disagreed.

Cutter reminded them, "The sheriff said there was no to-do in town."

"That supports what you said yesterday," Willa told him. "Remember? You suggested that he rode out with the men who did this to him. He might have been coerced to leave Jupiter with them, or he might have been taken unawares."

"What about you?" Zach asked Willa. "What did you see when you were out there?"

"A pair of varmints," she said without hesitation.

Israel's brow furrowed but everyone else nodded. "Varmints?" he asked.

"Two-legged kind," Happy explained. "Malcolm and Eli Barber. Father and son."

Zach said, "Malcolm owns ranch land north and a bit east of here. A large tract of it shares a boundary with Pancake Valley."

Happy grunted and refolded his arms hard across his chest. "There's not a thing we share with the Big Bar ranch."

Willa looked sideways at Israel. One side of her mouth angled upward in a faint but clearly sardonic grin. "No love lost between our families."

"I'm getting that."

"I'd just as lief shoot them as look at them," said Happy.

"I told Mal that you would."

"You *talked* to them?"

"Couldn't very well ask them to leave without speaking, now could I?"

Happy harrumphed this time.

Zach got to the bigger point. "What were they doing on this side of the fence?"

Willa recounted her brief conversation with Malcolm and the aftermath. Happy and the ranch hands were as skeptical of the Barbers' explanation for their trespass as Willa had been. Only Israel did not have an opinion.

"Once they were gone, I rode up to Monarch Lake just to make sure they had not been doing mischief."

"Huh. Mischief." The manner in which Happy said it made it a curse. "Is that what we're calling it these days?"

"It's what *I'm* calling it," said Willa. "I circled the lake and I saw nothing to suggest anyone was attempting to divert the flow again. Everything was the same as the last time I was there."

Happy was not placated. "I wouldn't mind seeing for myself."

Willa was sorely tempted to forbid it, but she held her tongue. He was still her father, and she owed him some measure of public respect. Besides, when he started drinking again, he might forget all about it.

Willa pushed back her chair and stood. She felt their eyes on her as she walked over to her coat and figured they probably thought she was leaving. She was not, though. She went through her pockets and came away with the knotted length of rope she had found near the spot where Annalea discovered Israel. She held it up for them to see, then brought it back and dropped it on the table.

"What do you make of that?"

Israel only looked briefly at the rope before he rolled back one sleeve of his chambray shirt and studied the friction burn that almost entirely circled his wrist.

"Yeah," said Zach, staring at Israel's wrist. "Looks right. I guess we know what it was used for."

"What about that knot?" asked Willa. "You know anybody who makes a knot like that?"

"Not a hitch for roping a calf," said Cutter. He raised both eyebrows at Israel and gave him a significant look. "Not a noose either."

Israel pulled his sleeve back in place. "Yes," he said dryly. "I'm aware."

Happy picked it up and turned it over in his hand. "Different, ain't it?" He gave it over to Zach. "What do you think?"

Zach shrugged. "Seems simple enough, but not as simple as a half hitch. That would have done the trick quicker, I think. Makes you wonder."

"It's a Portuguese bowline," Israel said.

Happy cocked an eyebrow at him. "You *know* what it is?"

"Sometimes it's called a French bowline." He pointed to the knot. "Gooseneck."

"And?" asked Willa.

Israel shrugged, sucked in a breath that he blew out slowly. "I've seen it used on riverboats."

"Riverboats," Willa repeated.

"Yes," he said dryly. "Boats. On the river."

Happy looked him up and down. "You been on the river much?"

"Some. The Mississippi. Thought I might find a story there, maybe write a book, but Samuel Clemens had that covered." When everyone but Willa regarded him blankly, he said, "Mark Twain."

There was some nodding then and murmurs of agreement.

Willa asked Zach, "Do you know anyone with riverboat experience?"

"Never heard anyone tell about it. It's interesting, though."

"I thought so." Willa took the rope from him and tossed it on the bunk on top of her coat. "I'll take it back to the house."

Israel followed the arc of the rope's flight and continued to stare at it.

Watching him, Happy said, "You think it's gonna give up some secret? Hell, maybe it'll prompt you to give up one."

Israel had no response for that. What he did was address Willa and ask, "What's next?"

Chapter Five

Of course she had the answer to what was next.

As Israel shoveled muck from Miss Dolly's empty stall, he reflected on that night eight weeks earlier and was moved to wonder why he had even asked.

The oddly sweet scent of manure filled his nostrils when he turned over the shovel. His mouth twisted in a wry smile. He was getting accustomed to the odor, but not so much that he was willing to breathe too deeply. His ribs alone no longer accounted for his reluctance because they had finally healed. From time to time he felt a twinge in the muscles around his shoulder, but Willa had been right about the pain fading quickly, and now he barely recalled that first electric jolt that sent him reeling.

Scrapes healed, scabs fell away, and every swelling receded. His battered features began to assume a different shape, one that suggested a handsome countenance might eventually be revealed. He knew what he looked like before, and he knew more or less what he could expect to see when the mottling across his face faded, but he avoided looking in the mirror until the day Annalea accused him of hiding behind an unruly beard and threatened to have Zach and Cutter take a razor to it. Because he believed she would make good on her threat and that they would take perverse delight in obeying this particular edict, he shaved.

When he was done, when he had wiped the smear of lather from his jaw and the dab from under his ear, he turned to Annalea and dazzled her with a single-dimpled smile that made her blink as wide as a barnyard owl.

Yes, he recalled thinking while he stared at his reflection. How he looked was a little bit important.

If Annalea's sister had changed her mind on the matter, she never hinted at it. When Willa deigned to notice him, it was usually to show him how to do a particular task and then to reprimand him for not doing it to her satisfaction. He was aware that she did not single him out for attention. How she treated him was no different than how she treated Cutter, although Cutter was masterful by comparison. Zach avoided reprimands altogether because he *was* masterful and because more often than not he was the one she turned to for advice.

Israel watched Zach a lot, although he was rarely charged with the same chores. He did the things that Happy had once told him would only require two hands and two legs. Israel could have added that they also required a strong back, but he kept it to himself because it smacked of ingratitude. He mucked stalls, pitched hay, dug postholes, walked horses, hefted feedbags, hung the tack, polished saddles, and made repairs to the bunkhouse roof and the front porch of the main house without hurting himself too badly.

At night he slept very well.

Happy asked him if he dreamed about revenge. Israel said no. He did not say that sometimes he dreamed about Willa. Neither did he admit that he sometimes dreamed about John Henry.

If that sad hound was not on Annalea's heels, he was underfoot. Israel could not shake him, which amused Zach. "It's like you have magnets in your boot heels and John Henry's got iron in his nose."

Israel set the shovel's edge against the floor so he could lean against it and regarded John Henry with a rueful smile. The dog reciprocated with a doleful examination. "Don't you have somewhere you need to be? Maybe a rabbit to chase?"

John Henry flopped on his belly and set his head between his paws. His long ears spread out on the ground while his raised brown eyes remained fixed on Israel's face. The dog watched him from under a pair of thickly wrinkled brows.

Israel sighed. "If you're going to stay with me, you need to learn how to use a shovel."

From the open barn door, Willa said, "Who is going to teach him? You? Right now that shovel is doing a fair imitation of a crutch, maybe a lamppost."

Israel managed not to jerk to attention, but only just. This was not the first time she had caught him unawares. Not only did she move with feline grace, but she padded around on silent little cat feet.

Just to confirm she was wearing boots, his eyes drifted from her face and took a meandering path to the floor. It was a brief but excellent journey, and at the end, yes, there were boots. His chuckle was silent, but it lifted his chest on an indrawn breath. Shaking his head, amused, he leaned more heavily on the shovel handle.

"What can I do for you?" he asked.

"It's the other way around this morning. Zach is headed into Jupiter. Depending on the weather, it could be a spell before anyone takes a wagon back to town. I thought I'd better ask you if there is anything you need."

He held up his bare hands. "Gloves. The pair Cutter gave me were fairly worn to start, and I've finally finished them off."

She walked over to him. "Let me see them."

"The gloves? I left them in the bunkhouse."

Willa pressed her lips together in annoyance. "No, your hands. Hold them up again."

He did, palms out. There was a lot that was familiar about the gesture. A little higher and it would have been surrender. Turn them over, and it was reminiscent of his mother's inspection before dinner. Neither was a memory he wished to revisit, and he suffered Willa's examination until she waved his hands down.

"You should have said something earlier, maybe before Christmas came and went. Something like that would have been a fine present instead of the dime novels Annalea said you should have, not that a few blisters are going to kill you."

"The dime novels were a good distraction from the blisters." Recovered now, he said it with a measure of dry humor, but if she heard it, she was not amused. She merely stared at him out of those black coffee eyes of hers without any hint of what she was thinking. He stared back, but it was all he could do not to shift his weight.

"You had soft hands," she said, pulling her gaze. "There were the scrapes and cuts, of course, but under that, your hands were soft. I don't believe you had a callus before now."

He looked at his palms. The skin across the backs of his knuckles had thickened and the fleshy ball of his hand was rough. His fingertips, too, were coarse. They rasped across the fabric of his clothes when he dressed. Oddly enough, he didn't mind.

"Even on the middle finger of your right hand," she said.

He frowned. "How's that again?"

Willa removed the leather glove on her right hand and rubbed the side of her middle finger with her thumb. "Right here. I would have thought a writer, a reporter such as yourself, would have a callus here. From holding a pen or a pencil. See? I don't. But then I am not much for writing."

"I have a gentle grip." He did not look away when she regarded him again, this time with a thoughtfulness that he suspected was meant to be unnerving. Israel promised himself that he would take the sharp end of a pencil to his eye before he'd show her that it was.

"So," she said at last, tugging on her glove. "A pair of gloves. What else?"

He plucked at his shirt. "One of these, and I think I have enough money for another pair of trousers."

"Don't worry about the cost. I'll pay."

"And make me your indentured servant? I don't think so."

One of her dark eyebrows lifted in a perfect arch. "Is that what you believe you are?"

"No. It is what I might become. I don't want to be any more beholden than I already am."

Willa screwed her mouth to one side as she slowly shook her head.

"What?" he asked. "What did I say?"

"I guess I don't know why you feel beholden. You've thanked everyone, Annalea more than once, and that balanced the books if that's what you were looking to do. It's a fact that folks in these parts tend to help one another."

"When you're not stringing them up."

"Or shooting them," she said without missing a beat. "Look. What Annalea did, what any of us did, none of it is extraordinary. I take you for a reasonably smart man, and I'd wager that you've known for a long while that you can leave anytime you have a mind to. Maybe you really do feel beholden, but maybe, just maybe, you're hugging that the notion to your chest because you don't want to go. Feeling like you haven't made it up to us helps you stay put."

Israel said nothing. He could not recall the last time he was silent because words failed him. Perhaps it had happened when he had been roped like a calf for branding and threatened with death by dragging, but he did not think so. He imagined even then, especially then because he would have been under pressure, that he had found the right words to mount an argument. That he had been unable to persuade his attackers to abandon their plan had more to do with the nature of his offense against them than a failure of his glib tongue.

Willa offered a single-shoulder shrug and hooked her thumbs under her belt. "Just something to think about."

"Hmm." She surprised him then by dropping her gaze and looking around, in fact looking anywhere but at him. She affected a casual stance, had spoken her last words as if they carried no weight, but then her eyes slid down and away, and in that brief unconscious gesture, she showed him something that he believed she would have preferred to remain hidden.

She was not indifferent.

Israel tucked that revelation out of sight so the knowledge of it did not show on his face. He waited patiently for her dark eyes to drift once more in his direction. When they did, he met them with interest, not a challenge.

"Anything else?" she asked. "Toiletries? Socks?"

"Boots. Mine are not going to last much longer."

She nodded but did not look down at them. "So you're going to stay."

"For now."

"All right." She took a step backward, started to turn, then hesitated and came back around. "Annalea will be glad to hear it. She's afraid you'll come to a bad end if you show your face in town."

"So she's told me."

A shadow of a smile momentarily changed the shape of Willa's mouth, angling one corner of it upward. "Of course she has. She doesn't know how not to say what she's thinking." The tenor of the smile changed to self-mocking. "I reckon she comes by it honestly."

"I had that in my mind."

She laughed abruptly, lightly, on a breath, and then the moment passed and her chin lifted and her features settled soberly. "When you're done here, go up to the house and ask Annalea to trace your feet. Wouldn't hurt for her to make a hand trace, too."

Israel had cause to wonder if Willa had overshot the mark when she characterized him as a reasonably smart man. He did not ask, but he did frown as he puzzled it out.

"So Zach can bring back boots and gloves that have a hope of fitting you decent."

"Oh." He noticed that this time when she smiled, it was more of a smirk, but even that shaped her mouth in splendid fashion. Belatedly, he realized he was staring. He pulled his gaze and hefted the shovel. "I won't be long."

She nodded shortly. "I've been thinking that it's time you show me what you can do on a horse."

He lifted the business end of the shovel. "Instead of what I can do behind one, you mean?"

"Something like that. I thought that after lunch you and I can ride out to where we found you. It's time. Probably past time, but then you haven't asked to see it either."

"I'm not asking now."

"I'm aware. Like I said. It's time."

Israel lowered the shovel. "I've thought about going there."

"Have you? Happy and I talked about it. He says that maybe you don't want to poke at your memory, that maybe there's things you suspect but don't want to know."

"What do you say?"

"I say you haven't asked to see the place because you remember more than you're letting on and you've got no pressing need to go."

"Huh. You know, I tend to be a suspicious sort. As a newspaperman, cynicism served the job, especially when I was asking questions at city hall, but I have to say, I can't hold a candle to you. So here's what I'm wondering. Are you just naturally distrustful or is it a consequence of experience?"

Willa regarded him without expression. "I'll see you at lunch."

Annalea wanted to ride out with Willa and Israel, but Willa said it would have to be another time and remained firm in the face of her sister's escalating arguments. She came within a hairsbreadth of sending Annalea away from the table, but Happy intervened with a quelling look in Annalea's direction and that was that.

That her father made an effort at all was impressive. Willa thought about that as she matched Israel's steps toward the barn. "He's changed some since you arrived," she said. "I don't suppose you've noticed, though."

"Whom are we talking about?"

Willa realized Israel had not been privy to the thoughts that preceded her statement. There were times she wondered about that. It seemed to her that he had uncanny prescience where she was concerned. She recalled occasions when her thoughts were barely formed and he was suddenly speaking on the exact subject she had in mind or he was beginning a task that she was only on the verge of giving him. It was disturbing.

He disturbed her. Her mind wandered when she was around him, the business at hand forgotten as she considered his eyes, his mouth, the loose-limbed way he held himself. Equally troubling, her mind wandered when he was not around. It was not so easy to identify the cause of the frisson under her skin or the ache that began in her chest and spread to that space between her thighs. His physical presence could not account for the whole of it. He exerted a subtler influence. What she finally acknowledged, reluctantly and unhappily, was that Israel McKenna reminded her she was a woman.

"I was talking about Happy."

Israel hunched his shoulders against a blast of cold air that sent an eddy of powdery snow in his direction. His eyes darted sideways. "I've noticed you rarely call him 'Pa' or 'Father.' Why is that?"

What it was, was something she did not care to talk about. "He prefers it to Shadrach."

"I imagine. He told me why he's been called Happy all his life, but it doesn't explain why you call him that."

"No. It doesn't." She had nothing more to say on the subject and waited to see if he would let it go or stir it with a stick.

"All right," Israel said easily. "In what way has Happy changed?"

"He pays more attention to Annalea," she said. "Or maybe it's that he gives her better attention than he used to."

"Why would my arrival bring about that kind of change?"

"I have no idea. I don't even know if you have anything to do with it, but you came, and he's different. I can't help but wonder why."

"Maybe he's not different at all," said Israel.

"What do you mean?"

"Maybe what's changed is how you see him."

"Hmm." She was inordinately relieved to reach the barn. "You're going to ride Gal. You think you can manage him?"

"I think I can." Galahad was a three-year-old black gelding whose name was shortened to Gal when he ceased to be a stallion. "I treat him like he's still a king," he told Willa. "And he treats me with contempt."

"I've noticed." She pointed out the tack she wanted him to use. "When you're on his back, you need to be the king and you need to let him know it. He'll respond to that. He still has plenty of spirit, but he's not wild and unpredictable the way he used to be."

"That's what got him castrated?"

"Uh-huh." Willa grinned as Israel paused, his hand hovering over the saddle blanket. "Makes you think, doesn't it?"

He looked over his shoulder at her, one eyebrow raised. "It does a lot more than that."

She laughed. She couldn't help herself. Laughter bubbled to her lips and spilled over like the froth on a cherry phosphate from Maxwell's soda counter. She was aware that not only was he still watching her from under that raised eyebrow, but he had somehow managed to raise it another notch. It was when the vaguely wicked grin appeared that Willa reined herself in. He ought not to look like that, she thought, or at the very least, he ought not to look at *her* like that.

He had remarkably brilliant blue-gray eyes. She had seen that at the occasion of their introduction, and her opinion of them had not changed. She could hardly admit to herself that it had been something of a relief when the one eye was swelled shut for a time. Owning to that made her seem weak in character, when the larger truth was that those eyes, or rather the way he looked at her out of them, made her weak-kneed.

She did not know what accounted for him being able to bring everyone else into his fold. He was not overtly charismatic, but he did have an easy way about him that she supposed people might call charming. Whatever it was, in the two months Israel McKenna had been at the ranch, he had captivated Annalea, earned Zach's respect, Happy's trust, and John Henry's devotion. Even Cutter had come around and stopped poking at him. No one called him Mr. Roundbottom anymore.

Willa thought of herself as a holdout, but there were times, like now, that she suspected she was merely holding on. Her laughter abruptly ended.

Israel watched her a moment longer. "All right, then," he said. "We're done with that." He picked up the saddle blanket and laid it over Gal's back.

Feeling a little foolish, Willa stood as though rooted. It wasn't until Israel asked if she needed help with Felicity's bridle that she was moved to go to her mount. She watched Israel out of the corner of her eye while she brushed Felicity before she settled a blanket on her.

Israel worked with an economy of motion that Willa admired. He moved easily and confidently around Galahad, with a familiarity that she had not observed before. He put the stirrup and girth over the saddle and then hoisted the saddle onto Gal's back. She opened her mouth to remind him to set the saddle so the horn was on top of Galahad's withers, and closed it again when he adjusted it to the correct position and made certain the saddle was lying evenly on the blanket. He released the stirrup, pulled down the girth, and then slung it under Gal's belly so that it fit behind the gelding's front legs. Gal snorted, moved a little restlessly, but Israel did not balk and Gal quieted. In short order, Israel fed the cinch strap through the rings, then tucked and tugged it to take up the slack.

He was already outside, mounted and waiting for her, when she finished. Willa stood at Felicity's shoulder and held the reins in her left hand. Some sixth sense caused her to look up suddenly, and she saw a hint of amusement in the line of Israel's mouth. He did not even try to mask it. In fact, his narrow smile became a grin and the dimple that maddened her with its irregular appearances showed itself at the right corner of his lips.

"Well?" he asked. "Did I earn passing marks?"

Willa felt her cheeks grow warm and did not thank him for it. She put one foot in the stirrup and her hand on the horn. With the unconscious agility and grace of long practice, she put a spring in her step that helped her swing her right leg up and over Felicity's back. She landed as gently in the saddle as a wren on a perch.

"Let's see how you ride," she said. "Then we'll talk about your grade." Eyes forward, her body a straight line from ear to heel, she squeezed Felicity with both boot heels and clicked her tongue. "Try to keep up."

It was not very long before she was flying.

Chapter Six

Israel could feel Galahad's muscles bunch as he prepared to give chase, but he held the horse back. Gal might have the strength and speed to catch Felicity, but not with Israel on his back. There was a surer way to come alongside Willa, and it was not to give her the race she wanted. It was to make her wait.

It was not exciting, but it was smart.

Israel held Galahad to an easy walk, making the gelding's rhythm his own so he was not working against his horse but with him. If Cutter was right, and he had ridden out with the men who tried to kill him, then eight weeks ago was the last time he had been on a horse. Before that, the best he could do was guess. It made sense that he had arrived in Jupiter by train; therefore, when he searched his mind going backward, he figured he had not ridden in well over a year. He reasoned he was going to be sore tomorrow, but he was damned if he'd let Wilhelmina Pancake know.

Israel and Gal eventually came abreast of Willa and her mount. Felicity was pleased to see Galahad and sidled close enough to nose him until Willa pulled her back. In contrast, Israel noted, Willa was in no manner pleased. She had her teeth set tightly enough to make a muscle tick in her jaw. Her anger ran to cold, not hot, so her face was not flushed with high color but drained of it. Her dark eyes glinted, but it was because they were frozen over. Her gaze, when it settled on his face, was implacable.

Israel was careful not to show that he was satisfied with this outcome.

"Well," she said finally, pulling Felicity around, "you stayed in your saddle."

He pretended to be oblivious to her sarcasm and went so far as to inject a touch of pride in his voice when he responded. "I did, didn't I?"

Willa snorted. She put her heels into Felicity's sides and said, "Walk."

Israel nudged Gal to do the same. "How far is it?" he asked.

"A mile and a bit."

He nodded. "I can't get a sense of the place in my mind. It's close to a stream?"

Willa waved a hand to indicate the land around them. "It looks like this. High grass, clusters of trees, mostly pine, a rise not too far distant, and yes, there is a stream. A run, we call it. Potrock Run. There was no powder on the ground then, but snow was in the air."

"How will you know the place now?"

Willa shrugged. "I just will. I've lived here all my life."

"Except for the time you were in Saint Louis."

Her head snapped sideways in his direction. "What?"

The sharpness she managed to summon for that single word caught Israel by surprise. His eyebrows lifted, but he said evenly, "I thought you were in Saint Louis for a couple of years, or did I misunderstand?"

"Where did you hear that?"

She posed this question less sharply than she had the previous one, but Israel could not miss that she was still guarded. He did not like giving Annalea up, but he did not see that he had a choice. Willa probably suspected the source of his information anyway. "Annalea mentioned that you attended a school for girls there."

"Hmm."

"I think it was in regard to her practicing good manners when you're around."

Willa turned her head to face forward once more. "Hmm," she repeated.

"She said you've threatened to send her there." Out of the corner of his eye, he saw Willa's shoulders relax. Still, it was a long time in his estimation before she spoke, and he wondered if she was regretting her initial response.

"Promised, not threatened," Willa said at last. "And I might do it yet."

Israel could not gauge how serious she was. He decided the wiser course was not to ask for clarification. He would have liked to ask her about the school, about her experience there, but he deemed both those subjects to be untouchable for the moment. Instead, he said, "I suppose you're familiar with every inch of your land."

"I don't know about every inch, but I have a good sense for the lay of it. If you're still here in the spring, you'll be able to ride out with Zach and Cutter for roundup."

Spring seemed a long way off just now. There had been two significant snowfalls since his arrival, but Zach had been quick to point out that neither should be confused with the heart of winter. They were sideshows, not the main event. "You'll take on new hires then, won't you?"

"Yes. At least four."

"Ever have a woman come looking for a wrangler job?"

"No. Never. Why?"

"Just wondering."

Willa glanced at him. Cynicism exaggerated the slant of her mouth so that it was almost a smirk. "Just wondering, hmm? You sure you don't want to tell me that kind of curiosity is part and parcel of being a newspaperman?"

"Former newspaperman," he said, "And maybe it is, but I'm not writing a story."

"Damn well better not be," she muttered.

Israel's chuckle stayed in the back of his throat, where he could cover it with an abrupt cough and clearing. He was aware of Willa's suspicious regard, but he gave her no reason to comment.

Willa's attention turned once again to the trail, and she pointed ahead of them and to the left. "There's the run. We'll follow it about a quarter of a mile. The place where Annalea found you will be around the first easy bend we come to."

Israel followed the line of her finger pointing to the run and then continued along the bank. He could not yet see the bend she was talking about. "I never got a good sense of what Annalea was doing out here."

"We probably seem farther away from the house than we actually are. This is just a meandering walk for her and John Henry, but I recall that she said she was looking for water."

"Well, she found Potrock."

Willa smiled, nodded. "I know. I pointed that out to her. She did not think it was very funny. She had some idea that she was going to discover an underground source. Apparently she found what she claimed was a divining rod and was using it to guide her."

"That would be the two-pronged stick she poked me with," he said dryly.

"You remember that?"

"I do. I would have been satisfied just then if she had left me for dead. Instead she gave me a good poke to see if I was done."

"Annalea is thorough."

"Hmm."

Willa drew back on Felicity's reins and the mare stopped. "Here we are."

Galahad also halted his forward progress. Israel slowly looked around, first in the immediate area where they were standing, and then farther afield. He noted the rise and ridge she had talked about, and knew from previous conversations that he had been dragged down from it, but the path he might have taken was unknown to him.

"Nothing about this place is familiar. Are you certain this is it?"

"This is it."

He nodded slowly as he continued to survey the ground around him. He pressed his left knee into Galahad's side and the horse turned right. Israel kept up the pressure, moving Gal steadily in a clockwise circle. He kept Willa as his center point when he widened the route.

She watched him, turning in her saddle to follow his progress. He made two loops before she asked, "Anything? Anything at all?"

"No."

"I'm sorry. Are you disappointed?"

"Some, yes. You?"

"Same. I thought . . ." She shook her head, released the breath that had lodged in her throat. "This probably had no chance of working."

He gauged that her sense of failure was as keen as his. Disappointment was merely the word they were hiding behind. "Maybe if we ride up to the ridge," he suggested. He watched her glance uncertainly in that direction and added, "What would be the harm? Unless you think we might run into your neighbors?"

"No, I don't think we are likely to meet the Barbers. Not now, not so long after the incident."

"Well, then?"

"All right. I intended we should go up there when we started out, but when you didn't recall anything here, it didn't seem as important."

He held her gaze for a long moment. "It is important, though, isn't it? Not about going up there. About me remembering."

She exhaled quietly. "I think so, yes. Don't you?"

He nodded. "What you said today in the barn, about me wanting to be beholden because it makes it easy to stay, well, I figure not remembering is about the same."

"And what you said about being an indentured servant," she said. "Maybe there's a bit of truth in it. You should have choices, and at the moment you don't. Not really. You're safe here, but you were on your way to somewhere, and maybe it's better if you know where you were going than if you don't."

Israel did not correct her impression that he did not know his destination. He had always known that. What he did not know was how he got off course, and he had to acknowledge, at least to himself, that his failure to remember might very well be intentional. How could he be sure unless he tried?

He wondered if the stirring in his gut was fear.

They rode in tandem, Willa and Felicity leading the way, the mare picking her way daintily among the rocks. Galahad was as surefooted, though not as particular about the route. Israel felt the strain in his thighs as he tried to keep his seat.

Willa took them past an outcropping of rock and stopped

when they reached a clearing. "This is where Cutter found the first evidence that you had come through here. The grass was trampled flat. He could tell there was a lot of movement. I saw the same the following morning."

Israel was quiet, trying to imagine it. He swung down from the saddle and handed Gal's reins to Willa. "I just want to walk around. Do you mind?"

"No. Do whatever you like. We'll wait over there." She used her chin to direct him to a copse of scrub and stunted pines.

Israel made a slow spiral, not so much examining the ground as examining his mind. He had never been one for introspection. That was his brother. Quill was the thoughtful one, the one who had changed paths over the years but never his purpose. Israel supposed it could be said of himself that he had kept to a single path, although no one, least of all he, would have described it as a straight and narrow one. The less he reflected on what had been his life's purpose, the better off he and everyone around him would be.

He stopped walking and stood very still. He closed his eyes and listened. He heard water trickling over stones and the snuffling of the horses. A breeze soughed through the pines. The branches stirred; needles fell. It astonished him that he could actually hear the needles as they brushed the ground. The peace of this place was overwhelming; everything about it at odds with what he knew had happened here.

A shadow of what might have been a memory flitted through his mind. Two men, not three, on horseback closing ranks, blocking him on either side, and his horse stamping the ground, rising up. A third man arriving, shouting, and then nothing . . .

He tried to fix the image in his mind's eye, but it had already disappeared and he could not call it back. It might not have been a true memory anyway, only one born of suggestion. There had been considerable speculation about what had taken place, and he had visualized it all as the others spoke. It was possible that was what he was recalling, nothing else.

Israel opened his eyes. He lifted his hat, raked fingers

through his thick hair, and set the hat back in place. Shaking his head, he started walking toward Willa.

"I'm sorry," she said when he was back in the saddle. "You stood there for so long, I thought that perhaps something was coming to you."

"Something did." He told her what happened.

"Let's go on," she said. "Not far. I don't want to get too close to the fence line. I'm not concerned about Mal and Eli, but we could see one of their hands. There is no point taking a chance that you might be known to one of them."

Israel agreed.

They rode for another half hour before Willa announced they should probably head back. Israel could not think of a reason to argue except that he wanted to stay out longer. The wild beauty of the land was a draw, but then so was Willa.

There had been no woman for him in a long time. But even for a man of his dubious character, it was not a good enough reason to seduce Willa, and that was supposing she could be seduced. He had his doubts.

"Happy wants to see you married," Israel said. "Did you know that?"

Willa blinked. "Jesus."

"Yeah," he said, grinning. "I wondered."

"What do you do to inspire people to give you their confidences?"

"I don't know. Whatever it is, it hasn't worked on you."

She pointed to herself. "Suspicious, remember?"

"I do." He was aware that she'd done something to increase Felicity's pace, although whether it was deliberate or unconscious, he didn't know. He urged Galahad to match it. "Happy told me that you've had proposals."

"Yes. More than I care to remember."

"And that you turned them all down."

"That's right."

Israel darted a sideways look at her. She was still staring straight ahead, stoic as a Spartan warrior, her profile as cleanly defined as if it had been cut in marble. It was only the pink flush under her skin that gave her warmth, and he doubted she was happy about that. Still, she hadn't shied away from anything he had said.

"Any particular reason?"

"For what?"

"For turning them down."

"Besides not wanting to get married?"

"Besides that."

"I didn't love any of them. A few of them I didn't even like."

"You figure liking a man is a criterion for marriage?"

"It's a good starting place." She put up a hand. "I want to hear what prompted this conversation with my father."

"I have no idea. Happy started it. I just followed along."

"I'm not sure you 'just' do anything." Her nostrils flared as she breathed in deeply and exhaled slowly. "Tell me what he said."

"I've already given you the gist of it."

"All right. *When* did this conversation take place?"

"The day after Annalea found me. It was in the afternoon. You came in just as Happy was getting ready to leave. Do you remember that he said we were talking about you?"

"*That's* the conversation you were having?"

"Not to put too fine a point on it, but Happy was doing all the talking. I was listening."

"I'll just bet you were. What else did he say?"

"I recall the words 'old maid' were used at least once." He thought she might take offense to that, but what she did was laugh. "You are a hard woman to figure out."

"I am a hard woman," she said. "End the sentence there. There's no satisfaction for you in trying to figure me out."

"There might be."

She grunted softly. "Anything else?"

"Was one of the proposals you turned down really Eli Barber?"

Willa's head snapped around. "Goddamn it. Was he drinking when he told you that?"

"No. He might have been hung over from the day before, but he was sober when he visited. Is it true?"

"Yes."

Israel realized he would have to find a way to make up

for his lie to Happy. He had played a hunch, something he was good at, and he had surprised the truth out of her. She would probably have it out with her father, and Happy would deny saying it, and eventually it all would come back on him. This was likely his only opportunity to learn more.

"Was Eli one of the men you didn't like?"

"What do you think?"

"I imagine so. Did he know?"

"I thought he did. I gave him enough clues."

"Why do you suppose he proposed?"

"There's no supposing about it. Not now. He wants the land, same as all the others."

"All of them?"

"Danny McKenney, that's Old Man McKenney's son, might have only wanted to bed me, but that just proves he's got rocks for brains. It's the land that's the prize . . ."

Israel waited, expecting to hear more. When she added nothing, he merely said, "Huh."

"Does my plain speaking offend you?"

He supposed she was referring to Danny McKenney wanting to bed her. In Israel's lexicon that hardly amounted to plain speaking. "No, I was thinking about the last thing you said. It sounded to me as if you meant to say more."

"I don't know what you mean."

He repeated her words. "'It's the land that's the prize.' Seemed as if you might be implying that you're not."

"Well, I'm not, but I don't know that I needed to hear it out loud."

"That's the thing," he said. "From where I'm sitting, not saying the words was the same as shouting them."

"You have an interesting way of looking at things. Hearing them, too."

"Is that a compliment?"

"I didn't mean it to be."

That made him grin.

She caught his quicksilver smile and flattened her own lips as she shook her head. "And a ridiculous sense of humor."

His smile deepened, carving a crescent dimple at the corner of his lips. He knew it was there because she was staring at his mouth. It was something she did from time to time, and he finally decided it was the dimple that drew her attention. Other women had commented on it. Willa didn't. She simply stared.

"So why do you think you're not a prize?" he asked, sobering.

"That's what you want to talk about?"

"Unless you'd rather not."

She shrugged. "I'm set in my ways, stubborn to a fault, and suspicious. You know I am. You've said as much."

"I wasn't arguing." That made her slant him a droll smile, and he asked, "Is there more?"

"I tend to have a serious nature, some might say humorless."

"I hadn't noticed."

"Hmm."

He chuckled. "Anything else?"

"You tell me."

He thought about it for a while. "You work hard, harder sometimes than any two men, and I suppose there'd be those who would find it intimidating."

"But not you."

"Lord, no. Shiftless suits me just fine." He went on, enjoying himself. "You're fair, but that could be a fault if you're always sitting in judgment."

"I see," she said.

"Then there's that responsible aspect of your character. You take on everything. That's practically selfish, is what that is." He added quickly, innocently, "Not that I mind."

"No," she said under her breath. "Not that you'd mind."

Israel pretended he didn't hear. "You're whip smart. So smart, in fact, that a reasonably intelligent man can feel downright stupid around you."

Willa blinked.

"Finally, you're easy to look at. Real easy, I'd guess you'd say."

"I wouldn't say it."

"That's all right. I'm saying it. Even when your eyes go narrow and cool the way they're doing now, it's not in me to look away. Not anymore. My mother called what you do staring daggers. I guess she knew what she was talking about."

Willa slowed Felicity to a walk. She said nothing for a time, then, "Let me see if I have this right: I'm intimidating, judgmental, selfish, and I make people feel stupid."

"Is that what you heard?"

"Mm-hmm."

"Then I guess that's what it is, although you left out the part about being easy to look at."

"That does not deserve comment, except I appreciate your mother's observation about staring daggers."

"You wouldn't if you'd been standing where I was when she said it. She tried to slap that look right off my face."

"Oh, I thought . . ."

"I know. You thought she was staring daggers at me."

"Then I don't imagine slapping you effected any change."

"No. More or less fixed that look permanently."

"Not permanently," said Willa. "I've never seen it."

"Unless my mother shows up, you probably won't."

"Ah. Is that why you've never asked any of us to send word to your family? You don't favor them?"

"I don't favor communicating with them. You haven't, have you?"

She shook her head. "You gave me your parents' address in the event you did not survive your injuries. Do you remember that?"

"I remember you badgering me for it."

"Well, you survived so I figured what you wanted to tell them was up to you."

"Good. They're used to not hearing from me." But he had promised he would write to them when he reached Temptation. They probably knew by now that he had never arrived. They would be disappointed, resigned, but not surprised.

"But you lived right there in Chicago," she said. "You said Herring wasn't far."

"It's been a lot of years since I lived in their pockets. I was eighteen when I left. That was fifteen years ago, and I don't make a habit of looking back. I will say, though, as rebellious as I got, I never once thought of calling my mother 'Pearl' or my father 'James.' Happy is considerably more tolerant than the good Reverend McKenna could ever be."

Whatever Willa might have said to that, Israel did not know. They had finally reached the ranch. She dismounted first and gave him Felicity's reins when he swung down. Without a word or a backward glance, she walked off to the house, leaving him to care for the horses.

Chapter Seven

Eli Barber eased back in his chair and unfolded his legs under the table. His arms were extended in front of him, and he hugged a heavy mug of beer in his palms. It was the fifth time he had been served a beer in just under two hours. The boneless slouch he affected was as much a necessity as a preference, and his heavy-lidded green eyes were vaguely unfocused.

He did not count himself as drunk past repair. If his father walked in, he could still snap to attention.

He regarded his companions and judged it was the same for them. Buster Rawlins sat on his right, thick and compact, tightly wound for all that he was matching Eli drink for drink. On Eli's left was Jesse Snow, considerably taller than Buster and loose-limbed with a wiry, flexible frame.

The three of them sat in one corner of the Liberty Saloon in the shadow of the staircase. Buster had already been upstairs, and Jesse swore he was contemplating the same, although he continued to stare at his beer with more interest than he showed for either of the girls flitting between the tables. For Eli's part, he did not want anything to do with them that did not involve getting a beer. His father told him a long time ago that a man didn't drink where he pissed. Or something like that. When Eli wanted a poke, he went upstream, or in this case, to Denver.

"I think you should ask her," Buster said suddenly, picking up the thread of a conversation that had died several beers earlier. His rheumy gaze slid sideways to settle on Eli. "That's what I think."

Eli screwed his mouth to one side. "Hmm."

"It's been, what? Seven, eight months since the last time?"

"About that." Eli knew the answer to the exact date, the precise hour, but he did not offer that information. "Maybe you should ask her."

Buster gave a shout of laughter. His hand jerked and a wave of beer slipped over the lip of his mug and dribbled onto his fingers. He licked them clean before he drank. "Wouldn't that be something?" he asked. "What the hell would I do if she said yes?"

Jesse continued to study his beer. His normally fair complexion was ruddy with the effect of drink, and his heavy eyelids sheltered unfocused brown eyes. With considerable effort, he managed to raise an eyebrow. "Fuck her," he said. "Then fuck her over."

Eli stopped hugging his beer and reached for Jesse's. He calmly poured it in the ranch hand's lap. "You're done."

Jesse did a fair imitation of a jack-in-the-box as he jumped up from his chair. Stupid from drink and with no coordination to speak of, Jesse's arms flung sideways and his knees buckled as soon as he got his legs under him. He stumbled backward, collapsed again, and worked his hands like windmills over the blossoming wet spot on his trousers.

"What the hell, Eli?" he said, still fanning the wet. "It looks like I pissed myself, and I'll have to ride back to Big Bar like this. It'll shrink my balls."

Eli was unmoved by Jesse's argument, but Buster said, "How will you know?"

Jesse ignored Buster and looked up from his lap to face Eli. "What? What did I say?"

Buster swiveled his gaze to Eli. "He really might not know." He grabbed his beer to keep it safe and said, "And I'm not repeating it."

"Leave it," said Eli. "We have time. You can still go upstairs and dry your pants while you take stock of the state of your balls. And they would probably thank you if you took Louisa or Mary Edith with you." Without giving Jesse an opportunity to argue, Eli raised one arm and waved Mary Edith over to the table. "Can you take this boy upstairs and dry him out? See to his trousers, too." He reached in his pocket, produced a handful of coins, and carelessly dropped them in her open palm without counting. "My treat."

Mary Edith tipped her head sideways to indicate Jesse, who was still flailing about in his chair. "I sincerely doubt it will be mine."

Eli chuckled and shooed her away. She managed to grasp one of Jesse's bony wrists and pull him out of his chair. Watching them go, Eli and Buster shared another laugh.

"He had it coming," said Buster. "Damn me if he didn't."

"You talking about the beer or the whore?"

"The beer. I don't think he has Mary Edith coming unless she warms herself up first."

Eli saluted Buster with his glass. "How many years do you have on me, Buster?"

"You're what? Twenty-five, six?"

"Six."

"Then I have exactly ten on you. Why?"

"I was just thinking, is all. I suppose age is of no account when it comes to kinship. Not kinship in fact. Kinship in feeling."

Buster's upper lip curled and he set Eli's ears back with a steady, knowing look. "Seems to me that maybe you're done, too. You're comin' around to maudlin."

"What if I am?" He took a gulp of beer and pressed a sleeve to his mouth to wipe it. "I'm not ashamed to admit that you've been more friend to me than hired hand."

"I reckon that's because I've known you near on all your life, what with my mama cookin' for your family and my daddy working alongside yours for as many years as he did." His palms folded around his beer. "Seems to me you've got a question in your mind about Jesse. Am I right?"

Eli set his drink on the table and sat forward in his chair. He nodded slowly, solemnly. "I don't feel a kin to him same as you. And there's but six months between us."

Buster shrugged his heavy shoulders. "Sometimes there's no rhyme or reason for what draws folks together. I figure Jesse for all right."

"You think so?"

"You have a different opinion?"

Eli removed his hat and dropped it on the empty chair beside him. He pushed his fingers through his hair, flattening spikes and making furrows in the field of wheat. "I'm coming around to one," he said. "I notice Jesse doesn't say much when he's sober or when he's drunk, but when he's drunk, he says things he shouldn't. That concerns me some. Doesn't make him good company."

Smiling narrowly, Buster nodded. "Maybe so." The smile faded, and he asked, "Are you really thinking about proposing to Miss Pancake again?"

"You can call her Willa. I won't pour beer in your lap for that."

"Well? Are you?"

"I'm thinking about it," he said. The truth was, he had never stopped thinking about it. It was always there at the back of his mind. He remembered clearly the first time he had asked her to marry him. It was the only time she had said yes. He had been twelve. She had been ten. They had solemnly pledged their troth at the fence line that divided their families. It was Willa's idea to do it there. She told him it was symbolic. He thought it was more than that. He thought it was heroic. They each carried knives back then, but when they decided to make a blood oath, they didn't use them. Instead, Willa cut her wrist on a barb in the wire and Eli followed suit. They put their wrists together, held them fast for several minutes to be sure their blood mingled before they drew back. Willa tore her kerchief in two and gave him half to stem the bleeding. They had been perhaps more enthusiastic in making their cuts than was strictly necessary. Eli could still find the scar that was a consequence of that bloodletting. He wondered if Willa could do the same. He'd never asked.

Their promise to each other lasted three years. Willa was thirteen when she left for the Saint Louis girls' academy. There had been no word from her before she went, not even a hint that she was going. Sometimes it felt to him as if she had been whisked away, but when he asked, casually of course, if Willa had wanted to attend the academy, his mother assured him that Willa was looking forward to it, and she had that from Willa's own mother.

It was only a year after that he left for college in Virginia, and Willa had not yet returned. He did not stay in the East long, but it was already too late to repair what time and distance had put between them. He did not understand that immediately, but Willa made sure he figured it out.

Her contempt for him was tangible, and while it twisted his heart in the beginning, he eventually came to despise her for it. It never changed the fact that he still wanted to marry her.

Fuck her, and fuck her over. Poor Jesse Snow had only said what he had been thinking.

"It sure would make your father happy if she finally accepted," Buster said. "The combined property would be the biggest spread in Colorado."

Eli had nothing to say to that. He picked up his beer and drank.

Willa was quiet at supper. Only Happy and Annalea shared the meal with her. Zach was not back yet, and Cutter and Israel elected to eat in the bunkhouse.

"I don't know why they couldn't eat with us," said Annalea. She plunged her fork into a dumpling that she had already pointed out was the size of an eyeball and held it up for inspection. Once she had fully examined it, she plopped it into her mouth and then moved it from one side to the other so her cheeks alternately ballooned.

Happy said, "Swallow the damn eyeball, Annalea." He stabbed a small link of sausage and waggled it in front of her. "And then you can eat one of these fingers."

Willa wanted to stab something, but it would have been an actual body part. "Don't encourage her, Pa."

Happy blinked and lowered his fork. "Pa? It must have been a helluva day if you're calling me Pa."

"Yeah, Willa," Annalea said, swallowing hard. "You're looking a mite peaked. Are you feeling all right?"

"I'm fine. Tired, is all." She eyed them both in turn. "And not in the mood for supper shenanigans."

"Shenanigans," Annalea repeated. "I *do* like that word.

Kind of comical, isn't it? I think it sounds exactly like what it is." She shoveled sauerkraut onto her fork and slowly raised it to her lips. She watched the fork approach until her eyes crossed, then she slanted a look at her father and mouthed the words "shredded brains."

Willa said tiredly, "Sauerkraut doesn't look a thing like shredded brains. More like you flayed and boiled someone's skin."

"Gross," said Annalea. "Sure, you can play, Willa."

That eased a chuckle out of Happy. He tucked into his food again. "You haven't said how it went with Israel."

"That's probably a conversation for later," she told him. She saw Annalea's shoulders fall. "That's right. I intend to exclude you."

"I am ten. You remember I had a birthday, don't you?"

Willa ignored that. "There was a moment on the ridge that he thought he recalled something, but there's been so much talk among us about it, that he was not confident that it was a true memory." When Annalea frowned, Willa explained, "You know, like how you insist you were there when Zach fell in the ravine over Blue Knob way."

"I have it clear in my mind."

"I know. But you weren't but three years old when it happened and nowhere near Blue Knob. You've just heard the story so many times you have images of it and that's what you're calling a memory."

Happy told her, "But you're just really looking through someone else's album of photographs."

"Well, that's disappointing," Annalea said around another doughy eyeball. "Not for me. I mean for Israel. I think he was hopeful."

In spite of what he had told her, Willa was not so sure. She let it pass. "He handled his mount fair to middlin'. Then again, Felicity led Galahad about by the nose so there wasn't much skill required on Mr. McKenna's part."

"Israel," Happy said. "He's told you to call him Israel. I don't know why you don't."

"Because Annalea's here, and I am trying to teach her—"

"Stuff that." Happy poked at another sausage. "You don't call him Israel when she's not around. You don't call him anything."

She blew out an audible breath and spoke sharply. "Why are people questioning what I call other people? When did that become important?" When Happy and Annalea simply stared at her, she dropped her eyes to her plate and applied herself to her meal. "Never mind."

Silence fell over the table. Annalea and Happy exchanged glances, but it was Happy who finally ventured to speak. "So about Israel's horse sense. What do you reckon?"

Aware her heart was racing, Willa took a moment to ease it into normal rhythm before she answered. "Mr. McKenna—Israel, I mean—has a decent seat. He's out of practice as a rider, but he wasn't hesitant or timid. I probably should have had Zach work with him before now."

"Why didn't you?"

"What I had Israel doing freed Zach and Cutter to do other things, and they're experienced trainers. Well, not Cutter, but he's coming along."

Amused, Happy said, "Well, he's got the part down pat where he's tossed and tumbled, I'll give you that. The boy's got rags for bones."

"True, and that's the other reason I didn't put Israel on a horse earlier. I couldn't see the sense of him risking another injury."

"Huh. Were you thinking that when you rode out of here hell bent for leather and dared to him to keep up?"

Willa opened her mouth and closed it again.

Happy was nodding his head. "That's right, Wilhelmina. I was coming around the barn and caught the tail end of that exchange. Now don't look at me like you wish I had been in the house drinkin'. I always took you for having a better heart than that."

Willa set her fork down. "I *don't* wish you were drinking, and wherever you are is fine. I shouldn't have challenged him. You're right. He might have been hurt. I wasn't thinking."

Happy whistled softly. "That's enough, girl. No need to

martyr yourself because you made a mistake. Good thing it doesn't happen often. Gettin' up and down off that cross will tucker you out."

Annalea stared at Happy. "Pa! You ought not to say things like that."

Willa had a significant look for Happy. "Listen to her. She's right."

"It's not supper table talk," he said. "I'll give you that, but it doesn't change my opinion."

They finished their meal with no more talk about Israel McKenna. His name did not come up again until Annalea was clearing the table and Willa directed her to leave the dishes and take pie to the bunkhouse.

"Don't overstay your welcome," she called out as the back door opened. "And don't forget to bring back their plates." This last was mostly lost as the door juddered closed.

Happy chuckled. "You want to wager on whether you get them tonight?"

"Oh, I'll get them tonight because I will have to go out there and drag her back." She fell silent, gathering her thoughts, and when she turned in her chair to face her father, she could not help being aware of his wary regard. He was anticipating a confrontation. She wondered if he was thinking about having a drink in his hand, and just as important, what she would do if he went looking for a bottle.

"Out with it," said Happy. "You look like your belly's on fire with all words you're not sayin'. Just say them."

"All right. When I was out with Israel, he asked me about the marriage proposals I've had. He said he learned about them from you. Is that true?"

Happy leaned back in his chair and folded his arms across his chest. "I appreciate you giving me the benefit of the doubt, but I expect you already know the answer. Israel's got no reason to lie about that."

"I see, but I don't understand. Why would you tell him about any of it?" She watched the tips of Happy's ears redden, but at least he wasn't patting himself down to find his flask. "He told me when you had the conversation. Why then? You were coming off a five-day drunk and it was still unclear if Israel knew his own name. What were you thinking would come of it?"

"When you put it that way . . ." He shrugged. "I worry about you."

"Since when?"

"Jesus. Do I really have to explain that? Since forever."

Willa stared at him, incredulous.

"It's insulting that you don't believe me."

"I'm sorry. I didn't mean . . ." Her voice trailed off. She sighed. "Maybe I did mean it. But that doesn't mean I should have said it. You surprised me. The drinking . . . it's been a long time since I thought you were paying attention."

"Well, I was." His chin jutted forward. "I have it in my mind to see you settled. Your mother and I talked about that. Talked a lot about it, actually. It was something we both wanted for you, to see you with a good man or at least a decent one. You have a right to know what that's like. When Evie died, I figured it was left to me to see it through."

Willa spoke softly. She had to because the urge she was fighting was to scream. "Are you telling me that Israel McKenna is not the first man you talked to about this?"

"I wasn't telling you that, but I suppose you could infer it."

"I *am* inferring it."

"Ah. Then you're not wrong."

Willa slowly slumped forward until her head rested against her folded forearms on the table. She closed her eyes. "Who else?"

"I might have said something to Dave Huggins."

"He left."

"Yes, but I don't think the prospect of proposing to you had anything to with that. He had a lung ailment, remember?"

She groaned. Loudly.

"I'd have to go back a ways to think of someone before that. Might've been Jinx Shreve."

"His name is John."

"Jinx suits, though, doesn't it? Yeah. He was the one. Knocked his drink right off the bar while I was talking to him. Almost got mine as well. He never proposed, did he?"

She lifted her head a fraction. "No. Thank God."

"You're upset."

Willa sat up and glared at him. "You *are* paying attention."

Happy wisely said nothing.

"How could you?" She placed her fisted hands against her middle. "It's humiliating enough that you invited men to propose to me, but to tell them about Eli, well, that is beyond humiliating."

Happy shook his head vehemently. "I never told anyone that Eli was one of your suitors."

That gave her pause. "Never? You didn't tell Israel?"

"No, and it will be a disappointment if you don't believe me. Did he say I told him?"

She reviewed her conversation with Israel in her head. "Yes, he did, but that was after I confirmed that Eli proposed."

"Then he took a stab in the dark and you walked into the point of his knife."

"Hmm."

"Wishing I was drinking yet?"

She sighed. "No. I don't wish that."

"I haven't given it up, you know. A nip now and again keeps my hands steady. I'm telling you so you don't set your expectations higher than I can climb."

"I understand." She rubbed her temples. "I do believe you about Eli. I suppose that means that Israel lied to me."

"What are you going to do about it?"

"I don't know." She said nothing for a moment, thoughtful, then quietly, more to herself than to her father, she said, "Maybe I'll tell him the truth."

Zach cursed his bad luck when he walked into the Liberty Saloon and saw Eli Barber and Buster Rawlins drinking at one of the tables. If they had been sitting at the bar, he might have been able to back out without being seen, but it was Eli's habit, learned from his father, to always sit facing the doors. The only bit of good fortune, as Zach saw it, was the absence of Malcolm Barber.

Zach touched the brim of his hat, acknowledging Eli and

Buster as he passed their table. He laid down his money on the bar and asked for a whiskey. He was on the point of picking up his glass when he heard Eli invite him to join their table. Judging Eli to be on the side of drunk that inevitably provoked a commotion, Zach swept up his drink and walked over. Buster kicked out a chair. Zach took it and sat.

"You fellas come here for supplies?" he asked. "I noticed the stock at the feed store was low. That your doing?"

"First come, first served," said Eli. "That's why you're here? Supplies?"

"Mm. Seems as if we're between storms. Can't be sure when I'll get in again."

Buster nodded. "You here alone? Miss Wilhelmina wouldn't happen to be with you, would she?"

"Now what business would you have for asking after Willa?" He saw Buster jerk without visible cause, which he supposed meant that Eli had kicked him under the table. He knocked back his whiskey and held up the empty glass to indicate to the barkeep that he wanted another. "She's back at the ranch," he said. "Looking after things the way she does."

"Been some time since she's left," said Eli. "Did she mention that we met up a while back? Must be more than two months now."

It was almost exactly two months, Zach knew, but he did not correct Eli. "She mentioned that she ran you and Malcolm off."

The beer in Eli's hand shook as he laughed. "I wouldn't characterize it as running us off." He set his glass down. "She was real polite about it, and we were obliged to be mannerly in return."

"Uh-huh."

Buster paid for Zach's drink when it was put in front of him. "You didn't have to do that," said Zach.

"Sure. I know. You'll get the next round."

Zach had hoped he could leave when he finished this one. He decided to nurse it. "Thanks."

Buster shrugged. "You ever find that extra man to help you through the winter?"

Zach initially came up blank, then he remembered the

story that Cutter had put out there to learn what he could about Israel. He had no idea if he recovered quickly enough to turn aside suspicion so he just shook his head and said, “Nope. Never did.”

“I asked around like I promised Cutter I would. No nibbles. Are you still looking?”

“I think Willa’s decided we’ll manage on our own. We’ve been doing it so far.”

Eli tipped his chair, balanced it on the two back legs, and regarded Zach as though from a great distance. “But you wouldn’t turn anyone away, would you? Say, if someone showed up looking for work?”

Zach regretted leaving the bar for the table. Hell, he regretted giving in to the urge for a drink. He answered Eli’s question the only way he could. “I don’t imagine we would, that’s supposing they have some experience and don’t mind hard work.”

Eli nodded and dropped his chair in place. “Good to know, Zach. We’ll keep looking for you, then.”

Chapter Eight

"Tell me what he said exactly." Willa was going over the books and bills of sale at the kitchen table when Zach walked in and made his report. When he was done repeating the conversation he'd had with Eli and Buster, there was a chill in her marrow and no color in her face. She nodded when Zach asked her if she wanted a drink.

He put a tumbler of whiskey in her hands and pushed aside the books. "Those can wait."

She nodded dumbly and pressed the glass against her lips. She sipped and was glad for the heat sliding down her throat and emptying in her belly.

Zach pulled out a chair and sat. His broad brow folded into deep furrows. "Eli was feeling no pain, Willa. He might have been talking to hear his own voice. He's been known to do that."

Willa gave him a clearly skeptical look. "Do you really believe that?"

"No," Zach said after a moment. "Probably not."

"Then be honest with me. I depend on that, Zach." She took another swallow. "So do you think Eli's going to send someone our way?"

"He never said it outright, but it seemed like he had it on his mind."

Willa gave a jerky laugh. "And I think we know it wouldn't be because he's trying to help us out." She set her drink on the table. "Have you had supper, Zach? Did you eat in town?"

"No. I came here straightaway."

She told him to stay where he was and then she set about

warming up the leftover kraut, sausage, and dumplings. He declined liquor so she brewed a fresh pot of coffee. "I think better on my feet," she said, leaning a hip against the sink. She kept an eye on the pan on the stove. "I'm concerned that someone's going to show up here looking for work and we won't know that he's Eli's man."

"Won't Eli want credit for it? He likes for you to think well of him."

"Perhaps, but what if he doesn't want credit? Wouldn't that be what he'd do if he's sending a spy?"

"A spy?" Zach showed genuine astonishment. "You mean because of Israel? You think it has something to do with him? I figured Eli for trying to impress you with his thoughtfulness or some such thing and make another run at marriage. That's what I was thinking, especially on account of that kick he gave Buster under the table."

"What kick? You didn't tell me about a kick."

Zach realized he had repeated the initial exchange that he'd had with Buster, but he'd neglected to describe the kick. He made up for that oversight now. "I didn't see it, you understand, but I don't think I mistook what was going on."

"So Eli did not want Buster asking after me."

"Seemed that way, but then I challenged Buster about it and maybe that's what Eli didn't like."

Her nostrils flared as she exhaled heavily. "I can tell you, I don't like it." She picked up a dishtowel and folded it around her hand so she could remove the coffeepot from the stove. She poured Zach a cup and replaced the pot. "Kraut's almost ready."

He nodded. "I'm real sorry about this, Willa."

"So am I." Thinking, she unwound and rewound the towel around her hand. "Lord, but I hope he doesn't have another proposal in him. How many ways do you suppose a person can say no?"

"You need to head him off at the pass."

"What does that mean?

"Get hitched," he said bluntly. "Eli would have no reason to ask you again if you were already married."

Willa stared at him. "That's not a serious answer."

"It isn't? Maybe you should sit down, Willa. I'll get my own supper." He stood and gently pushed a chair toward her. She dropped into it, not hard, but slow and easy, and once she was down, he pushed it up to the table. He took a plate from the china cupboard and heaped it with food before he joined her again.

"Not only is it a serious answer," he told her, "it's also the most obvious one."

"Has Happy been talking to you about this? I'm just hearing that he's so bent on seeing me settled that he's been approaching matrimonial candidates."

"You're just hearing that? You didn't know?"

"Of course I didn't know. I would have put a stop to it. Dammit, Zach, he asked Jinx Shreve to consider it. Jinx Shreve! Can you imagine? He's spastic when he gets close to work or a woman!"

Zach could not quite suppress a grin. "I'm trying to put it out of my mind."

That prompted Willa to smile as well, although not for long. She stared at Zach, at his open, ruddy face, at the concern expressed in his dark and kind eyes. There were more short gray wires in the stubble of his beard these days, and a few more creases at the corners of his eyes, but he still had a big heart and sturdy, broad shoulders, which she had been leaning on for years.

It only seemed proper that she give him the right of first refusal. "What about you, Zach? Will you marry me?" She allowed that her timing left something to be desired. Poor Zach had a mouthful of hot coffee, and it seemed to Willa that he might spew before he managed to swallow. "Sorry," she said, watching him choke it down. She leaned over to clap him on the back when he began to cough, but he quickly put a hand out to stop her. She tossed a dishtowel at him instead so he could dab at the tears in his eyes.

"Jesus, Mary, and Joseph," Zach said when he could catch his breath. "Maybe you really do think better when you're standing."

She shrugged. "Shall I assume your answer is no?"

Zach swiped at his eyes again and then laid the towel

across his lap in the event he had further need of it. "Hell, yes, my answer is no. Jinx is a better choice."

"No, he's not. I like you."

"Well, I like you, too. Love you, in fact, but not in the way a man should love a woman he's set on marrying."

"Do you think you're too old for me?"

"Age ain't got nothing to do with it. It doesn't matter that I'm old enough to be your father. It matters that I feel like one toward you."

Willa lowered her eyes, nodded. "I feel the same. Not like a father, I mean like a—"

Zach put down his fork and laid a hand over hers. "I know what you mean."

She smiled jerkily, ruefully. "I guess Happy never suggested that you should be a suitor."

Zach removed his hand and leaned back. "Actually, he did."

Willa's head snapped up. "He did?"

"Mm. We didn't discuss it. He brought it up and I put him down. He'd been drinking so he just sort of folded. It was a long time ago. If I'd asked you then, I might have been your first."

No, she thought. He'd forgotten about Eli. Eli had been her first. "How long ago?"

"Soon after your mother died. So I guess it's been five years."

Willa's throat thickened, and she was relieved she had nothing to say because she couldn't have spoken just then. She got up and poured a cup of coffee for herself and drank it while Zach finished eating.

When he was done, he took his plate and fork to the sink and dropped them in a pan of water. "Unless you need something, I guess I'll go on over to the bunkhouse."

"I think they're playing cards. I sent Annalea out with pie after dinner and I sent Happy out after Annalea. They haven't come back, and I haven't minded." She waved a hand over the ledger and papers cluttering the far side of the table. "But their continued absence suggests penny poker."

"Thanks for the warning. Annalea took me for two dollars last time."

"Stop letting her cheat."

Zach grinned. Standing behind her, he put one large hand on her shoulder and squeezed lightly. "Good night, Willa. Give a holler when you want Annalea back and I'll send her over."

Willa tipped her head back to look up at him. "Would you ask Israel to come here? No hurry. He can play out his hand."

"He'll be over directly then. He doesn't play cards."

"He doesn't?"

"Never. Can't get him to sit at the table."

"Huh. What does he do when you and Cutter and Happy are playing?"

"Damnedest thing. He reads."

Israel knocked on the back door and waited for Willa's invitation to come in. He had expected her to call out, but she opened the door, stepped aside, and ushered him in. He brushed snowflakes off his shoulders and tapped his boots against the side of the house before crossing the threshold.

"I didn't realize the weather had turned," she said, looking out. Pale yellow light from the bunkhouse illuminated the quietly falling snow. She stood in the doorway a moment longer before she backed into the kitchen and shut the door. When she turned and saw that Israel was standing beside the table, hat in hand, she inclined her head toward the empty hooks to the left of the door. He hung up his coat and hat and removed his gloves. He stuffed those into the pockets of his coat.

"Are those the gloves Zach picked out for you?" asked Willa.

"Yes. He just gave them to me."

She nodded and pointed to a chair. "Please, sit."

He did.

Willa also sat but not before she bent down to look at his boots under the table. "Those aren't new."

"I didn't take the time to try out the new ones."

"I told him there was no hurry."

"He said that, but I thought there might be more pie here."

She gave a short laugh. "No, you didn't."

"No," he said, smiling briefly in return. "I didn't." He looked around while he waited for Willa to announce the reason she'd requested his presence. This kitchen was not as ordered as the one he recalled from his childhood. In that kitchen the dry goods were kept alphabetically and the seasonings were all labeled in his mother's copperplate hand. The space he occupied now was infinitely more inviting. It was not merely the residual heat from the great iron stove that gave it its warmth; it was also the gently scarred china cupboard and the mismatched cups and saucers on display there, the plates soaking in dishwater, the fragrance of freshly brewed coffee, and the chair under him that wobbled ever so slightly when he shifted his weight. He rocked it back and forth several times. "Do you want me to fix this?"

"What?"

"This chair wobbles. Do you want me to fix it?"

"No. Why would I want you to do that?"

"Because it wobbles," he said patiently. "And I'm assuming you asked me here for a purpose."

"I did. Of course I did." She sat down abruptly, straight-backed, and folded her hands on the table. "What were you reading?"

"Pardon?"

"Zach said you don't play cards. He says you read instead. I wondered what you were reading. More dime novel adventures?"

"Oh. I see." He didn't see at all. It occurred to him that she had been drinking. There was an empty tumbler at her elbow that might not have been Zach's. "Your father brought me *A Tale of Two Cities* from the house."

"You like Dickens?"

"Usually. I'm not sure about these particular high-minded characters. Too much nobility for my tastes."

"That's right. The Quill effect. I forgot."

"How's that again?"

"You don't like saints."

Frowning, Israel raked his fingers through his hair. "What am I doing here, Willa? If this is about this afternoon, then tell me what I did and I'll apologize."

"You didn't do anything, at least nothing I can think of."

Israel almost suggested that she give it time, and it would come to her, but he choked off the words. He rose instead and found a glass and a bottle and poured himself a drink. When she pushed the tumbler at her elbow in his direction, he gave it a generous splash. He sat down, touched the rim of his glass to hers, and then drank. After that it was a matter of waiting.

The pads of Willa's fingertips turned white with the pressure she forced on her glass. "Zach saw Eli Barber in town today. Had a drink with him actually. Eli was with Buster Rawlins, the ranch foreman who works for the Big Bar. There was some conversation, not much, but enough passed between them for Zach to get the impression that Eli might be planning to send someone out here, someone looking for work."

"All right."

"I don't think you understand."

"Oh, I'm sure I don't." He took another swallow. "Go on."

"Eli would be much more likely to hire every vagrant passing through Jupiter just to make sure they never reach our spread. Looking out for the Pancakes is not characteristic of his behavior. The opposite, in fact." She carefully repeated Eli's conversation as Zach had recalled it to her.

Israel listened, and when she finished, he felt the full force of her expectant expression. What he did not have was a well-considered response. "All right," he said again, more carefully this time.

"All right? Do you have any idea what he's planning?"

"No. None. Do you?"

Her shoulders slumped and she stared at the drink in her hands. "No."

"Then . . ."

"You realize there is a possibility that he knows something about what happened to you. I'm not prepared to say he bears any responsibility for it, but he *was* out there poking around the day after Annalea found you. And he had his father with him. That's never good."

"So you think he suspects I'm here and he's looking for some way to confirm it."

"That occurred to me, yes. You could be in danger."

He ignored her last statement and spoke to her first. "Anything else occur to you?"

She hesitated, sipped whiskey, and then turned to him, lifting her chin a mere fraction higher than it had been before. "Not to me. To Zach. He thinks that Eli is looking around for a way to impress me and chanced upon this."

"And a good impression," said Israel, the light beginning to dawn, "would be the preamble to another declaration of devotion and an eventual proposal of marriage. Is that right?"

"Yes."

Israel had to lean in to hear her reply. "Did you say yes?"

This time she nodded.

"Well, if I understood your objections this afternoon, then you'll tell him no and that will hold him off. How long since he last proposed?"

"Six months ago, perhaps a little longer than that."

"Then it will hold him off for another six months or so."

Willa finished off her drink and set the tumbler down. It thumped dully against the tabletop. "What if I don't want to hold him off this time?"

Israel wondered if he blinked. He didn't think he had but in every other way he was at attention. The hairs at the back of his neck were standing up, and something cold that might have been his blood was slithering under his skin. There was a breath lodged in his throat, and he felt his heartbeat stutter to a stop, then resume a moment later with a thud loud enough to concuss him.

"You're going to tell him yes?" he asked, carefully neutral.

Willa blew out a breath, all exasperation this time. "No, I'm not going to tell him yes."

"But you said—"

"I said I don't want to hold him off any longer. That

doesn't mean . . ." She paused, hearing the words again. "Oh, I see why you're confused . . . I wasn't clear, was I?"

"Not remotely." Israel was moved to consider what method might work best to encourage Willa to stop talking. Choking her was undeniably a solution to the problem, but kissing her would give him so much more pleasure. He had just decided on option two when she started talking again. He poured another measure of whiskey in his glass and sat back to listen.

"I don't merely want to hold him off," she said. "I want to stop him altogether. I am weary of the shadow he casts. It has weight and substance and darkens my thoughts, my life. I've had enough. I want to be done with his proposals once and for all. I want to be done with him. Is that clear enough?"

Israel was struck by her vehemence, but he did not allow himself to respond to her urgency. Calmly, he said, "I think so, but don't forget I told you I wasn't good with a gun. If you're asking me to kill him, I might not be—"

Willa snatched the glass from his hand and set it down hard beside hers. "I am not asking you to kill him. Are you truly recovered from your concussion? I am asking you to marry me!"

This announcement was followed by a profound silence. Israel did not know how long it was before he heard the sound of his own breathing. Sometime later, he heard hers. The thrum in his ears came after that, dull at first, then louder, clearer, like the rush of water spilling from a pump, intermittent in the beginning and finally steady with no hint that it would ever stop.

He stared at Willa, watching her mouth, waiting for her lips to move around the words she would use to take it back. There were no words, though. Her lips did not so much as twitch.

Israel spoke because he decided one of them had to and it seemed the onus was on him at the moment. "Are you certain you don't want me to kill him?" He dodged the tumbler she threw at his head, but then she picked up the glass and droplets of whiskey splattered his shoulder as it sailed past his ear. He threw up both hands to defend himself even though she had no more weapons within easy reach. "All right," he said. "I'm sorry. I misjudged your sincerity."

"Misjudged my sincerity," she muttered, glaring at him. "And stop laughing."

He knew he wasn't laughing. The opposite was true. He'd purposely set his mouth in a flat line to smother any hint of amusement, and his jaw ached because he was holding it so tightly. His breathing was controlled, steady and even, and he did not look away once. He was presenting her with his soberest look, and she was accusing him of . . . well, perhaps it was only his mostly sober look because his shoulders *were* starting to shake.

He sucked in a deep breath and fought to hold it.

"Go on," Willa said, resigned to the inevitable. "Just let it go."

Oddly enough, her words had the opposite effect. The pressure in his lungs eased and the urge to laugh went with it. He was able to find the gravity of the situation that had eluded him before.

"I apologize," he said. "I should not have . . ." He shook his head, and for the second time that day, words failed him. "I apologize."

Willa studied him for a long time. Finally she nodded.

Israel said, "I realize I am about to state the obvious, but it still needs to be said. You don't know me, Willa. It begins and ends there. It is hard for me to imagine that you are so desperate, so lacking in choices, that you see no alternative except to make a proposal." He pointed to himself. "And to put that offer to me? You'd make a better match with Zach. You like him."

"I asked him. He said no."

That effectively shut Israel's mouth.

"That's right. I asked, he said no, and I sent him to the bunkhouse to get you."

"Zach didn't mention that I was your second choice."

Willa's jaw slid sideways as she regarded him unbelievingly. "Are you really going to pretend that you're wounded? You *laughed* at me, and you've been furiously trying to think of a way to say no that will end this. Well, you did, and it's ended. I won't ask again. I believe the feeling you're groping for is relief."

Israel waited a few moments to be sure Willa was not going to come out of her chair or at the very least, order him to the bunkhouse to send Cutter back. Before she looked away, he caught and held her gaze. There was a glittering sheen in her dark eyes that reflected the lantern light, but he had no way of being certain what provoked her tears. Frustration with him? Disappointment in him? Regret that she had posed her question?

So she would be sure to hear him, or more important, so she would be sure to listen, he spoke quietly, gravely. "I did not say no." He waited then for his words to have impact. The change in her features was subtle, but whatever she had been expressing before was being replaced by uncertainty. A small vertical crease appeared between her eyebrows as they pulled together. Her mouth parted just enough for her to suck in the lower lip. She worried it with her teeth. A flush crept up from her collar and spread slowly across her face, and her nostrils pinched slightly as she breathed deeply through her nose.

"You did not say yes."

"That's right. I didn't. But what's important here, at least as I see it, is not to get ahead of ourselves."

Willa continued to regard him warily, but she did nod.

Israel took a breath and released it slowly. "The order of events here is that a very short time ago Zach returned from Jupiter and related a conversation with Eli Barber that alarmed you."

"Concerned," she said. "I was concerned."

"Uh-huh. Seems that it raised every one of your hackles, but if you want to characterize it as concern, I'll accept that."

"You're laughing at me again."

Dead calm, he said, "No, I'm not."

She was quiet, thoughtful, and then, "I do not know how to take you sometimes."

"I understand. And that speaks to my earlier point that you don't know me. That's something you need to consider carefully. I was trying to say that there hasn't been much time between when Zach spoke to you and when you put your proposal to me. 'Hasty' is one word that comes to mind. 'Impulsive' is another."

"You probably have a lot of words at the ready, you being a writer and all."

The absolute aridness with which she spoke made him grin. "Well done. You see how you can poke at me and I don't take offense?"

"I don't know why not. I was trying to offend you."

That merely broadened his grin. He watched her eyes drop to the dimpled corner.

Willa dragged her eyes away from his mouth. "Can you be offended?"

"Mr. Roundbottom," he said. "That stung."

"Of course. You think a lot of your good looks. That was a poke at your vanity."

He shrugged carelessly and cocked an eyebrow at her. "My Achilles' heel."

Willa slumped back in her chair and shook her head. Laughter bubbled. "Do you recall what you said about me making a better match with Zach?"

"Because you like him. I remember."

"Mm-hmm. Well, I suppose you should know that I don't dislike you."

"Ah. You don't dislike me. That's a tad left-handed, don't you think?"

"I prefer cautious. You've warned me about hasty judgments."

"So I did." Israel knuckled his jaw. "Do you need my answer now, Willa? If I say no, will you ask for Cutter? If I say yes, will you have a preacher here in the morning?"

"No," she said. "No to both those things."

"Then there's still time to think this through. For both of us. You might decide that turning down Eli Barber's regular proposals is preferable to marrying me. I might decide it's better to move on than put you and your family in danger."

She stared at him but said nothing.

"Well? I have to tell you, I'm not used to being the sensible one in the room. I don't know if I can hold out. I wanted to kiss you real bad a little while ago."

"That's as good a reason as any to wait."

Israel's mouth quirked to one side. "That's not flattering."

She ignored that. "You're right. There are things I haven't thought through." She held up a finger as one of them occurred to her. "Are you married?"

Apparently he did not answer quickly enough to suit because he heard the tattoo of her boot against the floor.

"It's yes or no," she said with a touch of impatience.

"It's not." In any other circumstance, he might have been flattered when her face fell, but he reminded himself that Willa was not necessarily eager to marry him, she was eager to be done with Eli Barber.

"It's not?" Puzzlement defined her features, and she stopped tapping her boot. "Oh. I see. Of course. You're engaged."

With careful attention to his intonation, Israel said, "No, you don't see. The short answer to your question is I don't know. The longer version is that I was not married—or engaged—when I was walking along Wabash. What happened between Wabash Avenue and Pancake Valley still isn't clear. I have no reason to believe I got married on the journey, but you need to know that I've wondered now and again if avoiding marriage is what got me into trouble. I'm leaning toward that being unlikely, not because I am man of good character, but because not that many days passed between the last thing I remember in Chicago and showing up here."

Willa rubbed her forehead with her fingertips. She closed her eyes briefly. "That's a lot to consider."

"It is."

"I've been foolish," she said.

"I don't think that."

She snorted lightly. "Then you're too kind or you're a liar."

"If you have to choose, choose the latter."

Her head lifted and she stared at him, frowning. "Do you mean that? Are you a liar?"

"I do mean it. And yes, I am. Frequently."

"But—"

"But I was not lying when I said that. You are perhaps the least foolish woman of my acquaintance, and I know that because I have a tendency to seek foolish women out.

I didn't find you. You found me, and I still don't know what accounts for the attraction."

"I never said I was attracted to you."

He gave her an arch look, one eyebrow lifted, his mouth similarly slanted. "I was talking about what attracts me to you."

"Oh."

"Mm-hmm. Oh. And there is another thing I think you should know." She did not flush, he noticed, no pink blossoms in her cheeks this time. She went white. He was afraid it confirmed something he had begun to suspect about her proposal. "I am attracted to you, Willa, and if you have some idea that I would marry you under any conditions that do not include consummation, then there is no reason for us to continue this conversation."

She smiled a shade weakly. "Yes, of course. Consummation."

He did not take that as agreement. Israel believed she was only repeating the word, testing the taste of it on her tongue. He had the sense that she found it bitter. "You understand what I'm saying, don't you?"

Willa nodded. "I understand."

"And?"

"I don't know. I wasn't thinking that it would have to be a real marriage. I mean it would be real in the sense that we would be married by law, but in—"

"But not in the eyes of God?"

"God? How can you speak of the eyes of God when you just finished telling me that you're a liar?"

"I'm not sure what one has to do with the other," he said. "Do you think I don't know He's watching? Judging?"

"It seems to me that you brought up the Lord's name to make a point in your favor, not because you are a Godly man."

"And you would be right, but I am the son of a minister so it comes fairly easily to me. For instance, 'A man shall leave his father and his mother and hold fast to his wife, and they shall become one flesh.' That's from the book of Genesis, chapter two, verse twenty-four."

Her lips parted but she had no words.

"I know," he said. "It astonishes me sometimes. That was not a verse the good reverend insisted that I learn. As a very young man, the idea of one flesh was intriguing." He shrugged. "So I learned what I could about it."

Willa made a strangled sound at the back of her throat.

"Are you all right?" Israel asked. She threw out an arm to stop him when he was moved to clap her on the back. He waited for her to catch her breath and relax before he said, "Here is another one. From Proverbs. 'It is better to live in the corner of the housetop than in a house shared with a quarrelsome wife.'"

"Hmm. I don't know about a corner in *this* housetop, but there's always a bunk for you across the way."

He laughed. "Good to know." He stood, stepped carefully around the glass and tumbler, neither of which had shattered when Willa threw them, and reached for his coat and hat. He started to put them on, stopped, and then came back to the table, this time passing up the chair where he had been sitting and going to Willa's side instead. When she turned, her knee brushed his leg, and with only a hairsbreadth distance between them, she was forced to tip her head back to look at him.

Israel dropped his hat and coat on the table. His hand continued its sweep toward Willa, glancing off her shoulder first, then the nape of her neck. His fingers curled around the loose braid that mostly confined her dark hair. It was as fine and silky as he thought it would be, and for the first time since he'd begun working for her, he was glad that his palms were not thick with calluses.

He applied very little pressure, but the tug was telling, and as it turned out, it was enough. She came to her feet of her own volition, and regarded him warily but unafraid. She never once looked away. Neither was she issuing a challenge. She seemed to be . . . what? he wondered. Then it came to him. She was waiting. Quietly.

He smiled. Her eyes dropped to his dimple, and that was when he kissed her.

Chapter Nine

Willa watched him closely over the next week and then only slightly less closely the week after that. She did not have a clear idea what she expected from him, but it was not indifference. She made it impossible for him to ignore her because she directed his work, and if he ever wondered if she was punishing him for that kiss with the hard, physical labor she assigned him, he did not call her on it. Sometimes she wished he would, not because it was true—it wasn't—but because it would have demonstrated that he was dissatisfied with mucking and digging and repairing. All of the work he did was necessary, so that was not an argument he could make, but he could have asked for work that would have challenged him and improved his skills, made him more valuable to the operation of the spread.

Israel had once claimed to be shiftless, but that was proof that he was a liar. He worked hard and he worked long. He followed directions, he rarely drank, and as far as she knew, he never played cards with anyone except Annalea.

He also had not shown the least interest in repeating that kiss.

Willa was not sure if she was disappointed, insulted, or relieved. There were moments that each of those emotions was keenly felt and times when it seemed to her that she felt them all at once.

As for Israel being uninterested in a second kiss, Willa accepted responsibility. She had not yet happened upon the right time to explain this to him, and the words that would fill out the explanation still had not presented themselves in any coherent fashion. She was aware that she occasionally avoided him because she feared she would simply blurt out that the fault was hers, that she had not been ready, and that perhaps she never would be.

Every time this last thought tumbled through her mind, and it came at her with alarming frequency, she recommitted to silence.

"I should have slapped him," she told Felicity, holding out a dried apple slice in the palm of her hand. "Or ground my boot heel into his toes. Either would have been clear enough, don't you think? I could have done both. The boot heel during and the slapping afterward."

Felicity set her nose against Willa's shoulder, nuzzling for more treats when Willa's hand dropped away.

Willa absently reached into her pocket for another apple slice and came up empty. "Sorry, girl. No more." Felicity pushed her shoulder again. "No." Willa placed her hands on either side of Felicity's nose and steadied her. "I said no."

Felicity responded to the pressure of Willa's hands and the firmness of her voice and took a few steps backward. Willa picked up the brush lying on the bench beside the stall and began grooming the mare. Felicity nickered softly and Willa patted her neck. "I didn't say no to him, did I? And you know what? I didn't want to." That was her secret, her shame. She only wanted to grind her boot into his foot or slap his face because she hadn't said no.

Willa's long brush strokes slowed and then stopped. Her hand rested on Felicity's flank. She had an urge to lean into the mare, and she gave in to it because standing alone had nothing to recommend it at the moment. She laid her forehead against the animal's neck and closed her eyes and breathed. The air was cool and pungent with odors that were familiar and somehow calming. There was Felicity's scent, tangy and humid, and it mingled with the smell of hay, leather tack, dust, manure, and weathered wood.

From just inside the doorway, Israel watched Willa. He had not expected to find her in the barn. He was under the impression that she had already ridden out when Zach sent him over. He was supposed to cut a few different lengths of rope and bring them to the bunkhouse, where he was finally going to get his first lasso-throwing lesson. He had been hinting around for weeks that he wanted to learn, but it wasn't until bitterly cold weather drove Zach indoors that there was time and opportunity for tutoring.

Now here was Willa. Willa, who had done a fair job of late creating a fence with more barbs than barbed wire. To stay or go was the question here, a question, Israel decided, that differed from the one that occupied Hamlet—but only in the matter of scale. Hamlet, though, had Shakespeare composing his soliloquy. The best Israel could manage at the moment was to clear his throat.

Willa spun around, clutching the grooming brush in front of her.

"I didn't mean to startle you," he said. "I wanted you to know I was here."

She nodded shortly.

Israel slid the rolling barn door closed, shutting out the harsh afternoon sunlight that had thrown his figure into dark relief.

It occurred to him that, before he shut the door, he should have asked her if she wanted him to leave. Her silence made the situation increasingly awkward, at least for him. He could not read her features, and the lack of expression was troubling.

"Why are you here?" she asked at last.

Israel did not think she sounded particularly interested. The question was posed as a matter of course, not curiosity. "I thought you'd left the door open when you rode out."

"But I haven't ridden out."

"I see that now."

She turned her back and reached for Felicity's bridle. "It's just as well that you're here. I wanted to speak with you."

The fact that she was not looking at him was telling. He considered approaching, considered offering to help, even considered taking the bridle out of her hands and wrapping her up with it, but he did none of those things. He stood his ground and kept his gaze steady on the back of her head.

"I was in love with Eli Barber once upon a time," she said, slipping the bridle on her mare. "I've been thinking that you might want to know that. I'm not sure that it's important, at least to the way I behaved when you kissed me, but it might be, so that's why I'm telling you."

Of all the things she might have said, this was easily the most unexpected. Israel decided the wisest course was to say nothing and let her go on. She must have sensed his presence because she didn't turn around, *and* she kept on talking.

"About Eli . . . we were young. I was Annalea's age. He would have been twelve. Our families had been feuding for a long time, and it was rather Romeo and Juliet of us to act in defiance of that. When he proposed, I said yes." She laid a blanket over Felicity's back and then hefted the saddle into position. "Neither of us knew quite what to do then, so I suggested that we take a blood oath right there at the fence line. It was all very dramatic." She glanced at the underside of her right wrist as she fastened Felicity's girth. "I still have a scar from where I cut myself on a barb. I think he might have one as well. I don't know; I never asked."

Israel did not have a mental picture of Eli Barber so he inserted his twelve-year-old defiant self into the ceremony, all unruly dark hair, long legs, and insolent smile. The image of Willa that he brought to mind looked a lot like Annalea. She wore a single braid, not two, and her eyes were darker than her sister's, but they were just as lively back then, and she looked at him with the purity of a child's joy. He would have opened a vein for her. If Eli had been moved to do the same, he probably did have a scar.

"What happened?" he asked without inflection.

Willa shrugged. "Family mostly. We kept our engagement a secret for years, but eventually we were found out. We didn't get married, and we didn't kill ourselves." She took Felicity by the bridle, finally turned, and began to lead the mare toward Israel and the exit. "I was thirteen when I was packed off to the Margaret Lowe School in Saint Louis. I wrote to Eli once a week for the first six months of my incarceration, but he never wrote back. It occurred to me that Malcolm and Edith were not allowing him to see my correspondence, but I believed, and I still believe, that he had a responsibility to initiate a letter. Something would have reached me eventually."

She came abreast of Israel. "By the time I returned home, he was at a school in Virginia. That presented him with an opportunity to write to me without interference from his parents. He did nothing with it. Eventually he came home, but my perspective was considerably changed by then, and I did not care. I had responsibilities, real ones, and when I looked at Eli Barber with fresh eyes, I did not particularly like what I saw. I tend to think it was the same for him." She handed Felicity's reins to Israel so she could put on her gloves. "It broke my thirteen-year-old heart when he didn't write, but a broken heart at that age is merely a rite of passage. Do you understand?"

Israel nodded. "Bea Winslow."

"Ah, yes." She smiled faintly. "The first girl you asked to dance."

"That's right. So you are not still grieving for him."

"No." She took back the reins and pointed to the door. "Will you open that, please?" As he walked away, she said, "No, I am certainly not grieving. You know he's proposed since then, and I've always said no. That is not going to change."

The door jerked unevenly as Israel pulled it sideways. The metal rollers emitted a high-pitched squeal as they moved along the track. He recognized it now as a cry for oil. That would be his responsibility, and he made an absent note to take care of it before someone asked him.

Willa's eyes lifted to the top of the rolling door. "You'll take care of that?"

And just like that, he was her employee again. "Yes, ma'am."

One of her eyebrows lifted, but she made no comment, and after a moment, she walked on.

Israel watched her, and when she was gone, he went looking for the oilcan.

That night he lay in bed on his back, his head cradled in his palms, his lashes at half-mast. Three bunks away, Zach was whistling through his nose. Beside him, Cutter ground his teeth.

Israel hardly noticed.

His thoughts were occupied by something Willa had said that afternoon and never got around to explaining, or perhaps never meant to. The snippet had stayed with him through supper, nagged at him during the lasso lesson, and kept repeating itself during card play with Annalea. After asking him to pass the bread plate three times, Happy demanded to know if he was taking a train of thought back to Chicago. Zach threatened to lasso his neck if he didn't pay attention. Annalea was perhaps the most direct. She threw her cards at him when he was too long taking his turn.

The way I behaved when you kissed me.

That's what Willa had said. He was recalling it out of context but that was hardly important, and it was going to keep him up all night if he didn't get an answer to what the hell she had meant by it.

Willa's eyes flew open and she sat straight up in bed. She did not know what had disturbed her sleep, but her first instinct was to look toward the bed where Annalea slept. The oil lamp, which Annalea insisted should remain burning until she fell asleep, flickered ever so faintly now, but its light was sufficient for Willa to make out the top of Annalea's head above the blankets. She listened closely for the sound of her breathing and heard nothing that provoked her concern, no labored breaths or congestion, no coughing or fevered murmurings.

Relieved that she had been startled awake by something other than a problem with Annalea, she turned back the covers and put her legs over the side of the bed. As soon as she set her toes on the floor, cold penetrated the soles of her feet in spite of the thick woolen socks she was wearing.

When the disturbance occurred again, Willa had no difficulty identifying what it was. She stood and padded quietly to the window. The scratching sound had come from there. *Where the hell is John Henry?* she wondered. The hound should have howled, should still be howling for that matter, but the space where he slept at the foot of Annalea's bed was empty, and he had not yet appeared.

Willa parted the faded blue gingham curtains and peered

out between the panels. Well, she thought, surveying the moonlit scene that confronted her, she had found John Henry and solved the mystery of why the traitorous dog had not made a sound.

He was cradled like a baby in Israel McKenna's arms having his belly rubbed and no doubt being told what a very good dog he was.

She wanted to bang her forehead against the glass but feared that the percussion would wake Annalea. Instead, she carefully raised the window a few inches and knelt on the floor so she could speak through the opening. The rush of cold air made her rethink her choice.

"What are you doing here?" she whispered harshly. "And don't tell me you're returning John Henry. I won't believe you. You probably stole him in the first place."

Israel stepped closer to the window. "I want to talk to you." His dark brows lifted a fraction. "Did you just growl at me?"

She thought she might have, but she was not going to admit it. "I'm coming out," she hissed. "And I'm taking John Henry back!"

She closed the window with more authority than she'd intended and immediately looked over her shoulder to see if Annalea was stirring. She was not, and Willa was able to release the breath in her ballooned lungs. Willa rose, and the curtains fell back into place, but not before Israel snared her attention with his careless and charming grin.

She quelled an urge to stick out her tongue because it was immature, and lacked dignity. That, and he could no longer see it anyway.

Willa shrugged into her heavy woolen robe and belted it tight. The hem of her flannel nightgown fluttered around her ankles as she hurried to the kitchen to find her boots. She sat down to yank them on and then bounced to her feet as though she had springs in her knees and was out the door moments after that.

Israel was not waiting for her on the back porch. He was also not standing in the yard where she could see him. Was he still loitering outside her window? Willa ignored the steps and jumped off the side of the porch instead and walked around the corner of the house. Israel was still there, although he had moved about four yards back from the window. She supposed that was his idea of being discreet.

Willa employed long strides to reach him, and when she did, she held out her arms for John Henry. One of the hound's long, black-tipped, brown ears was draped over Israel's arm, and his belly was still exposed. He would probably howl if Israel passed him over now. Willa dropped her hands to her sides and was immediately beset by a shiver. She folded her arms in front of her and tucked her hands under her armpits. In another moment, her teeth would begin to chatter.

"I'm here. What is it?"

He looked her over. "We can't really talk here, can we? You'll freeze."

"Exactly my thought. Hand over John Henry so I can go back inside."

"I'll put John Henry in the house, but you and I are going to talk in the barn."

"I'm not going into the barn with you."

"Why not? We were there this afternoon."

"That's right. It was afternoon, not the middle of the night."

"It's not the middle." He stopped scratching John Henry's belly to put up a hand to halt her protest. "All right. I'll concede that it's night. My point is that it is a difference without distinction. We'll have privacy and warmth in the barn just as we had earlier."

"Yes, but—" She hesitated, glanced warily in the direction of the barn, which loomed like a great black hulk against the night sky, and then shook her head. "It's not a good idea. Whatever it is, it can wait until morning."

"Not if I am going to be able to sleep tonight."

If he had reported this to her as a complaint, Willa would have summarily dismissed it, but it was not issued as a grievance, only as a matter of fact, and since she had some experience with sleepless nights of late, she had a measure of sympathy for this state. Some of that must have shown in her expression because he angled his head toward the barn and lifted his brows once more in question.

"All right," she said at last. "But let me put John Henry in the house first."

"I don't think that's a good idea. John Henry should come with us. You can take him back when we're finished. Besides, if someone wakes and wonders where you are, you can say you were looking for him."

It seemed reasonable, but that only made Willa question the soundness of her thinking. "I don't think anyone is going to miss me," she said, falling into step beside Israel. "Happy was tippling last night, so he won't wake until coffee's on, maybe not even then. And Annalea slept through you scratching at the window."

"That was John Henry." Israel took one of the hound's short forepaws in his hand and waved it at Willa.

A bubble of laughter swelled in her throat and she snorted softly to cover it. "I don't understand you," she said when she could trust herself to speak. "Is there anything you take seriously?"

"Is there anything you don't?"

"That is not an answer to my question."

"Nothing gets past you, does it?"

Willa set her teeth together hard, but she freely admitted to herself that it had as much to do with the cold as with Israel's failure to respond in a straightforward manner.

When they reached the barn, Willa pulled the door open because Israel was still cradling John Henry. It moved soundlessly on the track. She looked up and then back at Israel as she slipped through the narrow space she'd made for them.

"Yes, ma'am. I fixed it."

She stepped to the side when he came through and closed the door. "Don't do that," she said. "Please."

"Do what?"

"Call me 'ma'am.'"

"Cutter does."

"I didn't ask Cutter to marry me."

"Well, there you have me."

"And you don't say it the way Cutter does. He's respectful. You're . . ."

"Not?"

"That's right," she said quietly. "You're not, not really."

"Hmm." Israel set John Henry down. "Stay where you are. I'm going to get a lantern. I don't want you to hurt yourself."

"That's kind of you, but I know this barn"—Willa paused when she heard his soft "oof" punctuated by "damn"—"better than you." She bent to scratch behind John Henry's ears as he rubbed his head against her leg. She whispered to the dog, "I do know it better, don't I? Hmm, don't I?"

"I can hear you."

She chuckled and stood, and her eyes gradually did as much adjusting to the dark as they were able. Narrow beams of moonlight slipped through cracks in the sides of the barn and she could make out the darker shapes of the loft ladder, the wheelbarrow, and the wagon. A bench was situated cock-eyed near the first stall, and she imagined that's what Israel had bumped into. She did not take everything seriously, and she could have told him that just then because his bump in the dark had made her smile.

Willa blinked furiously and shielded her eyes when the lantern light suddenly appeared in the same direction she was looking. Israel turned back the wick until the light was reduced to a soft glow that only bathed the area immediately around him. For Willa, it was like a beacon, and she started toward it, John Henry at her side.

"Watch out for the bench," Israel said as she neared it. "It jumped in front of me."

"I heard," she said dryly. She took an exaggerated step sideways to show him she was skirting the bench. John Henry went under it. Several of the horses nickered as she passed their stalls, many more slept undisturbed. Felicity put her nose over the stall door and Willa rubbed it. "No treats, girl."

Israel lowered the lantern when she reached him.

Willa looked right and left and wondered what it was about this particular place that had made Israel choose it. They were standing in the aisle with stalls and benches on either side. One of the benches was covered with grooming brushes, files, a horseshoe, and a couple of nails. The other held a double stack of horse blankets. Before she could ask if he meant for them to talk here, he pointed to the bench with the blankets.

"You take some, I'll take some."

Since she was shaking with cold, his suggestion had a lot to recommend it. What he intended to do with them, though, had her raising her brows.

"That's an empty stall behind you. There's also the hayloft and the wagon bed. You choose."

"I choose to go back to the house." And in the event he misunderstood or pretended to, she added, "Without you."

"All right, then we'll just stay where we are." He hung the lantern on a nail and picked up one of the blankets. He snapped it open and whipped it around Willa's shoulders like a cape. She clasped the tails in one fist to keep it secure. He shifted the rest of the blankets to the floor except for one that he spread across the bench. "You can sit there," he told her. "Do you want another for your lap?"

"Yes, please." As soon as she sat down, he tucked another blanket around her. She huddled under them, breathing in the scents of horse and leather and not minding in the least.

Israel cleared a space for himself on the other bench and chose one blanket to put under him. He sat and stretched his legs, crossing them at the ankles. John Henry nosed around Israel's boots for a few moments and then settled himself beside them. "And here we are."

Willa gave him one of her better cynical looks, the corner of her mouth ever so slightly pulled to one side, her eyes fixed on his face with a dead-on stare. "You had these benches in mind when you walked back here. I know you did. So why did you ask me to choose between the stall, the hayloft, and the wagon bed?"

"Optimism?"

She made a dismissive sound at the back of her throat.

"Very well," he said. "Are you all right? Warm enough?"

She was neither of those things, but she did not want to delay whatever discussion he meant for them to have so she said, "Yes."

He nodded once. "I want to ask you about something you said this afternoon."

Confident that he could not see her tense beneath the heavy blankets, she kept her expression carefully neutral. It was beyond extraordinary that Israel wanted to discuss Eli Barber.

"You mentioned your behavior when we kissed . . . it keeps—"

Willa could not help herself. She interrupted. "When *you* kissed *me*. I recall saying 'when you kissed me.' I was clear on that when I said it and when it happened."

"Oh." Israel removed his hat, set it beside him, and rested the back of his head against the stall. He regarded her from under his lashes, shielding her from the amusement in his eyes. "So that's important to you. That I initiated the kiss, I mean."

"It's accurate."

"It is. I kissed you first."

"Mm-hmm."

"And you kissed me back."

Willa felt her throat closing. She made a strangled sound. She wanted to ask him why he wasn't talking about Eli Barber but knew her voice would not support the question.

"As first kisses go," he said, casting his mind back, "I thought it went well." He began to tick off points on his fingers. "We did not bump noses, which can sometimes be funny, but is unfortunate when there is injury. And yes, it's happened to me. Another point in our favor was that it was a whiskey kiss. We'd each had a glass, remember? No mingling of sour mash and milk, say. Third, you have a splendid mouth with an intriguing slant that fits quite nicely against mine. I think you must have noticed that. Neither of us was aggressive with our tongues, and a chaste kiss is a good beginning, I always think. Are you sure you're all right, Willa? You sound as if you might be choking."

"Mnh."

"And finally, that kiss lasted for a good long time. I was not counting, but I have an uncanny sense for it, and I would put the duration of that kiss somewhere between the time is takes Cutter to get thrown from the new mare once he's seated in the saddle and the first eight measures of Bach's "Jesu, Joy of Man's Desiring" played at a moderate tempo."

Willa stared at him, blank and unblinking. She suspected

her eyes were as round and as large as silver dollars, but under threat of death, she would not have been able to close them.

Israel asked, "You're familiar, aren't you? No?" He hummed Bach's masterwork, pitching it low and perfect, but only the first eight measures so that it ended abruptly. "I have always liked that piece." He held up his hands, wiggled ten fingers. "Piano. Twelve years. You didn't guess that, did you?"

Willa shook her head, but the movement was barely perceptible.

Israel dropped his hands to his sides again and curled his fingers lightly around the edge of the bench. His features settled solemnly into place. "I'd like to hear your version of that kiss," he said. "I'd like to know what you mean when you talk about the way you behaved."

Frozen in a manner that had nothing to do with the cold, Willa was silent.

"I've been wondering," said Israel, "if there is something you think you did wrong. Or perhaps you're thinking you should not have participated. You did, though, and rather sweetly."

Willa jerked slightly. The blankets shivered around her.

"Ah." This time it was Israel whose shake of the head was almost imperceptible. "Would you have preferred that I not kiss you at all?"

Willa found her voice, or rather she found *a* voice, one that had a distinctive rasp to it and was unlike anything she had heard coming from her throat before. "Yes," she said. Then, "No." And finally, "I don't know."

"It's that confusing, is it?"

"Yes." This time the voice was one she recognized. "I'm sorry, but yes."

"That's all well and good, except there is no reason that I can think of for you to apologize."

She shrugged. The blanket around her shoulders slipped and she drew it back, but it slipped again. Before she could tell Israel she did not require his help, he was off the bench and resettling the blanket around her so that it covered the front of her like an armor breastplate and opened at the back. When she leaned against the wall, he tucked it in. She was several degrees warmer almost immediately, or at least it felt that way. Then again, it might have had something to do with Israel's hovering presence. He stayed where he was, looking her over, and she was reminded that this was exactly how he stood close to her in the kitchen moments before he kissed her.

There was no kiss this time. He backed away without looking and John Henry had to scramble to avoid being stepped on.

"Hey, boy," Israel said, bending to scratch the back of the dog's head. "Aren't you the clever one to be looking at where I'm going?" He straightened and returned to the bench, where he and John Henry both resumed their positions.

"Aren't you cold?" asked Willa once he was comfortably and casually stretched out.

"I can tolerate it. Anyway, sometimes being cold is what's called for." When Willa frowned, he said, "It's all right. You don't have to understand." He thrust his hands into the lined pockets of his heavy coat. "Have you changed your mind about your proposal?" he asked. "Maybe you regret making the offer."

She supposed she should have expected the question, but oddly enough, she hadn't.

"I'm asking," Israel said, "because you haven't said another word about it. I was following your lead, but I don't figure that excuses me from bringing it up, so that's what's on my mind. For now."

It was the "for now," or rather the intentional way he said it, that caused Willa's heartbeat to falter first then knock hard against her chest. She was not accustomed to feeling ridiculous, but when her mind kept wandering back to the kitchen, back to that kiss, it was exactly how she felt.

"I haven't changed my mind," Willa said.

"Mm. Regrets?"

"No. You?"

"It's not quite the same for me, is it? I didn't give you an answer that night, and I haven't made up my mind about it yet so I can't really change it. I don't have regrets, though. Not about you putting the question to me and certainly not about the kiss."

"I thought we were done talking about that."

"The kiss? No. Why would you think that? Is that something you regret?"

"You're just coming at that question a different way. I don't know how I feel about it. I don't know how I am supposed to feel about it."

"Supposed to? Are you under the impression there is a right answer here?"

Willa breathed in deeply through her nose. A moment later her lips parted with her slow exhale. "I've been kissed before," she said.

"Of course."

She looked at him sharply. "Why 'of course'?"

"Because you said 'yes' to Eli. In the three years you kept your engagement a secret, I supposed you and he eventually followed up on that blood oath."

"Oh. Well, I didn't like it."

"Perhaps if you and he had been older."

"I didn't like it," she repeated.

"All right."

"So I didn't expect I might come to a different opinion."

One of his dark brows kicked up. "And . . ."

"I did. Come to a different opinion, that is. I liked it."

Israel removed one hand from his pocket and held up an index finger. "Just to be clear," he said. "How long ago did you begin entertaining this new view?"

Willa did not try to hide that the question puzzled her. Her brows folded together. "It's been two weeks," she said flatly, wondering why he didn't know that.

"Ah. So we *are* talking about the kiss in your kitchen."

"*I* am. I have no idea what you're talking about."

But then she did. Before he could explain himself, it came to her that he was wondering about the man who was responsible for her new perspective. He hadn't known he was that man. Perhaps he had been hopeful, optimistic as he said earlier, but he wasn't sure, and now she was not sure she should have told him.

"Never mind," she said, giving him a narrow-eyed look. "I understand why you were asking, and I certainly hope you do not mean to crow or strut or beat your chest. I liked the kiss just fine, but maybe for all the practice you've had, I should've liked it better."

Chapter Ten

Israel gave a shout of laughter that surprised even him. Willa's head snapped back against the stall wall with a resonating thump, some of the horses snuffled, others nickered, Galahad snorted loudly, and John Henry raised his head and gave Israel an unhappy look before he settled his nose on his paws again and closed his eyes.

"You know, Willa, if any other woman told me that for all my practice maybe she should have liked the kissing better, I would take it as a challenge. But it's you, so I expect you meant nothing more by it than to put me in my place, maybe keep my head from swelling so big that my hat won't fit."

"It's your pride I was swiping at," she said a shade defensively. "That other thing you said about putting you in your place, that wasn't my intention."

"Wasn't it?" he asked. "You do it frequently."

Instead of denying it outright, she said, "I do?"

He shrugged. "All part and parcel of you being the boss lady, I expect. You probably can't help it."

She sat up straight. "Do the others think like that? That I put them in their place? Does Cutter? Lord, does Zach?"

"I can't recall that you've ever done it to them. Certainly not to Zach. Maybe Cutter when he first came, but I can't speak to that. You didn't ask about Happy, though."

Willa's silence was telling.

"I suppose he struggles the same as I do," Israel said. "I realize Happy's lost his way in a bottle, and me? I've just lost my way. That's why any place you put me right now mostly feels tolerable, but you should know that it won't always, and that time will come sooner if we're married.

Happy says you will never give me a part in running this ranch. Is he right?"

"Yes."

"Huh. I didn't believe him."

"I'm not going to give you anything. You have to earn it. Happy's different. He has to earn it back."

"That's fair."

"Happy doesn't always think so."

"No, I don't suppose he does."

"Did he tell you he almost lost the valley to Malcolm Barber shortly after my mother died?" When Israel shook his head, Willa went on. "He started drinking—hard drinking—when she first took ill with the cancer. That was four months before she died, and he slipped away from us before she did. She said she understood, and perhaps she did, but I didn't. We needed him. *She* needed him. After Mama was gone, so was he. He spent weeks at a time in Jupiter. I don't know if he was whoring, but he was drinking and gambling, and that attracted Malcolm's attention. Mal got my father into a high-stakes poker game, probably with no coercion whatsoever, and proceeded to strip him of his cash on hand, his money in the bank, his horse, his saddle, and when there was nothing else left, Mal put the promise that I would marry Eli on the table."

"The promise that you would . . ." Israel's voice faded away. He shook his head to clear it. "You're not married to Eli, so what changed?"

"In spite of Happy's condition, he still had enough sense not to agree to that wager. He straight up offered the deed to the ranch instead."

"Jesus," Israel said under his breath.

"Yes. He had it in his mind that he was saving me, naturally with no thought to the fact that he was risking everything I loved."

Israel could only imagine one outcome, but he had to ask. "What happened?"

"He won. Full house, three queens, two sixes. Mal had a spade flush. A good hand, but not good enough this time. Folks watching the card play told me later that there was a suspicion that Mal cheated to get his flush, but no one dared call him out, and it wasn't their place anyway. They were bystanders to that little drama, and only Mal and Happy were still in the game. Zach arrived late, too late to intervene, and I swear to you that having to stand there helplessly while the hand played out just about killed him. He brought Happy back and told me what happened. I thought he was going to quit, and I hardly could have blamed him if he had. I wanted to take a whip to Happy, but he was so pathetic, crying and slobbering all over himself, begging to be forgiven, promising to never take another drink, that I fired a shot at his feet instead and walked away."

"Mm-hmm."

"He stopped crying," she said.

"It's a wonder he didn't stop breathing."

"That would have been my second shot."

She said this last with considerable dryness, but Israel was not entirely convinced that she didn't mean it. He didn't ask her, though. There should be mystery, he decided.

"I think I understand what Happy needs to do," he said. "I'm still wondering what you expect from me." He stopped her before she charged ahead with a list. "Not as one of your hands, Willa. As your husband."

Her lips parted and then closed.

"You understand there is a difference, don't you? As the first, I work for you. As the second, I work with you."

She slowly nodded. "Yes, but you still have to learn all the same things. Riding, busting, mustering, herding, branding, shooting, digging, shoveling, mending, planting, weeding, accounting, canning, and cussing." She sucked in a breath. "I'll give you the last. You have a fair grasp there."

"I'm decent with a shovel, too."

She laughed on a breath. "Sure, there's plenty you can do, and plenty more you can learn if you have a mind to. Frankly, I've been wondering. I meant what I said. I won't give you anything."

"And I meant what I said," he told her. "That's fair."

"It'll be no different in the bedroom."

That made his eyebrows climb his forehead. "At the risk

of you taking another swipe at me, I am relatively confident there are things I can do in the bedroom. I won't list them. It would embarrass even me." If he had not been watching her closely, he might have missed the wash of color that suffused her skin. Her cheeks glowed gold and rose in the lantern light.

Smiling to himself, satisfied with this result, he said, "Zach is teaching me how to throw a lasso."

"He is?"

"And I've seen a lot of the property at one time or another, riding out with Cutter or Happy."

"When have you done that?"

"At night. Had to do it then, otherwise you would have known, and we were all busy during the day so there really wasn't time. And I guess I should tell you about some things I can do. For instance, we had a garden back in Herring. A big one because my parents were in favor of eating and sharing the fruits of my labor. Quill's, too. He wasn't exempt from the planting and weeding and canning. Preserving as well. You didn't mention that. You also didn't mention butchering and smoking meat. My father liked to hunt, and he took Quill and me when he thought we were old enough. I know how to dress a deer, prepare venison and jerky, so I guess I would be a help in the smokehouse no matter what meat you're preparing. Hunting is also how I know I'm not much good with a gun. Now my brother, he was a savant. By all accounts, he still is. And about accounts? I can keep them. I know about credits and balances and receivables. I had to learn it for the church and the missions. I am not without skills you need here. True, I can't rope worth a damn yet and I've never mustered or branded or herded, but Zach will bring me along. He swears he's going to make a cowman out of me."

"I had no idea," she said somewhat distantly.

"I know."

"And you play the piano."

Israel ginned, dimple flashing. "Not much call for that here. Not any call really."

"There's a piano." Willa's wistful smile transformed her face when it reached her eyes. "It was my mother's. She played. Beautifully, I think. She taught Annalea some tunes, but I never had an interest, nor do I believe I had any talent for it."

"A piano? Where is it?"

"In the front room. I don't suppose you've been in there."

"Never past the kitchen."

"Perhaps that's something that can change. Annalea hasn't touched the keys since Mama died. No one has. If she heard you play . . ." Willa shrugged. "Maybe . . . maybe it would be good to have music in the house again."

Israel drew up his legs and leaned forward, setting his forearms on his knees. He loosely clasped his hands together as he regarded Willa openly and with no apology for making her squirm.

"I want to kiss you, Willa. Does that surprise you?"

She pressed her lips together and shook her head.

"Does it alarm you?"

"A little." She lifted her chin and added quickly, "But not because I'm scared."

"No. Of course not. Does anything scare you?"

"There are . . . things."

"Spiders?"

"Now you're mocking me."

"I'm not."

"Hmm. Are you going to kiss me?"

"I'm working up to it. You scare me."

"I do not."

"Yes, you do. Come here." He sat up and made a pocket for her between his knees. He held out his hands, palms up, fingers curled slightly toward him. The invitation was clear, and he was in no expectation that she would take him up on it, but in spite of that he waited, and then waited longer, and finally, when he was at the point of withdrawing, he said her name softly. "Wilhelmina."

She shrugged off the blanket that lay across her shoulders and breasts, the one that he had tucked around her to protect her from the cold, and quite possibly from him as well. When she stood, the blanket across her lap fell to the barn floor. She stepped over it, hesitated, and then took a breath and the last three steps to close the distance between them.

She laid her palms against his. His fingers slipped under the sleeves of her robe and her shift and circled her wrists. Just as before, he exerted very little pressure to bring her closer.

Israel eased her onto one of his knees. She wobbled a bit there and pulled her wrists away so she could grasp his shoulders. He slipped an arm under her calves and lifted, bringing his knees together so she was securely in his lap. He placed one hand on her hip, the other at her back. A shiver went through him.

"You *are* cold," she said. "Let me get a blanket."

He shook his head. "I'm the opposite of cold." He watched her think about that, watched the traces of perplexity fade as she worked it out. Her brow smoothed, one corner of her mouth lifted, and her black coffee eyes filled with the light of comprehension.

"Oh," she said.

He laughed low in the back of his throat. "Yes. Oh. Are you all right?"

She nodded.

"Good. I was thinking that maybe this time you could kiss me, and we'd see how that goes."

"But this was your idea."

"So is this. You begin. I'll follow." He waited, eyebrows raised in patient expectation. He was careful not to challenge her. She would not have hesitated to meet that, but it was not what he wanted. He could sense her caution, just as he had sensed it in the kitchen, and what he wanted was her trust. Everything he had said about the kiss they shared was true, but then he had not mentioned that he suspected she had been anxious, perhaps even afraid, and what followed was her proving that she wasn't. He did not believe he was the sole source of her wariness. There was something else that made her pause, something that she reflected on before she could move ahead.

It happened now. He could see it was not a puzzle that occupied her; it was a memory. Her eyes were distant, vaguely unfocused, but they moved slightly as though she were reading or reviewing an image in her mind's eye. It did not last long, and it would have been easy to miss if he had not been looking for it, and it was easy to forget when her mouth touched his.

She sought his lips tentatively at first, brushing them so lightly it was the warm whisper of her breath that he felt, not the pressure of her mouth. When his lips curved in a faint smile, she tilted her head and put her lips to his again, this time matching the curve. Her mouth opened and she sipped on his upper lip. Her fingers tightened on his shoulders as she sought purchase. She held on as though she thought he might dislodge her from his lap.

It was the very last thing Israel wanted. He held her firmly, and when her mouth covered his again, he applied pressure in return. Her lips parted and then so did his, and the kiss that had been so sweetly started became lusty and carnal. Her mouth slanted across his and the tip of her tongue traced the line between his lips and along the ridge of his teeth. He sucked it into his mouth, twisting his tongue around hers, teasing her with forays and retreats, forcing her to explore and expand her awareness of him.

It was clear to Israel now that Willa had to know he was the one she was kissing. Above all else, she had to know that, and it meant familiarity with the taste and heat and smell of him. When she broke off the kiss and buried her hot face in the curve of his neck and breathed deeply, he was satisfied with that because to his way of thinking, it meant she was learning. He was also selfishly relieved that she did not remain there long.

Her mouth came back to his. Her lips were damp, succulent. She tasted of peppermint and more faintly of whiskey. He heard her breath catch and he liked that little hiccup, liked it for reminding him that it was something they shared. The breath that wasn't trapped in his throat, she had already taken away.

She briefly hummed her pleasure against his mouth. It was light and soft and it tickled his lips. It was not, thank the Lord, "Jesu, Joy of Man's Desiring," but the thought that it could have been made him choke back a chuckle.

Willa pulled back, searched his face, suspiciousness in hers. "What was that?"

He made a show of swallowing hard. "That was ticklish."

"What? What was?"

"The humming." And to keep her from thinking about it too deeply, he put his lips against hers and did the same. He felt the change in the shape of her mouth under his. She was smiling, and then she hiccupped again, but this time it was because she was trying to hold on to a laugh. He knew because he felt the first stirrings of it with the hand he had against her back.

He raised his head. "'Jesu, Joy of Man's Desiring'?"

She nodded. "You?"

"The same thought." Israel blinked when Willa smiled again, this time brilliantly. It touched every part of her face, but most especially her eyes. He drank it in, but not all of it. He did not believe he deserved all of it. "So there *are* things you don't take seriously. I suppose I was hoping that kissing was not one of them." His smile was a shade rueful. "Do you think we can come back from that lapse into humor?"

"Oh, I think so." To prove it, she cupped his face in her hands and kissed him hard on the mouth.

"I guess we can," he whispered when she put a hairsbreadth space between them. "That is very good to know."

Willa briefly touched her forehead to his and released his face. She returned her hands to his shoulders as she drew back and sought a more comfortable position on his lap.

Israel gritted his teeth and winced.

"I'm too heavy for you," she said.

"No. You're not." He moved his hand from her hip and slipped it under the curve of her bottom. He shifted her in his lap until they were both satisfied with the fit, he perhaps more so because she was pressing in an agreeable way against the bulge in his trousers. Israel moved the hand he had resting on her back to her nape and made a half circle around her neck with his thumb and fingers. His thumb did a slow up and down pass from the base of her ear to the knob of her collarbone. He brushed loose tendrils of hair out of the way.

Israel bent his head and kissed her where his thumb had been. He sucked gently, heard her whimper, and moved on, kissing her once on the jaw, her cheek, and then the corner of her mouth.

He kissed her deeply, slowly, with heat blossoming in his belly and in his groin. She answered in kind, which made him think it was no different for her. She was a glowing ember in his arms, bright, hot, sizzling when he touched the damp edge of his tongue to her skin.

Israel felt her hands move from his shoulders to the uppermost button on his coat. She stopped there, fingers hesitating. He looked down and saw that she was tracing the circumference of the button with a forefinger. His eyes lifted and caught her staring at him.

"What do you want to do?" he asked.

She was a long time answering. "I'm not sure I should say. You might think me a whore."

"A whore? Willa. I would not think that. Ever."

"You might." She shrugged as if she had decided it no longer mattered. "I want to touch you," she said, grasping the button and deftly pushing it through its hole. "Do you mind?"

"No. Not unless you will think me a whore."

Willa did not laugh, but the shadow of a smile passed quickly across her face. "A rogue," she said. "There's an old-fashioned word for what you are. Maybe scoundrel. Rascal, I think is a better description. Yes, definitely rascal."

Israel had been called all those things, sometimes with amused affection, sometimes in punishing, strident tones. He'd also been called much worse: good-for-nothing, reprobate, degenerate, and sinner. Annalea had wondered at the outset if he was a villain, and he had not denied it.

By the time he glanced down again, Willa had three buttons undone and her hand was inside his coat working the buttons on his shirt. When she had room to slip her fingers inside, she tugged on his undershirt, pulling it up until she could slide her hand beneath it and lay her cool palm flat against his hot skin.

The contrast in their heat made him suck in a breath, but then her palm began to slowly warm and he released it during the transition.

"You are like a forge. Metal would glow on your chest." Her hand jumped when his chest rumbled with quiet laughter. "No wonder you didn't need a blanket."

He let her go on believing she had nothing to do with the heat. While she dragged her fingers from the hollow between his collarbones to just above the buckle of his belt, he fiddled with the knot keeping her robe closed. She did not appear to know he had undone it until his hand was under the curve of her breast. Her flannel nightgown was still a barrier between them, but his warmth slipped through as if there were no impediment, as easily as water through a sieve.

Israel regarded her inquiringly when she raised her eyes to his. Her bottom lip trembled almost imperceptibly. The widening and darkening at the center of her eyes was easier to see. She did not tell him to remove his hand. She did not tell him to stop.

His thumb made a slow pass across the tip of her breast. The nipple was already budding, but it stood at attention when he brushed over it. Her lip stopped trembling because she bit down on it hard.

"That's all right?" he asked low in his throat.

"Mm."

He kissed her again, openmouthed, with hunger. She arched into him, filling the cup of his palm with her breast, and then suddenly she was a wild thing in his arms, squirming, changing position so that she straddled him, her knees resting on the bench on either side of his hips. It seemed to Israel that if she could have crawled under his skin, she would have done it. He didn't mind for himself, but he was afraid for her.

Their mouths fused, parted, came together again. They shared heat and air and desire, all of it equally, and then he was on his feet, carrying her, his hands cupping her bottom, her long legs wrapped around his hips. In three long strides he had her back pressed flush to the stall door opposite them. Her fingers were scrabbling at her robe, her gown, tugging hard to put them out of the way. Israel could not reach his belt, not without setting her down, and he was not going to do that. She pushed against his groin, grinding, and he felt himself swell and harden and thought he might come in his trousers like a schoolboy looking at his first French postcard, and then . . . and then John Henry sank a mouthful of teeth into his boot.

Israel growled deep in his throat but then so did John Henry. He tried to shake the dog off but lost his balance as soon as he was one-footed. Willa began to slide down the wall, and he hoisted her back up as if she were a saddle, which might have worked if she were a saddle, but she was a woman, all woman, and her forehead banged hard into his nose.

Israel's eyes watered with the force of the blow. Willa had to stop clutching his hips and find her own way down. When her foot touched the floor, John Henry nipped at her ankle.

"Hey!" she said, nudging him out of the way while she rubbed her forehead. "He bit me."

"I bet he bit me harder." Closing his eyes, Israel gingerly investigated the topography of his nose with a thumb and forefinger. It did not seem to be broken or bloody. "Damn, that hurt."

Willa shimmied once so that her nightgown fell into place, and then she closed and belted her robe.

Israel blinked several times to clear his eyes. He saw the knot Willa had tied in her belt and knew there would be no opening that robe again tonight. He glared down at John Henry. Willa placed her fingers on one side of his chin and urged him to look at her. He did.

"Are you all right?" she asked. "If it's any consolation, your face is as manfully beautiful as the angels sculpted it."

Amused, Israel let her grip his chin and tilt his head this way and that while she regarded him with a critical eye. For all her self-possession, he wondered if she knew her face was a glorious shade of sunset red.

"Lord, but you're pretty, Israel McKenna. It's a shame, if you ask me, and I will wager that those fine looks got you out of more than half of the scrapes you got into."

Israel thought the tips of his ears might be turning pink, but he quelled the urge to run a hand through his hair to find out. "Why don't you sit down, Willa?" She was as wobbly on her legs as a foal, although she did not seem to be aware of that either. He guided her to the bench she had been sitting on earlier and she dropped like a stone. There was even a whoosh as air left her lungs when she went down.

He scooped one of the blankets off the floor, shook it out,

and wrapped it around her shoulders. She was shaking now, not much, but enough for him to see that she was beginning to take an accounting of her situation and all that had come before it. Israel did not imagine that was going to go well for him.

He sat down beside her and nudged her shoulder very gently. He spoke quietly, a husk in his voice. "Breathe. It will be better if you just breathe."

She answered with a faint nod.

"Is there something I should apologize for?"

"No." Her voice was pitched just above a whisper. "Not if you want to live."

He smiled a trifle crookedly. "I suppose it's good that you have a sense of humor."

She turned her head and cocked an eyebrow at him. "I'm serious."

His crooked smile faltered, but then she turned away, and when she was facing forward, she dropped her head on his shoulder. "I guess you are," he said.

"Mm."

They sat without speaking for a time, heartbeats slowing, breaths coming more regularly. There was more stirring among the horses but even they quieted eventually.

"If we're going to be married," he said at last, "then I'm glad our first time together wasn't in the barn."

"And if we aren't going to be married?"

"Then John Henry will never be able to make it up to me."

Willa chuckled soundlessly. She pointed to the hound. He was lying at their feet again, looking up at them under a heavily wrinkled brow. "He looks apologetic," she said.

"No. He looks sorrowful, not sorry, and I think he's got a taste for my boot." He raised his right foot and angled it to show her. "New one."

"John Henry improved it," she told him. "It looks like a boot that's been lived in, not Sunday-morning-only wear. I bet you had a pair of shoes like that growing up."

"I did. I had to polish them every Saturday night until they gleamed and wear them until they pinched. Usually longer. My parents are frugal. I blame it on being Presbyterian." Israel liked the weight of her head on his shoulder.

It felt comfortable and something more than that. It felt right. He did not understand that. He had spent years avoiding this sort of complication, and now that the complication was resting her head on his shoulder, he felt at peace.

"No one's showed up in Pancake Valley looking for work," said Israel. "You have to wonder if that was ever Eli's intention."

"I don't have to wonder. I know."

Israel thought how like him it was to poke at the peace. He would always skip stones on the calm and glassy surface of a pond. "What about the proposal? Is that something he will do here or does he wait until he sees you in town?"

Willa looked up at him briefly and then resettled her head on his shoulder. "It's hard for you to let a thing just rest, isn't it?"

Israel gave a small start but not so small that Willa could have missed it. "I was thinking the same thing," he said, and that he had admitted it aloud surprised him. "If there was freshly poured concrete somewhere in Herring, I dragged a stick through it."

She chuckled.

"I'm serious. It's in my nature."

"Huh."

"You don't believe me? You would be the first."

"Oh, I believe that you would disrupt a sleeping baby just to create a commotion, but that doesn't mean it's in your nature. It could merely be a habit of long standing."

Israel shook his head and said curtly, "Don't make excuses for me."

"I wasn't. I was offering an alternative explan—" She stopped. "I see. You'd rather believe it's in your nature. You feel no obligation to try to change that."

"I am trying to deal honestly with you, Willa, and trust me, *that* goes against my nature. I want you to know what you're getting if I say yes to your proposal."

"Do you?"

Israel missed the presence of her head as soon as she lifted it. He was aware of her shifting on the bench, swiveling so she could study him. He only gave her his profile.

"Tell me, Israel, where were you really going in Chicago on the last day you remember?"

It needed to be said, so he said it. "I was on my way to buy a train ticket."

"All right. That makes sense. Now tell me where you were coming from."

And this, most of all, was what she needed to hear. Israel turned his head so she could look into his eyes. Without inflection, he said, "The Cook County Jail. I had just finished serving my time."

Chapter Eleven

Willa woke up groggy from a poor night's sleep, but after sitting on the edge of the bed for a few minutes and pretending to listen to Annalea chatter, she shook it off. "I am going to ride out with Israel this morning and give him an opportunity to show me what he can or can't do with a gun. I'll probably take him to Beech Bottom. Would you like to ride along? You could pack some food and blankets, if you like."

Annalea beamed and bounded out of bed. She hopped around, mostly because she was excited, but some because she was barefooted and the floor was cold.

Watching her, Willa bit back a smile and said, "Chores and then breakfast. Oh, and you should find your socks. One of them is under the bed. I think John Henry is sitting on the other."

At the mention of his name, John Henry lifted his head and looked from Willa to Annalea.

"And take John Henry out with you when you feed the chickens," Willa said.

"Can he come to the bottom with us?"

"No." For a moment it looked as if Annalea wanted to argue, but then she seemed to think better of it. If that was any indication of how the day was going to go, it would be very good indeed.

With that in mind, Willa made a first attempt to wake her father and discovered he was already up, had the stove fired, and the coffeepot set to brew. He was sitting at the table in the chair closest to the stove, warming himself and watching that coffeepot. She could not fail to notice that he had shaved this morning and also combed and slicked back his hair. He was wearing a clean shirt, reasonably clean trousers, and spit-shined boots. Willa's eyes wandered to the galvanized pail beside the stove. It was filled with kindling where it had been almost empty the night before. It seemed that Happy had been at his chores.

"Good morning," she said.

"Mornin'." He moved his stretched-out legs so she could get around the table without having to step over them. "I was thinking eggs and ham this morning. I brought a nice cut from the smokehouse, but I figured I'd wait for Annalea to gather up some eggs. Those chickens don't like me."

"They don't like anybody except Annalea." Willa put out the iron skillet and then took plates and cups from the china cupboard and set them on the table. "I have outside chores first," she said, "but I'll be back to make breakfast. I wouldn't mind if you looked for me coming back, maybe had a cup of coffee ready." When Happy nodded, Willa went to get her boots. She sat down at a right angle to her father to put them on.

Happy folded his arms across his chest and regarded Willa down the length of his nose. "I heard you come in the house last night, and that was after you were already in once. What took you outside?"

Willa did not flinch and she did not look up. She concentrated on getting her left foot in the correct boot. "John Henry."

"He got out?"

Eyes downcast, she nodded. "I found him nosing around the coop. He made me chase him all the way to the barn. I don't know what got into him."

"I'll be darned. Wonder how he got out."

"Can't say." She elected to pull on the second boot very slowly. "Did you step out last night? Maybe he slipped through the door and you didn't notice."

"Except for hearing you, I never stirred. Funny, though, that he was so frisky, leading you on a chase that way. Not like the little fella to do that. I wonder if there's varmints in the barn."

"There are always varmints in the barn," she said dryly. She sat up straight, rolled her shoulders, and finally looked at her father. She lifted her chin in the direction of the stove. "Better check your coffee before it burns."

Happy did not jump to his feet. He as was slow to unfold his arms and legs as he was to shift his gaze from Willa's face. "It couldn't hurt to have a look around the barn today, maybe find what attracted John Henry's sniffer."

"Sure," she said. "I'll do that."

Happy turned toward the stove. "I have it in my mind to do it myself."

Willa stared at her father's back and said nothing. She had not heard this particular voice from Happy in a very long time, but she recognized it immediately as the one he used when he would entertain no argument.

On her way to the barn, Willa saw Zach leaving the bunkhouse. She waited for him and told him about her plans to ride out to the bottom with Annalea and Israel. He was in agreement that it was time but advised caution when it came to putting a gun in Israel McKenna's hands.

"The only account we have that the man is a poor shot is his own," said Zach. "Could be he's just being modest."

Or lying, she thought. Israel McKenna was a damn hard one to figure out. Last night he told her about his eight months in prison followed by four more in the Cook County Jail and his release on the day he had been walking along Wabash, but except to say he had not murdered anyone, he offered no explanation for his confinement, and she had not asked. Willa didn't know if he would have told her, or if he had, if it would have been the truth, but she was more certain just then that she did not want to find out.

"Maybe," she said in response to Zach's observation. "I'll be careful." They talked guns as they walked. Zach suggested she take Happy's old Colt .45 that he kept clean but hadn't pulled the trigger on for years, and plenty of the long ammunition for it. She agreed that they should probably know if the gun could shoot straight. As for the rifle, Zach was in favor of the Remington; she was partial to the Winchester. She decided to take the Winchester and leave behind the weapon that Zach preferred.

"You're still expecting trouble from Big Bar?" asked Zach. He opened the barn door and let Willa enter first.

"Aren't you?"

"Well, I guess you don't ever *not* expect trouble from them, but it's crossed my mind that I figured things wrong."

"Hmm. Does that mean you think I shouldn't have asked Israel to marry me?"

Zach's hat tipped cockeyed as he scratched behind his ear. "I'm still puzzling that one out. I expected you'd put that proposal to someone from town. That Knowles fella, for instance, the one that works at the mercantile with his father, or maybe Ben Coldsmith. He's about your age and a widower. Good-lookin', too. Not as handsome as Israel, I'll grant you, but then not every man can look like one of God's fallen angels."

Willa laughed out loud at that dead-on description. "Well, he hasn't said yes."

"Can't puzzle that out either. Didn't take him for a fool."

"Zach," she said patiently. "You didn't say yes."

He reset his hat on his head and gave her a lopsided grin. "You have to hire smarter hands, Willa. That's a fact."

She chucked him lightly on the arm and then walked to Felicity's stall. She spoke to Zach over her shoulder. "You think you're smart enough to figure out what Happy's up to?"

While she made a surreptitious inspection of the barn, primarily in the area where she and Israel had been sitting, then embracing, and then sitting again, she told Zach about Happy being the first one up and dressed for the day in a manner that made her think he had something other than chores on his mind.

"He didn't tell you anything?" asked Zach.

"I didn't ask. I figured if he was shaved and cleaned up just because he wanted to be, I shouldn't call attention to it. It'd seem as if I were suspicious."

Zach caught her eye and held up a finger in the manner of one addressing a point of order. "Um, I believe that, in fact, you *are* suspicious."

"Well, of course I am, but I'm trying to act as if I'm not."

"Huh," he said, scratching behind his ear again. "Seems like you're goin' at the thing sideways, but then I always did think women like a meandering path."

* * *

The ride to Beech Bottom also took a meandering path, but the steep angle of the descent made it the safer route coming and going. Willa knew Felicity could negotiate the more direct trail because she had done it before, but then they had been trying to rescue a calf that had wandered away from her mama and was frozen with fear on a narrow ledge of rock. There was no urgency now and unlikely to be any. The cows had been herded out of the bottom before the first snow so they would not be trapped without sufficient food or water, or worse, killed in an avalanche.

Willa was satisfied that Israel and Annalea and their mounts could manage the route she had chosen. She only felt the occasional need to glance back and make sure they were following. Annalea was the caboose of their little train, a position she insisted upon because she believed that Israel might need guidance from time to time, and she could do that better if she were behind him. Not only did Israel not take issue with Annalea's assessment, but he accepted it with equanimity.

If Willa had thought Annalea would not get wind of it, she would have told Israel that she liked him for it, then again, Annalea's sole purpose on this ride was so there would be nothing to get wind of.

Israel was agreeable to riding out when Willa suggested it to him after breakfast, and he was amenable when she told him there would be target practice, and he was patently amused when he learned Annalea would be joining them.

"Chaperone?" he had asked.

Willa was not surprised he had seen right through her ploy but a little surprised that he had called her on it. No matter what he said, he was not afraid of her. A faint smile lifted one corner of her mouth as she reflected on it. At least he had not called her a coward, and she was fairly certain that applied.

The day was unusually warm for the middle of January, and the bowl-like nature of the bottom circulated a gentle eddy of wind but protected them from gusts. The trail was mostly dry, pockmarked where small rocks had been kicked up and overturned. There were patches of ice that Willa steered Felicity around and warned the others about.

When they reached the wide flat of the bottomland, Willa chose a site close to the spring. Water spilled steadily from an underground source and into a pool that was not completely iced over, although the hard glaze was creeping from the edges to the center. She dismounted and saw Israel was still in the saddle, looking around, eyeing the small, shrubby trees that formed a thicket along the circular edge of the clearing. There were taller trees of the same variety beyond the thicket, some of them twenty, twenty-five feet tall with glossy, rich brown bark and slender, drooping branches.

"Water birch," she told him.

He turned to her. "Ah. So it's called Beech Bottom because . . ."

Annalea swung down from her horse. "Because my granddaddy Obie named it before he got down here to see what was what. That's what Pa told me. Obie had the naming of everything on Pancake land."

There was no mistaking the pride in Annalea's voice. Hearing it made Willa smile. She told Israel, "Grandpa Obie said the land spoke to him, and he never changed his story and he never changed the name of anything, no matter that the facts did not support it."

"Like Pancake Valley not being a valley," said Israel.

"You noticed," Willa said dryly. "Yes, like that."

Chuckling, Israel dismounted. He landed lightly and patted Galahad on the neck. Over his shoulder, he asked Willa, "What's next?"

Willa directed the activity. Annalea was charged with finding a satisfactory location for the two coffee cans she had strung together and looped around her saddle horn. She wasted no time skirting the edge of the pool and heading into the thicket. While she crashed around in the brush, Israel took the reins for all three mounts and, as Willa instructed, took them to a place where he could not possibly shoot one of them. When she looked up from loading her gun, he was still walking.

"You don't have to go that far," she called to him. "I thought you'd figured out that I am not always serious."

He stopped, turned. "And I thought you'd figured out that sometimes I am." He led the horses another thirty feet and hitched them to a tree. By the time he walked back to Willa, Annalea had reappeared from the thicket dragging the dead trunk of a birch behind her. The rope with the coffee cans attached was slung around her neck so the cans banged and bounced against her as she pulled. "What is she doing?" he asked Willa.

"Give her a moment."

Annalea dropped the log when it was completely clear of the thicket and then rolled it toward the pool, stopping a few feet from the edge. She stood back, critically regarding its placement, straightened it, and then took the rope from around her neck and cut it with her pocketknife. She set a coffee can on each end of the log, balancing them carefully, and backed away. When neither can toppled, she spun around to face Willa, arms akimbo. "How's that?"

"Very good, now get over here."

"Maybe she should wait by the horses," said Israel.

"You cannot be *that* bad of a shot."

Israel shrugged.

When Annalea came around and stood beside them, Willa told her to find a place to spread out a blanket and work on lessons from her fifth year primer. "You remembered to bring it, didn't you?"

Annalea thrust out her lower lip. "You're truly going to make me do lessons?"

Willa did not deign to answer. She merely lifted an eyebrow and Annalea slunk off toward the horses to get her bedroll and books from her saddlebag. Watching her go, Willa shook her head. "I'm going to have to send her back to school in Jupiter in the spring. She wants no part of it, but I worry that I'm not giving enough attention to her studies. Happy promised to help out, but you can imagine how that is. It's still mostly when he feels like it, not when she needs it. Zach does not have time, and Cutter says he doesn't read or do sums as well as Annalea."

Israel accepted the Colt she held out to him by the ivory grip. "Why haven't you asked me?"

It struck Willa then that she had never considered it. "I don't know. Maybe because I didn't know if you were going to stay through the winter." That explanation seemed inadequate, and she felt heat rising in her face as he stared at her.

"Maybe because you didn't want me in your house," he said quietly.

Willa shook her head hard enough for her braid to swing forward over her shoulder. "No," she said firmly. "That's not it. You've been in the house."

"Kitchen table in," he said. "I didn't know about the piano in the front room, remember?"

"Well, Cutter and Zach don't traipse through the house either. You work for me. You have living quarters."

"Are you listening to yourself, Wilhelmina? You asked me to marry you, and I don't know the color of your goddamn couch."

She flinched, blinked, and drew in a sharp breath. After a moment, she spoke, but softly, not trusting herself to manage her temper above a whisper. "Maybe you should give me back the gun." She held out her hand.

"Gladly." He placed the Colt squarely in her palm, put distance between them by retreating a step, and rubbed the back of his neck.

Frowning, Willa stared first at the gun, then at Israel. "You don't want to do this, do you? I think you just picked a fight with me to get out of it."

Israel did not look away, and he also did not deny it.

"Well, damn," she said under her breath.

He made a noise at the back of his throat.

Annalea looked over the top of her primer and yelled, "Is someone gonna shoot or are you two just gonna keep on jawin'?"

Willa sighed deeply. "Gonna. Jawin'. Do you see why I am worried she will grow up stupid as a stump?"

"She might think it's more important to learn to shoot," he said after a moment. "She can see you set a lot of store by it."

His comment put Willa's attention back on the Colt. "I do. I hadn't realized how much, but you're right. I do. It's important for me to know that she can protect herself."

"Could you? Protect yourself, I mean. At her age?"

"I knew how to shoot," she said a shade defiantly.

Israel's blue-gray eyes narrowed when she looked up. "I didn't ask if you could shoot. I asked if you could protect yourself. It's not quite the same."

Willa felt herself go from hot to cold. Very cold. If there were any color left in her face, she would have been surprised to learn of it. She had lots of thoughts but no reply, and because it seemed prudent to do something, she began to lower her hand holding the gun.

"Hey!" Annalea shouted out again. "What about the shooting? Isn't someone gonna shoot?"

Israel caught Willa by the wrist and took the gun from her. "It's loaded?"

"Yes."

And because she spoke so softly, he checked it anyway. "All right. Stand off to the side." When she didn't move, he did, taking a position four feet to the left of her. He raised the Colt, held it steady, and squinted as he studied the targets. They were about two yards apart, one yellow, one green, both with bold, black lettering. "Yellow one," he said, and fired.

When the sound of the shot died away, the yellow can was still nicely balanced on the log.

Willa said calmly, "That was high, I think. And a little to the left."

Annalea hollered, "You missed!"

"Thank you," he said under his breath. To Willa, he said, "Green." His eyes narrowed on the target and he squeezed the trigger.

"Still high," she said.

He lowered the gun. "Well, I didn't hit the horses." He held out the Colt to her, shrugging when she didn't take it. "I suppose you want me to practice, but I'm telling you, it's mostly a waste of ammunition. I shot a buck once when I was hunting with my father, but it was not a kill shot, and Quill had to do the merciful thing and finish it for me. I never shot a squirrel, a pheasant, or a rabbit. Now I can add that coffee cans are safe." He added mildly, "Although I understand they're not good eating."

A slender, rueful smile touched Willa's mouth. "No, not good eating. Would you mind taking aim at the yellow can again? You don't have to shoot. I want to see something."

Israel obliged her, raising the gun as though drawing from the hip. His eyes shifted sideways when Willa stepped closer.

"No," she said. "Keep looking at the can as if you were sighting it."

He did, eyes narrowing in concentration until she put a hand on his and told him to lower the gun. This time when he looked at her, her head was angled in a thoughtful pose. "What?" he asked. "My grip? The way I stand?"

She shook her head and took the gun from him, holstering it. "None of that. It's the way you look at a thing when it's distant from you. Have you owned a pair of spectacles in the past?" Willa could not recall that she had ever been on the receiving end of such dismissive regard. He might as well have sneered at her. "I suppose not," she said.

"I don't need them."

"Uh-huh." She pointed to the yellow can because the black block lettering was clearer than it was on the green one. "Read what's stamped on the yellow can."

Israel did not turn his head to look at the can. "Coffee," he said. "It says coffee."

She raised an eyebrow. "That's what you want to do? Read what it says, Israel."

Sighing heavily, he turned, squinted, and said, "Coffee."

Willa said, "Finch's Best. The word 'coffee' is on the other side. Do you want to try the green can? I'll give you that it's more difficult at this distance."

Israel shifted his attention to the opposite end of the log. "Cortana."

"It's Cortana, all right, but that's not the side that's facing us. It reads 'coffee.'"

Israel gave her a sour look. "Trickery. I thought that would be beneath you."

She shrugged. "Can you even see the cans clearly?"

"I can see them just fine."

"I don't think you have any idea just how well you're

supposed to be able to see them." She waved to Annalea, gesturing to her to join them. "And bring your primer." When Annalea ground to a halt in front of them, Willa took the reader from her hand, opened it to a random page, and held it up for Israel. "Start anywhere. Just a few sentences."

He took the book from her. "I don't believe this," he muttered, but he dutifully began to read. "'Before the berry can be used, it undergoes the process of roasting.'" He stopped, looked at Willa oddly, and turned back a page to see what subject he was reading about. "Coffee. This about coffee."

She held up both hands in the universal sign of innocence. "Happenstance. I swear. Go on."

He found his place and continued. "'The amount of the aromatic oil brought out in the roasting has much to do with the market value of the coffee, and it has been found that the longer the raw coffee is—'" He stopped because Willa plucked the book out of his hands and returned it to Annalea.

"No wonder you don't like that reader," she told her. "Thank you, and you can go back to the blanket."

"But—"

Willa pointed to the blanket and Annalea left, making a dramatic show of dragging her feet. "Your near vision seems to be just fine, which I expected it to be since you read a lot, but then you don't play cards, so I wondered if there was something I didn't understand. You didn't need to change the distance of the book from your eyes the way Happy sometimes does. I guess you're good there."

"Your professional opinion, Dr. Pancake?"

Her mouth flattened momentarily. "Sarcasm? That's your best defense?"

"It's early moments yet. I will have a better strategy presently."

In spite of herself, she laughed. "While you're thinking about it, tell me how long you've had this problem."

"You're the one who says I have a problem."

"Israel. You must have suspected. What about when you were in school? Could you see what your teacher wrote on the board?"

"Yes," he said. When Willa's dark stare narrowed and never wavered, he added, "Mostly."

"Hmm," she said, finally satisfied. "Could your parents have afforded spectacles if you'd said something?"

"My father wore them to read and write, so, yes, they would have found a way to get a pair for me."

"Then I'm imagining you didn't want them because they'd point to a flaw in your pretty face."

"Not quite. I didn't want them because I didn't know a boy who didn't become a target wearing them. There is something about a pair of spectacles that makes bullies want to punch you in the nose. I have a lot of respect for my nose."

She regarded it critically. "It's a very nice nose, I'll give you that, but I've told you before that a break would add interest, if not character."

Wincing slightly, he rubbed the bridge of his nose with a forefinger. "I'll keep that in mind," he said drily.

"Mama wore spectacles. She didn't need them for fine work like sewing, but if she had to see who was riding down the road toward the ranch before they got to the porch, she put on her spectacles. Same when she wanted to watch what was happening in the corral when she was standing at the kitchen sink. We didn't bury her with them because Annalea had it in her mind that God would fix Mama's vision, and she would be able to see us just fine from heaven." Willa's lips lifted in a brief, somewhat sardonic smile. "I'm fairly certain Happy never believed it."

"I think that's probably right."

She nodded. "The point of telling you about Mama is that I can put my hands on those spectacles in less than a minute after we return to the house. You can try them on, see if they help some, and if no one punches you in the nose, we'll figure out a way to get you a pair of your own."

"So your mind is made up on this."

"Yes." She realized he was studying her, head cocked to one side as he grazed her features with his brilliantly colored blue-gray eyes. "What?" she asked. "What is it?"

He smiled a little then, his gaze never leaving her face.

"I can't say for certain, but it seems to me that you're sounding a lot like a wife."

"Oh." A crease appeared between her eyebrows. "What does that mean? Should I apologize?"

Israel laughed on an indrawn breath. "No. It means that the time's come to make it a fact. For all kinds of reasons, Wilhelmina Pancake, I need to be your husband."

Chapter Twelve

There was less than an hour of daylight left when Israel, Willa, and Annalea returned to the ranch. Annalea knew nothing about the agreement that the adults had come to. There was no handshake, no display of affection. Israel had chuckled but mostly because Willa was dumbstruck.

He'd led her back to the blanket, where they sat with Annalea and ate from the repast she had packed in Willa's saddlebag. There was ham left over from breakfast, hard-boiled eggs, a thick heel of bread, and apples. They held their canteens under the fresh, cold spring water cascading from the rocks and drank their fill. Annalea read to them from her primer, although not from the chapter on coffee, and answered questions about her reading to Israel's satisfaction. Willa remained quiet, observing only.

When the blanket ceased to provide a sufficient barrier between the ground and their backsides, they packed everything with the intention of returning right then, but because Willa caught Israel eyeing the rifle in her scabbard, she asked him if he wanted to try it out. He had, after all, shot a buck once.

If she had challenged him, he would have declined, but her wry humor had him agreeing to it. That began a round of target shooting in which even Annalea was eventually able to participate. Her success was on par with Israel's, but Willa was the undeniable champion, striking down the targets so often that Annalea finally refused to set them up again. Willa bowed out of the competition after that and took care of repositioning the coffee cans, a task that, to the sheepish amusement of Israel and Annalea, required infrequent attention.

They dismounted at the entrance to the barn. Zach came

out to meet them and helped Annalea. He sent her inside to care for her mare before she could launch into all the particulars of her outing. If Annalea suspected she was being maneuvered out of earshot, she did not say so. Willa, though, knew very well what Zach had done. She arched an eyebrow at him and waited.

"It's Happy," said Zach. "Not long after you left, he saddled Lightfoot and headed out. I assume to Jupiter, but I can't know for certain. I couldn't get a word out of him about his intentions. Tried comin' at it a few different ways, but he shrugged off all my questions. Cutter doesn't know anything either."

"And Happy's not back." It was statement, not a question.

"That's right. I figured I would go into Jupiter and have a look around when you got back."

"Do you know if he had any money?"

"Couldn't say. He wasn't drinking, though, and he didn't take his flask."

"Both those things are to the good," said Willa. "I'll check the old flour tin to see if there's much missing. I don't think he would have gone anywhere with empty pockets. Go on, Zach. Unless you want to send Cutter."

"No, I'll go. I have more experience bringing Happy home."

Willa nodded. The truth of that made her want to weep like an orphaned child.

Israel and Cutter were invited to the house for dinner. It was Annalea who wanted them at the table. In a frank declaration, Annalea told her sister she was not fit company, and she also declared the same to Israel and Cutter when she asked them to come up from the bunkhouse.

Israel was forced to agree with Annalea. Willa's efforts to behave as if nothing were wrong only underscored the fact that something was. Her smile was forced, her laughter a bit too bright and brittle, her eyes never quite meeting his or anyone else's. She was deeply unhappy, and quite possibly, he thought, afraid.

Cutter excused himself as soon as he scraped the last crumb

of applesauce cake from his plate. No one asked him what he was in a hurry to do. Annalea used John Henry as her motive to leave the table, carrying the dog out the door because he needed to walk. She seemed to miss the irony there.

Israel offered to clear the table, but Willa told him that she would do it, and since she was tense with pent-up energy, he didn't try to help. Instead, he leaned back. He smiled to himself when the chair wobbled. It took him back to the night she proposed. No one had ever gotten around to fixing it. Maybe no one would, and maybe there was a reason for that.

"Was this your mother's chair?" he asked suddenly.

Willa paused halfway to rising. "Yes. Why do you ask?"

"A stray thought."

"Hm." She finished getting to her feet. "But that reminds me . . ." She excused herself and left the kitchen.

Israel had a fairly good idea where she was going and what she would be bringing back. She did not disappoint. In less than a minute, she returned holding her mother's spectacles. She separated the wire stems and held them up for his inspection. He did not take them from her immediately. They looked too delicate for him to hold comfortably. The stems were gold-plated, as was the bridge, but the lenses were frameless, making them all but invisible.

When he did not reach for them, she turned them around and settled them on his nose, carefully bending the earpieces so they fit snugly behind his ears. She straightened and tilted her head this way and that to study him. "Look up," she said, pointing to her face. "At me. Hmm. Not bad. Wait. Don't move."

Israel watched her disappear into the pantry and return holding something behind her back. She skirted the table in a way that kept it hidden from him, and when she was on the far side of the kitchen, she revealed it, holding it up in front of her chest. "Can you see this?"

Even without the glasses, Israel would have had no difficulty making out that Willa was holding a jar of preserves. From the color alone he could have narrowed the contents to something in the deep blue or purple family: elderberry, blueberry, plum, or grape. What he could not have told her with certainty was that she was holding blackberry preserves.

"Blackberry," he said.

"You don't sound pleased about it. Your vanity really has no bounds. Would you like a mirror?"

He shook his head. "No, I might punch myself in the nose." That raised her slim, slanted smile and Israel did not mind at all that it was at his expense. He wiggled the glasses up and down on his nose instead of raising and lowering his eyebrows while he studied her mouth.

"I'm not giving them up," he said. "Not now that I can see you still have a truly splendid mouth all the way over there." He was prepared for her to throw the jar of preserves at him, but she surprised him by setting the jar on a shelf behind her and walking toward him.

"What about now?" she asked when she came to stand beside him.

Israel looked over the top of the rimless lenses. "Still splendid." He removed the spectacles because he did not need them to see her clearly anymore, and he set them on the table. He circled her wrist with his fingers but did not attempt to pull her onto this lap.

"If it's my answer to your proposal that is making you so unhappy, then you need to tell me. I don't think it is, though, and that makes me believe it has something to do with your father. Am I right?"

"Mostly. It has everything to do with my father." Without any encouragement, she dropped onto his lap. "I thought he was doing better. I really did. After all this time, you'd think I would know better than to allow myself to hope, but I had an inkling, and it's hard to ignore an inkling." A tear slipped over her cheek and she hastily brushed it away. The mouth he had called splendid turned rueful and watery. "You should probably rethink your answer. Look at the family you'd be taking on. My father's a drunk, Annalea is like a pebble in your shoe, John Henry's no kind of hound dog, and most days I'm afraid Zach and Cutter will realize I'm not up to running this place. It's occurring to me that Eli Barber deserves us. You don't."

Israel touched the side of her chin and turned her face toward him. "Really? And what do you think I don't deserve?

I like your father, Willa, he's not a mean drunk, and sober, he is a good storyteller and makes sense. There are times your sister is a pebble in my shoe, but I swear I've learned to walk better when that pebble's there than when it isn't. As for what Zach and Cutter might realize, it will never be that you aren't up to managing this spread. I know that because you are up to it, and I had an inkling I might earn the right to stand beside you someday. I'd count it as maybe the best thing I've ever done. Like you said, it's hard to ignore an inkling."

She sniffed. Her smile wobbled.

Israel groped for one of the crumpled napkins on the table and handed it to her.

Willa blew her nose into the cloth and balled it up in her fist. "You didn't mention John Henry," she whispered.

"Well, truth is, my feelings toward the dog are mixed. You're right that he's no kind of hound, but last night he rose to the stature of Cerberus." When she regarded him blankly, he explained, "That's the three-headed dog that guards the gate of Hades. When you think about it, John Henry was rather fearless. I don't think he knows he's stubby-legged and wrinkly."

Willa's laughter had no sound, but Israel felt the vibration of it ripple through her chest. He waited for her to go still again, and then he said, "You heard what I said last night about doing time in a Cook County cell. I thought you believed me. Did you?"

"In spite of you being a liar? Yes, I believed you."

"When you invited me to ride with you today, I thought you meant to press me for details, then you told me Annalea was coming with us, and I realized it was unlikely that it was your intention. But your sister's presence aside, I did wonder why it wasn't."

"You didn't tell me about your crime last night. I have to trust that you'll tell me when you're ready, or I have to accept that you'll never tell me. I can't exactly force it out of you."

"Are you sure it isn't because you really don't want to know?"

She hesitated a beat too long. "Maybe I don't. Last night I didn't. You've been clear all along that no one's ever mistaken you for a saint, but as long as you haven't killed anyone, and with your aim, I am inclined to believe it would have been an accident if you had—"

"I haven't killed anyone."

"Well, then, that's in your favor."

"You do realize the Lord sent Moses down from the mountain with Ten Commandments, don't you?"

Willa grinned. "Sometimes I forget you are a preacher's son."

"Minister. My father is a minister and I am a minister's son. The distinction is important to him. A preacher is a Bible-thumping, snake-handling, speaking-in-tongues individual who never attended seminary. The Reverend James McKenna delivers fire and brimstone from the pulpit in an erudite fashion. You see the difference?"

Willa's smile deepened. "All right. You are a minister's son. The up-to-no-good one if I understand correctly. Exactly how many commandments have you broken?"

Israel counted them soundlessly on his fingertips. "Seven."

She whistled softly. "Perhaps you could tell me the ones you've obeyed."

"No killing. No other gods. No graven images."

"Oh my."

"Mm-hmm." He regarded her soberly. "That's what you're getting, Wilhelmina, and I'm damn sure you don't deserve it."

Willa's reply was cut short by the sounds of horses and men approaching the house. She sat up straight, removed herself from Israel's lap, and went to the back door. When she stepped outside, Israel was right behind her.

A fingernail of moon provided enough light for Israel to easily identify Zach and Happy as they rode up to the porch. There was a third man, unknown to him, who was following in a buggy. Annalea and Cutter emerged from the bunkhouse and were hurrying toward them, while John Henry trotted ahead of the pair in pursuit of the buggy wheels.

Israel heard Willa mutter something under her breath that sounded like, "Prepare yourself," but he wasn't certain if she was speaking to him. Still, he sidled closer and had the odd thought that perhaps he should have put on the spectacles. He would have liked to have had a sharper picture of Mr. Buggyman's face.

Willa ignored her father and Zach and stepped off the porch to greet Mr. Buggyman as soon as he brought his conveyance to a halt.

Israel heard her speak clearly this time but still wondered if he heard her correctly.

"Pastor Beacon." She held out her hand to him.

Beacon leaned over the side of the buggy and placed his gloved hand in hers. He had an almost perfectly round face, a chin that protruded like a doorknob, and eyes that seemed to be perpetually astonished. They tended to lend him a very merry look even when he was not smiling. He was not smiling now, and for once he looked harried and vaguely put out in spite of the wide eyes.

"How lovely to see you," said Willa, removing her hand from his firm grip.

"And you, dear. I think. Your father insisted that I accompany him back. Rather forcefully, I might add."

"Gun?" asked Willa.

"Shotgun. He thought it was fitting and believes he'll have the use of it here directly." He used his buggy whip to point past her to the porch. "Is that the fellow there?"

Seeing Pastor Beacon indicate him with a flourish of his whip, Israel dropped down one step. Out of the corner of his eye, he was aware that Happy was dismounting. It took him a moment longer to register that Happy was pulling a shotgun from the leather scabbard. By the time he turned his head, his eyes every bit as astonished as Pastor Beacon's, Happy had the shotgun aimed squarely as his chest.

Israel raised his hands slowly, not with any hope of deflecting buckshot if Happy decided to fire, but to indicate in no uncertain terms that he was surrendering. He had some experience with it, of course, but he usually was plotting escape in the back of his mind. He was not thinking about that now. From the presence of the parson, Israel was able to make a reasonable deduction about Happy's intentions.

When Pastor Beacon gasped, Willa spun around to look for the cause. Her blood ran cold when she saw the shotgun in her father's hands. She strode over and put out an arm for the purpose of forcing him to lower the gun.

"Don't you dare," Happy snapped, jerking the barrel out of her reach and then steadying it again on Israel. "Put your hand down. This is business between men, Wilhelmina. Between me and Israel. I got it in my mind to do right by you this time. I'm sure there'd be folks who'd say I shoulda done it years ago if they knew the truth, but I let my pride overrun my common sense and that's what makes me suffer so."

"Stop it, Happy," Willa said sharply. "I mean it. Stop talking." She looked to Zach and then over her shoulder at Pastor Beacon, who appeared to be frozen in place on the padded leather seat of his buggy. "Has he been drinking?"

Zach shook his head, but the pastor spoke up. "Not a drop, Willa, and I offered him drink when he came to the parsonage."

Happy set his jaw. "I'm clearheaded and my eyes are wide-open. I am not going to take the chance that you'll be put through it again. Not without your mother here."

Willa's hands fisted at her sides. Her chin rose belligerently. "I swear, Happy. Stop. Not another word."

He did not look at her, keeping his eyes steady on Israel, but when he spoke, he addressed his remarks to Willa. "You go inside. And take Annalea with you. I won't say anything I shouldn't, but I want to have words with Israel here. You understand?"

"I understand what you're saying. I don't understand why you're doing it."

Annalea broke away from the light hold Cutter had on her shoulder and ran past Happy to Israel. She put herself on the step below where he was standing, offering her slight frame as a shield. The action stunned everyone into silence so it was Annalea who had the presence of mind to speak up first.

"This ain't right, Pa. You ought to be able to say what you want to say without a shotgun. Mr. McKenna ain't done nothing to you." When Willa groaned softly, Annalea's eyes shifted to her. "What?"

"You are hurting my ears, Annalea."

"Huh?"

Israel decided it was safe to lower his hands. He used them to grasp each of Annalea's pigtails and then tugged just hard enough to make her tip her head backward and look up at him. "Your sister cannot help herself. There is a shotgun pointed at us and she wants to correct your grammar."

When Israel released Annalea's braids, her head did not immediately drop. She continued to stare at him a few moments longer and said in a voice that was eerily calm and adult-like in its intonation, "That is just not natural."

This pronouncement made even Happy smile. "There's a truth from a babe's mouth. Now, you git, Annalea. In the house with you."

She remained firm. "Are you going to shoot me, Pa?"

Happy did not have to answer because Willa stepped forward, took Annalea by the elbow, and pulled her up the steps, across the porch, and into the house. The door banged shut behind them.

It seemed to Israel that no one breathed. He knew he certainly didn't. He imagined the shotgun was getting heavy in Happy's hands but the aim remained steady. Israel tore his eyes away from the barrel and kept them on Happy. "About that business you want to discuss . . ."

Happy nodded, swallowed. "That's right. We have business. Preacher Beacon, you best step down from your buggy now so Cutter can take it to the barn. Zach, you take care of our horses. What I got to say is for Israel, and this man of God is goin' to hear it."

Israel thought that Zach appeared more reluctant to leave than Annalea had been, but Cutter was philosophical about it. Beacon made an awkward descent from the buggy because he was short-legged and considerably rounder at the waist than at his hips. Cutter was patient, though, and waited to be handed the whip before he climbed into the buggy.

Zach started to follow but stopped after a few feet and appealed to Happy's better sense. "If you have to have the shotgun, at least point it at the ground. How's a man supposed to think when he's facing a load of buckshot?"

"I don't want him thinking," said Happy. "I want him doing. Buckshot encourages doing."

Israel considered telling Zach that it was all right to leave, that he and Happy and Pastor Beacon would come to terms, but doing so would have undermined Happy's authority and might have provoked a blast of buckshot after all. The wiser course was to say nothing, so that was what he did.

Happy waited until the buggy was gone and Zach was out of earshot before he lowered the shotgun and changed his grip to hold it like a baby in his arms. "I'm not putting it away," he told Israel. "Not yet. Just so you know."

Israel nodded.

Happy used his chin to gesture to Beacon. "Come over here, William. I'm not going to shoot you. Never was, and you damn well know it."

"You were effectively convincing," William Beacon said. To underscore this, he stepped around Happy so that he was standing closest to the butt end of the shotgun and not the barrel.

"This here is the man I told you about," Happy said to Beacon. "Mr. Israel McKenna. Hired him on, like I said, about two and a half months ago now. Gave him fair work and wages and such hospitality as a man warrants when he's living on your land. He's not going to tell you different. Isn't that right, Israel?"

"That's right, sir."

Discomfited, Beacon greeted Israel by clearing his throat and offering a short nod.

Happy went on, his attention all for Israel again. "I heard Willa leave the house last night. Late. I told her that this morning. You know what she told me?"

"No."

"She told me she left to find John Henry. Funny thing about that is she didn't mention running into you in the barn."

Israel knuckled the underside of his chin. "That's a funny thing all right."

Happy grunted softly. "See, I failed to mention to my daughter I got to thinking about it after she left, couldn't fall back to sleep like I wanted, so I took it in my mind to get up and find out what was what. Saw light flickering in the barn. Coulda been a fire for all I knew, so I had to investigate. You understand?"

"I do."

"Got me an eyeful of everything I didn't want to see. It wouldn't be proper for me to repeat it, especially in front of William, especially since I already gave him the gist of it when I visited."

"Then you are right," Israel said carefully. "It would not be proper."

"I didn't do a thing about it last night. For the life of me, I couldn't think what I wanted to do or should do. Went back to the house, tossed and turned some, woke early, and suddenly had the answer clear. You're a smart man, Israel McKenna. Clever, too. I figure you know why I went to see the parson and why I insisted he come back with me."

Israel nodded. "Yes, I have a good idea."

As if he suddenly felt the weight of the shotgun in his arms, Happy hefted it once and then resettled it. "I'm going to insist that you marry Wilhelmina."

"Yes, sir."

"And I've got my reasons for it. Good ones."

"I'm sure you do."

"So arguing about it is as pointless as a warm ball of candle wax."

"Candle wax. That *is* pointless."

"I love my daughter, Israel."

"I know that."

"And if you hurt her . . ." He allowed the threat to go unfinished.

"I imagine a quick death would be too good for me."

Happy smiled, but it was grim. "Like I said, you are a smart man."

"Are we doing this now?" asked Israel. "In the morning? Does Willa have a say? I admit we hadn't gotten around to discussing details. I don't think she would have chosen a pastor from Jupiter." His gaze swiveled to William Beacon. "Nothing against you, Pastor, but we would have had reasons for looking elsewhere."

"My congregation is in Lansing. That's a ways north and east of here."

Happy said, "William used to have a church in Jupiter.

It's been five years since he moved to Lansing. He was a regular visitor back when Evie was ill. Rode out several times a week to see her. He's the first one I thought of when this came up, seeing as how a preacher from Jupiter might present a problem. And to your question . . . we are going to do this now. William's brought the papers and the family Bible's inside. It will be a proper wedding, legally registered and performed under the eyes of God."

"Then that's that." Israel folded his arms casually across his chest and regarded Happy candidly. "Who is going to tell Willa?"

Happy finally looked beyond Israel to where Willa's face was framed in the kitchen window. "She's clever, too. She knows what's going on."

Israel made a half turn on the step and looked over at Willa. In response to her lifted, questioning eyebrows, he smiled a trifle guiltily and shrugged his shoulders. When he turned back to Happy, he asked, "The front room?"

"As good a place as we've got for a thing like this. You and William go on in. I'm going to fetch Zach and Cutter from the barn. Now that it's settled, we should have witnesses outside of the family."

Israel stepped aside to allow Pastor Beacon to precede him into the house. They were both still standing on the porch, their backs to the yard, when the shotgun went off. Beacon staggered sideways in real astonishment, but Israel pivoted in the direction of the blast and was quick enough to catch Happy in the act of lowering the gun. Seconds later, Zach and Cutter came out of the barn on a run.

Happy waved to them, signaling that everything was as it should be and that they could return. He put the shotgun under one arm and started heading back. It was a short walk because he had only traveled thirty feet from the house. He had the grace to grin sheepishly as he approached. "Just seemed easier to bring them in that way."

Beacon had one hand over his chest, and he kept it there as Happy climbed the steps. "You about killed me with that, Happy."

"I shot nowhere near you."

"You know what I mean."

Happy laughed. "You have to buck up. Go on. Open the door. Have a care Annalea doesn't fall on you when you do. She'll be right there."

She was. In spite of Willa's warnings to step away, she stumbled forward when the door opened. "Sorry, Pastor Beacon."

"No harm done." He patted her on the back and then took her by the shoulders, turned her around, and urged her back inside.

"Is there going to be a wedding?" she asked, moving to the table as everyone else filed in. "Willa says there's going to be a wedding. A real shotgun wedding. Is that right, Pa? Israel? Will somebody tell me what's going on?" She had to keep backing up so there was room for all of them to be standing in the kitchen.

"You have to stop talking, brat," said Israel. He went to Willa and stood beside her, shoulder to shoulder. He nudged her surreptitiously to look at her sister. Annalea had backed herself against the far wall and was standing beneath the shelf where Willa had placed the jar of blackberry preserves. The jar was directly above Annalea's head, looking very much like it had been put there for the sole purpose of shooting it off, much as an apple had been balanced on the head of William Tell's son. To put that image out of his mind, he told her, "Yes, there is going to be a wedding."

That confirmation had predictable results. Annalea pushed away from the wall and launched herself at her sister, wrapping her up in a fierce hug, pressing her head against Willa's chest hard enough to make her gasp. She flung her head backward then, pigtails flying, and looked up at Willa, her expression the very definition of earnest.

"You want this, don't you? I think I found him for a reason. For just this reason. Am I right? Did I do a good thing?"

"Yes," Willa said, slipping her palm over the back of Annalea's head, smoothing the flyaway strands that always worked themselves loose from her braids. "Whether or not this was the fated outcome, you did a very good thing." She bent, kissed the top of Annalea's head, and then said to

Happy. "I know it's not in you to be patient, but if you had waited a day or so, Israel and I would have told you that we planned to marry. We were getting used to the idea is all."

Happy snorted. "Getting used to the idea? I planted that seed the day after he arrived. It should have taken root before now because, God knows, his head was not crowded with any other thoughts back then."

Israel pressed a fist to his lips to check the urge to laugh. He looked sideways at Willa and said behind his knuckles, "It's truc."

"Mm-hmm," she murmured and set Annalea from her. She eyed the shotgun that Happy was still cradling. "Will you put that down now? Set it by the door, or put it back in the rack if you like, but I refuse to be married with a shotgun pointed at Israel's back."

Happy shifted his slight, rangy frame as though he meant to challenge her. Instead he leaned the gun in a corner beside the door and grumbled something under this breath that sounded like it had been his intention to keep it pointed at Willa.

Pastor Beacon reached inside his coat and tugged on his clerical collar. He cleared his throat and managed to make it sound significant. "Perhaps we should proceed to the front room."

To Israel's amusement, Happy insisted that he and Willa lead the way. There would be no ducking this ceremony. Israel had been escorted by federal marshals who were less attentive than Happy Pancake.

"I finally get to see the front room," Israel said in an aside to Willa. Her beautiful mouth flattened, and she flushed. There was also a flash in her eyes, more glint than sparkle, which he could not quite interpret, but since she had not tried to make a break for it, he chose to be encouraged.

The least he could do was go into this marriage hopeful.

Chapter Thirteen

Willa stared at the bed. "He changed the sheets," she said under her breath.

"What's that?" asked Israel. He was sitting on a ladder-back chair, one leg raised and bent sideways at the knee as he worked off a boot.

She pointed to the bed. "Happy. He changed the sheets and made up the bed before he left this morning. He had to have done it then, and he did it in anticipation of us spending the night here."

"I think it's proof that we did not stand a chance." With a short, final grunt, he wiggled the boot off and dropped it on the floor. "The shotgun was good for insurance, though."

Willa felt her knees wobble. Before they gave way, she sat down near the head of the bed. The house was quiet now. She could hear the steady ticking of the mantel clock in the front room. It was a sound she hardly ever noticed anymore. She had forgotten how soothing it was, how regular and reliable. She needed that just now. Tonight would be the first night in almost ten years that she would not hear Annalea's soft, sleepy murmurings in a bed next to her.

As a matter of course, the wedding ceremony had been brief. Happy took her by the arm and tucked it under his elbow, holding her in just that way until Pastor Beacon asked who gives this woman. Her father had spoken in smooth, tenor tones, clear and resolute, his voice uninhibited by whiskey. Words were exchanged then. At each of the pastor's prompts, she repeated vows, none of which came from her heart. She imagined it was no different for Israel, although he spoke more slowly and with consideration of the weight of the words. His eyes, his remarkably sentient blue-gray eyes, never left hers, and she found herself quite unable to look away.

The kiss was awkward. It did not seem to matter that they were familiar with the mechanics of one; they misjudged the distance and the angle. It was more of a collision than a kiss, but it gave the witnesses something to rib them about and put air back in the room.

She signed the document Pastor Beacon presented to her. Israel did the same. It was duly witnessed, folded, and tucked inside Beacon's vest for registering the following day. She did not feel any more married for having signed it than she did when Beacon made his final pronouncement and introduced her to people she knew, some of them all of her life, as Mrs. Israel McKenna.

There were toasts afterward, some solemn, most only mildly ribald in deference to Annalea's presence, all of them requiring a measure of participation from her and Israel. Happy produced a bottle of Kentucky bourbon from under the piano lid that he had been saving, in his words, for an occasion of enormous consequence. It was good liquor, and provided a sore temptation to Willa to drink herself senseless, but she refrained, choosing to do no more than sip when she was pressed to raise her glass. It did not surprise her that Israel exhibited the same caution, but Happy's careful imbibing was a revelation. When it was time for everyone to go to their respective beds, Happy was still standing without wobbling and walking without weaving.

"He thought of everything," said Willa. She picked up a pillow and hugged it to her chest. "Did you hear Annalea? She's thrilled that she gets to sleep in the bunkhouse tonight."

"That will last until Zach starts snoring. She'll be back before morning."

"I doubt it. She sleeps like the dead."

"Are you worried about her?"

Was she? Oddly enough, she didn't know. "Sleeping there . . . all the men." Once the words were out, she could not call them back, and she was aware that Israel's stare had gone from mild interest to penetrating. With no conscious thought, her grip on the pillow tightened. What she said, though, was, "She'll be fine. I'm just used to her being here."

"If it matters to you, I heard Cutter tell Zach he was going to bed down in the barn loft. Apparently sharing space with Annalea reminded him a little too much of home. He has a lot of sisters."

A brief smile lifted Willa's lips. "Four, by my count. There are a couple of brothers, too."

Israel shucked his remaining boot and studied the imprint of John Henry's teeth for a moment before he set it on the floor. "I can go and get her if you like. If she's already asleep, I'll just carry her back."

Willa shook her head. It was a sincere offer, she saw that, but accepting it would have been unfair to Annalea, Israel, and even to her. This was her wedding night, and if she examined her anxiety to the root of it, she would not find Annalea. "She can stay put. There will be less fussing in the morning."

"And John Henry's with her."

Quiet laughter bubbled. "Yes. She has John Henry. You were insistent about that."

"I was thinking about my ankles. I don't wear boots to bed."

A single glance at the pair on the floor beside him filled her face with heat. She remained composed enough to say, "I don't sleep with them on either."

"Then we have that in common. It's as good a place to start as any. What else don't you wear to bed?"

Willa judged that if her face had been warm before, it was flaming hot now. He was set on provoking this reaction from her, and she told him so. Israel's eyes widened a fraction, but Willa suspected that the surprise and innocence in his expression were feigned.

"It's teasing," he said. "Not provocation."

Willa was still uncertain. "Teasing?"

"You're warmer now, aren't you? And you're thinking about what I asked, maybe even wondering what else I don't wear to bed. You might be considering what it would be like to ease the stranglehold you have on that pillow and slip it under your head. Or quite possibly under your bottom. Women do that sometimes to angle their hips, or men do it for them. It makes for better—" He caught the pillow easily when she lobbed it at his head. Grinning, he smoothed it out and tossed it back. "Perhaps you'll smother me with it later. Something for you to look forward to once the preliminaries are out of the way."

Willa's hands fisted in the pillow. "Preliminaries?"

"Consummation," he said. "You remember, don't you? We talked about it. If not for John Henry, it would be behind us and you would not be sitting over there as if you were anticipating a blow. It's not flattering. I am not going to attack you, Willa. I thought that was understood."

She pressed her lips together, but her fingers uncurled. Lifting her chin a few degrees, she put the pillow behind her. "Last night . . ." She stopped and deliberately cleared her mind of everything but what she wanted to say. When she began again, her voice was quieter but recognizably more confident. "Last night was a succession of spontaneous moments, and I acted—reacted—impulsively, perhaps even instinctively, to every one of them. I was suspicious of your intentions when I accompanied you to the barn, skeptical when you wandered deep inside it to find a lantern, but amused by your transparent attempt to get me into the loft or the stall or wagon bed. You were clever about that because what you let me see wasn't what you really wanted, and then we were talking, just talking, and you asked me to come to you, and I did. It wasn't planned, not by me, and I don't think by you either."

She looked around the room that Happy had made ready and then vacated for her wedding night and gestured to all of it so Israel would understand her meaning. "All of this . . . it feels deliberate and forced and uncomfortable."

"This is where your parents slept."

"Yes. I suppose that's part of it. I haven't had any time to accustom myself to the idea, although I'm not sure I want to."

"Then we will need a new bed."

This was said in a manner of such practicality that Willa had to laugh. "All right," she said. "We'll do that first thing in the morning."

"We will do that tonight."

Her eyebrows lifted. "I wasn't serious."

"Well, I damn well am. Stand up."

For no good reason that she could think of, she did. So did Israel. He went to the foot of the bed, took a fistful of sheets, blankets, and the down-filled comforter in each hand, and yanked all of it off the mattress in a single sweeping motion. There was considerable fluttering and snapping until he had everything bundled against his chest.

"You take the pillows and bring the lamp," he said. "Follow me."

She had a thought that her eyes might be as round and as wide as Pastor Beacon's because she certainly was astonished. Again, without quite knowing why she was falling in with his plans, she scooped up the pillows and followed in his wake. His footfalls were padded by the thick socks he was wearing. Hers were not nearly so silent. Her boots tapped lightly on the wooden floor, which she supposed kept him from glancing back to see if she was behind him.

There were not many places in the house that he could take her. There was the bedroom she shared with Annalea, the kitchen and the adjoining pantry, and a cubby that her grandmother and mother had used for sewing and for storing a cornucopia of threads, needles, bolts of cloth, and every sort of whatnot, but was now a repository for all of that plus items no one knew what to do with. There was also a room with a desk, two chairs, an oak filing cabinet, and shelves for books that after fifty years in the valley still had too much space on them for anyone to mistake it for a library. Happy called it a study. Willa referred to it as her workroom. Annalea knew it as where-Pa-goes-to-drink.

And finally there was the front room. In homes Willa had visited when she lived in Saint Louis, she had heard the room referred to as a parlor, a drawing room, sometimes a salon. Some homes had all three, although the purpose of that had eluded her then and still eluded her. The front room was a serviceable name for what it was, a gathering place for the family, a place to welcome guests, and it was situated along the full front of the house. They rarely used it anymore, tonight's ceremony being an extraordinary exception.

But it was back to the front room that Israel led her. There was a stove in one corner that had gone cold hours earlier. After the first toast, Happy had declared there should be a fire in the hearth because on such a momentous night as this, a home needed more than heat. There needed to be sparks and crackling flames. Willa had smiled rather numbly in response, but at Israel's nudging, she lifted her glass and sipped.

There were no sparks now, literally or figuratively. Willa felt a little cold inside. Because Israel's hands were full, he tipped his head to indicate the rocker positioned to the left the fireplace. "Sit there. Hold on to the pillows if that helps."

If it seemed as if she took his suggestion, it was only because the rocker had always been a place of comfort and she had no intention of surrendering the pillows anyway. She set the lamp on a side table and adjusted the wick for more light.

Israel dropped the bundle of linens and blankets in the middle of the long, thickly upholstered couch. "It's claret," he said.

"Pardon?" His back was to her and she was sure she had not heard him properly. The thought of a glass of wine chasing the whiskey she had already drunk made her stomach roil.

He turned around and pointed to the curved back of the sofa. "The couch," he said. "Not as deep a color as burgundy, not as red as a cherry. Claret."

She stared at him, unblinking, and her thoughts fell back to their somewhat heated exchange in Beech Bottom. "I think you mean my goddamn couch."

There was no hint of embarrassment in his quicksilver smile or in his short laugh. "That's the one."

Willa's cheeks puffed as she blew out a mouthful of air. "What are we doing here?"

"Well, I am going to improve on what's left of this fire, and you, unless you have a mind to do something else, are going to watch me."

It bothered her some that she did watch him. He exerted

no effort to compel her attention, and yet he had all of it. She did not watch him build the fire; she simply watched him. He moved with unconscious grace, lightly and fluidly. There was a rolling rhythm in his step when he strode across the yard. More than once she had stopped what she was doing to take it in. He had never caught her at it, but Annalea had, and she made gooey, smacking noises until Willa threatened to throw her in the watering trough.

Israel had not merely healed since he arrived in the valley, he had become strong. Incarceration was not meant to be kind, and it hadn't been to him. It was not easy to tell in the beginning, but beneath his bruises, his skin was pale and pasty. When healthy color should have returned, he had almost none of it. Work had been a balm for him. His shoulders had filled out, straightened, and muscles, not bone, defined his arms and chest and back. If he was aware of the transformation, it was probably because his shirts fit a bit more snugly or tasks that he had once performed with labored breathing no longer stressed his endurance.

It was a pleasure to watch him hunker in front of the fireplace. The match he struck bathed his flawless profile in a flash of golden light, and when he set it against the kindling, the glow enveloped him. He regarded the fire for several long moments, mesmerized perhaps, or merely thoughtful, the threads of silver at his temple glimmering like ice, and then he suddenly turned his head toward her and met her eyes.

She did not, could not, look away from one of the Lord's fallen angels.

"I'm not sorry that we're married," she said.

"Then that's something else we have in common. Probably should keep a list."

"You start it. I'm too tired."

"Later. I'm tired, too." He stood, brushed his hands off on his trousers, and inspected them. "I'll be right back."

Willa smiled to herself when she heard the pump in the kitchen and the sound of running water. Ranching had not made him any less fastidious. She was still smiling when he returned to the front room.

"What?" He halted in the archway and leaned casually against the frame, arms crossed, one foot on top of the other.

"You," she said, as if that single word explained everything. "I swear you could muck stalls all day and leave the barn smelling only of leather and newly mown hay."

"'Cleanness of body was ever deemed to proceed from a due reverence to God.'"

"Is that from the Bible?"

"Francis Bacon. Or put another way, cleanliness is next to godliness. Even out of proper context, my mother was a believer. Nails. Hair. Shoes. And definitely behind the ears." Shrugging, he pushed away from the wall and went to the couch. "I was a better student of tidiness than Quill. Mostly he looked like an unmade bed." He pulled the down comforter from the bundle of linens and held it up. "For the bottom, I think."

Before Willa could ask him what he meant, he was snapping it open and spreading it wide across the floor in front of the hearth. The displacement of air fanned the flames. The embers grew brighter, glowed brilliant orange, and the tongues of fire twisted and fluttered and licked the stack of wood.

He did the same with both sheets and then added the quilt and wool blankets. When there was nothing left on the couch, he turned down the top sheet and then held out his hand. She thought he meant for her to put her hand in his, but then he said, "Pillows."

Realizing she was getting ahead of herself, she flushed a little and tossed both pillows to him, one after the other. He laid them out side by side and looked to her as if for approval. She nodded and came to her feet without being invited to do so. She bent over the lamp and turned back the wick. "Less light now, I think."

"All right."

Willa thought he might extend his hand again or invite her to come stand beside him, but he did neither. He knelt on top of the blankets and began to unbutton his shirt. She felt rather foolish standing there with her arms hanging at her sides, so she unfastened her belt. It was akin to putting the cart before the horse because she had not removed her boots, and her trousers were not coming off until she did.

No one had thought to ask her if she wanted to put on a dress before the ceremony, and it certainly had not occurred to her. Now she rather wished it had. She had several pretty dresses that she visited in her wardrobe from time to time. Cutter's mother, acknowledged to be the finest seamstress in Jupiter, had made all of them, and she was not shy about telling Willa that she needed to stop admiring them and actually wear one. Now Mrs. Hamill would have it from her son that Willa had not worn one to her own wedding.

She couldn't help it. She sighed.

"What is it?" asked Israel.

She simply shook her head. How to tell him it was a stray thought too depressing to run down? She carefully balanced herself on one foot while she removed the first boot and then shifted legs and did the same with the other. She put them beside the rocker before she unfastened the fly of her trousers and shimmied out of them. She kicked them to the side and looked down at herself. The wrinkled tails of her shirt hung almost to her knees and her cotton drawers ended a few inches below that. If it had been colder this morning, she would have been wearing a pair of long underwear, or maybe a union suit, but she had plucked the drawers out so now she was showing the small length of naked calf that was between the hem of her drawers and the tops of her thick woolen socks. She doubted it was a fashion Israel was used to seeing in the bedroom.

Willa dropped down to the bed he had made for them, first to her knees, and then lower until she was sitting cross-legged in front of him. Her entire left side absorbed heat from the fire, and she shifted just enough to feel more of the heat on her face and neck. She closed her eyes briefly, savoring the warmth and the moment, and never felt Israel's hand coming toward her or passing behind her until he had the tail of her thick braid in his fist.

He pulled it forward so that it lay over her right shoulder and released it only after he had dragged his fist lightly down the length of it. "You don't know how often I've wanted to do that or how much I want to see your hair unbound. Will you do that for me now? Unwind it?"

She was silent while she gave the request the consideration it deserved, but in the end she said, "No." And then, "You do it."

Israel exhaled a long, slow breath punctuated by a crooked, vaguely guilty smile. "I had prayed."

Willa started to laugh softly but the sound was aborted when her breath hitched. He did not give her a chance to change her mind; his fingers were already tugging the tightly knotted rawhide string that kept the plait mostly intact. He undid the knot far quicker than she ever had, but then perhaps it was because he was more motivated.

Israel's fingers slipped between the braided chains of hair, unwinding them slowly from the bottom up. Her hair revealed itself as one silky wave after another, a tide of dark water cascading under his fingertips, across his palm, and around the back of his hand. Strands of it circled his wrist, brushed his skin with the delicacy of a hummingbird at rest.

When the last three cords were unwound, he carefully combed them with his fingers, and where his fingers dipped more deeply and skimmed her shirt, he stroked her from shoulder to breast.

Willa held herself very still. It felt as if a shiver might go through her but it didn't, not then. Instead a pinwheel of sparks skittered through her belly, and where Israel touched her, his fingers left a wake of fire.

Israel's hand drifted to her knee and lay there lightly. His eyes searched her face, and she wondered about the view he had. Did she look anxious, eager, or perhaps afraid? She felt some measure of all those things, but then she reasoned that every woman since Eve, regardless of experience, likely felt the same.

Israel changed position so that he mirrored hers and sat cross-legged opposite her. He took her hands in his, brushing the knuckles with his thumbs. "You look as if you are entertaining very deep, possibly very dark, thoughts. Is there something you want to say or maybe ask?"

Willa's tongue cleaved to the roof of her mouth. Even if she had a thought she could pluck and present, she would not have been able to speak it aloud. Israel seemed to have correctly interpreted what was happening because he rose suddenly in a single fluid motion and disappeared into the hallway. He was not gone long and returned somewhat triumphantly with two glasses and what remained of the last bottle of whiskey Happy had brought to the table.

"I think a drink is in order," he said, dropping easily into the cross-legged position he had abandoned moments earlier. "I could use one, and I am realizing that we never toasted each other." He splashed both glasses with whiskey and set the bottle aside.

Willa accepted the glass he handed her and turned it so the firelight reflected in the amber liquid began to dance.

Israel nodded his head toward her glass. "Go on. Take a drink first to loosen your tongue, then we'll toast."

Willa sipped the whiskey, and now the fire inside it danced on her tongue. She let it play there before she swallowed. As heat lined her throat, she said, "It's occurred to me that all the usual things have been said tonight."

"There are no rules. Say what is unusual."

"All right." She raised her glass and was glad to see that her hand did not tremble. "To you, Israel Court McKenna, for having the uncommonly fine sense to accept my proposal. I mean to be a good wife to you, and I hope, a better friend." When his hand did not rise, but rather seemed suspended, she extended her arm several more inches and touched her glass to his. She thought it might have been the soft clink of the glasses that made him start. He withdrew his hand and drank, taking all of it in a single swallow.

Willa drank then, too, and when she lowered her glass, she felt her smile waver as uncertainty tapped her heart. "I probably should have—" She stopped because he was shaking his head.

Israel put his empty glass beside the bottle and set his elbows on his knees. He folded his hands and regarded her frankly. "I am not prepared to hear you take it back. Not any part of it. It was perfect. I did show uncommonly fine sense, which is noteworthy in and of itself, but in this particular situation it is toastworthy."

"Toastworthy?"

"It's a word. I'm a writer, remember?"

"Uh-huh. You know I don't believe you." To underscore that, she gave him an arch look. "About either of those things." She picked up the bottle, poured a finger for each of them, and indicated it was his turn to say something unusual.

Israel raised his glass. "To you, Wilhelmina Pancake McKenna, for not believing me, but trusting me in spite of it, for not knowing me, but accepting me nonetheless, for being my wife, for wanting to be my friend . . ." He touched his glass to hers. "For becoming my lover."

Willa swallowed hard, and then she drank. She examined her empty glass before she put it aside. She took his as well and met his darkening eyes with the same candor that he had shown her. "To becoming," she said softly, and leaned forward and kissed him.

Her hands went to his shoulders. She gave a tentative push, then a harder one, and felt the vibration of his low laughter as he allowed her to tumble him. Never breaking the kiss, she followed him down, and lay partially on top of him, her breasts flattened against his chest.

His arms came around her, cupping the swells of her bottom cheeks, squeezing just enough to make her squirm, and then his hands slid to the small of her back, fingertips pressing at the base of her spine. She felt tingling all the way to her nape, where the shortest tendrils of hair stood up. When he moved his hands again, this time it was to learn the shape of her back and shoulders with his palms. Her shirt rucked up, but he did not dive under it to tug at her camisole or dig fingers into her flesh.

Although the fire warmed the crown of her head, Israel's hands were far warmer. He did not have to apply friction to produce heat. It settled on her every time he touched her.

She raised her head, reluctantly removing her mouth from his. It felt like a sacrifice. "I don't mind being on top of the covers," she whispered. "But if I had my druthers, I'd like to be under them."

"Cold, are you?"

That he would think that made her laugh softly. "The very opposite," she said.

He lifted one dark eyebrow. "Then?"

"Cowardice, I think."

"I doubt it. Let's call it modesty."

She nodded, a smile hovering on her lips. "You would have made a fine writer, you knowing so many ways of saying a thing."

Chuckling, he raised his head and brushed her mouth with his, then he took her by the shoulders, caught both of her legs in one of his, and turned her onto her back. What followed that accomplishment was a wrestling match with the sheet, quilt, and blankets to get them from under her and under him and then settle all of it over them. When it was finally done, she was the one chuckling.

Israel raised himself on one elbow and looked down at her, suspicious. "Hm?"

"You're winded."

"Am I?"

Willa's smile deepened when he paused to listen to the sound of his own breathing.

"Perhaps a little," he conceded. "And that's amusing because . . ."

"Because they're *blankets*." She paused then, and when he began lowering his mouth to hers, she whispered, "The next time they resist, shoot them."

He covered her lips with laughter. This kiss vibrated, tickled, and when there was no air to share between them, they broke away, gulped for breath, and came together with a kiss hot enough to fuse their mouths.

Willa's fingers scrabbled at the buttons that were still done on his shirt and fumbled with the fly of his trousers. He found the hem of her shirt where it was twisted around her waist and slipped his hand under it. She wore no corset, but his hand slid beneath the cotton camisole as well and lay against her ribs just below her breast.

She stiffened for a moment, her fingers quieting, her heartbeat thundering, and let the anticipation of his touch roll through her until she knew she could accept it, knew that she wanted it. She abandoned his fly and found his hand instead. She guided him to her breast, and when he covered it with his palm, she covered his hand with hers and held it there.

That was when she shivered, only it was more than that, and she knew it immediately but had no name for what it was. She had not been fully aware of how taut she had become until every thread of tension snapped at once and what followed was the rippling of release.

He tore his mouth away from hers and there was no hiding from his remarkably keen gaze except to close her eyes, so that was what she did. Her teeth pinched her lower lip, but that was all part of the shuddering response, not an attempt to control it. A whimper rose in her throat, a small mewling sound that she tried to swallow as soon as she heard it.

"It's all right," he said, his voice not much above a whisper. "Let me hear it. I want to hear it."

She gasped, letting go of her lip. Thin threads of heat spiraled in an ever-widening circle from the nipple budding under his palm all the way to her womb. She felt the contraction, the fisting deep inside her, and came to know both profound pleasure and abiding emptiness.

Her body sagged; the moment of weightless abandon was gone. She opened her eyes. He was still watching her, a faint smile revealing the mercurial dimple. His hand still lay over her breast, but now it was filled not only with her flesh but the steady thudding of her heart.

"You're winded," he said.

Willa's sigh was blissful. It was answer enough.

Chapter Fourteen

They could not shed their clothes quickly enough to suit either of them. He tugged. She pulled. One of the buttons on his shirt came off in her hands. She held it up to the firelight and promised that she would sew it back on for him, and they laughed because they both knew that she wouldn't. He took the button from her and tucked it under his pillow and the disrobing resumed.

It was hardly important for them to be naked, except it was what they wanted. Regardless of ownership, Willa held up each item of clothing outside of the covers and waved it as though a victory had been won before flinging it aside.

"Are you drunk?" Israel asked. His face was buried in the curve of her neck and shoulder, but before he had targeted that specific spot, he saw her spinning one of his socks on her fingertip and letting it fly.

"I think so," she told him, moaning a little as his teeth scraped her skin. "But I don't believe we can, um, blame the, oh, the whiskey."

He raised his head. "Really? I believe—"

Willa placed her hands on either side of his face and drew him back to her neck.

"Iamfladdered," Israel murmured, his mouth pressed to her neck. "Veryfladdered."

"Mm." Willa threaded her fingers into his hair. She sifted and stroked and he made a throaty noise against her shoulder that could only be interpreted as satisfaction. She was in full agreement and told him so in a husky voice that quavered ever so slightly.

Israel slipped under the covers. The air was humid with

the scent of their musk. He breathed deeply and settled his lips between her breasts, tasting her with the damp edge of his tongue before he moved to her areola and took her with the hot suck of his mouth.

Willa released Israel. Her hands dropped to her sides and her fingers curled in the sheet under her. Her neck arched. "Oh!" Pleasure that was so intense it was almost pain jangled her nerves. She rubbed one of her feet along the length of his calf. To her surprise, and regret, he stopped what he was doing and came out from under the covers.

"You still have a sock on."

Her eyes widened. It might have been an accusation if she couldn't see that he was amused.

"Take it off."

Now she blinked owlishly. What amusement had been in his voice was gone. He gave her the command in a tone that had weight and consequence. "Goodness," she said softly. "It's a sock, not a fig leaf."

Israel stared at her just long enough for the rejoinder to register, and when it did, he gave a shout of laughter before diving deep under the covers to retrieve said sock. She did not make it hard for him, which he appreciated, and proved it during the slow journey back up her body toward the firelight. By the time he emerged from under the blankets with his prize, he had intimate knowledge of the long, smooth curve of her calf, the soft, sensitive underside of her knee, the firmness of her inner thighs. He had pushed his tongue into the sweet, damp folds of flesh between her legs and teased the little bud that was wet with her honey. He had been careful to see to the breast he had not attended earlier, and when his lips closed over this nipple, she made such an exquisite sound of pleasure that he was compelled to stay a bit longer than he had planned.

Willa tore the sock from Israel's fingers when he dangled it above her. She waved it in a circle and gave it a toss. It flew straight into the fireplace, where it lay over a log and briefly smothered the flames before it burst into a tail of gold and orange light.

The smell of burning wool was not particularly pleasant,

but neither was it a deterrent. The light illuminated their features and was reflected in the darkening centers of their eyes.

Israel nudged her lips. She opened them. And when he climbed on top of her, she opened her legs as well. He lifted them, coaxed her into wrapping her legs around him and cradling him between her thighs. She pressed her fingers into his shoulders, and he waited to be sure she did not mean to push him away. For a moment, only a moment, he wasn't certain if she knew what she meant to do, but then, just as she had done in the barn, she seemed to come to some conclusion, and this time, thank you Jesus, John Henry was nowhere around to interfere with it.

Taking himself in hand, his cock hard and throbbing with every beat of his heart, Israel pushed into her. She was as slick and as warm as he'd known she would be. She was also tight and part of her was pushing back. He stopped, held himself still.

"Are you all right?" There was a lot of grit in his voice. It was difficult to get the words past a throat that seemed to be closing.

Willa pressed her lips together, nodded.

"No," he said. "You have to say it."

So she said it, her voice no less strangled than his had been. "Yes. I'm all right. Go on."

He did go on, levering himself on his elbows, and driving his hips forward. She rocked under him, made an odd sound that was not quite protest, but not pleasure either. There was no retreat from this, and Israel did not try. His concession was to go as carefully as he could, slow but hard, and draw the rhythm from her so that she might match his.

He grabbed a pillow and stuffed it under her hips when they were raised. With her pelvis angled toward him, he was able to go deeper, and there was no question that she would take all of him or that she wanted to. She rose against him to welcome his thrust and contracted around him each time it seemed as if he would withdraw.

Her hips rolled, lifted, fell, and she flung her arms wide like a pagan sacrifice. She stretched, arched, closed her eyes so she could not see the terrible beauty that was his face as he hovered above her, denying himself the pleasure of release that she had already known.

But she then discovered that she hadn't known it, not this way. The shudder that had rippled through her before when his hand had merely covered her breast, the one that made her smile and sigh in a most satisfied manner, was no more than a hint, a tease, of what could be.

The cry lodged at the back of her throat escaped, her eyes flew open at the raw animal sound of it, and fierce pleasure rocked her so hard that she thought her skin might not be able to contain it.

"Please," she whispered, and it was for him that she said it, not for herself. Her hands found his shoulders again, smoothed the bunched muscles. His thrusts quickened as he abandoned rhythm for the steady pumping of his hips.

She held on because it was what she could do now, and when he gave a shout, it was her name that she heard first and then God's.

When Willa woke, she was alone.

She sat up slowly, disoriented at first, and needed a moment to get her bearings. The fire was still quite warm at her back, so she reasoned that either she had not been asleep long, or Israel had recently added more logs. The lamp on the side table was no longer burning, but from where she sat, she could not tell if the oil was gone or the flame had been extinguished. She looked around and had to shake her head when she saw the clothing scattered around the room like so much flotsam. Her shirt was draped over the arm of the couch and she leaned across the blankets to seize it. She was closing the last button when she heard the back door open and close. Foot stomping followed, all of it in place, which satisfied Willa that it was Israel who had come in and not anyone else. He was the only one who bothered wiping his feet at the door. She was still grinning about that when he finally appeared under the archway wearing only his shirt and socks and carrying a tray of food, some of it left over from their picnic that afternoon.

Israel stopped there. "Ah. Awake and already finding something amusing. I have no idea if that bodes well for me, but I do like your smile."

"I was thinking that you are a contradiction."

"I am?" He entered the room and set the tray on the floor at what they had decided was the head of their bed. "I woke up hungry. I thought you might want something, too."

"Hmm. Ravenous." She held up the covers for him.

Israel crossed his legs and simply folded to the floor. He tucked the blankets around Willa first and then himself while she investigated the tray. She selected two small wedges of sharp cheddar cheese, and when she gave him one, he asked, "Do I want to know how I am a contradiction?"

"I don't know, do you?"

He did not take long thinking about it. "Tell me."

"All right. It's hard to square the man who spent a year behind bars with the man who wipes his feet when he comes in the house."

"Huh." Israel bit off half the wedge and chewed as he considered that. "You're right. That *is* hard to square." He bent toward Willa, kissed her on the lips, and said, "Unless you keep in mind that my mother liked a very tidy house and mud in the hallway or on the carpets was not tolerated."

"So your mama made you sweep it up yourself."

He laughed shortly, ironically. "Something like that."

Willa shook her head. "No," she said, frowning. "Tell me exactly, not something like it."

Israel hesitated then he shrugged. "Quill and I came home from fishing once, forgot to clean our shoes in our excitement to present our string of catches, and Mother got out the rug beater and used it on us before we spent the rest of that Saturday using it on the rugs."

Willa winced. "She swatted you with it?"

"It's a beater, Willa. Not a swatter. She bent us over the kitchen table with our trousers around our ankles and whaled on us." He took a slice of apple from the tray and bit into it. "As often as I stood in defiance of my parents' rules, that was one I rarely broke again."

"What about your brother? Did he also learn that lesson?"

"After a fashion." Israel grinned, remembering. "He wasn't always a saint. The next time he forgot to clean up before he walked in the house, I told my mother that I had done it and took the consequences. He was so scrawny back then, it hurt just to think of him getting beat like that. There were other times that I stepped in for him. I guess it seemed more right than wrong because even if I wasn't around to get him out of a scrape, I was in trouble with our parents for not being around. Hard to fault that logic when you're ten." He finished off the apple and shrugged. "Funny thing is, I might have set him on the straight and narrow by taking responsibility. He became the good son to keep me from always claiming to be the bad one."

Willa studied him. He seemed more philosophical than bitter. "So you protected each other," she said. "In your way."

"In our way," he repeated. "Yes, I suppose we did." He chose another slice of apple, but this time he fed it to her. "You might think that Quill received accolades for his accomplishments. He served in the Army, graduated from Princeton, and . . ." Israel caught himself and his voice trailed off.

Willa prompted. "And?"

"And he is largely ignored by our parents except when he is called upon to step in to help me. You can appreciate that I had a lot of time to reflect on that in the last year or so, and it finally came to me that my father thinks Quill's soul is safe from the ravages of hell, but mine is in danger of being lost forever. For a minister of my father's particular ilk, I might be a disappointment, but I am also his particular call to arms. As a father, he is dedicated to correcting my faults; as a minister, he dedicates himself to my salvation."

She smiled crookedly, reprovingly. "And you have dedicated yourself to keeping him busy."

"Not quite. More like giving him a purpose. My mother, also. She is committed to fretting, and she draws sympathy from her friends the way others draw water from a well. I am very good for her."

Willa gave him an arch look. "You don't mean that."

"I do." When she continued to regard him with narrowing eyes, he said, "Mostly I do."

She was quiet, thoughtful. Her features relaxed. "You've never told me so much about yourself."

"Hmm. I'm hoping to make you think twice before you try to square any more contradictions."

"Ah." She chose a biscuit, sliced it, and drizzled both halves with honey. She held one out to Israel. When he took it, she said, "After hearing all of that, I'm trying to square why you weren't in jail for murder."

His mouth was open, prepared to bite into the biscuit, but he stopped short of that. He likely would have choked. "There's something I hadn't considered. I don't see myself being bored with our conversations." He appreciated that her short laugh was deeply amused. She bit into her biscuit. A bead of honey clung to her lower lip, but before he could do anything about it, and really, there was only one thing he wanted to do, her tongue peeked out to take a swipe at it. "That's my job," he said, staring at her mouth.

Willa dabbed at her lips with her fingertips and then examined them. "What is?"

"It was honey, not a crumb, and it's my job to lick it away, not yours." She blinked at him and firmly pressed her lips together.

His mouth took on a wry twist. "That's not quite the response I was hoping for."

Her lips suddenly parted on a sharply indrawn breath. "Well, it was rather surprising."

"That I said it?"

"That it's a job."

Laughter rumbled in his chest. "As I said, I don't see myself bored with our conversations." She rewarded him a smile that settled in her fine, dark eyes. It was more satisfying than the biscuit, and that was very good indeed.

When Israel finished off the last biscuit bite and brushed crumbs from his shirt into his hand and dropped them on the tray, he got up and added a couple of logs to the fire. He poked at them until the flames began to flicker around the bark before he returned to bed. This time he stretched out on his side under the covers and raised himself on one elbow.

Willa finished her biscuit and licked her fingers. When he appeared to be fascinated by her tidiness, she said, "Not your job."

"It could be."

"You are incorrigible."

"So I have been given to believe."

Willa did not hear any regret in his voice, which she supposed was the point. "I didn't mean to fall asleep earlier. I must have done it very quickly. I don't remember anything after . . ."

"After?"

"You know, just after."

"Uh-huh. It's all right. You were tired. We both were. I slept some, too."

"You went out. I heard you come in."

"Mm. Answering nature's call. But that was after I nosed around the kitchen looking for food and made the tray. I wasn't particularly quiet. There were a couple of times I thought I might have woken you, but when I checked, you were still asleep."

The idea of it prompted Willa to yawn abruptly. She covered her mouth after the fact and smiled a shade guiltily, most of it behind her hand.

Grinning, Israel patted the space beside him. "Lie down. Unless you want something to drink. Do you? I can—"

She placed a finger over his lips before he could finish and shook her head. "You don't want to spoil me, Israel, at least not all at once. If I'm thirsty, I'll get a glass of water from the kitchen. On my own. You'll like me better if I do that."

"All right," he said when she removed her finger, "but I might as well tell you, I like you better than fair to middlin' now."

Willa slid under the covers. She did not stretch out beside him but lay curled on her side, her knees drawn toward her chest, and a pillow folded thickly under her head. "Is that sweet talk?"

"What do you think?"

"Sounds like it's skirting the edges. You ought to be careful. If Happy gets wind of it, he'll be crowing louder than our rooster. He's already so full of himself about this that he's likely to burst."

"You're peeved at him, aren't you?"

"Peeved? Yes, some. I don't like being pushed in a direction I was already going. What did he say to you outside anyway? I couldn't hear all of it for trying to keep Annalea from hearing any of it."

Israel cast his mind back to the encounter. "You need to understand I was a tad hard of hearing myself on account of the shotgun leveled at my chest, but the gist of it was that he saw us in the barn, and not when we were engaged in conversation."

"Well, damn, he lied to me."

"That's what you are taking away from what I just told you?"

"I'm ignoring that." She huffed a little, blowing away a strand of hair that had fallen over her cheek and mouth. "I asked him if he had been out last night. This was after he told me this morning that he'd heard me come in and was questioning my story about John Henry getting out. He told me he hadn't left the house. In fact, he told me he hadn't stirred except for when I came in. I can't say that I like it that he lied to me."

Israel stared at her, confounded. He did a finger rub behind his ear as he tried to find the logic.

"What is it?" she asked.

"I think you just gave me a concussion." When she wrinkled her nose at him, clearly not amused, he said, "I'm serious. You hurt my head when you do that. Did you hear yourself? You're peeved because your father lied to you when you lied to him about John Henry."

"That wasn't *my* lie. That was yours. You told me to say it."

Israel fell quiet, thinking, then he said, "I am not going to win this argument, am I?"

"Not if you were Daniel Webster."

After another pause, he said, "All right. I can accept that."

She chuckled. "You're good at that," she said quietly,

reaching for his hand. When she found it, she threaded her fingers through his. She saw that he had no idea what she was talking about. "Good at making me laugh. You have a way of taking a jab at me that stings some but doesn't leave welts. I didn't expect that you'd be good for me that way, but you are."

"Is that sweet talk?"

She squeezed his fingers. "My idea of it anyway."

Israel eased his hand from hers and reached above his head to push the tray closer to the fireplace and away from them. "I want you to think about how I plan to use that honey, but for now . . ." He leaned over her, nudged her knees down, and when she was stretched parallel to him, he cupped her buttocks and jerked her close. He guessed that she was expecting it, but her breath hitched anyway, and he liked that he could do that to her.

"Give me your mouth, Wilhelmina."

A moan slipped past her lips. Her eyelids were heavier than they had been a moment before, and she had no peripheral vision to speak of because Israel was the center of all she could see. She gave him her mouth.

She kissed him, her tongue making a sweep of his upper lip, the lower one, and then slipping deeply inside to meet his. The rhythm of the kiss meant something to her this time because it was the rhythm of their bodies joining, the thrust and parry of battle where the outcome would inevitably be a draw.

His kisses were a narcotic. Willa had no other explanation for the drugging effect of them. Her limbs felt oddly weighted, their movements deliberate but sluggish. It was as if she were underwater, swimming leisurely, but always headed upstream against a slow-moving current.

She quivered.

Israel pulled away long enough to remove his shirt over his head and then remove hers. As a precaution, he toed off the socks and pushed them out of the way. He managed to accomplish this in the moment before she began to rub against his chest and make murmurings that simultaneously hinted of need and promise.

Israel lifted her upper leg and placed it over his. He thrust his hips into the pocket he made for himself. She twisted sinuously and then they were belly to belly with only his cock between them. He found her hand, took her to it, and held his breath waiting for her fingers to curl around it. She did more than make a fist; she squeezed.

"Ah, um, yes. Like that."

She did it again. Her hand slipped to the root and she cupped his balls.

Israel closed his eyes and grit his teeth.

She opened her hand, pulled it away. "I'm hurting you."

"Now you are." He took her hand and put it where he wanted it. "Go on. I'll tell you when it's enough." He kissed her on the mouth. "More likely, I'll show you."

And that's what he did, eventually sliding into her when she made him so hot, so hard, that it wasn't a choice but critical to his state of being. He had meant to go carefully, but intention was not enough to make it so, not when his need was greater than his good sense.

She was ready for him, slick and snug, and accommodated his entry with little difficulty this time. He wanted to stay where he was, just like this, breathing her musk and the smell of her sex, their sex, and being aware of nothing so much as the glove-like fit of her around his cock, but then she moved and what he wanted changed. He found her wrists and held them on either side of her head as he toppled her. Her laugh was deep and throaty and he smothered it with his mouth. His lips pressed hard against hers. His hips did the same. She pushed back, squirmed, and finally was able to gasp for breath.

He kissed the corner of her mouth, her temples. He nudged her nose and bit the lobe of her ear. He arched, driving deep, and hearing her whimper, he did not think he could have enough of her. She said his name, and it was as if she had pulled a trigger. As always, her aim was dead on.

He came noisily, and to his mind, clumsily, as he juddered like a wagon on a corduroy road. In quick succession, he lost his grip on her wrists, spilled his seed, and fell heavily against her.

Israel lifted his head, spared a glance for Willa, and then

shoved away from her, turning on his back and flinging a forearm over his eyes.

Willa needed to catch her breath because it felt as if Israel had driven the air out of her lungs when he collapsed on her. She turned her head, saw he had his arm across his eyes like a blindfold, and was reminded of coming upon him lying near Potrock Run. He had tried to shut the world out then in just that way.

She looked around for her shirt and saw that he had not flung it far. Stretching, she was able to reach it with her fingertips and drag it toward her. She sat up only long enough to put it on, and in that short of a time, she began to shiver.

She would have welcomed Israel's body heat, but he did not invite her to share, and she did not believe he would appreciate the intrusion. She clamped her teeth to stop the chitter and lay as still as she was able, staring at the ceiling. It did no good to wonder what he was thinking; she had no idea, and since it was her strongly held opinion that he should say something first, she cast her mind elsewhere.

Of all the things she might have chosen to think about, her thoughts settled first on her lips. They were slightly tender, a little swollen, but in a pleasant sort of way. She touched them tentatively with the tip of her tongue, and confirmed that his kisses had changed the shape of her mouth, at least for now. Her breasts were similarly tender, but she gradually became aware that there was also an ache, not in any way painful, but niggling nonetheless. That ache made her want to touch her breasts, to cup them in her hands in the same manner he had. It was not fair that he had left her with this ache, this *need*, not after he had shown her there could be something more.

Willa suppressed the urge to tell him so. She would not make herself ridiculous in his eyes or her own. Instead, she wondered what the dark stubble on his jaw had done to her skin. He had probably brushed pink color into her everywhere his mouth had grazed, and the thought of it, just the thought of it, put heat into her flesh and brushed her a deeper shade of rose.

Annoyed with herself for that train of thought, she deliberately took another tack.

Her wrists were vaguely sore. She did not think he realized how firm the grip was that he'd had on her. She had not minded in those first moments, but then he hadn't released her, and she could own that that had made her struggle in earnest, not in play. She acquitted him of not knowing that either. How would he guess at that when there were so many things he didn't know? She could own that, too. She had not been any more forthcoming about her past than he had been, perhaps even less.

Under the covers, Willa absently rubbed her wrists.

Israel lifted his forearm and then he lifted the blankets. The fire cast light under them, enough for him to glimpse Willa massaging her wrists. She had already stopped by the time he lowered the blankets. He did not hide behind his arm again, but he did swear under his breath. In the quiet of the room it was as if a gun had gone off.

He turned on his side, supporting himself on an elbow. "Let me see them." When she merely angled her head in his direction, he added, "Please."

"There is nothing to see."

"How do you know? You haven't looked at them."

"I just know," she whispered, shrugging.

Israel waited. Sometimes he could wait longer than she could, and this was one of those times. After a long minute that the mantel clock obligingly ticked off, she slid her hands from under the covers and raised them enough for him to see her wrists. It still was not sufficient for him, even when she twisted them in the firelight to improve his view. He put out a hand but stopped short of circling one of her wrists. "May I?"

"They're not bruised," she said. "They are not even chafed."

Israel did not withdraw his hand. He left it there, hovering.

"Very well," she said, and sighed.

His fingers curled around her forearm, not her wrist, and brought it closer to him for inspection. She was right. Her skin was neither bruised nor chafed, but that did not mean it wouldn't be tomorrow. He gave her back her hand and examined the other one. It was also unmarked.

He said, "If there is a bruise tomorrow, I want to know." He tucked her hand back under the covers.

"Why? Why would you want to?"

"I just do. I've never . . ." He stopped, searched her face. He could see that her question was sincere, but that did not mean he understood it or could answer it. "I just do."

His words simply hung there, hovering much as his hand had done earlier.

Willa finally addressed the silence. "Do you believe you hurt me?"

"I know I did."

"Am I permitted to have an opinion about that?" When he did not respond, she went on. "It's true that you surprised me, not so much when you took me by my wrists, but when you held me down. I wasn't, um, I wasn't prepared for that. I didn't realize it could be part of . . . part of, um, what we were doing. I might have struggled some. All right, I *did* struggle, but that was because I wanted you to let me go, not because I didn't want you."

Israel shut his eyes briefly. "Jesus." He actually flinched when Willa touched his face, and she had merely laid her hand against his cheek.

"Look at me," she said.

When Israel opened his eyes and met hers, she greeted him with a smile that he could only describe as bittersweet. It made him ache some to look at it; it was that beautiful.

"You didn't know," she told him, withdrawing her hand. "And I didn't tell you. I should have done that. I should have done more than say your name."

"You should not have had to. I was rough. I was . . . clumsy."

"Were you? I thought you were, um, enthusiastic."

In spite of himself, a chuckle briefly vibrated in his throat. "Well, there's a word for it."

Willa took a deep breath and spoke as she exhaled. "It's occurred to me that because of your incarceration, it's likely been a long time since you had a woman under you."

The chuckle that was still tickling the back of his throat froze into a tangible lump that nearly choked him. He managed to swallow it, but only barely. He said wryly, "What took place a couple of hours earlier notwithstanding."

"I hadn't forgotten," she said primly.

"And again, I am damned with faint praise."

"Will you let me finish?"

There were a number of ways he could have responded to that, but he let them all pass and merely nodded instead.

"So I was thinking that it must have placed a great burden on you to behave with such restraint the first time you, um, you—"

"Had a woman under me?"

"Hmm, yes." She pressed her lips together, musing. "So I don't think you should be so troubled about losing yourself like that the second time."

"And that's what you think I did? Lost myself?"

"It seemed so."

"What if I told you that I lost myself in you?"

"Well, if it's true, then you will have reason to regret that you convinced me you are a liar, because I wouldn't believe you."

"Huh."

She nodded, repeated the word softly, "Huh."

Israel observed her shiver as a ripple in the blankets. "Do you want me to make a bigger fire?" he asked.

"Only if you intend to burn down the house. I want you to move closer. You're a furnace. I'm not."

He obliged her, inching toward her until she took him by the hand and pulled his arm across her waist. Accepting the invitation, he fit himself neatly against the contour of her slender frame, and when he thought he could not get any closer, she did. "You *are* cold. Maybe some more clothes?"

"No. My shirt's enough now that you're here. Anyway, you'd probably just take them off again."

"Probably," he said with a wry smile, "being as it's been so long since I—"

She stopped him with three fingers placed over his lips. "I know it amuses you to say it again, but restrain yourself or find other words."

"Oh, there are plenty of other ways of saying it. I didn't figure you for wanting to say or hear them."

"You're right. Just restrain yourself, then."

"There's consummation, which has come and gone, so I

don't think we can properly use it again to describe continuing acts of carnal knowledge in the context of our marriage."

Willa gave him a reproving look. "Since you cannot help yourself, let me be clear that there will be no acts of carnal knowledge *outside* the context of our marriage. We took a vow on it. At least I think we did."

"Oh, we did. Forsaking all others was the agreement. I'm clear on that."

"Good."

"Sex outside of marriage is a sin against your own body. I'm paraphrasing, of course. First Corinthians, chapter six, verses eighteen to twenty. My father had a number of sermons on the theme of fornication."

Willa stared at him. "Sometimes I simply don't know what to say."

He grinned. "I know. Now about those other words . . ." He tapped them out on his fingers, every tap against the curve of Willa's hip. "There are five that come to mind immediately."

"I felt six," she said. "I'm sure I felt six."

"One of them I won't say."

"All right. I know that one. Tell me the five you will."

"Besides carnal knowledge and now, fornication, there's coupling, covering, mating, intercourse, and making love."

"Good Lord."

"Do you have a preference?"

"Hmm. Well, covering is what our studs do to the mares, so I'm not sure I like that. Coupling makes me think of trains."

Israel made a strangled sound but still managed to say, "That might not be entirely bad."

She gave him a withering look. "Mm-hmm." She turned thoughtful. "Mating makes me think of rabbits."

As quickly as he'd come the last time, Israel was not in favor of it either.

She said, "Intercourse is what we are doing now."

"Well, yes, but—"

"And to call it making love seems presumptuous at this juncture."

"When you put it like that . . ."

"Until something else occurs, I suppose we are left with fucking."

Now it was Israel's turn to stare at her. A sly shadow of a smile touched her lips while her black coffee eyes regarded him with such innocence that it could only be feigned. He released her hand and reached above him for the tray he had carried in earlier. Without looking, he groped among the plates for the little crock he wanted. When he had it in hand, he held it between them for her to see, and then said exactly what was on his mind, "It is fortunate for you that I don't have soap, but a blessing to me that I have honey."

Chapter Fifteen

Eden Ranch
Temptation, Colorado

Quill McKenna carefully reread the letter from his father before he placed it on the table, smoothed the creases, and slid it sideways to his wife.

"Do I want to read it?" Calico asked. "Your father has a way of riling me that makes me want to reach for my gun. How he manages it the whole way from Chicago, I will never understand."

"Well, it's a mixed blessing that he and Mother have no plans to leave. The trade-off is that it's up to me to do something."

Calico ran her finger across the Reverend McKenna's salutation. His handwriting made her think he favored using spiders dipped in ink over a fountain pen. She did not pick up the letter, preferring to study her husband instead.

There was no question that he was troubled. There were furrows in his sun-licked hair where he had plowed it with his fingers, and his smile, the one that still dazzled her with its brilliance, was notably absent. She did not think she could tease a smile out of him now if she tried, and that made her sad and then angry, and the person who most angered her wasn't the reverend, it was his firstborn son.

She reached for Quill's hand and put hers in its curve. He didn't respond to the overture until she lightly squeezed his fingers, and then he looked at her with his very fine blue-gray eyes and somehow managed to assure her that he would be all right, that everything would be all right.

Calico removed her hand, picked up the letter, and read. The gist of the request was more or less what she thought it would be. It had now been almost three months since Israel had been released from the Cook County Jail, and no one in the family had heard from him. His parents had seen him the morning of his release, given him funds for new clothes, incidentals, a train ticket, and a modest amount of pocket money for him to buy food on his journey. He had no choice but to accept what they gave him, but the reverend made a point to write that Israel had taken it most reluctantly, and here was proof, then, that his son had changed. Israel had been humbled by his incarceration, and too humiliated to permit them to escort him around to the shops while he made his purchases. They had wished him well there, prayed for him in front of the police sergeant's desk, and stood as guardian angels might as he walked away.

It was all very affecting . . . and calculating. It was supposed to move Quill into action, which was the exact thing he was opposing.

Calico set the letter down and idly ran her fingers through her hair where a thick length of it had fallen over her shoulder like a rope of fire. Feeling Quill's eyes on her, she looked up and smiled ruefully.

"I don't know what to say," she told him. "Except, perhaps, to apologize for asking you to give him a chance." She thought about that. "*Another* chance, I should have said."

"I didn't need convincing," he said. "You have nothing to apologize for. It was hardly generous to offer him a job here when he got out. He would have had to work hard, harder for that matter, than he ever has. Israel had always gotten by on the strength of his wits, not on the strength of his back." Quill took a deep breath and let it out slowly. "I wonder if I should have tried to get him a job in Stonechurch, in the mines. Ramsey would have hired him as a favor to me . . . and you."

"That's not a favor you want to abuse, and anyway, it would have been cruel to your brother."

"I was thinking it might have been crueler to Ramsey.

Israel would have organized the men into a union inside of six months and then made off with their dues."

Calico had to laugh. From everything she knew about Quill's brother, it sounded perfectly plausible. "Well, you didn't put that job on the table, and he accepted your offer to come here, where he knew you'd be keeping an eye on him. I think he wanted that."

Quill snorted.

"I mean it. I saw the letter he wrote to you. He was grateful. Sincerely. I believe that."

"Then you would be one more among the hundreds of people Israel gulled because he made them believe he was sincere."

Calico did not like that. "I am not an easy mark, Quill. You know I am not."

"And Israel would see that and use it against you. It's what he does. It's what all confidence men do, and he's very good at it."

"He just spent a year behind bars."

"He should have had three and all of it in prison. Instead he served only eight months there and spent the last four months in a county jail close enough to my parents that they could make sure he had decent meals and clean clothes. His incarceration was just one long con."

"You don't believe that."

"I do." He paused. "Mostly."

"Maybe you're right," she said. "Maybe it was a con, but does that matter now? He's missing—"

"He's gone underground."

Calico ignored the interruption. "And no one knows where he is. He should have arrived in Temptation a few days after he left Chicago and—"

"*If* he left Chicago."

Again, Calico pretended he had not spoken. "He had instructions on how to reach us. I know you were worried when we didn't hear from him."

"I felt foolish, not worried. If anyone can land on his feet, it's my brother."

Calico did not let that pass. She said quietly, "I know you. You felt betrayed, not foolish, and you *were* worried in spite of what you felt. You didn't send any of the hands into town to ask after him. You went yourself."

"I haven't made any inquiries since," he said. "And I waited more than a month before I broke the news to my parents."

"That's hardly surprising when you had to know that would put the burden of finding him back on you. Haven't they always applied to you for help when he got into trouble?"

"No. Not always. Only when he got into trouble with the law."

Calico nodded. "I'm sorry. I overstated it."

Quill shrugged.

"I mean it," she said. "I'm sorry. I know what you and Israel are to each other, and what both of you are to your parents is more complicated than I stated. But don't you see, Quill? What you just said about them only asking you for help when Israel's in trouble with the law, they must suspect something of that nature."

"It's hard not to, wouldn't you say?" he asked, his tone dry as dust. "Calico, you realize, don't you, that he could be calling himself anything now? He could be anywhere."

Calico set her hands flat on the table and braced herself as she rose to her feet. It momentarily gave her the advantage of height and she made good use of it. "Mr. McKenna," she said firmly, "did you or did you not marry Calico Nash, a bounty hunter of some repute?"

A glimmer of a smile touched his features. "I did."

Calico blinked. The mere flicker of Quill's smile could make her stop and take notice. In spite of the momentary drift in her attention, she persevered. "And did your wife, not above four months ago, track Grant Hollis Daily and his two cronies to a hotel in Goliath, Nebraska, after their pictures were posted in the local sheriff's office because they foolishly shot up a bank in Cedar Falls, Colorado?"

"I seem to recollect she had some help."

Calico huffed a little. "I was getting to that."

"Then yes. She was instrumental in running the miscreants to ground."

Mollified, she said somewhat wistfully, "And she recalls it was a very nice hotel there in Goliath."

Quill's blue-gray eyes danced. "Her grateful assistant recalls the same."

She did not flush easily, but she did so now. To recover, she put starch in her voice. "And did she not also uncover a plot to kill Ramsey Stonechurch in the not so distant past and end Nick Whitfield's reign of terror?" Before he answered that, she quickly added, "With help."

"Hmm. She did."

"Then armed with those facts, isn't it reasonable to suppose that she might make a fair job of tracking down an aimless brother-in-law before he invites trouble to his table? With assistance, of course."

"Of course."

When Calico sat again, this time it was on her husband's lap, not because she meant to unduly influence him to come around to her way of thinking, but because she liked it there. "Well?"

He did not answer immediately. His eyes fell on the letter from his father and then lifted to meet Calico's. "Israel protected me, too," he told her. "Plenty of times when we were young."

"I know," she said softly.

"It took me longer than it should have to steer clear of trouble so he wouldn't take another punishment for me."

"It was the kind of trouble that all boys get up to. Mischief really. You weren't a criminal, and back then when it was early days yet, neither was he."

Quill's short laugh held no humor. "My parents did not think it mischief. Shoes not shined to my father's standards, dirt tracked in on the carpets, a bed made up but too wrinkled to pass inspection, a Bible verse misquoted, swinging our feet under the pew when we should have been listening, those are the things that brought out the strap, or the switch, or the wooden spoon. Sometimes the rug beater. And that was only disobedience at home or in church. School yard antics or a report of misconduct from someone in the community, well, those behaviors were given considerably more attention."

"All in the name of doing right by you," she said, shaking her head. She took one of his hands and laid it over her belly. There was no swelling to speak of yet, but there would be. He said he was looking forward to it. For herself, she was not so sure. Still, she kept his hand there, fingers splayed, just as if they both could feel the life beating inside her. "We will endeavor to do better."

"Yes," he said. "That is a promise I can keep."

"And little Hephaestus here needs to know that his father is a good man and that is uncle is not a bad one."

"Hephaestus? You're calling him Hephaestus?"

"Or her."

"Still, Hephaestus? Isn't that the Greek god of—"

"Fire. Yes. I have heartburn all the time now."

"Oh. Appropriate then." He kissed her on the mouth when she smiled cheekily at him. "Now about our child's uncle . . ."

She knew him well enough to finish his thought when his voice faded away. "We are going to find him."

"We are damn well going to try."

Willa turned away from the stove with the coffeepot in her hand. She poured a cup for Israel and one for herself, and then replaced the pot. Instead of sitting down to drink, though, she remained at the stove pouring batter and flipping flapjacks.

"I've been thinking that maybe you're right," she told him. Without looking back, she added, "I bet your ears just perked up."

"And you'd win that bet. You keep denying that you have eyes in the back of your head, but Annalea and I think you are lying." Leaning back in the wobbly chair, he sipped his coffee and watched her over the rim of his cup. Three weeks to the day since they were married, and he still made good on every opportunity he had to look at her in the quiet moments, the ones like now when there were only the two of them in the kitchen, or like last night when she was brushing out her hair in preparation of joining him in bed.

She moved with unconscious grace, whether she was stretching after sitting curled in a chair while she read, or swinging down from the saddle after a long ride. And in bed . . . well, he would not think about that now. Turning his mind in that direction would likely lead to doing something about it, and doing something about it almost guaranteed burned flapjacks. Better not to tread too closely to that slippery slope. He was unusually hungry this morning.

"Tell me what I'm right about," he said.

"Maybe right about. Maybe." Willa slipped the turner under a flapjack that was browning at the edges and set it on top of one of the two stacks she was building. "I want to hire someone to cook for us and help Annalea with a few of her chores around the house. She rarely complains, but I think that's because she wants to make herself so necessary that I won't send her to school in the spring."

"If that's true, it's clever. Annalea has a certain evil genius that I admire."

Willa gave him a quick look over her shoulder. "You haven't told her that, have you?"

"No." He set his lips against the cup and muttered, "Not in those words." Israel thought he glimpsed a smile before she quickly turned her head. He took a swallow of hot, strong coffee and lowered the cup. "Will you want to hire a man or a woman?"

"I hadn't got to thinking that far. I suppose it could be either. Now that Happy's taken to staying in the bunkhouse until we can build on, there's an empty bed in Annalea's room. A woman could sleep there and live in the house. A man, though, could bunk with everyone else and wouldn't be underfoot in the evening. What do you suggest?"

"I say choose the one who can make the best fritters."

"That's your standard? Fritters?"

"Everything else being equal, yes."

Willa placed a short stack of flapjacks in front of him. "You must be hungry."

"Hmm." Israel set his cup aside and reached for the little pitcher that held the molasses. He drizzled thick brown syrup over the cakes and then cut into them, making a precise equilateral triangle. "Aren't you going to eat?" he asked, lifting a forkful to his mouth.

"You are not the only one I am feeding this morning," she reminded him. Her concession to eating was to pick up her cup of coffee when she returned to the stove. "The rest of them will be marching in before you know it. You merely finished morning chores first."

"I was motivated. I knew what you were going to make, and I didn't tell anyone else. Figured they could find out on their own." She shot him a reproachful look, which only made him grin. He took another bite, savored it, and swallowed. "Before they all get here, there's something I want to talk about."

"Oh?"

He might not have seen her stiffen if he had not been trying to gauge her reaction. She always did it when he approached her straight on. It was not that she would have preferred a manipulative approach; it was just that since the marriage she seemed to have developed an edginess when she sensed he was about to speak seriously. The only word he could find for it was dread.

As a favor to her, he plunged ahead rather than draw it out. "I can't stay here, Willa." She fumbled with the turner and a flapjack dropped to the floor. "I'll get it," he said, extending an arm to put her off. Before he bent over, he saw that it was not a matter of beating her to the flapjack but of beating John Henry. Stealthy as a fox, the hound appeared from under the table, snatched the flapjack, and returned to his den.

Israel exchanged an amused look with Willa and saw that John Henry's appearance had been a good thing for her. The tension that had pulled her shoulders taut was slipping away.

"I'd like to get off the spread, out of the valley. It wouldn't have to be Jupiter, probably shouldn't be. I was thinking Lansing. We could pay a visit to Pastor Beacon, have a look around. You might even find someone there you could hire as a cook or another hand since Eli hasn't done anything about sending help your way."

Willa kept her head bent over the griddle. "So when you said you can't stay here, you didn't mean you were leaving for good."

"Well, no," he said, surprised. "Is that what you thought?"

She spun around, the turner raised menacingly. "What other construction was I supposed to put on it?"

Israel kept one narrowed eye on the turner and the other on the quiver in Willa's lower lip. Calmly he said, "What other construction? The one I meant, of course. The leghorns roam farther than I do. Snow's been a consideration the last couple of weeks, but Cutter says the road is passable now for the horses, if not for the wagon." Deciding she was not going to threaten him with the turner, Israel shifted his attention back to his plate. He shook his head as he picked up his fork. "You really thought I was talking about leaving for good? I never figured that. I told you once that I would stay through the winter, which I'm hearing can last until about the middle of April, but I said that before we were married. I was under the impression that marriage meant I would be sticking around a lot longer than one winter. I didn't guess that you were still thinking along different lines."

Willa lowered her arm. She pivoted back to the stove and removed two flapjacks and poured more batter. "It catches me unawares," she said, her head bent. "It crosses my mind that you'll say you've had enough, that you're going to go wherever you were going when you took the detour that brought you here. Sometimes when you ride out with Zach or Cutter, I think that'll be the time you don't ride back."

Something sizzled on the griddle and Israel did not think it was the batter this time. There was a tremor in her hand and another rolling down her spine. He pushed away from the table and stood. "Wilhelmina."

She sniffed. "Don't call me that. Not now. Not with that tone."

Israel came up behind her, took the turner from her hand, and made quick work of the flapjacks while she had to stand there, effectively trapped and just a little bit helpless. Once the griddle was clear, he turned her in his arms, careful not to press her against the stove, and said, "What tone?"

"The patronizing one."

"That tone was concern."

She sniffed again. "You overshot the mark."

"All right. Perhaps I did, but that doesn't mean I'm not

concerned. You took vows, Willa, and while I realize they were not deeply felt, I reasoned you would honor them as a contract, if not as matter of belief. Was I wrong?" When her gaze shifted to a point beyond his shoulder, he ducked his head and followed it so she could not avoid him. Once he had her in his sights again, he said, "Well? Was I wrong?"

Willa shook her head.

"Then I am asking you to accept that I will at least honor them in the same way. I know what it's like to walk out on people who are depending on me." He smiled humorlessly. "Run out is more accurate. I'm telling you that so you'll know I've had the experience and that I've made a different choice this time. I wouldn't have agreed to marry you otherwise, not for the ranch, not to get into your bed, not even for Annalea, and God knows, she was relentless in singing your praises."

Willa brushed away a tear that hovered on her eyelash. She reached behind her, found a towel hanging from the oven door, and used it to erase the tracks on her cheeks. "She was? I didn't know about that."

"I didn't think you did, and I wouldn't have said anything if I didn't need it to support my case."

Her smile was a trifle watery. "Support your case," she repeated softly. "You talk like a lawyer." Her eyes were immediately suspicious. "Are you one? Because I will never believe you were a reporter."

"I don't know if you intend to insult me or the profession, but I am not a lawyer, have never been a lawyer, and have no intention of becoming one; however, that does not mean I haven't made a study of them. There's not much else to do when you're on trial." She made a little sound at the back of her throat that might have been protest or perhaps surprise. He spoke to both. "That's right. I don't want you to forget that I did time. It's who I was, Willa. Not who I am." He paused as she searched his face, and it was not hard to imagine that she was wondering what she could trust. He took a breath, released it slowly, and gave her the plain truth of the matter. "That's not quite right. I mean it's not who I want to be."

Without any urging, she leaned against him, rested her

cheek on his shoulder. "We'll ask Happy about the route he took to Lansing. If we don't have another hard snowfall in the next few days, maybe we can ride out that way like you want. I've only been there a few times, but I remember a bakery that made excellent Scotch wafers and jelly jumbles. We could bring a few dozen back."

"There can't be a better reason for going."

She tilted her head up and caught his eye. "There might be. I've heard Lansing has a rather fine hotel."

Chapter Sixteen

Eli Barber slugged back the whiskey his father poured for him and held out his cut glass tumbler for another.

Malcolm regarded his son for several moments, debating, and then shrugged his broad shoulders and poured exactly as much as he had the first time. "Sit down, Eli. If you're going to drink like that, you need to start out on your ass." He observed Eli's belligerent expression, and added, "If you're of a mind to argue with me, then you're not getting more. Your choice."

Eli sat. The chair was old, a relic in dark walnut from the settling days, as Malcolm liked to refer to them, and the curved spindly legs with their ball and claw feet shook when he landed on the faded bed of needlepoint roses. His grandmother planted that garden he was sitting on years before he was born, but Eli felt no particular attachment to it. He would have used the chair for kindling a long time ago, but his father was peculiarly sentimental about it, which he learned when he suggested tossing it. The lecture about history and birthright and reverence for the contributions of family was long and tedious and painful because he had to sit at attention in the very chair he wanted to toss.

He was not at attention now. He slouched in the chair but stopped short of rocking it back on two legs. Peripherally aware that his father was watching him closely, he purposely stared at his glass instead of drinking from it.

"I don't believe it," he said. "I don't."

"Since I am certain you are not calling me a liar, son, I imagine you're having that argument with yourself."

"Could you have misunderstood?"

Malcolm carried the decanter of whiskey to a table beside the sofa and set it down. He sat on the sofa, glass in hand, and propped his feet on a stool. His boot heels sank comfortably into the brushed velvet upholstery. Like the sofa, it was dark emerald green, slightly shiny in places familiar with his boots or his ass.

"Misunderstood?" he repeated heavily, raising his glass. "That doesn't seem likely, does it? I had it from Mrs. Hamill. That's Cutter Hamill's mother."

"I damn well know who she is."

"And you know Cutter works for the Pancakes."

Eli did not respond to that. His father was driving a point home, and Eli already felt as if he had been skewered.

"If you had gone to Jupiter with me, you could have had it from her yourself."

"I was there last week. Buster was with me. We had a chat with Mrs. Hamill outside the mercantile. She talked about Cutter, about all of her children, in fact, and she had some gossip about Birdie Cuttlewhite taking ownership of a recipe that was actually Sarah Barker's. Now if she dug deep enough into her tattle bag to tell us that, don't you think she would have mentioned that Willa Pancake got married?"

"Hmm. That's a fair point, Eli, and it likely would be correct if young Cutter had visited his mama and imparted his news before you and Buster saw her, but he didn't. The road between the Pancake spread and town had some waist-high drifts, according to Mrs. Hamill. Took the warming lull to make it passable again and then only barely. A man less motivated to see his mama than Cutter would not have made the trip."

"I'm sure she was thrilled," Eli said sourly. "And thrilled to tell you."

"That was my impression."

Eli waited, knowing there was more to hear and both wanting and dreading to hear it. His father's silence was purposeful, a punishment for having been questioned, and Eli saw his choice was to ride it out or abase himself and ask for the information.

To delay the moment of inquiry, he nursed his drink while he thought about finishing it in a single gulp and pitching the glass in the fireplace. In his mind, he could clearly hear it shatter, along with every hope he harbored about his future with Wilhelmina.

He darted a surreptitious glance at the scar on his wrist as he lowered the tumbler and felt a wave of anger where once he had only known longing. His fingertips whitened where they gripped the glass.

"So when were these nuptials?" asked Eli.

"A few weeks back," Malcolm said offhandedly, as if there had been no charged silence between them. "Three. Four. Mrs. Hamill did not tell me a specific day, and since I could not think why it would matter, I didn't ask."

"Huh." Eli absently pushed back the fringe of hair that had fallen over his forehead. "That's some kind of news you brought back. Did you hightail it out of Jupiter or take your time so you could savor the thought of telling me?"

Malcolm hiked up a single sandy-colored eyebrow, but his tone remained mild. "I am going to let that pass, Eli, because I know you're disappointed."

"Disappointed," Eli repeated softly. He lifted his head to meet his father's green-eyed stare with his own. "What about you, Father? Are you disappointed? In me, perhaps?"

Malcolm did not reply. Instead, he reached for the decanter and pulled out the stopper, and then he held the whiskey out for Eli, inviting him to have more. When Eli leaned forward and extended his glass, Malcolm poured generously before he swept the decanter away and added a finger to his own glass.

Eli stood abruptly, remembered his father's edict about sitting, and strode to the fireplace in defiance of it. Encouraged when Malcolm said nothing, he picked up the iron poker and stabbed at the logs, turning one of them so the bright orange glow on the bottom was exposed. The sparks pulsed. Like his anger, the fire's heat came at him in waves. Suppressing the urge to slam the poker against the mantle, he put it down and turned to face his father. What he did not do was return to the chair.

"You know I intended to propose to her again," he said.

Malcolm nodded, thoughtful. "I had an idea you were

entertaining the notion. It came to me not long after we saw her up on the ridge. Remember that day? It's been more than a few months now. You woke up that morning with a sore head. Revelry and overindulgence, I believe you told me."

"That's right," Eli said, resting his shoulder against the mantelpiece. His father was no longer looking at him. Malcolm's eyes had shifted to his glass, and he was regarding it as though it held all the mystic qualities of a crystal ball. "It was good to be back home. I celebrated my return with a couple of our men that I came across in Jupiter."

"Yes. I recollect thinking when you crawled home that night that a week in Saint Louis had not taken the wind out of your sails."

"I didn't realize you sent me there for any other purpose save ranch business, which I concluded satisfactorily."

"You did, but I always have it in the back of my mind that you will revel and overindulge where you are little known and return to Jupiter and Big Bar shrewd and sober."

"I take my whores in Denver," he said. "And now Saint Louis. That should count for something. It certainly demonstrates that I do listen to you when the subject is women and whoring."

"Drink makes you bold, doesn't it, son? And I am going to make allowances for it. We both know that what you said is not entirely true. You learned the lesson about whores well enough, but you don't know a damn thing about women. If you did, Willa wouldn't be someone else's wife right now."

Eli closed his eyes. Under his breath he said, "Shut up."

"She is spreading her legs for someone who isn't you, Eli. Is that the picture you have in your mind? You should. You should have pressed her the day after we met up with her on the ridge, and the day after that, and the day after that, and the—"

"Shut up!" Eli did throw his glass then, not into the fireplace, where the glass would have splintered and the whiskey would have burned blue, but at his father, where the glass thudded solidly against Malcolm's chest and the whiskey spilled over his vest and droplets splattered his face.

Malcolm gave a start when the glass hit him, but then he

calmly removed the empty glass from where it had fallen in his lap and placed it beside the decanter. He wiped his chin with the back of his hand and finished off his drink. He set that glass aside also.

"That was unfortunate," he said. He sighed deeply. "You should leave, Eli. Now."

While you can. Although his father had not said the words aloud, Eli heard them as if he had.

He straightened, tugged on the sleeves of his jacket to improve the fit across his shoulders, and nodded once in Malcolm's direction. All of it was done to give the impression that he was leaving because he wanted to, not because he had been threatened.

He was already out of the room when he heard his father howl with laughter that was as condescending as it was cruel.

"Just like that you're leaving?" Malcolm called after him when he could get a breath. "Don't you want to know the name of the man in her bed?"

Eli did not pause; he did not answer. He kept on walking, his father's laughter ringing in his ears.

The first thing Israel did after he opened the door to Room 204 was to sweep Willa off her feet and into his arms. That he took her completely by surprise was evident when she squealed and grabbed him by the collar of his coat.

"What are you doing?" she asked, frantically looking around for where he was taking her. "You didn't close the door."

He obligingly backed up, kicked the door shut with the heel of his boot, and then made for the bed. "Take off my hat," he said. "Then yours."

"Why? Oh, never mind." She removed his hat and flung it in the direction of the bed. It skipped across the comforter and fell to the floor on the far side. She did the same with her hat, although it teetered on the edge of the bed before it finally slipped to the floor.

"Not a bad toss," he said, striding forward.

"You're going to drop me like a sack of flour, aren't you?"

"I wasn't, but . . ." He chuckled when her arms went

around his neck. "Well, that's okay, too." He lowered her carefully to the bed, and when the mattress was under her, he told her she could let him go. He released her also but did not straighten. Instead, he bore her down using only the pressure of his mouth. When he heard her moan softly, he sat up halfway, his arms braced on either side of her shoulders, and smiled at her. "Nice, isn't it?"

"Uh-huh." She looked at him from under lashes that were only marginally raised. "Oh. Did you mean the kiss? I was referring to the mattress. I don't know if I've—"

Israel kissed her. He had to. It was an imperative, and he did not draw back until she moaned again. "You have a sassy mouth, Mrs. McKenna."

"I know. Did you bring the honey?"

Laughing, he sat up fully and encouraged her to move over and make room for him. When she did, he stretched out beside her and rolled onto his back. He wriggled his shoulders and then his entire frame until he created a sweet spot for himself. "It *is* a nice mattress."

"Are you comfortable?" she asked dryly. "There was a moment there while you were squirming that you put me in mind of John Henry. He twists something fierce when he's settling down beside Annalea."

"Well, John Henry has a certain charm. I am choosing to be flattered by the comparison."

"Of course you would be."

Israel found her hand, slipped his fingers through hers so they made a fist, and gave it a little shake. He looked at her out of the corner of his eye and saw that her grin had faded. She was pensive.

"A penny for them," he said.

"Mm. I was thinking about the register downstairs. Mr. and Mrs. Israel McKenna. I watched you sign it without the slightest hesitation. It struck me that I might not have done the same. Not done it as quickly, I mean. Do you suppose you are more married than I am? Is that even possible?"

"I don't know," he said, treading carefully. "What do you think?"

"I'm not sure. I know you thought hard about it before you

said yes, but once you made up your mind, once we were married, you took to it like a bumblebee takes to a blossom, like it was natural to you. I don't think it's natural to me. Not yet." She turned her head toward him. "You carried me across the threshold. That's what you intended, isn't it?"

"Yes. I was correcting an oversight."

"I didn't think of it, not once, and you, well, it was like you had it planned all along. Are you certain you weren't married before?"

Israel stopped staring at the ceiling and swiveled his head in her direction. "I'm certain." He saw she was trying to determine if she could believe him. "I'm *certain*," he repeated.

Willa nodded. "I'm sorry. That will teach you to think twice about offering to pay for my thoughts."

"Hmm. That's right. I owe you a penny."

She chuckled. "I'll record it under accounts receivable."

Israel said, "Or you could take it out in trade."

Now she gave him a full-throated laugh. "Are you trying to be helpful or are you merely hopeful?"

"Can't I be both?"

Willa took her hand from his and flung herself at him. "Come here, you wicked man." When she was more on top of him than not, she began planting kisses. His ear, his neck, the space between his eyebrows that creased when he was thinking deeply, she put her mouth to each place. Sometimes she lingered, as she did when she came to the corner of his lips, trying to tease the dimple to show itself. Sometimes her lips darted, alighting as briefly as a hummingbird in search of sweeter nectar.

"Should we remove our coats?" he asked, his breath hot in her ear.

"Soon." She breathed the word more than she said it and then said it again, this time against his mouth. "Soon."

Israel was agreeable, especially when she did a fair imitation of John Henry as she wriggled over him. He slipped his hands under her coat and cupped the rounds of her bottom. They were soft, beautifully curved, and eminently squeezable right up until the moment he whispered, "Mrs. Roundbottom, I presume." That was when her head jerked up and her buttocks tightened rock hard under his palms. "Huh," he grunted quietly. "Just as I thought. You're not much for the name either."

"It doesn't apply," she said, mildly nettled.

He grinned. "Not at the moment, it doesn't, but there are times, Wilhelmina . . . oh, yes, there are times."

She heard this last spoken with such reverence that she could not help but be complimented by it. She relaxed under his palms. "Like this? Like now?"

He nodded. "Plump as rising dough."

Laughing, she slapped his hands away. When they rested at the small of her back, she said, "That's better. I'll let you know when you can put your hands on my round bottom again." She lowered her mouth to his, nudging him with her lips, not teasing him with her tongue. Not yet. She played his lips as if his mouth were a fine instrument, which in many ways it was. She blew on them softly, sipped them, hummed against them. She drew the lower one between her teeth and bit down gently. He moved a shade restlessly under her; she liked that.

"We can take off our coats now." She touched her forehead to his. "And a lot of other things besides. You first." She rolled off and lay on her back, cradling her head in her hands as she settled in and prepared to watch him.

Israel sat up and began unbuttoning his coat. "I suppose you want your penny's worth."

"Taking what you owe me in trade was your idea, so I sure do."

Swiveling, he threw his legs over the side the bed and stood. The room was sparsely but adequately furnished for the transient guest. There was a stove in one corner giving off a fair amount of heat. A copper kettle with a rich verdigris patina and filled with split wood was situated at an angle beside the stove, assuring that the room, with very little effort, would remain warm. Nearby were a rocker and a footstool, both of them plainly made but serviceable. A small square table stood on the right side of the bed and a long bench seat with a colorful quilted pad on the lid sat at the foot of it. The room also had a trifold painted silk screen secluding the corner of the room closest to the stove.

Curious, Israel folded his coat over his arm, dropped it on the bench seat, and walked over to the screen. He looked over his shoulder at Willa, one eyebrow cocked. She had risen high enough to prop herself on her elbows, and she returned his gaze, clearly interested herself. He held up a finger and peeked behind the screen. He looked back at her again, smiled, and then disappeared.

"You are going to owe me that penny—with interest—if you are taking your clothes off back there."

Israel looked at her over the top of the screen, the lower half of his face hidden from view. "It is remarkable how you have embraced certain intimate aspects of marriage."

"It surprises me, too."

Israel shook his head, but behind the screen, he was grinning. When he stepped around it, once more in Willa's full view, only a hint of his smile was left, but what was there was full of cunning. "The washstand is back there. Basin, pitcher, towels, and fresh water. More importantly, there is a tub. I take it all we have to do is ask downstairs and someone will be charged with filling it. It's big. Bigger than we have at the ranch. There might even be room for two of us."

"There'd probably be more room in it if at least one of us wasn't wearing any clothes."

It was hard to argue with that logic, so Israel went over to the stove and stood beside it as he removed his jacket and vest and pulled his shirt over his head. He sat in the rocker to take off his boots and socks, and then stepped out of his trousers. He placed everything but his boots neatly on the bench seat before he shrugged out of his thin flannel undershirt and dropped the drawers that were now riding low on his hips.

He walked unself-consciously to the side of the bed while she tracked his movements with heavy-lidded and darkening eyes. "Well?" he asked.

"You are an astonishingly beautiful man, Mr. McKenna," she said huskily. "And you know what part is worth every penny you'll ever owe me?"

Israel stared at her hard. The faint smile playing about her mouth warned him away, but he said, "I am going to regret this, but damn if the devil in me doesn't want to know. All right. Tell me."

"The part where you fold all your clothes and put . . . put them . . . put them all . . ."

He pounced as her voice dissolved into peals of bright, joyful laughter. He pinned her with scissor legs and by making a fist around her rope of hair. She was free to pummel him if she liked because he did not grab her by the wrists, but she had begun laughing in a little hiccuping fashion and appeared to have no strength to fight back. It might also have been that she had no enthusiasm for doing so.

Israel leaned in so his face hovered inches above hers. "Are you quite finished?"

"I think—*hic*—so." She regarded him guiltily. "Sorry. I'm—*hic*—trying. I really am—*hic*."

Shaking his head, making a genuine effort to appear solemn, even stern, but failing so miserably that she began chuckling, Israel lowered his mouth until he could feel her breathy giggles, and then he tickled her until she begged him to stop. When he finally obliged her and rolled onto his back, she curled on her side, hugged her ribs, and gasped for breath.

"That was cruel," she said when she could speak.

"Mnh."

She stared at his profile, saw his lips twitch. "Do you know what would be more cruel?"

"What's that?"

"If you don't help me out of these clothes. Because frankly I don't have the strength."

"All right," he said, rising to his elbows. "But I am not folding them."

Laughing, she flopped onto her back and beamed up at him.

Israel made short work of her clothes, pausing only to torture her as much as he saw fit, but never as much as she deserved. She should be grateful, he told her, that he did not have the stamina to draw it out that long. And Willa, between gasps of pleasure and hitches of laughter, assured him that she was.

Israel pulled back the covers so she could wiggle under them. It was not until she was naked, perfectly so, that she had a stab of self-consciousness and wanted to be beneath the covers. He obliged, rising to his knees and tugging on the blankets to get them down and then over. Before he dived under them, he asked her about the curtains. Did she want him to close them?

Willa looked to window, frowned slightly at the cloudy gray light pressing against the glass, not because the day was overcast, but because she was reminded that it was still early in the afternoon. They had never had the opportunity to be intimate during the day while they were at the ranch. There was always the threat of intrusion, mostly from Annalea, even when they found themselves with time and opportunity.

"No," she said defiantly, as if she were taking a stand against the light. "Leave them open."

"Rebel," Israel whispered. He gave her a thorough kiss before crawling under the blankets and hoped she felt rewarded for her decision. That had been his intention. He wanted to see more of her, not less.

She turned to him once he was settled and did not question his decision to pull her leg across his. She was familiar with mounting and straddled him easily when she realized it was what he wanted. Her hair fell in two long waves on either side of her face, a dark curtain of modesty and mystery where it covered her breasts. Israel's fingers slipped between the waves, sifting and combing. He cupped the side of her face, and his thumb brushed her lips until they parted. When she sucked on the tip, bit it gently, it was as if she had found the single thread that would unravel all of him.

He pulled his hand back sharply before he was undone by her teeth and her Circe smile. He slipped his fingers under her curtain of hair and dragged them lightly over her breasts. The nipples stood erect under his thumbs, and those sweet little buds did not bite back. When her sorceress smile faded as she pressed her lips together, he chuckled deep in his throat, and the sound of it was vaguely wicked even to his own ears.

Her fingers were busy as well. They flitted over his chest, never alighting for long, but always exerting enough pressure to keep from being ticklish. When she traced an imaginary line from his breastbone to his navel, his skin retracted in anticipation of her touch and for a moment he didn't breathe.

He was not helpless to stop her when she took him by the wrists and removed his hands from her breasts, but neither was he persuaded any good would come of denying her anything. When she had borne his hands down to the mattress, she threaded her fingers through his to keep them there. The handclasp was an effective restraint as she bent over him and kissed him at her leisure.

Israel returned the kisses as he was able, but those were fleeting moments as she frequently left his mouth to attend to him elsewhere. She kissed the pulse beating in his throat and used the tip of her tongue to trace the sensitive cord in his neck. She blew a kiss against his ear that made him shiver. She told him to close his eyes, and when he did, she teased him with the unexpected, kissing the underside of his jaw, his temples, his forehead, even pressing her lips to his collarbone, before she settled them briefly on his eyelids.

When he opened his eyes, her face was close, and her eyes were so dark now that even with daylight as a companion, they were like black diamonds, fathomless, yet radiant. Yes, she had contradictions, too.

She nudged his lips, whispered against them. "I want you inside me. Show me."

Israel stretched his fingers, and she released him, sliding her hands along his forearms as she began to sit up. When he was free, he slipped his hands under her buttocks and lifted her. "Go on," he said. "Take it."

She reached between them, between her legs, and made a fist around his cock. She looked at him, momentarily uncertain, but when he nodded, she began to lower herself, guiding him, guiding her, and her hand came away and then he was inside her and she was all around him.

She closed her eyes briefly. He stroked her thighs, and when she began to lean forward, he caressed her buttocks. She tentatively lifted her hips and then pushed back. She squeezed him and opened her eyes when he groaned.

"Go on," he said again. "Watching you ride is a singular pleasure."

Moaning softly, she found his hands and brought them to her breasts. She rubbed herself against him, and it was not long before it was not enough. She covered him so he could take the tip of one breast into his mouth, and when he did, when he sucked and teased and tasted, she began to rise and fall with the rhythm he drew out of her.

Israel let her go at the first sign that she wanted to pull away. She was slightly out of breath but not in a way that was concerning. It was more in the way of a compliment, and he had a knowing smile for her when she sat up and took notice of his mouth.

"Beast," she said under her breath, and then she began to take him on a long ride.

She came noisily, without inhibition, and he liked her for it. Hearing her like this, so deeply satisfied that she could not help giving it sound, was a rare occurrence in their bedroom. In spite of her experience with Annalea being a sound sleeper, she was never so confident that she wanted to test it. Sometimes it happened in spite of her intentions, primarily because he would not let her go quietly, but she was more embarrassed than pleased in the aftermath, and he had to be careful not to press her too often.

For now, though, she was quite content to be tumbled onto her back and let him have his way with her, just as if he hadn't already had his way. He came when he was deep inside her, and he, who had often painfully tried to avoid any possibility of a child, wondered if perhaps this time he had got her with one.

They lay side by side, shoulders touching, breathing slowly, both of them with their eyes set drowsily at half-mast. After a few minutes, Willa lifted his arm so she could make a cradle for her head in his shoulder. Once she was comfortably nested, he was able to bring his arm around her.

She murmured something that Israel could not properly hear. "How's that again?" he asked.

"Mm."

"Oh. Nothing profound, then."

A brief, silent laugh shook her shoulders. "No. Nothing

profound." She rubbed her cheek against him. "But you know what would be?"

"No."

"That tub you talked about earlier, filled with hot water, ribbons of steam scented with lavender or spice, a thick sponge, floating soap, and a stack of towels warming beside the stove."

"I don't know if that meets the definition of profound," he said. "But you paint a very nice picture, although I have to tell you I'm not partial to scented bath salts."

"I am."

"Then you can put them in after I get out."

"The bath is for me," she said.

"Not if I'm the one getting up, getting dressed, and going downstairs to make it happen."

"Oh."

"Uh-huh." He started to rise, but she pulled him back. "It can wait."

He shook his head. "No, I need to get up anyway. There's something else I want to do. It won't take long, but I have to leave the hotel. I've seen the size of the tub. I'll be back before it's filled." He gently removed her hand from his arm and slid out of bed.

"May I know what you'll be doing?"

"I'd like to tell you when it's done." He could see that she did not particularly care for his answer, but he began to dress in spite of it. She was quiet and obviously unhappy, and that resonated uneasily with him. He sat on the bench to put on his boots. "I didn't have to tell you I was going to leave the hotel, but I did because I knew if you learned it on your own, you would wonder about every promise I ever made to you. That's precisely what I don't want you to do. I'm coming right back."

Willa sat up, drawing the covers with her as she raised her knees to her chest. She nodded, but it was reluctantly given. "I can't help but wonder if those are the same words you spoke to someone else."

He paused, tucking in his shirt. "What do you mean?"

"I mean those might be the very words you said to someone

before you rode out to the ridge with men who probably intended for you to die there. I can't seem to put it behind me, which is more than passing strange since it happened to you. But there you have it. It still knots me up inside. Life is that fragile and there is not much ahead of us that we can ever know for certain."

Israel sat down on the bed beside her and took her hand. "Listen to me, Willa," he said quietly, willing her to look at him. "'And which of you by worrying can add a single hour to his life's span? If then you cannot do even a very little thing, why do you worry about other matters?'"

"'Consider the lilies . . .'" she said softly. "Yes, I know. Matthew?"

"Mm-hmm. It's there, but I was quoting verses in Luke."

She smiled a trifle crookedly. "Seems that if two disciples saw fit to write down what their Lord said, they are words to take to heart."

"Hmm. Quill told me once that I interpreted the whole passage wrong, or perhaps took it too much to heart. He said when the Lord provided, it did not mean that He provided only for me, nor did it mean that whatever was provided was mine for the taking. There was very little I worried about in those days, which is not precisely what was meant either."

"It must be useful to know so much and employ it at will."

"Are you talking about me or my brother?"

"Both of you, I imagine. You had the same father . . . and mother."

Sober, he said, "We did, but Willa, we employed what we learned in very different ways."

"I think I understood that."

He bent, kissed her on the mouth, and allowed himself the privilege of lingering. When he drew back, he heard himself ask without any forethought of doing so, "Do you want to come with me?"

Surprised by the offer, her lips parted. "Really?"

"Yes, really." His eyebrows lifted as her smile erased every vestige of concern from her features. Anticipating her answer, he stood and tugged on her hand. He was slow to register her resistance until he heard her speak.

She said, "No."

"No?"

"Uh-huh. No."

"But I thought—"

"It was enough that you asked." She loosened her hand from his and shooed him away. "I don't understand it either, but there it is. You go, and I will supervise the filling of the tub to an acceptable height and see that it's hot enough to still be warm when you return."

"All right." He finished tucking in his shirt and slipped into his vest and jacket. He found his hat on the floor where she had tossed it and stooped to pick it up, beating it lightly against his thigh as he straightened. He took his coat from the bench seat and folded it over his arm and stood there at the foot of the bed, making a memory of her as he might if he were taking a photograph.

"But just to be clear," he said. "I am still not requesting scented salts."

Chapter Seventeen

Buster Rawlins held up his horse when he heard Eli shout from behind him. He turned in his saddle as Eli's gelding slowed to a trot. He looked over horse and rider, giving more attention to the horse than the rider, and when he was satisfied that neither was hurt, faced forward and waited for Eli to come abreast of him.

Buster pulled down the scarf covering the lower half of his face and grunted a greeting.

"Morning to you, too," said Eli. He lifted the collar of his coat and tucked his chin lower. The wind was bitterly cold, and riding into the face of it had beaten ruddy color into his cheeks.

"You're up early." Buster dug his heels into his mare's sides and she started forward. "Keep up," he told Eli. "You're likely to freeze in place if you don't. Damn brisk out here."

"Brisk. Yes. It's that."

"So what are you doing out here? Not like you to come looking for work."

"I need your help."

Buster shook his head. "Not if it means crossing your father. I know you had an argument with him the other day. I'm not getting in the middle of that."

"How do you know we argued? Did he tell you?"

"No, and neither did anyone else. Do you think after all these years of spitting and scratching at each other that I can't tell when you've been at it again? Putting on that face the way you do when you're with him in public, and him doin' the same thing, well, it's been a long time since I was fooled by it. Guess you both have your reasons, so it's not for me to question, but if you suppose I am going to put myself in the line of fire, go suppose somewhere else."

Eli gave Buster a sharp look. "He *did* speak to you. I bet you didn't give *him* that speech."

Buster shrugged. Up ahead a dozen cows were huddled around a standing pool of water that was most likely frozen over. He had an axe with him to break it open. He hoped he had patience enough not to use it on Eli's head.

Eli persisted. "What did he say to you?"

"He said that Willa Pancake got herself hitched."

"Did you believe him?"

"'Course I did. Didn't you?"

"Not at first."

Buster simply shook his head.

"Did he say who she married?"

"Nope."

"Did you ask him?"

"Nope. I wasn't that eager to prolong the conversation, but I will tell you, I don't think he knows."

"Why do you say that? He led me to believe he did."

"Now that'd be like him, wouldn't it? But I had a different impression is all, like maybe Mrs. Hamill didn't tell him because Cutter never told her." Buster stopped and dismounted when he was ten feet from the cows. He gave Eli his reins. "You might as well make yourself useful since you're here. Don't let her wander off." He took the axe he was carrying in his scabbard in place of a rifle and found an opening between a pair of broad-boned beauties that he could slip into. He butted and shoved and elbowed his way forward. The beef was not inclined to move.

Eli remained in the saddle, watching him. He called out above the lowing protests of the cattle. "Well, someone has to know. That's why I want you to ride into town with me. I figure if we ask around, the two of us, we'll find out who stepped in where he shouldn't have."

"Now, see? You and I are about to have a difference of opinion, Eli. Who's to say he wasn't invited in?"

Eli urged his horse forward so he did not have to pitch his voice so high to be heard. He sounded like a boy whose balls hadn't dropped. "I'm noticing you're considerably more amiable when you've had a few drinks."

"Isn't everybody?"

"Not Mal. He's rattlesnake mean. It's only after a few becomes one too many that he gets soft in the head and just a little soft in the heart. You've probably never seen him like that."

"No. Never have. Don't think I want to." Buster raised the axe over his shoulder and brought it down hard on the thick crust of ice. It cracked but didn't break. He shoved back on the cow trying to push him forward and brought the axe down again. This time it sank deep and water sprayed between the cracks. "Got it!" Buster crowed.

"Good for you."

Buster spent another five minutes chipping away at the ice, digging out big chunks and whipping them aside like so many skipping stones. He got out of the way as soon as he was done because one of his brown-eyed lovelies was determined to push him into the drink.

He walked back to his mount, put the axe away, and took his reins from Eli. He swung up in his saddle. "There are a few other places I need to get to and do the same thing. You're welcome to ride along."

Eli didn't see that he had any other choice, not if he was going to persuade Buster to assist him. "Hyah," he said, and his horse fell into step beside Buster's. "Where to next?"

"The fountainhead at Cook Hill. I want to be certain it's still flowing."

"Why isn't Jesse Snow doing this?"

"Because then I'd have to ride out to make sure it was done. He's good when you're in close and keeping an eye on him, but he can't be left alone for long. Jesse does like a shortcut." He gave Eli a sideways glance. "I guess I'm wonderin' why you haven't corralled Jesse for a ride into town. He wouldn't hesitate."

"Maybe you were too many sheets to the wind when we talked about Jesse back a ways, but I recall saying that his tongue gets to wagging when he's had a few. God knows what he would say. I want information, but I don't want to become a laughingstock trying to get it."

"Understandable." Buster pulled the brim of his hat lower. "I'm recollecting you were thinking about sending Jesse over to the Pancake spread. What happened to that?"

"Truth?"

Buster smirked. "No. Please lie to me."

"I thought he was too good-looking to put in Wilhelmina's way."

"Lord, Eli, but she has you by the balls."

"You're the one who said I should have another go at proposing to her. That's what you said, or have you forgotten?"

"I said it because I could tell you were thinking it. Does your father know you were going to take another shot?"

Eli's chuckle was humorless. "Don't you realize yet that he knows everything? He told me once I should steal her away, make it look like she came willingly, and not return until she was my wife, legal, bedded, and if I was fortunate, with my child in her."

Buster screwed his mouth to one side and he scratched the stubble on his jaw. "Well, damn. I did not know that. It's no secret that he wants the valley. Always has, and that strip by the fence line, he wants that real bad, but I didn't know he entertained notions about you running off with Miss Willa."

"The irony is that he put a stop to Willa and me seeing each other when we were kids. I guess he couldn't see the advantage of me taking up with her back then or maybe he just hated all the Pancakes so much he didn't want any association with them. He and I have never talked about it. I suspect he had a hand in Willa leaving the valley back then, but I've never asked him. I wouldn't believe him if he denied it so there's no point."

"Huh. Guess I never knew the particulars. You can play your cards close, just like your father, when you have a mind to."

Eli said nothing. The comparison to his father, even a relatively complimentary one, stung more than usual coming from Buster. When people commented on the similarities between father and son, Malcolm was the yardstick and Eli was the ruler.

They were approaching the foot of Cook Hill when Eli

finally broke the silence. "So? Are you going to ride into Jupiter with me?"

"I'm still thinking. I guess I want to know what your plans are."

"I told you. I want to know who he is."

"And?" The word hung in the air while Buster studied Eli.

"And . . . nothing." When Buster slowed and then held up his horse, Eli did the same. "What? Do you think I'm playing my cards close to my vest now? I'm not. I just want to know who he is."

"So you don't have any thoughts about making her a widow? Because I'm not having any part of that. I am still harborin' regrets about that other business. I can't help but think I should've tried harder to put a stop to it. I wish I'd understood how serious you were before it was too late." He put up a hand to prevent Eli's interruption. "I blame myself, not you. Don't worry that I'm going to talk because I'm not. It's just a damn good thing you told Jesse to stay put and take away the body. There'd been hell to pay if Malcolm had seen it when he rode up to the ridge with you."

"It would have been worse if he found out what the fellow did and I had not seen fit to set it right. C'mon, Buster. You know it's true. *That's* why you agreed."

"That's why I went along to a point. I'm not sure that I ever agreed." He snapped the reins. "Listen, thinking on it now as I am, I can tell you that if you want to ask after Miss Wilhelmina in town, you should do it on your own or take Jesse with you. I'm not going."

Eli frowned. "Do you mean that?"

"I do. See? I think a lot more clearly when I don't have a glass of beer and a shot on the table and a warm and willing woman waiting for me."

Willa was preparing to dip her fingers into the tub when she heard the knock. "Your timing is uncanny," she said, opening the door. "Mrs. Putty's twin boys just carried away the last four buckets."

Israel's eyebrows lifted a fraction as he looked her over.

She was wearing a towel. Only a towel. "I passed them in the lobby," he said, trying to slip through the narrow opening she gave him. "Now I understand why they looked as if they'd been struck dumb."

Willa looked down at herself and told him with some asperity, "I was not wearing this when they were here."

Israel's brows rose even higher. "Then I'm surprised they were still breathing. You about stopped my heart when you opened the door."

"Fool," she said, not unkindly. She took him by the sleeve and pulled him through. It was an awkward entrance because he had several parcels in his arms but modesty prevented her from opening the door wider. As soon as he was inside, she shut the door, turned the key, and then turned to him. Her attention immediately wandered to the packages. She pressed her lips together and regarded him expectantly.

He chuckled. "Greedy wife. These are not all for you. Some are for sharing."

"Then they're all for me, and maybe I'll share some."

"All right, that will work." He walked to the bed, where he dropped everything. In his absence, she had made a half-hearted effort to make up the bed. The covers were straightened if not smoothed, and the pillows had been plumped but were resting cock-eyed against the headboard. It made him smile to see it. When he turned, she was standing right there as if she had been peeking around his shoulder, which was probably the case. That merely deepened his smile. He kissed her on the crown of her head, her hair soft against his lips. "Have at them," he said. "I am going to wallow in the trough."

"Enjoy," she said absently and sat down on the bed to make her first selection.

Israel had undressed, folded the screen and moved it aside, and was sliding into the tub before Willa finally placed a parcel in her lap. Up until that moment her inspection had been eyes only. She actually kept her hands behind her back as if she needed to restrain herself from touching or shaking.

Watching her, he wished he could have done more. His smile was a little rueful. "Remember that I'm not a rich man," he said. "I don't know what you think might be in them, but there's nothing there that will leave you breathless or bite you."

Moved by his thoughtfulness, savoring the anticipation, Willa fingered the twine tied around the flat, brown paper parcel while she looked at him. "I don't care what any of it is. That you did it is enough."

"Go on. Let's see if that's true."

She nodded and turned her attention once more to the parcel, tugging on the loose bow that held it all together. She turned the present over, carefully folded back the paper, and lifted what she found inside.

"It's a scarf," Israel said helpfully when she merely stared at the poppy red wool without unfolding it. "It's long, too. I figured you could wrap it around you three or four times to keep the chill off your neck when you're riding. Plus, it's red. I picked the color because it suits you and because it will help me see you from a long way off in case I'm not wearing the spectacles." When she still did not speak or give any indication that she meant to examine the gift, he added, "Of course, if you'd rather have a different—"

Willa looked over at him then. Tears hovered on the edge of her lashes, but she did not blink them back or knuckle them away. "Shut up," she whispered. "You have to shut up." She pushed the paper and twine off her lap and unfolded the scarf, draping it over one arm and running her hand along the length of it. Standing, she wound the scarf around her neck twice and let the tails fall, one in front, one down her back. She continued to finger it, and although her eyes had dried, her smile was still a trifle watery.

"It's lovely," she said. "Really. Thank you."

"You're welcome." He spoke gravely because the moment seemed to demand it.

That changed when she said, "I notice you're not wearing your spectacles."

"No. Not in the bath. Not as rule."

"Hmm. But you can see me?"

"Mm-hmm. All the way over here."

"How about now?"

Israel was appreciative if not entirely surprised when it

happened. He could have expected that another woman might have removed the scarf, but his wife was cleverer than that. She removed the towel.

"Yes," he said with the same gravity as before. "I can still see you."

"Good." She approached the tub, dragging the towel by her fingertips. "It pains me to remove this, but I really have no choice." She dropped the towel on the floor and unwound the scarf, careful to keep the tails out of the water. She hung it over the folded screen. "Move over."

Israel barely had time to comply before she was disturbing the water. In spite of the length and height of the tub, it was a tight fit, but they made the necessary compromises until she was mostly cradled between his legs and the back of her head lay against his shoulder. His arms rested on either side of her along the rim of the tub, while her hands rested on his bent knees.

"Thank the Lord for floating soap," he said as the bar of Ivory bobbed on the rippled surface of the water. Laughter rumbled in his chest when Willa made a halfhearted grab for it and it jumped out from between her fingers, as slippery as a frightened hop toad. "I don't suppose anyone's figured out how to keep it in your hands."

The soap drifted away, and she let it go. She set her palm over his knee again and gently massaged it. "Tell me why you had to leave. You said you would when you got back."

Amused, he asked, "The presents didn't move you off the scent?"

"Not for a moment. Is that why you brought them?"

"No. I'm ashamed to admit they were all an afterthought."

"Even the scarf?"

"Afraid so. Not that I didn't mean you to have it as soon as I saw it, but I didn't go looking for it. Maybe that makes a difference to you."

She was quiet, thoughtful, and then she leaned her head a little to the side and looked up at him. "No. No difference. You saw it, thought of me, and decided to have it. You know, Israel, you are a better man than you credit."

He started to deny it, but she cut him off when she stopped

massaging his knee and squeezed it as if her fingers were pincers. "Ow!"

Willa released her grip. "Accept that I believe it," she said. "Even if you don't."

Israel tried to remember if anyone had ever spoken up for him as she had. No one came to mind. He waited until she was no longer looking at him before he said, "I left so I could post a couple of letters."

"Post letters? But Cutter or Zach or even Happy could have done—" She stopped. "Oh, I see. I don't suppose they could, not if you didn't want anyone to know where the letters were going. That's it, isn't it? You didn't want any of us of to know."

Israel did not deny it. "One of the letters was to my parents. The other one was to Quill."

"You told me your parents live in Herring. I could have written to them at any time, but I respected your wishes, and I—" She sighed deeply, shaking her head. "They don't live in Herring at all. That was a lie."

"Yes."

"Do you believe your lies?"

"Sometimes. It's easier if I do."

"Do they even live in Illinois?"

"Yes." She had stopped massaging his knee for the second time, but at least she wasn't pinching it. "I couldn't trust you then, and when my back is to the wall, I lie."

"Forgive me, but it seems as if you don't trust me now."

Israel said nothing.

"Israel?"

"What about you?" he asked quietly. "Do you think you will ever trust me with your secret?" Holding her as he was, all but surrounding her with his body, he felt the tremor that slipped under her skin.

"Why not secrets?" she asked. "It is not particularly flattering that you think I have only one."

As a defense, it was good. Israel almost said as much because he admired her for not folding her hand right there. "You think a woman should be more mysterious?"

"Something like that."

"All right," he said.

"Why are you so agreeable? It's aggravating."

"Yes," he said dryly. "I can appreciate how agreeing with you would set your teeth on edge." He tilted his head to look down at her. A muscle ticked in her jaw. "And they *are* on edge." Before she snapped at him, he said, "You didn't allow me to finish. I was going to say, with no expectation that you will follow suit, that my parents live in Evanston. Quill lives on a spread near a little town called Temptation."

When she showed no reaction, he guessed she had never heard of it and probably did not know it was in Colorado. The state was full of little towns unknown to one another. "He owns the place, has for a few years. Calls it Eden. I've never seen it, but I've been imagining that it must be a lot like Pancake Valley."

"Not a lot like," said Willa. "A little maybe. There is no other place a lot like Pancake Valley."

"At the risk you of aggravating you, I'll agree."

"Those letters, Israel. What did you write?"

"Did I tell them I was married? No. And I didn't tell them where I am. I wrote that I regretted not writing to them earlier, which you will know is a lie, and I explained that I was detained by unavoidable circumstances, which you will know touches on the truth. I told them I was well—true—and that no one in law enforcement was after me—also true, at least as far as I know—and that I would write again when I was certain my situation was settled."

"And isn't it settled?"

Israel's hands moved from the rim of the tub to Willa's shoulders. His thumbs caressed her damp skin. "I think we need to dust the cobwebs off those secrets. If you don't send me packing, then it's settled. It will be up to you. I know I'm not leaving."

"You can't know that."

He gave her shoulders a gentle shake. "I *know*, Wilhelmina." Then more quietly, "I know."

She closed her eyes. "Tell me. If you think you're ready, tell me."

"I love you."

Chapter Eighteen

Willa simply ceased to breathe. Her heart stuttered once and then began to thump hard against her chest. She felt her face flame and heat rush to her fingertips and then to her toes. Her skin was suddenly so hot that the bathwater was like ice. She would have jerked around in his arms so that she could see his face, but the close confines of the tub and Israel's hands on her shoulders prevented her from hurting them both with wild thrashing.

In spite of Israel's heat, and her own, Willa shivered. She was grateful when he began to rub her upper arms.

"Of all things you might have said . . ." She did not finish the thought, and he did not press her.

Once her heart quieted, she felt his. It thudded dully, a heavy sound against her back, and she imagined she could hear the echo of it in her ears.

"Are you wondering if it's true?" he asked.

"No." She closed her eyes. She felt his chin move back and forth against her hair. It was as intimate as his kiss. "I believe you." It seemed to her that he went perfectly still, not frozen precisely, just still, and she understood then the depth of his uncertainty. She doubted that he thought of himself as particularly brave for uttering those words, but he had made himself vulnerable, and that was not the act of a coward. "It matters," she said, "that you told me."

Israel nodded but said nothing.

Willa covered one of his hands with hers. "I had no expectation that we would ever come to this pass."

"That was fairly clear during the ceremony."

"I hardly knew what I was saying then."

"I understand."

"You were in possession of yourself."

"Perhaps it seemed that way."

"Weren't you?"

"I was merely ready. I don't think you were."

"I was the one who proposed."

Israel placed his lips against her hair and kissed her lightly. "I haven't forgotten, but I don't think you prepared yourself for me to say yes. In the end, you were the one who was forced. I wasn't."

"I don't know why you would say that."

"Do you recall your father muttering something about the shotgun being for you?"

"Yes. And I pretended not to hear."

"So did I, but I never believed he was speaking tongue-in-cheek."

"More like foot-in-mouth." She immediately regretted her attempt to make light of the moment because Israel responded with gravity.

"Yes. From your perspective, I'm sure it was."

"You're talking about my secret again, aren't you?"

"I am."

"My secret is not that I love you." She felt his heart thud once and then thrum steadily. Her fingers tightened infinitesimally between his before she went on. "It couldn't be my secret unless you understand that it was one I was keeping from myself. I didn't know, Israel. I didn't. It's what I meant when I said I had no expectation that we would arrive at this pass. Can you appreciate that it's a revelation to me? To feel this way . . . to realize that someone feels this way about me . . . it's beyond overwhelming." She released his hand and sat up to the degree she was able. She turned her head to look at him and met the arrested expression in his blue-gray eyes fearlessly.

"I've known love, Israel. I have loved and been loved in return by my grandparents, by my parents . . ." She drew in a small, silent breath and said, "And by my daughter."

Nodding slowly, Israel laid his fingertips against her flushed cheek. "There it is," he said gently.

She searched his face. “You knew.”

“I suspected.”

“And the other?” she asked. “That I love you? Did you know what I didn’t?”

“No. Does that surprise you?”

“A little. Sometimes it seems as if you know my mind before I do.”

“Not about this, and probably not even as often as you think I do. I’m not a mind reader, but there are ways to read a face. I suppose you could say that I’ve made a study of it, and I’ve learned that you cannot give away what you don’t know.”

Willa cupped one hand and swept water toward her. The bar of soap floated in her direction. She caught it and carefully handed it to Israel. “My back,” she said, leaning forward to present it to him. “Before the water cools. You can tell me about this study of yours. Why would you do it?”

“Then there’s nothing you want to say about Annalea?”

“No.”

“Or about love?”

“No.”

“Hmm.”

“Are you laughing?”

“No.”

Willa did not believe him, but he was already rolling the soap down her spine so she did not try to catch him out. “About the study,” she prompted.

“It wasn’t a formal study, you understand, just something I did because it was useful in the course of meeting people, especially when it was necessary to maneuver and manipulate them.”

Willa lifted her head so sharply that her neck cracked. “You held an elected office! That’s it, isn’t it? You were part of a corrupt political scheme.”

Israel pushed her head back down so he could lather her nape. “Lord, you say it as if you’ve found the Holy Grail. No, I have never aspired to be on anyone’s ballot. Right church, Willa, wrong pew.”

“Then what?” she asked plaintively. “Why would it be

necessary to influence people so they don't suspect they are being influenced?"

"For no other purpose than getting something I wanted, and mostly what I wanted was their money."

She fell silent as his words penetrated. "Oh," she said.

"Oh," he repeated just as quietly. "Do you know what a confidence man is?"

"Yes," she said. "I think I understand now." She reminded herself that she had invited him to tell her, that she had wanted to know, but it now felt like a lie she had told herself and made him believe.

"Then to be clear, Willa, I will say it so you do not have to. I made my living—a relatively good living—gaining people's trust in order to relieve them of at least some of their worldly goods." He stopped soaping her back and waited.

Willa set her hands on either side of the tub and lifted herself out of the water. Still without speaking, she stepped out of the tub and then chose a warm towel from the stack on the stove and wrapped it around her. Aware that Israel was watching her but unable to meet his eyes just yet, she dragged the rocker within a few feet of the tub and sat down. Folding her hands in her lap, she stared at them.

"Are you praying?" he asked.

She shook her head.

"Perhaps you should."

Willa's head came up. "And who should I be praying for? You? Me? All of my worldly goods?" She saw her words strike him as if she had used a whip, but his flinch was confined to his eyes. He accepted her rebuke as a stoic might or as a man who owned that it was deserved. "Was it all lies? Am I one of your marks? That's what a man like you calls a person like me, isn't it? A mark. What can I expect now that you own my heart? Have I risked Annalea by putting that truth in your hands?"

Israel did flinch then, all of him. The rapidly cooling water rippled. He dropped the soap and started to rise.

Willa put out a hand. "No. Stay where you are." When he neither raised nor lowered himself, but remained where he was as if caught, she added, "Please. It is a small advantage to be where I am and you to be where you are. I need that right now."

Israel eased back into the water. "All right."

Willa lowered her hand, and she set it on her lap without folding it into the other. "Start anywhere."

"Then I will begin with Annalea," he said. "If you cannot put the idea to rest that I would betray that confidence, that I would use her to hurt you, or hurt her to use you, there is no reason for me to go on. You will never be able to hear me out if you believe I could do that."

"You have yourself to blame," she countered. "From the beginning you warned me you were a liar. You told Annalea you were a villain. You made certain we knew you were not a good man."

He fell silent but did not turn away.

Willa found the quiet as unbearable as staring into his eyes. "Say something!"

"What do you want from me, Willa? A defense? Words that will explain it all away? I have nothing like that to offer. No excuses. That is the promise I made to myself when Annalea found me. It doesn't mean that I haven't lied, only that I am not going to justify it."

Willa rolled the rocker forward and sprang to her feet. It was still rocking when she retrieved a second towel from the stove and threw it at him. Without sparing a glance to see if he caught it, she stalked to the window and stared out, wrapping her arms around her in a hug that she hoped would be comforting but only made her feel alone. There was some part of her thoughts dedicated to wondering why she was dry-eyed when she wanted nothing so much as to dissolve into a puddle of her own tears.

Israel heaved himself out of the tub and wrapped the towel around his hips. Water droplets spattered the floor as he walked to the stove. He took another towel, rubbed his hair and chest dry, and then slung it around his neck. He did not approach Willa.

"I employed several different schemes," he said, his voice pitched low. "I secured small loans and used them as collateral to secure larger loans and used them to secure . . . you see where that is going. I gathered investors to purchase property that was not mine to sell. I oversold shares in projects doomed to fail so when the bubble burst, I did not have to return money to the speculators. My most successful play, in terms of money collected, was also the one that eventually put me behind bars. I was a Bible-thumping, gospel-quoting, brimstone-and-fire-raising preacher to seven different congregations in three different states, and I raised money every Sunday morning and Wednesday evening on the promise that each tent church would be replaced by a permanent house of worship on a foundation so solid that Simon Peter himself could not have found it wanting. When I judged that I had collected as much as a congregation could offer, and not a penny more, I fled. I reasoned that I was not greedy; after all, I performed a service for the worshipers by presiding at births, deaths, weddings, baptisms, and delivering sermons that kept them to the right of every wrong. Also, I arrived in their communities with my own tent and left it behind when I went."

Wincing, Willa hugged herself tighter. Outside the window, the sky was still gray with no hint that the sun would show itself. That was fine with her; it matched her mood perfectly. Across the street, a mother with an infant in her arms and a toddler in tow stepped out of a dry goods store and started toward the apothecary. The child was giggling and the mother was smiling at her wriggling baby. It hurt Willa's heart to watch them. "What you've done, Israel. It's wicked. Shameful."

"Yes," he said. "And yes."

"Is that the worst of it?"

"That is for you to decide. I also spent a great deal of time playing cards on Mississippi riverboats."

"Are you a cheat?"

"No, not since I was bucking the tiger in my youth. I don't need to. I'm just that good."

Willa heard no pride in his voice. He said it merely as a statement of fact. "Then stealing from your parishioners is worse."

"Do you think that will be God's judgment?" he asked.

"I don't know, but it's mine." She breathed in and out once. Slowly. "It seems as if a judge and jury somewhere agreed."

"Well, they didn't know the totality of my crimes so it would have been difficult for them to compare. Different victims. Different jurisdictions. Some people never knew they had been gulled. Some people are too proud to report that they were."

Willa hung her head. "I have no words. None."

Even though she could not see him, he nodded. "Do you want me to go?"

Instead of answering, Willa stepped closer to the window, and dropped her palms to the sill. Hunching her shoulders, she pressed her forehead against the glass. Behind her, she heard Israel step away from the stove and pad softly to the bench seat. He began to dress and she did nothing to stop him. She stood exactly as she was until the door closed behind him.

The soft click of the lock sliding into place was the thing that moved her toward the bed. She pushed the parcels and packages aside with a sweep of her hand and then turned back the covers. She lay down, not in the space she had previously occupied, but in the space that had been his. She breathed in deeply, filling her nostrils with every nuance of his male scent, spicy with sweat and leather and sex, and then, overwhelmed by the ache in her chest, she began to weep.

In time, she slept.

Israel walked without purpose or direction, numb to the cold, numb to feeling. His aimless tour of Lansing would have brought him back to the hotel in less than thirty minutes if it hadn't been for January's Saloon and Saint Luke's Church.

The saloon was not crowded. Two or three men sat at just a third of the tables. One table was occupied by a single man, and another stood alone at the long bar. As a stranger, Israel expected to be watched, and he sensed eyes following him as he made his way to the bar and ordered a whiskey. Except for the barkeep, no one spoke to him, and he appreciated that. He did not desire conversation. The one he was having with himself was equally unwelcome. It was his hope that the whiskey would put that voice to rest.

He finished the drink at the bar and ordered another, which he took to one of the empty tables. He removed his hat, dropped it on a chair beside him to discourage company in the event someone decided to make his acquaintance, and nursed the whiskey. Voices droned on around him; occasionally there was laughter. It barely penetrated his consciousness. That was why Israel gave a start when someone appeared at his elbow as though materialized by some magician's trick and spoke to him.

"May I join you?"

The voice was familiar but not immediately identifiable. It was not until Israel looked up and directly into a round face and a pair of astonished eyes that he recognized Pastor Beacon.

After a moment's hesitation, Israel nodded and used the toe of one boot to nudge an empty chair toward the minister.

Beacon sat and placed his glass on the table. When Israel eyed it, he said, "Sarsaparilla. I keep my spirits in a sideboard in the dining room at home."

Israel nodded again, this time appreciatively. His father did the same, although he could not recall hearing that Reverend James McKenna ever crossed the threshold of any establishment serving liquor by the glass.

Beacon asked, "Is it impertinent of me to inquire what brings you to Lansing?"

Impertinent? At the moment it just seemed damn nosy. Israel swallowed the urge to say as much, reminding himself that he had suggested paying a visit to the pastor when he first raised the idea of going to Lansing. "No particular business," he said. "Taking advantage of the break in the weather to get out of the valley."

"Spending the night?"

"Could be. It wasn't the plan. We left early this morning."

"We? Happy's here?"

"No. Willa. She's at the hotel."

"Ah."

"Ah?"

"Straight to the point, then," Beacon said. "Was this your first significant argument?"

Israel's eyes slid sideways. "What makes you ask?"

"Experience. I know the look of a man who's kicking himself. How long have you been at it?"

"About an hour."

"Hmm." Beacon was able to give his slow nod the weighty consequence of a sage. "Then you probably want to stay out at least another hour."

"I don't think another hour, a day, or even a year will be enough time to make this right."

Beacon sipped his drink. "Well, there's your faulty premise. Time doesn't make it right. You have to do that. Time just gives you a chance to think . . . to pray."

Israel turned the tumbler in his hands. "I'm not much for praying."

"Maybe not while you're nursing that drink, but when you've had enough of that, you might consider walking over to the church. Door's open. It's quiet. No one's there but God." Beacon rose, picked up his drink in one hand, and set the other lightly on Israel's shoulder. "Just something to think about."

It was dark when Willa woke. The room was quiet, still, and yet she sensed Israel's presence. She did not lift her head, but her eyes surveyed the area in her line of sight. She found him sitting in the rocker but outside of the stove's meager firelight. Both he and the rocker were merely deeper silhouettes than the shadows around them.

"You're awake," he said.

His voice barely broke the silence. It drifted toward her as if from a distance much greater than the ten feet separating them, like the sough of the wind high in the treetops. She wondered how he had known she was awake but thought perhaps it was no different for him than it was for her. Each of them, they just *knew*.

"Have you been here long?" she asked. Her voice was thick and husky, almost unrecognizable as her own. He knew how she sounded coming out of a deep sleep. This was different. Even without seeing her face, he would know she had been crying.

"I had a Shaker tune running through my mind. 'Simple Gifts.' Do you know it?"

"No."

"It's not quite a minute long." He hummed a few measures for her, tapping his fingers on the arm of the rocker as if accompanying himself on the piano. "I was on maybe the ninth go around when I realized you were awake."

"You have a rather unique way of marking time."

He shrugged. "It was just what was in my head. I've always found it hypnotic."

Willa sat up slowly and leaned back against the headboard. She felt as if she'd been drugged. She pressed three fingers to the faint hollow of one temple and began to massage it gingerly.

"Do you want me to light one of the lamps?" asked Israel.

"Lord, no."

"I didn't think so, but I thought I should ask."

The pressure of her fingers began to ease the dull ache in her head. "Where did you go?"

"I walked some. Nowhere in particular. Just walked. I ended up in January's."

"The saloon."

"Yes. Mostly to get out of the cold, but a little because of the liquor."

Willa felt her lips twitch. It was unexpected, even unwelcome, but there it was. Israel could do that to her, not because he tried, but because it was his gift.

"That's where Pastor Beacon found me. I was nursing my second drink, contemplating a third, and he suddenly appeared at my elbow."

"Not an angel on your shoulder, then."

"Not quite, more like my conscience. He invited me to use his church, and then he left. 'Just something to think about,' he said. So I did, and then I left."

Willa did not try to keep the surprise out of her voice. "You went to Saint Luke's?"

"Hmm. I did. It was the first time I've stepped inside a church in at least six years. A church like that, I mean, one not of my own making. It actually crossed my mind that the Holy Ghost might stop me at the door, but that didn't happen. The opposite, in fact, I was welcomed."

"Someone was there?"

"Not exactly, but yes."

She thought about that. "Oh."

"Mm-hmm. It set me back on my heels. Maybe it's the reason Pastor Beacon always looks so astonished."

Willa realized her headache was gone; she stopped rubbing her temple and laid her hand over her knee. "So the Lord lives in that house. What did you talk about?"

"No talking," he said. "Not by me. I just listened."

"And here you are."

"Yes. I was never going anywhere. Did you understand that when I walked out?"

"Not immediately," she said. "But eventually, yes."

"I wasn't entirely certain you would want to see me again, but there was never any thought in my mind about staying away. I love you, Willa. I want to be your husband, and I understand if what I've told you means that you do not want to be my wife. It was selfish of me not to share all of it before we were married. I knew that, and I chose to do what was in my best interest, not what was in yours."

Willa pulled her hair to one side and began to plait it as she considered the full meaning of what he was saying now. "You said something like that before, about needing to be my husband. Why? Why is it in your best interest?"

"Don't you know, Willa? You settle me. It's unlike anything I've ever known, this sense that I am where I belong, and where I belong isn't a particular place. It's wherever you are. You make me want to be a steadfast man, a better man . . ." He paused and then added with wry humor, "Maybe even a reasonably smart man."

Willa's quiet chuckle tickled the back of her throat. He'd remembered that she had once called him a reasonably smart man, and it had not quite been a compliment.

"I don't know, Israel," she said, shaking her head slightly.

"I'm not sure if I should be flattered or troubled. I don't want the responsibility for you staying . . . how did you say it earlier? On the right side of wrong? I think that responsibility should be yours, whether you're with me or whether you're all the way over there."

She heard the rocker creak and saw his silhouette shift in the chair. "That wasn't an invitation," she said. "I don't know when I will be ready for that. I'm still hurting, Israel. My head. My heart. I am not blameless here. I know that a lot of what I feel I brought on myself. You did not give me particulars, but it's not as if you didn't warn me. I cannot recall any one moment where I lowered my guard, and yet it happened. You asked me once if cynicism came naturally to me or if it was born of experience. I can tell you now that it was the latter, so accepting that I put it all aside for you, well, that's difficult right now. I thought I was smarter, you see. And I'm not." Her voice broke and she fought for control. On a thread of sound, she said again, "I'm just not."

Israel did get to his feet then. His destination was the window, not the bed, and he stood much as she had earlier, looking out over the street and clearing his mind. "This afternoon you said I owned your heart. Did you mean that?"

"Yes."

"But it's against your will now, is that it? You're telling me you wish it were different, that feeling the way you do makes you less in your own eyes, not more. Not clever, not sensible, maybe even foolish and weak and—"

"And human," she said quietly.

"Hmm."

"Are you smiling?"

"A little."

"Then I suppose you better light the lamp. I don't like missing that." Willa imagined that his smile deepened, but she did not wait to find out. Before he finished searching for a match, she was out of bed and on her way to the washstand.

By the time lamplight made it possible to see clearly, she was able to present a face unmarked by tears. It was not possible to hide all the evidence that she had been crying. There was nothing she could do about puffy eyelids or the red tip of her nose, but running a damp washcloth over her face gave her back a measure of composure.

Israel lowered the lamp and returned it to the bedside table.

Willa stood still for his assessment, her chin lifting ever so slightly when he finished and his eyes held steady on her face.

"As fetching as you look in that towel," he said, "I think you should dress so we can go downstairs and get a meal. We're not going home now that it's dark, and Mrs. Putty told me earlier that she would be serving dinner in the restaurant until eight if she didn't run out of pork chops and fried apples before then."

Willa's mouth watered and her stomach rumbled and still one of her hands lifted to touch her face in a self-conscious gesture. She pursed her lips when Israel raised an eyebrow at her. "What?"

"How you look," he said, unable to keep the humor out of his voice. "Seems as if it's a little bit important to you."

Her hand fell away. "Not amusing."

"A little bit amusing."

Willa whipped off her towel and threw it at him. He was still chuckling as she finished dressing and even now and again as he escorted her to the dining room.

Chapter Nineteen

"Come away from the window, Annalea," Happy said. "They won't be home tonight. Not this late. You can stop looking for them. Don't know what you think you'll see out there anyway."

Annalea came out from behind the curtains, clearly reluctant to leave the space she had occupied for the better part of the last hour. "They've been gone all day." She walked over to the piano bench, dragging her feet in dramatic fashion every step of the way. She sat down heavily but did not face the piano, choosing to stare gloomily at her father instead. "I barely had any time to talk to them before they left."

Happy rattled the two-week-old newspaper he was reading and gave Annalea a narrow-eyed look over the top of the broadsheet. "Hard to believe you didn't get at least a couple hundred words in edgewise."

"Maybe I did, but that's not the important part. The important part is that they promised they would be back tonight." Annalea's fingers curled on the bench on either side of her. "I'm telling you, Pa, this marriage is not what I thought it would be."

Happy returned to reading and said absently, "I collect you had expectations."

"Sure, I did. For one thing, I didn't think I'd be sleeping by myself every night. It's not that John Henry isn't good company, but I miss Willa. Feels funny to turn over and not see her in the other bed. She's been there my whole life."

At the mention of his name, John Henry raised his head, regarded Annalea soulfully, and when she paid him no mind, he settled comfortably back on the rocker.

"Her place is with Israel. A married woman sleeps beside her husband." He raised the broadsheet so it covered his face and he cleared his throat. "She talked to you about that, didn't she?"

"Yep, but she never said it would be every night. I'm telling you, Pa, I never thought it would be every night."

Happy did not ask for clarification of "it." Annalea might have been speaking of Willa's sleeping habits or something else entirely. He carefully folded the paper and laid it on the sofa beside him. "You said 'for one thing.' That leads me to suspect there might be at least one other thing, a second thing, you understand."

"Oh, there is. Willa still wants to send me to school in Jupiter in the spring. I thought Israel was on my side, but since he married her, he takes up with her on everything." She thrust out her lower lip. "I liked him better when he had a mind that wasn't hers."

"I see. Anything else? If not, maybe you could play something for me. Any one of the pieces Israel was teaching you would be fine. You have your mother's touch on the keys now that Israel's mostly got the thing tuned."

Annalea opened her mouth to speak and shut it abruptly. She cocked her head, cupped her ear, and listened. "Do you hear that? They're coming! It's them. I know it." The piano bench shook when she jumped to her feet. Ignoring Happy's admonition to wait for him, she ran to the front door and flung it open. She teetered when she reached the lip of the porch, brought up short by the single horse and rider approaching the house.

Recognizing neither of them, she set her hands on her hips, her stance more belligerent than welcoming. It was a rare occurrence that a stranger wandered into the valley and right up to the front door, so she figured he had a purpose and that it was her business to discover what it was.

"Who are you?" asked Annalea. The stranger tipped his hat to her, but then his gaze lifted to a point over her head and she realized her father was standing behind her. She looked over her shoulder and saw he had his shotgun. John Henry was there also, head up and watchful. She had felt quite brave facing the stranger, and now she felt quite safe.

She swung her head; her pigtails flew sideways before they fell down her back. "And what do you want?"

"Name's Samuel Easterbrook. And I do apologize for coming upon you after dark this way. Truth of the matter is, I stayed overlong at a neighboring spread. Big Bar, it was called."

Happy said, "We're familiar."

"Fellow there, a Mr. Malcolm Barber, invited me to rest a spell as I'd been riding all day."

"Now that don't sound like Mal," said Happy. "Annalea, you best step aside. If I hear more of this, I might just have to shoot something."

Annalea moved far to the left but stayed on the edge of the porch. "Pa. I see Zach and Cutter coming."

Samuel Easterbrook raised his hands. His horse stirred restlessly. "There's no need to run me off. I'm not lookin' for trouble. Fact is, I'm here on account—"

"What's going on?" asked Zach, holding up the lantern he was carrying. He was slightly out of breath from the dash across the yard to the front of the house, and the lantern wobbled in his hand. He stopped eight feet from the porch while Cutter leaped up on it from the side and stood protectively at Annalea's shoulder.

Happy said, "We're just determining that. Girl, you go on inside now and take John Henry with you."

"All right," she said. "But we'll be watching from the window."

"Wouldn't expect otherwise." Once Annalea was safely in the house, if not out of earshot, Happy addressed Samuel Easterbrook. "Go on. You were saying that you're not looking for trouble."

"That's a fact. I've been riding a few days now, coming from Stonechurch. You know it?"

"I reckon we all know it," said Happy. "It's a mining town. You don't look like any miner I've ever seen. For one thing, never knew one to wear a Stetson."

"I'm not *from* there. It's where I come from. I'm lookin' for a fellow that went through there a while back. Tracked him there. Now I'm tracking him here."

"Here?" asked Zach. "To Pancake Valley?"

Samuel Easterbrook slowly lowered his hands as he shook his head. "To Jupiter, and then to the ranches around these parts. I got myself turned sideways after I left Big Bar, and if you don't think that pains me to admit, you should think again. I understood there was a more direct route I could have taken, but Mr. Barber's son . . . Eli, is it?"

Zach, Happy, and Cutter all nodded in unison.

With the confirmation, Samuel went on. "Eli. He told me the shortcut would most likely get me shot. Said you folks were a mite touchy about riders coming over the ridge from Big Bar." He eyed Happy's shotgun. "Hard to see how he was wrong when I made a point to arrive from the road and still confronted this reception."

Happy did not apologize. "No one's shot you yet. It makes no sense that you'd come here after dark."

Samuel shrugged. "The Barbers were hospitable but not generous. No one offered me a place to bunk so I had to move on. Do you mind if I get down from my horse?"

"As a matter of fact, I do," said Happy. "Now, Mr. Samuel Easterbrook, I'm real clear on your name, but this tracking business is muddy to me. You some sort of lawman? And if you answer yes, you better be prepared to show me a badge."

"Not a lawman. And no bounty hunter either. Did some scouting for the Army a ways back, and I got a letter from a friend asking me if I'd look into this fellow's disappearance. So that's what I'm doing. A favor for a friend. And from what I've been through, it'll be years before I'm satisfied that he's paid me back in full."

Happy did not respond to any of this immediately. Instead, he told Zach to pass the lantern to Cutter and then directed Cutter to sidle on over. "I want a better look at who I'm talking to," said Happy.

Cutter stood directly above the steps and held up the lantern. Samuel Easterbrook's face was bathed in light. Happy saw nothing remarkable about the man's features. He was clean-shaven with no scars or birthmarks. There was no cleft in his chin, no prominent Adam's apple. His eyes were neither placed too closely together nor too widely apart. His mouth was set in a straight line; his nose was a gentle slope. Happy supposed that he had a face that women generally found appealing but not distinguished or even interesting after some time had passed. Happy judged Easterbrook's height to be about the same as Cutter's, making him taller than Zach or him. He sat too heavily on his horse's back, not putting enough weight on the stirrups. Happy wondered if he was tuckered out or just lazy.

"All right, Cutter," said Happy. "You can lower that now. I've got my measure of Mr. Samuel Easterbrook."

"Sam," he said. "Just Sam."

Happy ignored the friendly overture. "So about this fellow who disappeared, the one you're looking for. Who is he and what makes you think he might have come this way?"

"Like I said, I don't know that he came this way in particular. I tracked him to Jupiter from Stonechurch. He got himself in a poker game up that way, and the men he played with recollected that he talked about going to a little town they'd never heard of before. Turns out that was Jupiter."

"Uh-huh. And his name?"

"Buck McKay. You ever heard tell of him?"

"Buck McKay," Happy repeated. "Nope. Can't say that I have. Zach? Cutter? You know a Buck McKay?"

"Don't," said Cutter.

"Never," said Zach.

Happy took a few steps forward so when he looked sideways, he could see Annalea at the front window. He called to her. "Annalea? You ever heard of Buck McKay?"

"Never did, Pa." Her voice was distorted by the glass but perfectly understandable.

Happy's attention returned to Samuel Easterbrook. "None of us. And you're looking at everyone here right now."

"Huh. Well, I guess that's that. I wasn't hopeful anyway. The man's a card sharp. It didn't set quite right with me that he'd stray so far from town, but you can never know where he might pick up a game unless you ask around."

"And so you have. Where will you go next?"

"Denver. Lots of opportunity there, and it's the most likely place he'd go since he didn't seem to find anything to his liking in Jupiter. That's assuming he ever made it there.

Can't find evidence to support that either. Could be it's all a dead end."

"Too bad, then, about that favor for your friend. Now who would that be exactly?"

"No one you'd know, but I can't see that there's any reason I shouldn't say. His name is Thomas A. Wyler. One of the Saint Louis Wylers. They're well known up and down the Mississippi. I don't know the exact amount of money Buck McKay owes Tom Wyler, but for Tom to ask me for help, I have to believe it is considerable. I'm thinking there will be a tidy reward if you come by information and pass it along."

"How would we do that?" asked Happy.

"Send it directly to Mr. Wyler. Thomas A., in Saint Louis. He'll find me."

"Not likely we'll ever know anything worthy of a reward, but we'll keep it in mind. I figure that completes your business here. How about I have Zach and Cutter escort you off the property, just so you find your way back to Jupiter. Wind's picking up. Drifts will make it harder for you to backtrack."

"That'd be fine, sir. I'd welcome the company."

Happy remained with Cutter on the porch until Zach brought the horses around. He stayed there in the lee of the house, watching them go, and only when they were out of sight did he finally step inside.

He overrode all of Annalea's objections about going to bed and tucked her in. She was full of questions but reluctantly accepted his offer to read to her in trade for not answering any of them. She was asleep before he had finished the first short chapter of *Nat Church and the Day at Deadrock*.

From his secluded shelter beneath a canopy of pine boughs, Eli Barber could see the trio approaching the Y in the road where Pancake land met the juncture of roads east and west. Two of the riders stopped there, while the third—the one in the middle and clearly the one being escorted to that point—rode on, choosing Jupiter as his direction. Eli could not hear any words being exchanged, but the parting seemed friendly enough. He stayed where he was until the pair of riders, easily recognizable to him as Zach Englewood and Cutter Hamill, turned around and headed back the way they came, and then he followed the single rider halfway to Jupiter before he made himself known.

"Jesus, Mary, and Joseph," said Jesse Snow. His head snapped sideways as Eli came abreast of him. "Where the hell did you come from? I swear I was looking for you."

"I guess you should have been looking harder. I've been tracking you for the better part of a couple of miles. What did you find out?"

"Not a thing. I should've gone in the morning like I wanted. I don't know why you had to have me go now."

"The way I remember it is that it took me all afternoon and into the evening to find you. You have a way of hiding when there's work to be done. I'm not sure we've seen the like of it before at Big Bar. You won't be long for there once spring comes."

"Maybe. And maybe not. I figure you got a couple or three reasons to keep me on, seeing what I've done for you."

Eli spoke carefully, calmly, believing his words would be better minded that way. It was something he'd learned from his father, although rarely something he could do in conversation *with* his father. "Have a care, Jesse. It's a dangerous error you're making if you think my father will ever take up for you over me, and if you think I'll take up for you to keep you from talking, it's a sure thing I'd see you dead first. You hold that in your mind when you're figuring that those couple of reasons will protect you."

He gave Jesse some time to absorb that before he said, "You never did satisfactorily answer my question about what you were doing around Monarch Lake and the ridge. Maybe you think that's a good place to hide out when you're supposed to be working, but you surely know by now the Pancakes like to think that's their land. Someone from there will shoot you as soon as look at you."

Jesse started to speak, but Eli cut him off.

"You can tell me later. Right now I want to hear about what happened at the ranch. Everything."

Jesse said, "I did like you said. I told them who I was, that I'm a hand at Big Bar, and since everyone knows you and Malcolm aren't welcome in the valley, I was asked to come in your stead."

"How'd they take that?"

"Well, they didn't shoot the messenger, so I guess you'd say they took it in stride. I told them you'd heard that Miss Pancake got married, and since she wasn't a regular in town, you wanted to make sure you extended congratulations. Naturally they were suspicious because of the timing—I told you they would be—and that's why Zach and Cutter saw me off the land."

"And?"

"And what? That's what I said. They pretended they appreciated the sentiments, and then I left."

Reaching deep for patience and finding little of it, Eli said, "And what is the name of her husband? Who the hell did she marry?"

"Oh, didn't I say? No, I guess I didn't. Willa wasn't there. Neither was her husband. The little girl, the one you said looks like Willa at the same age, came out to greet me first. Her mouth is full of sass, I can tell you that. Then Happy appeared right behind her, shotgun in hand and a squirrelly-looking dog at his heels. Then Zach and Cutter showed up. No Willa. No husband. No one said I got it wrong when I offered your congratulations, but no one hollered for them either. I figure they were off somewhere."

"Damn, Jesse. Couldn't you have inquired after them?"

"It's like this, Eli. The shotgun, and Happy's predisposition to use it, made me think questions would not be encouraged. I tipped my hat, accepted their escort, and got the hell away from there. I've been looking for you ever since, and here we are."

"And here we are," Eli said dully. "I don't know one damn thing more than I knew from my father yesterday."

"You could've asked around Jupiter on your own instead of hunting me down to go with you."

"And if you hadn't been so goddamn hard to find, we would have already asked around Jupiter."

"Seems like you're purposely missing the point of you doing it on your own."

"I didn't miss a thing, but I don't answer to you. It works the other way around." Eli raised the collar on his coat. "Since you spent the day avoiding work, and I spent the better part of it looking for you, we are not going to be able to slip into Jupiter in the morning. You better partner up tomorrow and the day after and make sure Buster hears you're working hard. We'll head into Jupiter the day after that. Don't disappoint me, Jesse. You understand?"

"I always do what you tell me, Eli. We're still good, aren't we? About what you promised me once we get to Jupiter."

Eli corrected him. "Not once we get to Jupiter. Once we are finished asking around in Jupiter. But, yes, drinks are on me. And so is your poke at Mary Edith."

"You said I could have her for the night if I wanted."

"Fine by me. Mary Edith might object, but that will be your problem."

Jesse said confidently, "Then there's no problem."

When they returned to their room after dinner, Israel invited Willa to sit on the bed while he picked up the parcels she had swept aside earlier and put them within her reach. She had the grace to look sheepish when he placed one in her hands.

"This one might be good to open first," he said.

Willa looked past him to where the folded silk screen stood. The beautiful red scarf was still draped as she had left it before she stepped into the tub. "I already opened a very good one," she told him.

"Well, this one has more practicality at the moment."

Intrigued, she began to pull on the twine. "Go sit over there," she said, pausing long enough to wave him away from the bed and toward the rocker. "I can't do this while you're hovering."

"Hovering. I didn't realize." Shaking his head at her peculiarities, he compromised by pulling the rocker within a leg's distance of the bed before he sat down. He stretched his legs and used the bed frame as a stool for his boot heels. She was staring at him when he looked up after getting comfortable. His expression was one of innocence perfected. "Not hovering."

"I am in awe of your ability to do what you're asked on your own terms." It was her turn to shake her head, and she did that while pulling the twine free. This parcel was bulky and the paper began to unfold as soon as she removed the twine. Her fingers scraped what was inside, and she recognized what she would find before it was completely revealed. Her fingers curled around the smooth cherry wood handle of a hairbrush. She held it up to admire, turning it this way and that before she pulled it through the loose tail of her braid. "It's beautiful. Thank you."

He pointed to the paper. "There are ribbons, too. I thought maybe sometimes you'd like something different than a rawhide string to keep the braid together. Or you could wear one in your hair when it's down."

She found them. He had purchased three. One black, one forest green, and one poppy red. She threaded all three grosgrain ribbons between her fingers and pulled them through. The ribbed fabric created gentle resistance against her skin. She smiled at Israel. "What made you think of these things?"

"Your hair," he said simply. "I think about it a lot."

She looked down at the heavy plait of hair hanging over her shoulder and wondered what about it could possibly capture his thoughts, but before she could ask, he directed her to another package, this one a square box about the size of her hands if she placed them side by side. "Did you go to the bakery I told you about?" she asked, suspicious. "Without me?"

"Just for this, and I don't know that it's the same bakery, but it is the only bakery I saw. I didn't buy cookies. I couldn't remember what ones you told me you wanted anyway. This is something else."

Willa tugged on the string, and when the knot would not give, she worked it off the box one corner at time. She was looking at him, a question in her eyes, when she finally lifted the lid and the aroma of almonds and oranges made her breathe in deeply. His eyes directed her to look down.

Inside the box was a small, single-layer cake, covered in

swirls of creamy white frosting and decorated with a ring of thinly sliced almonds and orange zest. Some of the icing was smudged on the cake and sticking to the sides of the box, and Willa reckoned that was her fault for pushing Israel's gifts out of the way when she threw herself on the bed. He'd had more respect for what he was carrying than she had.

Willa put a forefinger inside the box, swept icing from the side, and held it up. "My job," she said and put the finger in her mouth and sucked it clean.

Israel stared at her finger when it reappeared. "I believe I said there were things to share. That's one I care about. That's our wedding cake."

"I know."

He saw her chin wobble a bit, as though she were feeling overwhelmed, but she covered it by dipping her finger inside the box again and thrusting her arm out to him. Quickly, before she could guess his intent, he was on his feet, carefully avoiding her outstretched offering, and removing the box from her lap. He returned to the rocker, set his heels on the bed frame once more, and situated the bakery box squarely in his lap.

"Keep your finger," he told her and dipped his inside the box. He came out with a gob of frosting that immediately disappeared inside his mouth.

"You took that off the cake," she accused. "Not off the side of the box."

"Guilty." He accepted responsibility but in a way that clearly communicated he had no regrets. "I'll hold this while you open the last one. It's still mostly hidden by the blankets."

Shrugging, Willa licked her finger clean before she rooted out the final gift. This one was neither wrapped nor boxed. What he was giving her was concealed in a black velvet bag no bigger than her palm. "This wasn't here earlier," she said. "I would remember the bag, and I'm fairly certain I would have chosen it first."

"You're right. It wasn't there."

She regarded him curiously. "That's all you're going to say?"

"It is. Open it. I can tell you're itching to."

"I am, and the fact that I feel no shame admitting it is a deep character flaw that I do not thank you for revealing."

Ignoring his chuckle, she fingered the braided silver string that kept the bag closed, teasing herself with anticipation for a few moments longer. She untied the knot and then spread her fingers inside the neck of the bag. Instead of reaching in, she turned the bag over and let what was inside fall into her open hand.

The gold band spilled into the heart of her palm. She stared at it, her lips parted for a breath she did not take. If the ring had been plain, it still would have been special to her, but this ring was engraved with delicate lacework, the likes of which she had seen only once.

Her eyes lifted and found Israel's. She made no attempt to blink back tears. They hovered on the tips of her lashes, blurring her vision until her fragile smile pushed them over the edge.

"This was my mother's," she whispered. "How did—"

"Your father wanted to give it to me the day after we were married. I told him to keep it until I was sure you would want it. He argued some because he didn't understand, but he did it anyway. When I knew we were coming here, I asked him for it. I thought maybe, just maybe, it was time. There were things you had to know before I could give it to you with any kind of clear conscience."

Willa used one corner of the sheet to swipe at her tears. When she was clear-eyed, she stared at the ring. "I'm glad you waited, Israel. It was the right thing to do. It means everything to me that you understood what I had not been able to grasp about our marriage. Those vows we exchanged, they meant something to you. This marriage *means* something to you, and you came into it not knowing if I would ever believe in it the same way. I think the risk you took was far greater than mine. In fact, I'm sure it was."

She extended the hand that held the ring exactly as she had when she'd offered him her frosted fingertip. "Your job," she said, meeting his eyes.

Without looking away, Israel closed the lid on the cake box and removed it from his lap. He sat up, abandoning the negligent stretch he found so comfortable for the posture the occasion deserved. Standing, he slipped one hand under hers, and used the other to pluck the ring from her palm.

He turned her hand over and began to slip the ring on her finger. "With this ring, I thee wed, and with it, I bestow upon thee all the treasures of my mind, heart, and hands."

She could not look at what he was doing for looking at him. It was not merely her hand he had turned over. It was her heart. She smiled up at him, and this time she did blink back tears. Her voice quavered slightly when she spoke, but in spite of that, her tone was dry. "Of course you would know the words."

Israel gave a bark of laughter that Willa silenced by grabbing his shirt and pulling him down on the bed. He did not try to resist, which made the kiss mutually satisfying, especially as quieted laughter continued to bubble between their lips.

It was some time before Willa had the opportunity to admire the ring on her hand. She lay tucked against Israel's side, her head on his shoulder, her arm raised so her hand and the ring were featured in the lamplight.

"Happy did not give this ring to my mother when they were married. There was no money for it then. What profits were made, and they were slim to none some years, were turned back in to the ranch. I think I was six when he gave her this. I have a memory of Mama sitting with me at the kitchen table, helping me with sums, and seeing this ring on her finger. If she had it the day before, I didn't notice it, but I don't think she did. There was something different about the way she was encouraging me to do my work, taking the chalk away from me more often so her hand was full in my view. When I finally did see it, she made out that it was a lovely but unnecessary gesture on Happy's part. She was thrilled, of course, but practicality would not allow her to say so. She was fiercely practical."

"The apple doesn't fall far from that tree."

Willa lowered her hand so she could jab him lightly in the ribs. "No, it doesn't."

Israel stretched his free arm toward the bedside table and turned back the lamp wick. With no moon to speak of, the room's light was once again reduced to the fire in the stove.

"We should leave early," he said. "Annalea was expecting us tonight. I promised her we'd be back."

"So did I. I don't think she'll understand that a broken promise is not a lie. I didn't, not when I was her age."

When she fell quiet, somewhat abruptly, Israel took advantage of the cover of darkness to ask, "Are you thinking about the promises you made to Eli?"

Willa did not rush her response. She offered a shade diffidently, "I was. But also the promises he made to me. It all seemed like lies afterward. I imagine he felt the same. I don't know how we could have felt differently, not then, not when we had so little understanding of consequences."

"You mean Annalea. She was a consequence?"

"Hmm." Willa turned a bit more on her side and slid an arm across Israel's chest. "A consequence and a complication."

"Eli doesn't know, does he?"

"No. And if I have my way, he never will."

"He'll never learn it from me."

"I know. I should have never let you believe I thought otherwise. I didn't, not for a moment, but talking about it is still one of those things that frightens me."

"You don't have to say another word."

"I think I do," she said quietly. "I think I need to tell you what I've never told anyone." She lifted her head a fraction. The meager light from the stove limned his features. He was looking at her, waiting but not rushing.

She said it again. "Not anyone."

Chapter Twenty

"There are only a few people who know Annalea is my daughter. Happy and Mama knew, of course. Zach worked for us back then. I don't know if anyone told him outright or if he figured it out on his own, but I'm confident he knows as much as my parents did. And now there is you. There were some other hands at the ranch, but except for Zach, Happy let them all go sometime after I left for Saint Louis with Mama and before she returned with Annalea."

"No one in Jupiter suspected?" Israel asked. "I know the valley is isolated, but she would have been seen occasionally in town."

"She made certain she was. That was the point of going there as often as she did in those days. She did not stay with me for the duration of my confinement. She traveled back and forth to visit, to see that I was well, but also to measure my progress. Her pillow pregnancy—and that is all that it was—matched mine. Friends discouraged her from going to see me when she was so close to term, but naturally she was insistent, and when she gave birth in Saint Louis, not one of them was surprised that the train ride had brought on labor. Mama took Annalea back to Pancake Valley, and I remained behind to be schooled in the way of young ladies, but mostly to make amends for my sin. Mama and Annalea visited occasionally, even Happy came once, but I was not allowed to return until Eli was sent away to college."

Israel fingers sifted through Willa's hair. "Was there ever any thought given to telling Eli?"

"Never. There was the valley to think of. My parents

were afraid, and rightfully so, that the Barbers would claim Annalea in order to lay claim to Pancake Valley as well."

"But doesn't that also work in reverse? That Annalea, as a Barber, has an equally legitimate claim to Big Bar land."

"Please don't refer to her as a Barber. I cannot think of her that way. She's mine. Just mine."

Israel kissed the crown of her head. "I understand."

"As for the other," said Willa, "you're probably right, but you can appreciate it was not a matter Happy wanted to discuss with a lawyer. I would have had to swear to the fact that Eli was Annalea's father, and I couldn't do that."

"No," he said. "I don't imagine you could."

"You think I loved him that much, don't you?"

"Didn't you?"

"It felt as if I did, but that is not the reason I couldn't speak up. It is not the reason I was protecting Eli. Here is what no one else knows, Israel. Eli is not Annalea's father. Malcolm is. Malcolm Barber raped me."

Israel closed his eyes. "Oh, Jesus."

"Mm."

"Sweet Jesus," he said under his breath.

As close as she was to him, it was not close enough to keep her from shivering. Willa thought she could crawl under his skin and still not be warm.

Israel tucked one of the blankets around her with no expectation that it would help. He did it because he needed to do something and he had no idea what that was.

"It's all right," she said, rubbing his chest with her palm. "I think 'sweet Jesus' is adequate. I don't know what else there is to say, and certainly there is nothing to do, although I doubt it feels that way at the moment."

"You're right. It doesn't feel that way. You never told your parents it wasn't Eli?"

"I never told them that it was," she said. "They assumed it, and it was better for everyone to let them keep on thinking it. Even at thirteen, I understood that. Happy would have gone after Mal, and mostly likely got himself shot dead for it. Or maybe Mal would've been killed, and Happy would have hanged. I don't know that anyone outside of my parents would have believed what Malcolm did to me. With so much bad blood between the families, there would have been plenty of folks speculating whether I'd been put up to it. Mal's father was alive then. Ezra might have believed me. He was as cruel a cuss as Malcolm, so he could have suspected his son was capable of it. The apple did not fall far from that tree either."

"Does Malcolm suspect he's Annalea's father?"

"You're a step ahead of yourself. In order for him to suspect that Annalea is his, he'd have to suspect that Annalea is mine. Happy and Mama covered those tracks. I don't think he's ever had a hint of it, and he's never given any indication that he has."

"Unless you look at Eli's proposals in a different light. Malcolm knew you would never have him. But his son? Maybe Malcolm's always believed that was a possibility."

It was a disturbing thought, one that she had never allowed herself to contemplate. She said, "He only had me the once. He probably doesn't even think it can happen with just the one time, and maybe he thinks my womb would expel his rape seed because, God knows, I wanted that to happen. I wanted to tear my insides out when I realized I was carrying his child. Devil child, that's what Annalea was to me before I met her, and then Mama took her away to raise as my sister, and that's mostly what she was to me until Mama died and Happy went a little crazy with grief. I had to be mother to her then. Sometimes father as well. I loved her the same, but differently, too. I try not to think of her as my daughter, for her sake, because it's safer, but also for my own because of the fear that still lives inside me."

Israel caressed the arm that she had slipped across his chest. He stroked it with his fingertips from wrist to elbow and back again and felt her relax, not only there, but everywhere her body was pressed to his. Perhaps what she needed just then was simpler than what he could do for her, perhaps it was what he could be for her: sanctuary.

He only had me the once, she had said. The words marched up his spine like a thousand fire ants and settled, burning as hot as a match head, at the base of his brain.

When the burn finally subsided, he felt as if he'd been branded. He saw that brand clearly in his mind's eye, the words of the Sixth Commandment, one of the three he had never broken. *Thou shalt not kill.*

For the first time, he wondered if he could hold with that.

Willa spoke into the quiet. "I went to meet Eli at the same place I always met him, not far from the fence, but on Pancake land. Sometimes we'd climb into the trees to talk, where we were certain we couldn't be seen. I was up there for a while, but he didn't come, and I climbed down. I wasn't concerned when he didn't show. Sometimes that happened because we had chores and studies and other things to keep us away. I wasn't expecting Malcolm Barber to be there when I swung to the ground. I will never know how long he watched me in that tree, waiting.

"Eli and I had kept our trysts secret for years. Our parents found out that we were meeting about a month or so before Malcolm showed up. As you might imagine, we were told to stay away from each other, and we knew this because naturally enough we met again and compared stories. My parents lectured me. Eli got a lecture from his mother and an appointment in the woodshed with his father. If I'd been given a choice of what Malcolm Barber might do to me back then, I would have asked for the woodshed.

"That's not as easy to say now, not when I have Annalea. Besides what Happy would have done had he known the truth, I had no illusions that my parents would want to raise Malcolm Barber's devil child. As much as I did not want to give birth to it, I did not want to be forced to give it away. I had some idea that I would need to protect people from the child, especially foolish people who might claim they wanted it. In the end, the only thing I had to protect from Annalea was my own heart, and there was never any chance that I would succeed."

Israel paused his caress at her elbow and squeezed lightly. "No chance," he said. "None."

That made Willa smile. It felt good, cleansing. "You love her, don't you?"

"I do. I'm fairly certain I loved her first. *You* were an acquired taste."

"Was I?" Her smile became a grin. "I think that's good."

"Mm. It probably is." He returned to stroking her forearm. "Caring about Annalea the way I do, I am reminded that she put a note in my coat pocket regarding several books she would like to read."

"Did she?"

"Also some ribbons and two handkerchiefs with lace borders if such can be found and plain if not."

"Well, isn't she a sly one? You better believe there is no such note in my pockets."

"I'm sure you're right, but I have a target on my back and a soft spot where I used to have a brain. She knows I will always owe her."

Willa did not try to argue the point. She couldn't, not when it was true for her as well. "All right," she said agreeably, sleepily. She closed her eyes. "We'll have cake for breakfast and shop before we leave. I think we should purchase something for Happy, too. Maybe a deck of cards. He'd like that. Do you know, Israel, if I had ever imagined a honeymoon, it would be exactly this."

Israel's shoulder and arm had no feeling left in them from where she lay against him, but not for anything would he have moved. This was who he wanted to be, the man who had earned the right to shelter her.

Falling snow impeded their progress back to Pancake Valley, so it was late in the afternoon before they arrived. Neither of them was surprised to see Annalea come charging out of the house to meet them. Before she had a chance to speak, Israel reached for her and lifted her onto his saddle.

"Hello, brat," he said, grinning. He gave her pigtails a tug for good measure. "You should have a coat on. Where is it?"

"Inside. You better hug me."

He did and then burst out laughing. "Are you really going through my pockets?" Before she could answer, he looked sideways at Willa and pretended to be appalled. "She's going through my pockets."

Willa shrugged helplessly. He'd earned the moment, so she let him enjoy it.

Israel drew back, caught Annalea by her chin, and said with mock severity, "If you're going to be a pickpocket, you have to choose better pockets to pick. What you're looking for is in your sister's saddlebag." Israel winced as she squealed with excitement in spite of the hold he had on her.

As soon as they reached the front of the house, he lowered her to the steps and told her to get inside, where it was warm. "Willa and I will be along directly."

He held up Galahad long enough to make sure Annalea got in the house and then he caught up to Willa on her way to the barn. "I thought she would be full of piss and vinegar because we stayed away so long."

Willa smiled. "I'm sure she will be eventually, but she knows we brought back things for her. That will help."

"So piss *or* vinegar, but not both at the same time. That's a relief."

Chuckling, Willa dismounted to open the barn door.

Israel also swung down and took up the reins of her horse as well as his and led them inside. "Did you hear what Annalea said before she went in the house?"

"No. I didn't know she said anything."

"I'm not sure I heard her right. The door was closing behind her, but I thought she said that we missed the excitement. I wonder what she meant by it."

"If that's what she said, it could be anything. Cutter might have finally beat Zach at checkers, or Happy could have drawn to an inside straight. Maybe Annalea mastered those scales you were teaching her last week. See? Could be anything." She took Felicity's reins from Israel and led her to her stall.

Israel followed suit with Galahad. He untied the girth strap and removed the saddle. "A little strange that Annalea was the only one to greet us. Where do you think everyone else is?"

"Happy is probably making supper and Zach and Cutter could be anywhere. There's plenty for them to do because we were gone." Willa finished removing Felicity's tack and blanket and picked up a grooming brush. "What I said about Happy drawing to an inside straight? That got me thinking again."

"Oh? What about?" Israel brushed Galahad in the long even strokes that the gelding liked and patted him on the jaw.

Willa stepped out of the stall so she could see Israel. "About poker. You don't play. You haven't since you've been here. Sure, you play a game now and then with Annalea, but she says you prefer Old Maid or rummy. You don't take a chair when Happy and the others invite you." Now that she had his full attention, she disappeared into the stall and began brushing down Felicity's glossy coat. "I guess it's been niggling at me since you told me you used to play cards on the riverboats. Hard to believe you played Old Maid then."

After a brief pause that made Galahad stir restlessly, Israel resumed brushing and calmed his horse. "Do you also recall that I said I'm a good player?" When she said that she did, he continued. "Sometimes being good can get you in as much trouble as playing with an ace up your sleeve. What I'm saying is that being good can look like cheating. I've been tossed into the drink from the Texas deck of a riverboat. That's the top deck. I was lucky not to get swept up in the paddlewheel, which I have to believe was the hope of everyone that I cleaned out that night. It's not that I gave up playing entirely after that, but that I chose the games more carefully. It wouldn't be fair for me to play here. I'd win too often, and it's not in me to purposely lose. I like your father and Zach and Cutter. I want it to stay friendly."

"What would entice you to play?"

"Here? Nothing. But I might enter a game if I saw someone dealing from the bottom. There's no point in calling him out if I can clean him out. There's something satisfying about besting a cheater."

Willa finished with Felicity and waited for Israel outside Galahad's stall, Annalea's gifts bundled under one arm. "I'm thinking that a lifetime in your company won't be long enough to figure you out. You draw a peculiar line, Israel."

"I didn't always draw one," he said, putting down the brush.

"I know." She slipped her free arm through the elbow he offered and they walked out of the barn together. "I don't suppose it will ever be a straight line, but the meandering one sure is interesting."

Chapter Twenty-one

Happy was standing at the stove, his head bent over the stockpot, when Israel and Willa entered through the back door. He did not look up until he had breathed in deeply. The aroma of ham and beans and cornbread filled the kitchen, but he preferred sniffing straight from the pot.

"You're not going to drown yourself, are you, Happy?" asked Israel.

Grinning, Happy set the lid back on the pot loosely enough to allow the scented steam to escape. He cracked open the oven door to peek at the progress of the cornbread. Satisfied, he closed it again. "I might. I figure it's that good. Welcome home. Annalea informed me you were back. Hear that?" He jerked a thumb in the direction of the front room, where Annalea was practicing her scales with a fluid ease that was rather impressive. "She's been doing that all morning. Teach her more tunes, Israel. Some Stephen Foster would be real kind to my ears about now."

"I can do that," said Israel. "Annalea mentioned we missed some kind of excitement. Is that it?"

"Is what it?"

"Her mastery of the scales." He pointed to Willa while he spoke to Happy. "Certain people think that might be considered excitement around here."

"Hell, no," said Happy. "Probably best that you both have a seat, and I'll tell you all about it."

Willa set Annalea's gifts on the table so she could remove her coat. After she stuffed her gloves in her pockets, she gave her coat and hat to Israel to hang up with his own.

"We have some things to give Annalea first, and then we'll

be back. And, Pa?" When Happy regarded her suspiciously, expecting trouble, she was prepared. She raised her left hand and showed him the ring. His eyes watered, and she wasn't prepared for that or the fact that hers watered as well.

"Thank you," she whispered.

She wanted to say more, but tears clogged her throat and made that impossible. Her wobbly smile simply dissolved and then her arms were around him and his were around her and they just stood like that until the ham and bean soup bubbled up under the lid and splashed them.

Israel watched as they jumped apart and away from the stove and saw that neither one quite met the other's eye, but he judged that the shift in the air could only be the start of something good.

He picked up Annalea's gifts and invited Happy to join them in the front room. Happy declined, saying he needed to watch the pot, and Israel let the lie go unchallenged. He put a hand at the small of Willa's back and nudged her forward. She was as much in need of a moment to compose herself as her father. Israel gave it to her before they walked in on Annalea because there would be no composure in the face of her excitement.

After much oohing and ahhing over half a dozen ribbons in the colors of a rainbow, two handkerchiefs with lace borders, a pair of ivory combs for her hair that she hadn't asked for but swore were exactly what she always wanted, and three dime novels with lurid covers and sensational titles, Annalea danced happily between Willa and Israel, throwing her arms around each of them in turn.

Israel and Willa returned to the kitchen when Annalea decided she was going to tie one of her old hair ribbons around John Henry's neck. They couldn't bear to watch.

Happy had cups set out for them, and poured coffee into each. "Expected you last night," he said. "Maybe that ring explains why you didn't come back, and maybe it don't. I guess I don't need to hear details as long as you're both satisfied with the bargain you struck."

"You're right," said Willa. "You don't need to hear details."

Israel picked up his cup. "So what is it that you think we should probably be sitting down to hear?"

Happy checked the soup, gave it a stir with a long-handled wooden spoon, and then moved to the sink, where he leaned back against it and folded his arms across his chest. Once he had assumed his comfortable storytelling stance, he began, "We had a visitor last night. Young fool showed up here after dark, said his name was Samuel Easterbrook, and claimed he was tracking down some fellow on account of a friend asking him to do it."

"You sure that was his name, Happy?" asked Israel.

Willa was alert to the narrow crease that had appeared between Israel's dark eyebrows. She watched him carefully over the rim of her coffee cup and waited for Happy's answer.

"Samuel Easterbrook," Happy repeated. "Yep. I've got it right. Made sure I said it once or twice so it would keep. Are you familiar?"

"No. Go on."

"Well, there was a couple or three things suspicious about him right from the beginning. Zach and Cutter and I talked about it after we showed him the door, so to speak, and they agreed with me."

"What sort of things?" asked Willa.

"I'm gettin' to that, girl. Can't be rushed. I need to keep it ordered in my mind." The wooden spoon in his hand distracted him for a moment as a heavy droplet of bean soup was set to fall. He quickly moved the spoon to the sink behind him and reassumed his position. "Sam—that's what he invited me to call him—said he was an Army scout a ways back. That didn't set right because he was so young. I made him to be a couple years older than Cutter, so if he was scouting for the Army, he must have been doing it when he was in short pants."

Happy's mouth pulled to one side as he regarded Israel. "You all right there, son? I thought you might've twitched some when I mentioned this Easterbrook fellow said he was a scout. You know somebody like that?"

"I might," Israel said evenly. He set his coffee cup down without twitching.

Happy grunted softly. "So Samuel Easterbrook not only says he used to scout for the Army, but he also admits that he got turned around on his way here from Big Bar, and that's why he showed up at night. He made light of it, but I had a hard time believing that even a former scout would admit to it. Where's the pride, I asked myself."

Willa unconsciously moved to the edge of her chair. She wanted to ask about Big Bar in the worst way, but she bit her tongue and hugged her coffee cup in her hands.

Happy's mouth worked back and forth as he considered what odd observation to reveal next. "Like I said, Sam visited Big Bar before he came here. Nothing particularly strange about that since he had already been to Jupiter to ask after his man and was visiting ranches in the area, but he stretched my imagination to unnatural lengths when he said Malcolm Barber had been downright hospitable. Welcomed him even, invited him to rest a spell since he'd been riding for days, coming from Stonechurch as he was."

Happy's eyes narrowed a bit as he examined Israel for the second time. "Now, see? There it is again. You're twitchy, son. What was it this time? Stonechurch? You recalling something finally?"

Israel did not commit. "I might be."

Willa stared at him, a frisson of fear tiptoeing up her spine. She was feeling twitchy herself now.

Happy said, "Sam told us that he was following a lead he came across in Stonechurch, something about a poker game. Apparently the fellow he's looking for is a card sharp. I can tell you, I was relieved to hear it. Seemed like it was a good piece of news, since up until then I had it in the back of my mind that he was looking for you, Israel, but since you're no kind of card player that I ever saw, I figured he was turning over the wrong rock."

He sighed heavily, looking from Israel to Willa and back again. "Looking at the two of you right now, I'm beginning to think maybe I'm wrong about that rock. The pair of you know something I don't?"

It was Willa who answered. "We might."

"Hmm. I'm noticing a certain sameness to the answers I'm getting."

Israel said, "It's probably nothing, Happy. Easterbrook must have given you the name of the man he's tracking, and you'd have told us already if it was my name, so who is he after? You committed that to memory, didn't you?"

"Sure did. Name's Buck McKay. Does that poke your memory some?"

Israel looked across the table at Willa and met her eyes before he nodded. "It does."

"Well, now we're getting somewhere," said Happy. "Though whether that somewhere is good or bad remains a question. Seems like you two might have the answer."

Israel asked, "Did he say why he was looking for this Buck McKay?"

"Sam disabused us of the notion that he was a lawman or a bounty hunter. He said he was doing a favor for the friend. McKay disappeared, and this friend wanted to know what happened to him."

"Huh. And the friend? Did you ask who that was?"

"Of course." Happy scratched the back of his head, thinking. "Give me a moment. It'll come to me."

The answer came from the hallway. Annalea said, "Thomas A. Wyler of the Saint Louis Wylers."

Happy's head immediately swiveled in Annalea's direction. His deep frown should have had her taking a step back, but she stayed where she was, mostly because she was ignoring him and speaking directly to Israel. Happy made it a point to bring her attention to where he wanted it. Reaching behind him, he picked up the wooden spoon and waggled it at her. "How long have you been standing there? This is no conversation for you."

"I only just got here." She pointed behind her to where John Henry was bringing up the rear. "See? He's just now catching up. Pitiful dog. Anyway, I guess I'm some use since I was there last night when Mr. Easterbrook introduced himself, and I'm the one recollecting the name 'Thomas A. Wyler.'"

Willa cast an eyeful of reproach at Annalea. "Mind the sass. It's dripping like syrup all over your words." She looked at Happy and then Israel. "Does it matter if she hears?"

Israel said, "She hears everything sooner or later."

Happy thought about it longer before he made a decision. "Take a seat, Annalea, and like Willa said, mind the sass."

Annalea flopped into a chair at the foot of the table. Her dark braids bounced over her shoulders and gave everyone a glimpse of all six of the new ribbons in her hair. John Henry, sporting a faded blue ribbon around his neck, padded into the kitchen and flopped with equal dedication under Annalea's chair.

Happy addressed Israel. "Thomas A. Wyler, just like she said."

Israel nodded once, grimly, and absently turned his coffee cup without making any move to drink from it. "Happy, I guess you have this pretty well worked out already. I thought at first that Samuel Easterbrook might be my brother, although I couldn't come up with a reason that he'd use an alias. Quill *was* in the Army. He mustered out years ago, and while he wasn't a scout then, he's done plenty of tracking since. If he ever got lost, I never heard of it.

"As for Buck McKay, that's one of the names I used from time to time, so it's evident to me at least, and probably to Willa since she knows just about everything now, that your visitor was looking to pay me a call. The problem is, I don't know why. I still don't have a memory that accounts for the time between walking along Wabash and arriving here."

Willa felt Happy watching her, not Israel, gauging her reaction to this news, not taking measure of Israel's quietly composed demeanor as he revealed it.

Happy said, "You all right, Willa? I've seen you with more color in your face than you have right now."

"It's not what Israel's saying that troubles me. It's thinking past that to what we are going to do about it."

Annalea said, "It's all right, Israel. Remember all the things you said to me when I found you? Maybe it's true that you were a bad man, but that's no never mind now. You're family. Pancakes protect their own."

Israel reached toward the end of the table and laid his hand over hers when she slid it in his direction. "I appreciate that, brat, but you're still going to have to go to school in Jupiter come spring."

Annalea's mouth opened and closed. For once, she kept it that way.

Israel patted her hand sympathetically before he drew back. "No one here is going to do anything. It's my place to take care of it. I never wanted trouble visiting you. Seems like that's happened."

Happy raised the spoon like a judge's gavel. "Just a minute. Let's not jump here. What's this about a card sharp? Is that you?"

"It is."

"I'll be darned," said Happy. "Don't that beat all."

Israel started to explain, but Willa interrupted and finished telling it for him. Out of the corner of her eye, she saw Annalea leave her chair. A moment later, she was at her side, and when Willa made her lap available, Annalea sat in it. It warmed her just then to have her daughter in her arms, and it was all to the better knowing that Israel understood how deeply felt the emotion was. When she finished telling Happy about Israel's Mississippi days, she asked Annalea if she had any questions.

Annalea stopped sucking on the end of one braid and removed the damp, spiky tail from her mouth. Her dark eyes, so like Willa's, narrowed when they fastened on Israel's face. "Did I win fair and square? That's what I'm wondering. Or did you let me win because I'm a kid?"

"You're a kid?" When she pursed her lips at him, he said, "Annalea, I don't *let* anyone win. Ever."

She continued to regard him suspiciously and then nodded. "Good thing. I have it in my mind that I am going to be a card sharp."

"Then we will have to talk," he said.

Over the top of Annalea's head, Willa gave him a quelling look.

Israel said to Happy, "There's couple of things about Mr. Samuel Easterbrook that don't settle with me as true. I can't say whether his name is Easterbrook or not. I never heard it before that I recall. I'm inclined to doubt the name because I am very familiar with his friend *Thomas A. Wyler*."

"You are?" asked Willa.

"Hmm. *Thomas A. Wyler* is a showboat that paddles up and down the Mississippi from Saint Louis to New Orleans.

Twice a year it hosts a floating poker game. Most players are invited, but not all. Someone who knows someone can get you in, and you pay for the privilege of sitting at a table. That's separate from the opening ante. The pots are big, the reward for taking it all can be substantial, but men have been known to leave the boat in tears for having lost what they could not afford to."

Willa looked sharply at Happy, who held up his hands and swore he was not entertaining any notions. She cocked an eyebrow at Israel and asked, "How did you leave the boat?"

He grinned. The dimple made a showboat appearance. "By the Texas deck the last time," he said wryly. "And you know it." He explained to Happy and Annalea what that meant. "Willa just wanted me to say it again. I suppose she thinks it's a good reminder; however, I sat at tables on the *Thomas A.* more the once. It was only the last time that I was flung overboard. They don't invite you back after something like that."

Annalea giggled. Happy chuckled deeply.

"Don't encourage him," said Willa.

Israel sighed. "Right. Don't encourage me."

Happy checked the soup, removed the cornbread from the oven, and told Annalea to set the table.

Willa asked, "Where are Zach and Cutter?"

"It was late when they decided to ride out to Monarch Lake. They had gone their separate ways in the morning, looking after the cattle and opening frozen watering holes, but Zach noticed some tracks on the ridge that made him think we had trespassers. He figured he'd wait for Cutter to get back and they'd go out together. That was shortly before you returned. I'd give them another hour or so. It's been quiet. No shots, so I'm figuring they're fine."

Israel thanked Annalea as she set the place in front of him with a bowl, spoon, and napkin, then asked Happy, "Does Zach think what he found has something to do with Easterbrook?"

"Hard to think otherwise, but no one's drawing conclusions. We always have to consider the Barbers when there's proof someone's been poking around over that way."

Willa lifted her bowl so Happy could ladle soup into it.

"Thank you. What did Easterbrook look like? Anything familiar about him?"

"Good-lookin' fellow, I suppose, but nothing to distinguish him from twenty other good-lookin' fellows."

Annalea blew onto a spoonful of soup. "Nowhere near as pretty as you, Israel."

Before Israel could comment, Willa interjected dryly, "I doubt that's Israel's concern."

Israel winked at Annalea. "It was a little bit my concern."

Annalea beamed at him and then gave Willa a reproving look. "See?"

Willa returned an identical reproving look then asked her father, "What else, Happy?"

Happy sat down with his bowl and dug in. Between shoveling hot soup into his mouth, he gave the best description he could of Samuel Easterbrook. Annalea filled in as she was able, but in the end they all agreed Easterbrook could be anyone.

Willa said, "It's passing strange that he'd say his friend was Thomas A. Wyler. Why would he do that?"

Israel shrugged. "Probably because when Happy pressed him for the name of his friend, Easterbrook needed to come up with something he could recall if he was tested, and he needed to come up with it quickly. There's no question that he's familiar with the riverboat, but whether he performed on it, worked on it, or played cards there, there is no way of knowing."

"Hmm." Happy slowed the intake of soup to his mouth and applied himself to buttering a square of cornbread. "I'm thinkin' about that bowline. You recall it, Israel?"

"Not when it was used on me, but I remember Willa showing it around. I don't know that it helps narrow down what Easterbrook might have been doing on the riverboat, but it seems to be more evidence that he was associated with it."

"And also associated with what happened to Buck McKay. We all understand that, don't we?"

"I'm clear," said Israel.

Happy and Annalea nodded.

Willa said, "Easterbrook suspects you're alive, Israel."

"Or he was trying to confirm that I'm dead."

"But why now? It's been months. And if you died out there, how would we know you were Buck McKay?"

"She has a point," said Happy. "You lived through that and we didn't know you were Buck McKay. Of course, another possibility is that Sam Easterbrook is only carrying four rounds in his six-shooter, if you take my meanin'."

Israel chuckled. "Not very smart and making it up as he goes along. I think I got it."

Happy said, "What do you imagine you might have done, Israel? What would it take to make Mr. Easterbrook want to do what he did and hunt you down after?"

"I can make some guesses, but the only way to be sure is to confront him."

Annalea frowned. "I'm not in favor of that. Even with Mama's spectacles, you ain't much improved as a gunslinger."

"Confrontation doesn't have to involve a gun."

"Uh-huh," said Annalea. "If you still think you can talk your way out of whatever you did, you didn't take to the lesson Samuel Easterbrook and his friends tried to teach you. Maybe that's not your fault, you being without a memory of that wild ride you were on at the end of a rope."

Israel stared at her while Willa noisily cleared her throat. Happy scratched behind his neck and cast his eyes at the ceiling.

"What?" asked Annalea. "Why's no one talking?"

The silence went on another few seconds before Israel finally broke it. "No one's speaking because you put it all on the table in language so plain there's no argument to be made."

"Hmm. Usually you try, though."

His mouth turned up at the corners. "I know when I'm facing a worthy adversary." He felt Willa's boot tap the toe of his under the table. He looked at her.

"We'll figure it out," she said. "Samuel Easterbrook is not a worthy adversary."

He nodded, and because of Willa, he knew it was true.

Willa sat on a padded stool in front of the mirrored vanity, brushing her hair and occasionally looking past her reflection to where Israel was sitting at the head of the bed. He was quiet; he had been since supper. Even when Zach and Cutter returned from their ride up to Monarch Lake, he had not inserted anything into the questions and answers that followed. It would have been easy to believe that he was content to allow everyone else to deal with the reality of the trespass onto Pancake land, but Willa thought she understood him better than that. He was plotting.

"Have you ever run from anything?" she asked, smiling when he required a moment to shift his attention from the inner workings of his mind to her out-of-the-blue question.

"Run? I suppose that depends on your perspective. I never ran from a fight, if that's what you mean. The folks I scammed over the years might characterize what I did as running away when I vanished on them, but to me, I was just done. The marshals would tell you I ran once while I was in custody. I call that an escape. I didn't try to get away because I was afraid of going to prison. I just had other plans."

Willa stopped dragging the brush through her hair. "You had other plans?" she asked, incredulous, but also a little amused.

"Uh-huh. And they didn't include prison."

"You, Mr. McKenna, were truly running your own game."

"I was." He offered no apology for what was in the past. "It's different now."

"Are you sure? You were thinking very deeply there. I suspect plotting."

"Oh, well, that's true enough."

"And . . ." She set the brush down and twisted her hair into a rope. "What do you have in mind?"

"I was entertaining the notion of inviting Easterbrook back to the valley. Maybe send Cutter into Jupiter so he can drop a hint or two about Buck McKay."

"Draw him out, you mean."

"Yes, but not only him. His friends, companions, associates . . . whatever you want to call them. I don't believe he'll come alone. I don't believe he came alone last night, but that's only supposition, not fact. We know that what was done to me wasn't done by a single man. It's hard for me to believe he's acting on his own now. There are two other men who have reason to be sure I'm dead."

"You certainly pissed in someone's soup."

"I must have."

Willa crawled into bed beside Israel. She lay on her side, head propped on an elbow, while he remained sitting up against the headboard. "Are we agreed that it was you who walked into the Viceroy in Jupiter looking for a room?"

"Yes. It seems likely."

"Mr. Stafford told Cutter you were carrying two bags. Tell me what you think might have been in them. You must have some idea even if you have no memory."

"It's likely that at least one of them held clothes. My parents met me when I was released and gave me money for clothes and sundries to make a fresh start. I don't remember buying anything, but I would have done that after I purchased my ticket. I told you that walking to train station is the last thing I clearly recall."

"I understand, but you know where you meant to go with the ticket. You've never said, Israel. Isn't it time you did?"

"You think it's important. It's not."

"So tell me."

The headboard thudded dully as Israel dropped his head back against it. He closed his eyes for a moment. "You're right. It's time. I've known where I was headed from the beginning. I just did not want to bring him into it. I thought—"

Willa could not let him finish without interrupting. "You're talking about Quill. That's where you were going."

"Yes."

"He's here? Temptation? His ranch is in Colorado?"

"Mm-hmm. By train, a couple hours south of Denver."

"So close," she said more to herself than him. "And you didn't tell him where you were when you wrote. I understand that you don't want to involve him in what happened after you left Chicago, but telling him where you are and what's gone on doesn't necessarily mean he'll arrive at the front door."

"You're wrong. It pretty much means exactly that."

"He was *expecting* you, Israel. Don't you think Quill will be worried? I would be."

"Worried? I don't know. Over the years he's learned to set his expectations fairly low."

"I don't think you're being fair to him." When Israel said nothing, Willa found his thigh under the blankets and ran her hand along it from hip to knee. "I'm not sure I understand why you were going to visit your brother. Of all the places you could have gone after your release, you chose there. Why?"

"He invited me. Quill asked me to come work for him."

Willa's eyes widened ever so slightly. "At his ranch?"

"I know," he said. "The irony is not lost on me either. I had it in my head that I'd learn about ranching, help him out, maybe even come to like it. I knew that his offer was partly prompted because he wanted to keep an eye on me. I guess I could have been insulted, being the older brother, but the hand he put out to me never felt like a slight. I was grateful for the chance, and I wanted to do right by him. I promised myself . . ." He fell silent for a time before he picked up the thread again. "I meant to be different. Dependable. Steady. Responsible. Accountable to someone outside of myself. During the time I spent behind bars, I made myself believe this leopard really *could* change his spots. And then I woke up in a place I'd never heard of, battered and bloody, and knew only one thing for certain: This time, I managed to disappoint even me."

"Oh, Israel, you don't know that you did anything to deserve what happened to you."

He lifted one eyebrow in a skeptical arch and said dryly, "History would indicate otherwise."

"But—"

"Don't, Willa. I'm not martyring myself, and I'm not looking for sympathy. Easterbrook knew me as Buck McKay. There are only two explanations for that. He either recalled me from riverboat days or I introduced myself to him as McKay. The former is actually preferable because one of the things I meant to do was put that name behind me. If I used it on the train somewhere between Chicago and Jupiter, it means I was playing cards again. That's not a good sign."

"I asked you this afternoon what it would take to get you to play. You told me that if someone were cheating, that could hook you. I think if you took up cards on the train, something like that must have compelled you. You might very well have taken the high road."

"As opposed to . . ."

"Getting liquored up and not know what you were doing."

His mouth curved sardonically. "Definitely a low road."

"Well, I'm just trying to make sense of it. I know you don't drink much, not to excess, but you just got out of jail. That'd be cause for a lot of people to celebrate until they were blind with drink."

"If I drank that much, then I wasn't sitting in a poker game. The two don't go well together, not if I mean to win, and if you recall what I told Annalea, I always mean to win."

"Maybe you were drugged. What about that?"

Israel chuckled. "You're reaching, but I appreciate the effort."

"It's not as far a reach as you seem to think. We know you made it to Denver because that's the only place you could have boarded the train to Jupiter. We also know your destination was Temptation, so something—or someone—influenced you to take the spur. You arrived with two bags, according to Mr. Stafford, and had none when we found you. It doesn't seem a stretch to me that you were drugged to get you on the train to Jupiter and robbed not long after you arrived."

"Robbed of what? My clothes?"

"Maybe Easterbrook and his friends thought you were carrying something more valuable."

Israel was quiet, mulling it over. "We just don't know, Willa. We can't. Other people hold answers to our questions, and I'm not so sure the answers matter any longer. Whether I am entirely at fault for bringing this trouble down on myself—and now all of you—or whether I merely contributed to it in some way, I am still part of it. What we are going to do about it matters. If you don't like the idea of trying to draw Easterbrook and his friends to the valley, then I need to leave for a while."

She stiffened. "I wondered when I would hear that."

"Then you've known all along it had to be said."

"I'm not opposed to trying to get Easterbrook here, but in consideration of Annalea's presence, I want to think about tracking him down."

"You heard your father's description of the man. Even with Zach and Cutter adding to it, the man could be almost anybody. Hell, Willa, they never saw the color of his hair. Maybe he was bald under his hat."

"We could backtrack, go to Stonechurch. Someone might remember him there because he was asking after you."

"That was all a lie, Willa. He was never there because Buck McKay was never there. Even without my full memory, I'm sure of that. What I know about Stonechurch is limited to the fact that Quill was there settling some business a while back, and there is nothing connecting me to Quill at that time. Easterbrook pulled the name of that town out of thin air."

"Or maybe you mentioned it to him when you were liquored up or drugged or simply exchanging pleasantries with a fellow passenger."

"Exchanging pleasantries," he repeated, amused.

"Why not? It's a long trip from Chicago to Saint Louis to Denver, and you don't have to try hard to engage people. It comes naturally to you. Is it so hard to imagine that you talked to a lot of folks on that trip?"

"Maybe I did. I'll give you that it seems more like me than getting drunk. There was not much chance for conversation in prison or jail, and not much that I wanted to say when I had visitors, so I probably was ready to exchange—"

Willa interrupted him when she suddenly pushed herself upright. "That's it, Israel. That's the question we should have been asking from the very beginning."

"I wasn't aware I asked a—" He stopped again, this time because she was vehemently shaking her head.

Willa laid a hand on his arm, partly to keep him from speaking, and partly to steady her excitement. "I sent Cutter into Jupiter the day after we found you, and I told him to ask after folks who got off the train when we thought you did. He inquired at the hotel and the boardinghouse and the saloon and got virtually nothing for his effort. It was the same when he spoke to Sheriff Brandywine. But the very first person Cutter went to was his mother, and when he asked her if she knew about anyone arriving from Denver, she mentioned the Cuttlewhites."

Israel nodded. "I remember. He spoke to them. They didn't know who got off the train."

"That's right, but Cutter should have asked them who they might have passed time with on the train. He could have asked them if they had a recollection of who boarded the train with them in Denver. Do you see? You could have spoken to them. They might recall you getting on even if they don't recall you getting off. They could have seen you with Easterbrook. We need to talk to Mr. and Mrs. Cuttlewhite, Israel. That's what we need to do."

"That's a lot of could haves and might haves."

"I know, but—"

Israel caught her chin, held it while he kissed her lightly on the mouth.

"All right," he said. "But can we sleep first? I'm sure the Cuttlewhites will appreciate my reluctance to leave this bed right now."

He caught her elbow before she poked him in the ribs and drew her down when he lay back.

"Why don't we see if you do?"

Chapter Twenty-two

The space beside Willa was empty when she woke. She sat up, bleary-eyed, and stretched her arms wide then high. It was on the point of remembering her conversation with Israel about paying a visit to the Cuttlewhites that she truly awakened. She threw back the covers, swung her legs over the side of the bed, and then danced on the cold floor until she put her feet into thick socks and found her robe.

She parted the window curtains to gauge the sunrise and realized by the sun's height and the clear white of dawn on the horizon, she had stayed abed longer than had been her intention. A little more distressing was the additional six inches of powder that had fallen overnight and the four-foot-high drifts that had been swept against the barn, the bunkhouse, and her windowsill. She did not remember hearing the wind beating against the roof, but then again, after Israel had finished appreciating her, she had slept like the dead.

Thinking about it now brought a wickedly satisfied smile to her lips and more than mere warmth to her cheeks. She saw proof of both when she sat at the vanity and regarded her reflection in the mirror. She was vaguely embarrassed by the pleasure she felt seeing herself as Israel must have seen her. Her eyelids were still heavy with sleep and only dark half-moons of her eyes were visible under her lashes. She touched her lips and found them tender, but still sweetly sensitive to the brush of her fingertips. Turning her head to the side, she was able to see a bruise on the curve of her neck. She remembered that he had suckled her there, sipped her skin until she whimpered and beat lightly at his shoulder with the heel of her hand. This was what had come of that, his brand, the sign he left to mark his territory.

She was not troubled by it because she imagined he could still feel where her nails had pressed crescents into his back and where her teeth had nibbled on his shoulder. Her marks might not be painted on his flesh the way his were on her, but she had to believe they were etched in his mind. It would take more than a blow to his head to make him forget last night.

Willa blinked when she realized that not only had she spoken that thought out loud, but that she was also mooning at her reflection.

"Who are you talking to?" asked Annalea, pushing open the door. She looked around. "Oh, it's just you. Well, I don't want any part of that conversation." She sat at the foot of the bed and then threw herself backward on it. "Pa says there's fried eggs and bacon in the warmer if you have a taste for that this morning. Don't see how you couldn't have known since the whole house smells like cooked pig."

As she had been otherwise occupied with thoughts of a carnal nature, Willa was only now able to receive the most excellent aroma of bacon. "Hmm. That must be what woke me," she said.

"Pa said your stomach would get you up. Israel wasn't so sure. He told us you didn't stir at all this morning, even when he gave you a shake."

Willa wondered if he really had tried to wake her. He could hardly tell Happy and Annalea that his appreciation had exhausted her. "Braid my hair, will you?"

Groaning as if this were an imposition rather than a task she genuinely enjoyed, Annalea heaved herself off the bed and went to stand behind Willa. "Two or one?"

"Just one, please."

Annalea picked up the brush and began pulling it through Willa's hair. "I've been thinking about Mr. Easterbrook. Seems funny how he showed up here, out of the blue and all. Even if Israel did something to provoke the man, that would have been a while back. What kind of man holds a grudge that long? That's what I asked myself."

"Well, the Pancakes and the Barbers have had a grudge against each other for a lot of years."

"Mm-hmm. It sorta got passed down, didn't it? Like your ring or Granny's rocker."

"Yes. Like that, I suppose."

Annalea returned the brush to Willa and then neatly separated her hair into three ropes of equal thickness. "So, I had Easterbrook's grudge on my mind and then my thoughts kinda slid sideways, you know, like they do when I'm doing one thing and my attention is stolen clean away by something else."

"I'm not sure that's precisely how that happens, but go on. Clearly you had a lot on your mind."

"I did, and I was doing some considerably hard thinking with it. That's how I got distracted by Mr. Eli Barber. See? I started considering his grudge, the long-standing nature of it, just like you said, and that's when I remembered something that no one talked about when we were sitting around the table last night."

"And what's that?" Willa asked, watching Annalea in the mirror. Her daughter didn't notice; all of her attention was focused on managing the braid and trying to talk at the same time. That made Willa smile. Annalea could not sing while she was playing the piano either. "What did you remember?"

Annalea plucked the red ribbon Willa held up for her and quickly tied off the braid. She admired it before letting it fall down the center of Willa's back. "I remembered the horse. No one said a word about it."

"You're right." Willa's stomach rumbled, and she knew it was the call of the fried eggs and bacon. She did not think she could indulge Annalea's flights of fancy much longer. She would have to bolt for the kitchen. "What about the horse?"

"It reminded me of Galahad. He was about the same size and just as black. It was dark, I know, but Zach and Cutter each had the lantern at different times, and I'm set on the fact that he was as black as Gal."

"All right. That could be helpful, knowing Easterbrook

was riding a black horse, probably a gelding and not a mare if he was as big as Galahad. Did you mention this to anyone else this morning?"

"No. I was conjugating while they were talking. I didn't have it quite clear then."

"I think you mean you were cogitating."

"Probably was doing that, too."

"Then I think we should let them know when they're around again." She started to rise, but Annalea dropped a firm hand on her shoulder that meant for her stay where she was. Willa's eyebrows lifted because nothing else could. "What is it?"

"The most important thing of all," Annalea said. "Mr. Easterbrook was riding a branded horse. I saw it clearly in the lantern light, and just as I know the horse was as black as Gal, I also know he had the Big Bar brand on his left shoulder. Everyone else was looking at Mr. Easterbrook, but I must have been looking at him and his horse. Hardly knew it myself until I got to conjuring it."

Willa hoped to heaven that her daughter had *not* conjured it, so she let that pass. "Big Bar? You're sure, Annalea?"

"Mm-hmm." She drew it the air with her fingertip. "Long bar beside an uppercase B. Everyone's shown it to me now and again, even you, and I've seen it on Big Bar cattle that get through a fence and into our herd. John Henry and me chased a few strays back in our time."

In other circumstances, Willa might have been able to muster a smile, but not now. Not when it concerned the Barbers. "You've never crossed the fence line, have you? Never gone onto Big Bar land?"

"No. Never. I wouldn't. Pa said the trolls would get me."

"Ah. The trolls. I'd forgotten. Did you ever believe him?"

"No, well, not for a long time, but I figured it'd be bad if I trespassed, so I never did. Not once."

"Good girl." Willa patted the hand Annalea still rested on her shoulder. "Let's go in the kitchen. I promise you, I'll eat quickly, and then we'll go find someone to tell. Hell, Annalea, we'll find everyone."

* * *

It was a slog through the new powder and drifts, some of them as high as Annalea's shoulder. Willa kept her close. Someone had already run rope lines from the house to the outbuildings in the event of a sudden squall. They'd all heard stories of people frozen twenty yards from shelter because they'd lost their bearings in a blizzard.

Annalea observed that anyone looking down on the ranch must see something that resembled a spider's web with all the buildings being tethered to it like so many flies. Willa couldn't disagree, and it was another reminder that Annalea saw things from a perspective that others missed.

Willa and Annalea crossed everyone's path except Israel's. When they inquired as to his whereabouts, Happy, Cutter, and Zach all had a different idea about where he'd gone. Not one of them believed he had left the valley, but that hardly reduced the area she would have to cover to find him. The only thing they agreed on was that he was strapped and carrying extra ammunition in his pockets. That certainly suggested that he had gone somewhere for target practice.

Willa decided that she would saddle Felicity and head out, while Annalea shared her very interesting observation with everyone.

Jesse Snow stepped outside the bunkhouse when he saw Eli trudging toward it. Today was not the day they had talked about riding into Jupiter. That was supposed to be tomorrow, but Jesse had a feeling that last night's squall had contributed to Eli changing his mind. The heir to Big Bar was just too damn impatient to follow his own plan. Eli was afraid that another storm would block the road and they wouldn't get to Jupiter inside of a week.

Jesse yanked up the collar of his coat and tucked his chin. He slapped his hands against his arms to keep warm while he waited for Eli and used his body to bar the way when Eli would have made straight for the door.

"Gotta talk here," said Jesse. "There are a couple of

fellows in the bunkhouse. Hammond and Keller. If you're looking for me, then we need to talk here."

"I'm looking for you. Where's Buster?"

"In the smokehouse with Adam Rockwell. What is it?" Just as if he didn't know.

"I want to go to Jupiter."

"Your father all right with that?" Jesse was not surprised that Eli took offense to the question. "Sorry, but I'm not crossing Malcolm."

"It was his idea. He's been waiting for some contracts. Weather's got him aching, so I'm going to ride in and see if they're there. Just that easy."

"And did you clear it for me to go? I know you ain't asked Buster yet, and he's also got to say it's all right with him."

"Buster won't raise an eyebrow. My father already approved it. There's nothing much for you to do around here anyway. The way I figure it, it's up to the cows to take care of themselves when it gets like this." He jerked his head toward the barn. "C'mon. Let's go."

Jesse sighed heavily and his breath made the cold air visible. "Let me get my hat and gloves. I'll be right behind you."

Quill McKenna put an arm around his wife's shoulders as they stared at the vast network of tracks on the map in the Denver rail station. East of the Mississippi the railroads were an intricate web, fanning out from business hubs on the Great Lakes like Toledo, Detroit, and Chicago, and on the Mississippi like Saint Louis and New Orleans. Farther west, the network dwindled to single tracks on a lonely journey across the Great Plains, the Rocky Mountains, and the Great Basin to the Pacific coast.

"If I stare at it too long," said Calico, "I start seeing double of everything. Have you ever been through Des Moines?"

"Yes."

"Then you know you don't want to go through it twice."

"Friendly people," he said. He put up a hand, staving off her attempt to contradict. Des Moines was not worth a dispute. "Just concentrate on Denver. We know Israel made it this far."

"If you hadn't thought to ask about a rolling poker game, I don't think the rail men we talked to would have remembered him. Until that game got underway, no one looked twice at your brother. From Chicago to Saint Louis, I get the sense he was about as noticeable as a penny in a change purse."

"True." Quill used his finger to trace tracks running from Denver to points west and south on the map. "I can't decide if I want to congratulate him for making it as far as Saint Louis without taking up a game, or if I should plant my fist in his face for not avoiding cards the entire journey." He shook his head, feeling frustration beginning to get the better of him. "Look at us standing here, better than a hundred miles from where we belong, trying to decide which one of these damn arteries he might have taken out of Denver."

Calico leaned into her husband as she followed the finger tracings he made. She said practically, "Well, we know he didn't arrive in Temptation, and we've made inquiries as we traveled from there to here, so I think we can safely eliminate that line."

"I'm going to pretend that's helpful," said Quill, "and there aren't seven other routes he could have taken. If he won at the table, and I told you that he usually does, then he might not have boarded another train immediately. He could have very well taken his winnings and found a fancy hotel and a fancy woman and stayed in the city until his luck or his money ran out."

Calico nodded reluctantly. "I was thinking along the same lines, but here is my suggestion for what to do about it. We are going to find a fancy hotel and get a room for a couple of nights while we ask around after your brother. We should be able to learn enough to set us on the right track—literally—especially now that we know Israel took up the name 'Buck McKay' again." She stepped away from Quill and searched his face. "That bothers you, doesn't it?"

He tried to shrug it off but Calico's sharpening green eyes told him he was unsuccessful. "Let's just say it makes me less hopeful for him."

"I understand. Maybe you'll feel differently after we find you a fancy woman."

Chapter Twenty-three

Willa had no difficulty picking up Israel's trail once she got beyond where the other horses had trampled the fresh powder, and it was not long after she found it that she heard the first shot. She continued to ride toward Beech Bottom, hoping all the while that he not ridden Galahad into the bowl.

He had not. Israel was easy to spot as soon as she came over the rise. He and Galahad were both dark figures in a vast white canvas. Seeking no protection against the occasional gusts of wind, Willa held Felicity back and watched Israel. He would have seen her easily if he had turned around, but his concentration was all for what he was doing.

From where she was sitting astride Felicity, it appeared that Israel was shooting into a bulky mound of snow that stood considerably higher than the snow around it. She had a glimpse of something black on the ground a few feet behind the mound but slightly off to one side. She squinted, realized that what she was seeing was Israel's hat, and pressed her gloved fist to her mouth to smother her laughter.

Israel Court McKenna had built a snowman. She admired the improvisation even as it made her chuckle. The Stetson, off to the side as it was, had probably been sitting on top of the snowman's head at one point, but whether Israel had shot his hat off by accident or design, or whether a gust had swept it away, she had no idea. In her heart, for his sake, she was rooting for the shot to have been deliberate.

Willa would have liked to move closer, but she did not want to give herself away. He had obviously left the ranch to avoid distractions as well as the scrutiny and advice his target practice would have invited. She could not tell if he was wearing the spectacles, but when she watched him draw and shoot dead center into the snowman's chest, she thought he was. He made three more good shots, all of them clipping the snowman, before he paused to reload. When he holstered the Colt and began walking toward his target, Willa realized she had to make a decision whether to advance or retreat. If she didn't choose the latter, Israel would see her as soon as he finished whatever he was about to do and turned to come back.

Retreat was an inviting alternative, but it wasn't her way, especially when she had Annalea's observations to pass along. Willa pressed her heels into Felicity's sides and advanced.

Israel picked up his Stetson, beat it against his thigh a few times to remove the snow, and then examined it for damage. He found the hole just above the braided leather hatband and resisted the temptation to poke it with his little finger. Nodding to himself, satisfied, he settled the hat on his own head instead of returning it to the snowman. He had a critical eye for his creation and began patching pockmarks. The fresh powder was useless for this task, but he dug deep under it and came up with wetter, heavier snow to do the job. He was nearly finished when he scooped up a large handful with a different intent in mind. Packing and rolling it into a ball, he pivoted sharply and threw it hard at Willa. It glanced off her shoulder, which was close enough to his target to satisfy him.

"Hey!" she called to him, still forty feet away. She pointed to her shoulder before she dusted it off. "How did you do that?"

"I didn't think about it." Israel touched one stem of his spectacles. "And these helped."

"I'm sure, but you're not wearing them behind your head. I thought I was sneaking up on you."

"Then you're not quite the Calico Nash you think you are."

She laughed. "No. I don't suppose I am, but then again, I don't make my living hunting bounties." She brought Felicity alongside Galahad before she dismounted. "I haven't read anything about her in the papers for quite a while. Used to be you'd see her name in the *Rocky* for collecting a bounty on one miscreant or another."

Before Willa could pose the question Israel could see that she was itching to ask, he said, "No. She never arrested me. I wasn't worth all that much as a bounty, and I worked outside her territory."

"Huh." She came up beside him, stood on tiptoe, and kissed him full on the mouth. When she disengaged, she was a bit less steady on her feet but in a very nice way. "Still, it's kind of odd that you'd mention Calico Nash."

"I was just making the obvious comparison. She's a woman. You're a woman." He looked Willa over, from her well-worn hat to the lived-in boots. "I imagine you both dress in a manner befitting your work, except I don't quite get a picture of her wearing a red scarf."

Willa smiled as she fingered it at her throat. "It's nice, though, isn't it?"

"Very fetching. And highly visible. I caught a glimpse of it out of the corner of my eye when I was making repairs." He used his thumb to point to the snowman behind him. "This fellow at my back is the appropriately named Mr. Roundbottom. I don't know his whole story, but I have it on my own authority that he is a bad man, wanted for crimes that are so heinous they cannot be repeated in front of gentle company such as yourself."

"Fool," she said, not unkindly. "I was watching for a while. From what I could see, you did very well. And your snowball pitch was quite excellent."

Israel was uncomfortable with her praise. He gave her what he hoped was a modest shrug. "Like I said, I didn't think about it. Quill used to tell me that was my problem, that I took too much time in consideration of the act. Of course, he didn't know about my eyesight, but even so, I think he might have been right. He said that I needed to do all my considering before I even set out with a gun. If I was carrying, I should have already decided I meant to use it. That way, there'd be no hesitation. Pulling the trigger would be second nature."

"Like when you threw the snowball."

"Yes, like that." He saw her eyes lift to his hat and knew precisely when she located the hole because she grinned.

"On purpose," he said, pointing to it. "Doesn't make a lick of sense to be proud of putting a hole in my own hat, but there you have it."

"Annalea was wrong about you not being much improved. Maybe you could be a gunslinger. Did you miss at all?"

He stepped aside so she could have a better view of his target and pointed out the patchwork. "I fired every round into him, not always exactly where I wanted, but I didn't miss him either."

"Impressive. I mean it. Take the compliment, Israel. You earned it." She picked up a handful of snow and started filling in where he had stopped. "Have you been practicing without anyone knowing? I can't even imagine how that would have been possible."

"I never fired the gun, but I practiced drawing and steadying my arm. As for taking aim and shooting, I did that up here."

Willa stopped what she was doing to look at him. At first she thought he was pointing to the ear stem of his spectacles again, but then she saw his forefinger was tapping his temple. "You practiced in your head?" she asked, straightening. "In your *head*?"

Her tone was so incredulous that Israel grinned even as his brow furrowed. "Don't you?" he asked. "Doesn't everybody sooner or later?"

"I don't know about everybody, but I can't say that I ever got good at anything by practicing it in my head."

"Hmm. That's interesting. I do it a lot. Always have, but never about handling a gun. Whatever it is that you're thinking, it's no good if you only keep it in your head. You have to try it out, see if you have the hang of it."

"And that's what you're doing here? Seems as if you might have worked out all the kinks."

"Maybe. I'll know better after a few more rounds. You know, Willa, I spent a good bit of time in jail mapping out the path I meant to take when I was released. I got to where I could see it as clearly as the lines on my own palm. I was thinking about that last night after you fell asleep, and you know what I realized?"

"What?"

"Either because of what happened on that train, or in spite of it, I'm precisely where I wanted to be."

Willa stared at him. She touched her throat. "Lord, but I love you."

She launched herself at him so fiercely that Israel didn't have time to welcome her. He rocked back on his heels, lost his footing, and dropped with a thud into the snow. Willa followed him down. The fresh layer of snow powder swirled around them, dusting their clothes and hair and eyelashes, but the hard crust under it was as unforgiving as the frozen ground, and Israel groaned as he lay sprawled against it.

"I hope you're comfortable," he said, staring past the snow smudging his spectacles and into her deeply amused eyes. He let her kiss the corner of his mouth and then his cheeks, melting snowflakes with her warm lips. "My backside is—"

"Shh," she said. "Let me finish."

He was hardly in a position to object, and he didn't really want to anyway. It was a damn shame there wasn't a decent shelter nearby, and he told her that as she was climbing off him. He accepted the hand Willa held out as he sat up and tried to rise from the depression they'd made in the snow. He stood, dusted himself off, and turned around so she could get his back. "What are you doing here? Didn't anyone tell you not to follow me?"

"No, no one did."

He grunted softly as she slapped him across his shoulder blades with rather more force than was necessary. "You must have had that look in your eye when you asked them where I was. I bet they didn't even try bluffing. Do you see now why I don't play cards with them?" That got him a handful of snow down his back. He jumped away from her. "Now that was just mean," he said, tugging at the collar of his coat. He jerked his head sideways. "Stand over there before I shoot you."

Unrepentant, she gave him a cheeky grin. "Is that what you're practicing in your head now?"

He removed his spectacles and cleaned them carefully with a handkerchief. "Let's just say it's tiptoeing across my mind's eye. Now go."

Still grinning, she went to where their horses were tethered while he returned to where he'd been standing to draw and fire.

Israel adopted a relaxed, yet watchful stance, removing Willa and her red scarf to the very corner of his peripheral vision. He pulled back his coat so the Colt was visible and within easy reach. He studied Mr. Roundbottom, imagining the man was studying him back. The way Israel saw it, it happened quickly. Roundbottom flinched first, telegraphing his intention to draw. Israel did not hesitate, and the bullet he fired pierced Roundbottom's black heart.

He did it five more times, every scenario playing out a bit differently, but all with the same result. He reloaded and backed up another ten yards and made four of six shots at a distance that he thought would have impressed his brother, perhaps even his brother's wife.

Willa cupped her hands around her mouth and called out to him, "Now you're just showing off."

He chuckled and thought he probably was. He checked his pocket for cartridges and found he had five left. He slipped them into the cylinder and then walked half the distance to the target. Fanning the hammer as deftly as he had ever fanned a deck of cards, his excess of enthusiasm exploded poor Mr. Roundbottom's head.

The shots echoed for what Israel thought was a long time, but then he realized that there was only silence around him and that echo he heard was in his head. He lowered the Colt slowly and let it hang at his side for a few moments before he holstered it. He closed his coat, buttoned it, and turned to bring Willa full into his line of sight. He was not surprised that she was staring at him as if he were a stranger to her. Just then he was a stranger to himself.

Willa stepped away from the horses and began walking toward him. He put a hand up to stop her. After a long minute spent mastering his heartbeat, he went to her.

"Who was that?" she asked when he was standing in front of her. "I don't believe it was Mr. Roundbottom you killed in that rather stunning fashion."

Israel turned to look at the shards of snow and ice that had been Malcolm Barber's head. He could not tell Willa that. It would frighten her. "You're wrong," he said. "I told you. Roundbottom was a very bad man." He met her gaze directly and watched as she began to doubt her interpretation of what she had witnessed. He was on the point of telling her the truth, no matter how she might take it, but then her scrutiny ended and she slipped her arms around him, pressed her cheek to his shoulder, and stayed there.

Israel's arms circled her. He was not her shelter now. He had instantly recognized what was different about this embrace. She was holding him. He was holding on.

They parted at the same time as if by unspoken mutual agreement and headed for the horses. Israel gave Willa a leg up for no other reason than he wanted to. As soon as he was in the saddle, they turned Felicity and Galahad and started home.

The wind struck them squarely in the face on the way back. No new snow was falling, but what was lifted into the air by each gust made it equally hard to see. They both lowered their hats and pulled up their scarves so only their eyes showed. Israel stopped once to remove the spectacles and put them in his pocket, and while carrying on a conversation was not possible now, he had no difficulty hearing Willa's short burst of laughter.

They were in the barn before they could properly talk to each other. Israel handed Willa a blanket and told her to put it around her and he would take care of the horses. She was shaking with cold, which served to shorten her argument but not stop her from mounting one. Israel fought back by prying Felicity's reins from Willa's frozen fist and ignoring everything she said.

Willa sat huddled on a bench outside the stalls while Israel worked. She found another blanket to put over her lap and legs. "I really did have a reason for finding you," she said when her teeth had stopped chattering.

"I figured. You want to tell me now?"

"Annalea told me this morning after you were gone that Mr. Easterbrook's horse had the Big Bar brand on its left shoulder."

Israel poked his head out of Felicity's stall. "Say that again."

"You heard me, you just can't believe it." She repeated herself anyway. "Annalea spent a lot of time putting it together in her mind. I'm thinking you can appreciate that perhaps better than anyone. I have no idea what Easterbrook's connection is to a Mississippi showboat, but that's in his past. The Barbers are paying his wages now. There is no other way he could have come by one of their working horses."

"Stole it?"

Willa closed that door with a highly doubtful look.

"All right. So you don't think that's likely. What is everyone thinking then? That he's acting on his own or that he was sent here by one or both of the Barbers?"

"The Barbers," she said succinctly.

"And?"

"We are divided on the 'one or both' part of your question, and if it's only one, which one. Happy thinks Malcolm is behind Easterbrook's visit. Zach, because of that conversation he had with Eli a while back, thinks Eli is responsible. Cutter made a case for it being Malcolm and Eli, along with Easterbrook, who took you for that ride."

"What do you think?"

"I know better than anyone what Malcolm Barber is capable of, and I don't see him as part of this. I believe that if you did something to rile Mal, he would have killed you where you stood. Even if I could be assured that he was part of the trio that got you out to the ridge, I cannot convince myself that he would have left you alive. Oh, I know they *thought* you were dead, but Mal would have made sure of it."

"So it's Eli, then."

"Yes. Only my opinion. We all have one."

"And the third person?"

"I don't know. Someone else from Big Bar probably, but we don't know everyone who works there. There's Buster Rawlins, who's been around for a long time. We know him on sight. Cowboys come and go; it's the nature of the work. Most of the hands that the Barbers hire come from somewhere else, same as our men. Cutter, being a local boy, is more the exception than the rule. That's why I kept him on."

"Does any of this connect to Monarch Lake?"

"We talked about that again. None of us can draw a straight line to it. I'm inclined to think it's a red herring."

Israel patted Felicity on the jaw and moved to Galahad's stall. "That's interesting."

"Hmm. Maybe 'distraction' would be a better word for it. I'm not sure how purposeful anything going on there is. You heard Zach and Cutter when they got back last night."

"I was at the table while they were talking about it," he corrected, removing Galahad's saddle. "I had other things on my mind."

"Well, they found evidence that someone had been out that way, but the wind swept snow across the trail." She shrugged. "Had they been able to follow it, it would have likely led them to Big Bar, not some rustler's hidey-hole. The important thing is that there was no evidence that anyone is trying to divert the water supply. How that could be accomplished at this time of year is a mystery to us anyway. If Malcolm still wants our water, he'll wait until the thaw or he'll make another legal run at it. On the other hand, it'd be very much like Malcolm to hassle us for the pleasure of it."

Israel began brushing Galahad. "This is not the first time that someone's ridden out from here to investigate a disturbance at the lake."

"As I said, it's a distraction."

"Mm-hmm. A dangerous one."

"I don't know about that."

"All right. A potentially dangerous one. What if Zach and Cutter had been out there when Easterbrook showed up? You and I weren't here. Happy and Annalea would have had to fend for themselves."

"I understand what you're saying, but fending for ourselves is what we do. It's what we've always done. You taking off this morning like you did, to do what you were doing, well, that says to me that you want to fend for yourself, too." Her slim smile appeared as he turned to look at her. "Not only for yourself, but for all of us."

Israel's eyes dropped to Willa's slanted smile. He put down the grooming brush and advanced on Willa, lifting her to her feet when he stood in front of her. "Your mouth, Wilhelmina, now that's a red herring."

Chapter Twenty-four

Eli Barber studied his cards for a long minute before he moved money into the pot. He was aware of the collective sigh that circled the table, and he looked up, settling his gaze one at a time on the three men who had waved him over to play. It occurred to him that they were regretting it. Not only was he winning, but he was taking his time doing it.

He had no reason to hurry the play along. His three companions at the table would all be going home tonight, while he would be going back to the Viceroy for the third consecutive evening. As he had anticipated, the weather had turned again. He had been wrong, though, about the ferocity of the storm. The roads out of Jupiter were blocked within hours of the first wave of snow and folks in town were mostly staying indoors or trudging through hip-deep drifts to get to the mercantile, the apothecary, or most often, the saloon. Even the train's arrival had been halted. Rumor had it that it was taking shelter in a snow shed somewhere east of Lansing.

Eli was playing with men he knew by name but did not know well. They were all better acquainted with his father, as was true of most people in Jupiter. Malcolm was everyone's friend, although no one's intimate. Eli was no one's friend and everyone's acquaintance. He knew he stood in his father's shadow, but he also knew, just as everybody did, that someday that would change. Folks in Jupiter had a long memory, and the older ones among them could recall a time when Malcolm Barber had been in *his* father's shadow. Eli accepted that and enjoyed certain liberties because no one who considered the future ever crossed him.

Eli followed the play around the table, and when it came

back to him, he set his cards down and turned them over. "A full house, gentlemen." He smiled and shrugged helplessly as they tossed their cards in mutual disgust. "Seems as if I win again." He used his arm to shovel his winnings toward him. "Another?"

They all nodded but with different degrees of enthusiasm.

"All right, then," said Eli. He passed the cards to Paul Beetleman on his left. Beetleman, a squat, square man with protruding lips, was a member of Jupiter's council and a funnel for information of what was going on in and around the town. Eli kept his voice casual and addressed the players at large instead of Beetleman in particular. "Any of you hear anything about how the Pancakes are faring this winter?"

It was Danny McKenney who answered. He sat deeply slouched in his chair, putting Eli in mind of Jesse Snow when Jesse had a few beers in him. McKenney, however, was merely spineless in body and spirit and never stood if he could lean and never leaned if he could lie down. Eli could not imagine how he had drummed up the courage to ask Wilhelmina to marry him, although the man was well suited to any position that called for kneeling.

"Haven't seen anyone from the valley in a while," said McKenney. "I swear they hibernate. My old man does same thing come winter. All of them like bears. You're lucky you got out when you did, Eli. You'd be holed up at Big Bar, just like your father."

"So I would."

Beetleman's eyes went to the stairs and followed them to the second floor. "Seems I recollect seeing one of your hands with you earlier. He's probably glad he got out as well. Can't imagine that he's not enjoying himself with Louise."

"Mary Edith," Eli corrected absently.

"What's his name?" asked Noah Cuttlewhite. Unlike McKenney, Cuttlewhite was sitting straight up, elbows tucked close to his sides, feet flat on the floor. This attempt to be taken seriously, as well as add inches to his height, was undermined by a jaw as smooth as a baby's bottom and a receding chin. "I think I've seen him around a time or two."

"Jesse Snow," said Eli.

"Guess he's not much for cards," McKenney said, studying his hand.

"Would you be," asked Beetleman, "if Mary Edith led you up those stairs?"

McKenney made a dismissive sound. "Can't afford her now. Eli has all my money."

"Surely not all," Eli said, looking at the pot. "You're still in, aren't you?"

"Barely." He threw a few coins in the middle of the table. "I did hear tell that Willa got her knot tied, if you take my meaning."

"I think we all do," said Beetleman.

Eli did not move, but he felt as if had suddenly snapped to attention. "How's that again, Danny?"

"Willa. She finally said yes. Couldn't believe it myself, not until I had it straight from Mrs. Hamill."

"Mrs. Hamill?" Eli asked. "Oh, of course. Cutter Hamill's mother. Yes, it would make sense that she'd know."

"You'd think so, wouldn't you?" It was Beetleman's turn to play and interject something into the conversation. "But she only knew that much. She said she couldn't pry a name out of her boy. For all we know, Willa Pancake might be married to Cutter himself. Wouldn't that twist his mother's corset?"

Eli smiled because the situation demanded it, not because emotion provoked him. It was the same every time he got close. Mrs. Hamill either truly didn't know, or she was keeping the secret so close that nothing short of threatening one of her children would get it out of her. Eli responded the same way he always did when he reached the end of this inquiry. In Jupiter, speculation was sometimes more useful than fact.

"Where do you suppose Willa met this fellow she married?" It was rare that anyone answered with more than a shrug. Eli had never been able to pose the question to someone who had actually asked Willa to marry him, but here was Danny McKenney, and even as indolent as the man was, he had probably spared some thought for the matter.

Cuttlewhite shrugged, but Beetleman said, "A drifter, most likely. No one from around here, or we would have heard of it."

McKenney closed his cards and tapped the corner of them on the table. "Probably someone passing through, looking for work, and ending up in the catbird seat. Still, I thought I should find out what was what on account of having thrown my hat in that ring a while back." His heavy-lidded eyes settled on Eli. "I figure that's something you and I have in common, which is probably why I brought it up in the first place. Hasn't been on my mind for a spell."

Eli was about to ask what McKenney knew, but he hesitated and Beetleman asked the question for him.

"Well, I figured if she was married, then someone had to do the deed. It's a legal contract, right? Maybe a religious one, too, although Willa hasn't much been one for church since her mama died."

Eli wanted to grab McKenney by his slack collar and shake information out of him. Drawing on a well of patience previously untapped, he sat there quietly and pretended a renewed interest in his cards.

McKenney shrugged his sloping shoulders. "So I did what made sense to me. I asked the justice when he was here if he performed the marriage, and when he said he didn't know a thing about it, I went to the preacher and asked. Abernathy only knew what I did and hadn't given any thought to how it had come about, but when I posed the question, it sure did tickle his curiosity. He reminded me the Pancakes set a whole lot of store by the preacher who was there before him. Remember William Beacon?" When he saw everyone nod, he went on. "So Abernathy supposed that it might have been Pastor Beacon since he's only in Lansing and that's not too far. If he's right, there'd be a record of it with the church and by now a legal record in the county courthouse."

"There's some good thinking," said Eli.

Beetleman and Cuttlewhite spoke up at the same time. "So what did you find out?"

McKenny regarded them as if they'd each sprouted a third eye. "Not a damn thing," he said. "It's one thing to ask after local folks, but paying for a ticket to Lansing, or God forbid, riding the distance on horseback, well, there's nothing I need to know that costs me money to get it—or puts calluses on my ass for that matter."

Beetleman shook his head. "It is hard to believe you are Old Man McKenney's son."

Far from taking offense, McKenney grinned. "I know. He says the same thing. Only my mama knows for sure and she's taking that secret to her grave."

Beetleman's chest swelled and shook with laughter. Cuttlewhite snickered. Eli smiled and was able to maintain it because he was seriously considering calling McKenney out for cheating and killing him right there. It was only out of respect for Old Man McKenney that he didn't.

Eli said in bored tones, "Is someone going to ask for a card? Whose turn is it anyway?"

Cuttlewhite stopped snickering. He held up a hand. "That's me." He asked Beetleman for two cards and then said to Eli, "I thought a player like yourself would be keeping track, even with conversation going on around you."

"I'm no card sharp. I don't even play around here much. Did you hear differently?"

"I never heard you called a sharp before, and I know you don't have a regular place at a table, but my parents mentioned they saw you in what looked to be a real serious game on the train coming from Denver. Someone told them it had been going on since Saint Louis. There was a train switch in Denver and the players made the switch, too. My mother didn't hold much with that, but Father told her it was dedication to a craft."

Eli forced an appreciative chuckle. "I'll keep that in mind." He waited for Cuttlewhite to finish looking at his hand before he spoke again. "When was this? I don't remember seeing your parents. I'd know them."

"Oh, it's been months now. They were visiting my sister. She had a baby. That'd be sometime in October. Mother didn't think you saw her or Father. They'd been warned by the conductor to pass through the car quickly so as not to disturb the gentlemen playing."

"How about that? I must really have been playing dedicated. I don't recall anyone passing through. Did your parents recognize anyone else at the table?"

"I don't think so. They didn't say, so I would guess they didn't. They thought the game might have broken up around Lansing." He whistled softly. "Saint Louis to Lansing. What I wouldn't have given to sit at that table."

McKenney said, "You can hardly sit at this one, Noah. I swear you're ready to either jump out of your chair or out of your skin. It's time for you to show us what you got."

The tips of Cuttlewhite's ears turned pink, matching the flush that slowly rose above his collar and disappeared under his scalp. He spread his cards in his hand and then set the fan on the table. "Three of kind. Anyone have anything better than that?"

Eli folded his straight and tossed the cards away without revealing his winning hand. It was time to gather his winnings and yank Jesse Snow from between Mary Edith's thighs.

Calico and Quill pored over another map, this time in the comfort of their hotel room. It was their third evening in Denver and they were feeling confident that they had enough information to take their search in the right direction. The weather and the trains were their current obstacles. Calico had suggested they buy horses and ride out, but Quill sensibly told her that would only happen over his dead body. She gave him the eye that said she was considering it, but then ruined any chance she would be believed by bursting into laughter. So now they waited, Calico less patiently than Quill, for the weather to break and the trains to move and sometimes for the baby to kick. Although they both knew this last was still months away, it was an event, unlike the others, that they looked forward to with more pleasure than trepidation.

The map was spread out on the bed, and they studied it from their respective corners, Calico in the southwest and Quill in the southeast.

"So we are decided," said Calico. "We will go to Lansing."

Quill nodded. "If we can trust what we learned here, then yes, that seems the next logical step. I admit that I entertained thoughts of finding him here, or at least learning that'd he stayed for a time and shared his plans with someone, but that does not appear the case."

"No, it doesn't. Israel was dedicated to the play."

Gaming and whoring, supplemented by the occasional vaudeville act from the East, was largely confined to three notorious streets in Denver: Holladay, Blake, and Larimer. There was so much territory to cover in the tenderloin that Calico and Quill split up, going door to door with an end agreement to meet at Bat Masterson's Palace Variety Theatre and Gambling Parlor. They secured a private box to watch the entertainment and discuss what they'd learned. A bottle of beer came at the dear price of a dollar, but since they were still there at midnight, they, like all the patrons, were treated to a free meal, which included their choice of succulent roast pork, prairie hen, or venison.

Their exhaustive search had turned up several important clues. Quill found someone at a gaming establishment called Chase's Cricket Club, who told him that not only did he know Buck McKay, but that he'd also had the pleasure of sitting at a table with him for part of the journey from Saint Louis to Denver. Mr. Adam Randolph left the game before Denver, but he did not leave the car, and he had some regrets about disembarking when he did because the game, as he described it, was a masterfully conducted symphony of card play.

Calico thought Quill made that up, but he swore he was repeating Randolph verbatim. It was obvious that the man took the game quite seriously. Randolph was able to recount several hands in the exact order of play, but other than Buck McKay, who turned out to be the masterful conductor of the symphony, he was less clear about the names of the other players. He thought there might have been someone named Davenport or Cavendish or maybe it was Ravenscroft. Another fellow, whose name he could not recall, said he was a barber. He was fairly certain there was someone named Elijah at the table, and another fellow, who stayed with the game when it moved to another car on another train, by the name of Groom.

It was not, Randolph assured him, a complete list of everyone who bought into the rolling game, but the names he offered were men he could still vaguely put a face to. Quill made notes of the descriptions, although they were rather less helpful than Randolph thought they were. Even Randolph's depiction of Buck McKay was suspect because Quill could not remember a time when his brother had ever sported a mustache. Quill had to allow that Israel's incarceration could have changed him at least that much, but there was also the fact that the features Randolph described more closely resembled the royal faces in a deck of cards.

Randolph did, however, impart one other detail that Quill believed he could trust. The players at the table when the train reached Denver all moved to the Jupiter line, and to a man they agreed the game would end in Lansing.

Calico spoke to a whore in Jennie Rogers's House of Mirrors, who recalled one of her lonely bedmates talking about a rolling game. Apparently it had excited the man to near exhaustion by the time he got to her, but he was still able to recount the game in excruciating detail while he poked her. Fortunately, he had stepped away from the table before he lost everything, and this bride of the multitude earned a generous tip that night. Calico also learned that the whore's companion had not gotten off the train in Denver like some of the other observers. He followed the game to Lansing, where it ended as the players had agreed. He stayed with the train to the end of the line and then rode back to Denver.

Calico's prostitute did not know the name of her pleasure-seeker, nor had she ever seen him again, but he had spoken so often of the man who had taken everything off the table that she only required a moment of thought to bring that name to mind: Buck McKay.

Quill folded the map and set it aside while Calico turned back the bedcovers. They spooned comfortably together, Quill's arm around Calico's waist. She snuggled her backside into the cradle he made for her and laid her arm over his.

"You know," she whispered, "Israel's winnings were considerable. Have you thought about what that means?"

"He did not do it by cheating."

"I didn't think he did. You said he was that good and I believe you. He started with a small stake. He only had the money your parents gave him to get a seat at the table, and from the accounts we heard, he walked away a much richer man."

"Are you wondering what he would do with all that money?"

"Yes. Aren't you?"

"No. I'm hoping I know. What I've been thinking about is the man who lost the lion's share of what Israel won. There was a player at the table with deep pockets and perhaps an ace up his sleeve; that's what drew Israel. I'm sure of it. Whoever it was played more or less anonymously. That, and the fact that many players came and went, is why we don't have a name to attach to him, but he is important, Calico."

Quill's chin rested against Calico's flame red hair. He said quietly, "The loser in a game like that is always important."

Calico threaded her fingers through Quill's and squeezed because she knew he was right.

Chapter Twenty-five

Annalea used both hands to pull the barn door open and struggled some to close it again. She looked around but didn't move away from the entrance. "Willa? Israel? You in here? Pa sent me to look for you on account of I was reading to him from my fifth reader, and he didn't much care for the information about coffee beans either."

"Imagine that," Israel whispered in Willa's ear. She had her face pressed into his shoulder, but he still could make out her smothered giggle. "Up here, Annalea. In the loft. Careful you don't miss a step on the ladder."

"Then I'm invited?"

"Sure." He grunted softly when Willa jabbed him with her fist as she bolted upright. "If you have that reader with you, leave it behind."

"Oh, I left it in the house. Pa says he might roast it with the potatoes, which I think is an excellent idea." She grabbed the sides of the wooden ladder and shook it to make sure it was well positioned. "Is Willa with you?"

"She is." Israel was watching her pull bits of golden straw out of her hair. As it happened, the bedding was satisfactory for people as well as the animals. He pushed himself upright and ran his fingers through his hair in an absent fashion, leaving it to Willa to pluck out the smaller pieces. He winced as she did this with rather more enthusiasm than was warranted.

"Hello," said Annalea when her head appeared above the lip of the loft. She cast her eyes from one to the other. "What are you doing up here?"

"I'm avoiding work," said Israel. "Your sister's talking about it. Spring planting. Driving the herd grazing by Settler's

Ridge to town when the thaw comes. Selling two horses to the livery in Lansing—there was an offer made while we were there—and inquiring after someone named Colonel Armstrong to find out if he is ready to take possession of the three that we've been boarding for him. Thanks to Cutter, there is elk venison to smoke, and it seems a pig will be ready for butchering as soon as Zach gets around to killing it."

Annalea shook her head at her sister. "Really, Willa, you do not know how to let a body rest. It's exacerbating."

"Exasperating," Willa said automatically.

"Exactly," said Annalea, unperturbed and unaware. Israel chuckled, and she smiled at him then accepted his help moving from the ladder and into the loft.

"Sit there, brat," he said, pointing to the blanket. "Beside your exacerbating sister."

"For goodness' sakes, Israel," said Willa. "Don't encourage her."

Annalea folded her legs and dropped beside Willa. "It's too late. Pa says I'm encourageable, so Israel must be doing something right."

Willa sighed. "Incorrigible. And you are, but I can't think of a single reason that matters at the moment."

Israel sat down on the other side of Annalea, looked over her head at Willa, and offered dryly, "Oh, good for you, Wilhelmina."

She gave him a sweetly sour look in return and lay down when Annalea flopped backward between them. A moment later, Israel joined them.

Annalea said, "This is nice. I come up here sometimes but always by myself. I can't bring John Henry with me so I don't stay long because he usually whines at the bottom of the ladder."

"I'm sure he does," said Willa. "Pitiful dog."

"He is, but I do love him so."

For a long time no one spoke, and the peace of those moments was something each of them absorbed and appreciated. Willa and Israel were under no illusions that it could last above a few minutes, and when Annalea began to fidget, they knew the fuse had been lit.

"Is no one going to say anything about the Barbers?" The words fairly exploded from her. "I can *hear* everyone thinking about them and no one says their names when I'm around. I'm the one who saw the Big Bar brand on Mr. Easterbrook's horse. I don't think you should keep secrets from me. What if I kept that brand a secret? What then? What if I flustrated you the way you all flustrate me? I bet there would be some words then."

"Lots of them," said Israel. Before Willa could insert a correction, he added, "I would be flustered, too, if I were that frustrated."

Annalea nodded. "Uh-huh. See, Willa? Israel understands."

Willa's voice, in contrast to Annalea's excited one, was calm, and the words were delivered in measured tones. "What is it you want to know?"

"What we're going to do," she said, marginally less agitated than she was a moment earlier. "That man works for the Barbers and he tried to kill Israel. It seems we should be doing something about that."

"There was some discussion about going to the sheriff," said Willa. "Tell him what we know and let him sort it out."

"That's no kind of way to do things."

"Sometimes it is," said Israel, "but maybe not this time."

Annalea was in firm agreement. "Without knowing what you did, it'd be like poking a hive for honey and disturbing a bear instead."

Israel knuckled the crown of her head. "Probably would. So what we're going to do is move you and your pitiful dog into town to stay with Mrs. Hamill for a while and invite the Barbers here for a parley."

Annalea held up one hand with two fingers extended. "Two problems. John Henry and I are not leaving and a parley is for pirates."

"A parley is a negotiation. Anyone can do it. Scalawags, scoundrels, and diplomats. As for leaving . . . you are."

Sitting up, Annalea twisted around and rose to her knees. She looked down at Willa and Israel, her narrowed eyes darting back and forth. She finally rested her stare on Willa and made her appeal. "You don't mean it, Willa. Say you don't. This is my home. I'm a Pancake. I should be here."

"It might not be safe for you," said Willa. It hardly mattered that Annalea was her spitting image; common sense dictated that she be kept away from the scrutiny of the Barbers.

"Safe? Do you mean you expect there will be a showdown?"

Israel's mouth quirked. "It's not the O.K. Corral, brat."

"It could be. We got a corral."

Israel looked over at Willa. "You take another turn."

Willa said, "We are not looking for a fight, Annalea. We are trying to stop one. What we want is an explanation. Israel wants to know what happened after he left Chicago, even if it means hearing something he doesn't like, and I want to come to terms with Malcolm about Monarch Lake, even if it means having to sit at a table with him."

"Did Pa agree to this? He still talks about shooting *Mal* . . . odorous."

"And that's another reason you can't be here," Willa told her. "I can't depend on you to call him Mr. Barber."

"Mr. Barbarian is more like it," Annalea said under her breath. In quick succession, she added, "*Mal* . . . content. *Mal* . . . ediction. *Mal* . . . adroit." She looked at Israel. "I've been studying up."

"Seems that way."

"Hmm. *Mal* . . . eficent."

"That's enough," said Willa.

"I'm just saying that you can make a whole lotta words mean something kinda bad if you put 'mal' in front of them. Ezra Barber should have thought of that before he named his son *Mal* . . . colm."

Willa covered her eyes with her forearm. Before she did, she saw that Israel had covered his mouth with his. "Enough, Annalea. You asked us to tell you about the plan, and we are getting an awful lot of guff in return."

"Humph." She crossed her arms in front of her. "If I can say just one more thing . . ."

Willa lifted her forearm enough to give Annalea a wary eyeful. "Go on. One more thing."

"Well, it seems passing strange that I tell you that Pa still talks about shooting Mr. Malcolm Barber, and all you pay attention to is me calling the man names. Sticks and stones, Willa. Sticks and stones."

Israel uncovered his mouth. "I'll hold her down, Willa. You tickle her until she wets herself."

Shrieking, Annalea tried jumping to her feet, but Israel was too quick. He snatched an ankle and pulled her down. Willa pounced. Annalea's fierce giggles filled the rafters with joyful noise.

Malcolm Barber looked over the letter that Buster brought him not above a half hour ago. He studied the lines and he studied between them, and he could not for the life of him see what he had to lose by accepting Happy Pancake's invitation. Happy had not penned the letter himself, but it was his signature at the bottom and that meant that he had approved the invitation.

Malcolm wondered how it had come about. Was it Happy's idea and Wilhelmina put it to paper, or was it Wilhelmina's idea and Happy merely added his name to it? The answer could assist him in identifying intent. Not being able to see a trap did not mean there wasn't one.

He had dismissed Buster upon receiving the letter and learning its origins. Zachary Englewood had carried it from Pancake Valley using the road and not the route over the ridge and barbed wire that would have been seen as trespass. Now, except for Harris Garvey rooting around in the kitchen in preparation for making supper, the house was quiet.

Malcolm set the letter aside and picked up his drink. He sipped, swore softly, and then sipped again. Eli had not returned from Jupiter. Malcolm accepted that the recent snowstorm was a factor, but he couldn't help thinking that if he had sent Buster after the contracts, he would have them by now. At the very least, Buster would have tried harder to get back to Big Bar.

Malcolm wanted to put more responsibility on his son's shoulders. It was time. Some fathers, his own included, would have said it was past time, but Malcolm had observed a reckless streak in Eli, as well as a petulance in his demeanor when he had to explain himself. That troubled him.

He had tested the waters now and then. Sending Eli to Saint Louis to complete negotiations on cattle pricing, specifically to fix those prices, had been one such test, and Eli had acquitted himself admirably, returning with the entire profit of that transaction. Encouraging Eli to pursue Willa Pancake with the same feverish intensity that he had shown as a youth was another test, but that one had ended badly. Malcolm had no regrets that he put a stop to that ill-advised affair in their childhood—both of them were absurdly naïve—but he did regret that ending it in the manner he did left young Willa with an abiding hatred and him with an abiding hunger.

Malcolm accepted that Eli's failure to bring Willa to heel was also his failure. And now with the disappointing, even disastrous, news that she had married, it seemed that revisiting those wildly satisfying moments they'd shared were something he should finally put behind him.

He had no idea how to do that. He had meant to punish her all those years ago, to demonstrate in the only way he believed his son's little whore would understand that he was not to be trifled with. She had been warned to stay away from Eli, and she had come anyway. How pretty she had been, perched like a chickadee in that old cottonwood, fiddling with her braids, humming tunelessly while she waited. The hem of her yellow dress fluttered as she swung her legs back and forth. He'd had a glimpse of long, smooth calves above her ankle boots and a peek at the young flesh of her thighs. The surge of lust she had provoked overwhelmed him, and it was then that he truly comprehended the grip she had on Eli.

He had beaten the truth out of his son before he went to find Willa. It had required half a dozen hard blows across Eli's naked buttocks to get his confession, but Malcolm believed he knew the ring of truth when he heard it. Willa had been spreading her legs for Eli for months.

So, yes, he had meant to punish her. And for a few days after he'd had her, he thought that's what he had done, but it had been borne home to him over the course of weeks, and months, and now years, that she had turned the punishment on its head. How else to explain that Wilhelmina still haunted his thoughts?

Malcolm's gaze slid from his glass to the letter. Maybe. Maybe there was yet some way he could influence her to come around and take Eli as her husband. It would not happen immediately, but in time she could be made to see the sense of it. And once the young widow took his son to her bed, it would not be long before he had her as well.

The corner of Malcolm's generously carved mouth curled as he reflected on Eli's recent success in Saint Louis. Perhaps his son would be a more appealing matrimonial candidate once Willa saw him as someone other than the clumsy lover who had betrayed her to his father.

Malcolm turned his attention back to his glass. He slowly raised it to his lips and gave over all of his thoughts to the matter of what Eli and that no-account Jesse Snow were up to.

"Who the hell is Israel Cord McKenney?" Eli demanded. He poked his forefinger at the offending name hard enough to slide the ledger to the edge of Pastor Beacon's desk. He let the pastor fumble to catch it before it toppled to the floor because he was already pivoting to face Jesse. "Do you know that name? Some kin to Danny McKenney?"

Jesse shrugged. "I'm still new to these parts. I'm not even sure I know who this Danny fellow is."

"Jesus," Eli swore under his breath. His eyes darted to Beacon. "Sorry, Pastor."

William Beacon's eyes expressed their usual astonishment. "If you'll have a seat, Eli, and give me a moment, I can explain. Your friend there, too. I do not care for people hovering."

Jesse murmured an apology and dropped into a chair more quickly than Eli.

Beacon turned the ledger so the entries were facing him. He waited for Eli to sit before he began. "This is my writing. My wife despairs of my penmanship, but then she does not have to read my sermons, only listen to them." He placed his finger beside the name that Eli had meant to abuse with his anger. "Here. This is Court, not Cord, and McKenna, not McKenney. Does that help?"

"Not a whit. Who is he?"

"I'm not sure I understand the question. He is Mr. McKenna. Miss Wilhelmina's husband."

"And I'm sure you understand a lot more than that. Where did he come from?"

"I performed a ceremony, Eli, not an investigation."

Eli felt heat rising in his face. He was damned if he was going to allow the bug-eyed Beacon to get the better of him, but belligerence still ran through his tone. "So where did you perform this ceremony?"

"At the Pancake homestead." Beacon held Eli's suspicious stare. "You were expecting another answer, I take it."

"Maybe." He'd hoped Willa and her intended had traveled to Lansing, been seen by other folks. He did not trust Beacon to give a good accounting of what transpired. Even a man of God could be a liar. "So you must have been there awhile, enough time to learn something about this Mr. McKenna."

"I think it's been a while since you've been to a wedding. Even in church, it doesn't take long."

Eli pointed to the book. "But it was all legal?"

"Oh, yes. I took all the proper papers. It's documented in the courthouse now, if you're interested. Of course, that'd be a ways to go on horseback since the train isn't running yet. I confess I'm surprised you made it here from Big Bar. I would have supposed the snow would have prevented that."

"We came from Jupiter."

"Still, a difficult journey. I understand your interest, given the number of times you asked after Willa's hand, but wouldn't it have been easier to simply inquire at the valley?"

Eli's chair scraped the floor as he thrust it backward and jumped to his feet. "We're done here," he said. "C'mon, Jesse. We have a name. That's what we came for."

Jesse stood, started to follow, then held up his hand. "I'll be right along. There's something I want to ask the pastor now that I'm here." He shifted back and forth on his feet when Eli hesitated. "It's kinda personal. Do you mind?"

Eli released a long sigh full of suffering. "Do what you need to do. I'll be outside."

Jesse waited until the door closed before he turned to Beacon. "It's not about my salvation, if that's what you were thinking, but it is personal." When the pastor merely turned over his hand, inviting him to continue, Jesse did. "This is just between you and me, right? Eli won't know what we discussed?"

"Not a word."

Jesse stood behind the chair he had been sitting in and braced his arms on the curved walnut rail. "I got my reasons for needing to know what this Israel McKenna looks like. If he's who I think he is, then I'm honor bound to tell Eli. It could be real important. I swear to you that Eli would kill me if I didn't say something, but I got to be sure. It's a man's reputation we're talking about."

"I don't think you have any reason to be concerned. He was a likable fellow and welcomed by all of them."

"Humor me, please," said Jesse. "If he is who I think he is, it's what makes him likable that makes him dangerous."

Beacon rubbed his chin and looked Jesse Snow up and down. The cowboy stayed still for it, but his eyes were restless. "Why don't you describe him to me, and then we'll see where we are?"

"All right. I guess I have to say right off that he's a good-lookin' fella. I don't know anyone who ever had a different opinion. He's got maybe an inch on me, so you know he's tall. Dark hair, dark enough that you could mistake it for black, especially since he's got these little silver wings at his temples."

"Silver wings?"

Jesse's eyes narrowed in response to the pastor's becoming fractionally wider. "That's right. But I got the feeling you know what I'm talkin' about. Silver threads." He straightened, pointed to one of his temples. "Right here." He paused, but Beacon said nothing. "Fair-skinned, though I'd wager that's changed some since I saw him last on account of him working the ranch."

"I never said he was working the ranch."

Jesse had relaxed enough to chuckle. "I'm not acquainted

with the Pancakes, but nothing I ever heard about them makes me think they'd welcome someone into their fold who doesn't know ranching."

Beacon did not confirm that one way or the other.

"If none of that seems familiar," said Jesse, "that's only because I ain't got around to telling you about his eyes. He's got these uncommonly colored blue-gray sparklers that'd pierce you as soon as look you over. It's a fact that women warm to him right off because he's got those eyes. There's no doubt in my mind that Miss Pancake did the same, but I'd be careful about concluding that she did all those other women one better by snaring him. If McKay was snared, then it—"

"McKenna," said Beacon.

Jesse looked at him blankly. "How's that again?"

"You called him McKay. It's McKenna."

"Right. A rose by any other name. Is that how it goes? I'm right about him, aren't I?"

"I don't know if you are right about him, but the description fits."

Jesse took a deep breath, nodded, and let that breath ease out of him. "Thank you, Pastor. That's all I needed to know. You can trust I'll make sure McKay's wife comes to no trouble because of him."

William Beacon stared at the closed door. "McKenna," he said as if Jesse were still in the room. "His name is McKenna."

Israel demonstrated the correct fingering for "Beautiful Dreamer" while Annalea followed every key strike with rapt attention. "I'll write down the notes for you. You have a good ear, but you should learn to read music." The sheet music Evie Pancake left behind had been printed on cheap paper and was yellow with age and rough-edged from turning the pages. Annalea was loath to touch it for fear of destroying it altogether. Early on, Israel had found a hymnal in the piano bench, but Annalea did not have much interest in learning those pieces, although she liked them well enough when he played them for her.

He stopped playing and they both looked up when Willa came in. He merely raised his eyebrows to pose the question. Annalea was the one who gave voice to it.

"Is he back?" she asked. "Zach's here?"

"He is." She removed her gloves, coat, and hat and placed them over the arm of the sofa to deal with later. "I just came from the bunkhouse. I'd hoped you would have started dinner, Annalea." She looked past Annalea to Israel. "And I thought you would be helping."

"Music sustains the soul," he said.

Willa ignored the mischief stirring in his blue-gray eyes. "Maybe so, but you need stew and a loaf of bread to sustain the stomach."

"She has a point, Annalea." He gave her a gentle shove to move her off the bench. "You start. I'll be in to help."

"I know what's going on," she said, standing. "A tick gets removed with more care for its feelings."

"No, it doesn't," said Willa. She swatted Annalea on the fanny as she passed. "But I'll keep that in mind the next time I am plucking one out of your scalp." When she was certain Annalea was out of hearing, she joined Israel on the bench. "Zach delivered the invitation, but he had to give it to Buster Rawlins. Buster wouldn't allow him to go to the house, but I have confidence that he will deliver the invitation."

"What about Eli?"

"Buster said he was in Jupiter collecting contracts for Malcolm. He'll do what Mal tells him to do."

"So Zach didn't stay for Malcolm's answer."

"No. We'll have to wait on that. Zach did stay long enough, however, to inquire after Samuel Easterbrook. Seems there is no such person working at Big Bar, at least no such person using that name."

"Ah."

"Zach shrugged it off, made out like he could have the name wrong since Easterbrook owed him money, and what man volunteers his proper name when he owes money to a stranger. Buster didn't blink, so I think Zach left no suspicions behind. Zach also asked if they'd been having trouble with rustlers at Big Bar. He told him we were experiencing some."

"All their horses are accounted for?"

"They are. Whatever else Easterbrook is, he is not a horse thief."

"Huh. I'd comment on the man's peculiar scruples, but that's better left in the hands of someone in a position to cast stones. I'm supposing that since Zach's only getting back now, he did manage to get into Jupiter. Did he cross paths with Eli there?"

"No. As a matter of fact, he didn't. He didn't speak to the Cuttlewhites either." One of Israel's hands still rested on the keys and now he depressed them in a dark minor chord. She laid a hand on his to keep him from playing it again. "He spoke to Noah Cuttlewhite. That's their son. He met up with Noah in the saloon, got to talking about this and that, and realized he didn't need to take it a step further. Noah knew everything his parents did, or rather, everything we wanted to know."

She removed her hand. "There *was* a rolling poker game on the train. It began long before the Cuttlewhites boarded in Denver, but they told Noah that they were hurried through the car where it was taking place, so they had only a brief look at the players. I think the pot received most of their attention because Noah described it as big as a platter and piled as high as a turkey. In spite of that, they also saw someone they recognized."

"Then it wasn't me."

"No. It was Eli Barber." Willa could not recall that she had ever seen Israel confounded, but that was the expression he turned on her. "That's right. You were playing at the same table with Eli. Israel, you might still harbor doubts, but I don't. You were in that game because of Eli. Everything Eli knows, he learned at the feet of his father. Malcolm tried to take the valley from Happy by besting him at cards, and I believe the folks who say he cheated to get what he thought would be a winning hand. Eli would do exactly the same. I think you observed him cheating and joined the game to even the odds for everyone."

"I don't know that my motives would have been as high-minded as that, but you're right, I could have easily decided to join a game like that."

"Good. That is settled more easily than I had dared hope. As for the rest, Noah said his parents thought the game ended in Lansing, not Jupiter."

"So Eli might have left the train early. Why would he do that?"

"Because he lost. That's what I think. He wasn't ready to go home." Willa's fingers wandered over the keys without pressing any one of them deeply enough to make a sound. "There's something else, Israel. Noah told Zach that he had almost the same conversation with Eli only a day earlier. Not only did Eli not deny that he was part of the game, he asked Noah if his parents recognized anyone else at the table. It could be argued that he was concerned they saw you later in town."

"A lot of things could be argued, but we'll stay with that. Did Eli share any particulars about the game, perhaps who won? Who lost?"

"I had the same question, but no, Eli didn't say. Noah admitted that he had not thought to ask as he was caught up in a game with Eli, Danny McKenney, and Paul Beetleman at the time. That means something to me, Israel. It means I'm right about Eli losing. He is not a noisy braggart when he wins, but somehow he always manages to let people know nonetheless. And when he loses? Not a word of it. Ever. That's why he didn't speak up. He lost, Israel, and you won. Everything on that table when the Cuttlewhites passed through, and more besides, was what was in the second case." She shook her head, chuckling lightly. "Maybe your winnings filled both cases. You might have had to throw your clothes out."

"It's hard to imagine pitching them was any kind of loss. Judging by what I was wearing when I walked into the Viceroy, it doesn't seem I bought anything in Chicago suitable for working on my brother's ranch."

Willa leaned over and bussed him on the cheek. When she came away, she was smiling. "I thought the very same thing."

Chapter Twenty-six

"Is that you, Eli?" Malcolm bellowed when he heard the back door open. "Get in here and bring those contracts with you. I want to see them first, and then you and I are going to discuss a few things."

Eli handed his outerwear to the cook and took the contracts folder to his father. Malcolm was behind the desk in his study, several ledgers open in front of him. Eli stood opposite and waited for him to put his hand out or indicate where he wanted the folder.

"Right here," said Malcolm, jabbing at one of the pages of a ledger.

Eli put down the folder. "I'm going to clean up for dinner."

"Sit. This won't take long." He looked up and looked his son over. "I guess you've been wearing those clothes the whole time you were gone."

"Yes, sir, and I am itching to get out of them."

Malcolm was unsympathetic. He pointed to the chair, opened the folder, and read through the contracts for unacceptable changes. The task required half the time he took for it, the main purpose being to make Eli squirm.

"It appears to be all in good order," he said, pushing the contracts and ledgers aside and folding his hands together on top of the space he had cleared. "You are slow in returning. Was there a problem?"

"Mother Nature."

"Hmm. I have something for you to read." He opened the middle drawer of his desk, withdrew Happy's invitation, and held it out. "I'll give you a moment."

Eli took it and read, and then read it again. "Do you take this seriously?"

"I do. I don't know why it's come to us now, but yes, I think it's a serious offer. Maybe Willa's marriage has something to do with it. The timing suggests it might."

"I don't—"

Malcolm interrupted. "Who the hell is Samuel Easterbrook, Eli?"

Eli blinked. "I don't know. Who the hell is he?"

"Zach Englewood delivered that invitation. Buster intercepted him before he got to the house and took it off his hands. Zach asked after someone named Samuel Easterbrook, said the man owed him money. Apparently the fellow told Zach he worked for us. Buster cleared that up, but it got me to thinking that this Easterbrook could have lied to Zach, or he could have lied to us."

"I never heard the name before. You want me to ask around the bunkhouse?"

"No. Buster will do that. I was wondering what you might know."

Eli shrugged. "You mind if I get a drink?" He returned the invitation to Malcolm's desk. "If I can't change my clothes just yet, a drink will serve to get my mind off what feels like a hair shirt."

Malcolm waved him to the decanters he kept on a side table. "I'm set on accepting the invitation, Eli. It's a chance to finally make peace with the Pancakes."

"If that's what you want."

"What I want is to have both ranches under a single brand."

"I don't see how that can happen now that Willa's married."

"You need to take the long view, Eli. Did you ever think how fine Wilhelmina would look in black?"

Calico stood beside Quill at the hotel's registration desk, looking around while he signed the ledger and took possession of the key. Two young men, identical in features, carriage, and attitude, stood at the foot of the staircase looking as if they meant to fight for the privilege of carrying her bag to the room. They were already elbowing each other in anticipation of Quill giving them permission.

"Boys," Mrs. Putty said, pointing two forked fingers at them. "Stop that. It's not a race."

Apparently it was, Calico thought, eyeing the twins up and down. She made a bet with herself that it would be the boy with the more pronounced cowlick who would win. He had a crafty edge. She turned around and slipped an arm through Quill's. Her yawn was so abrupt that she did not have time to cover it.

Mrs. Putty, diminutive in size and fussy in demeanor, was instantly sympathetic to her guest's fatigue. "Oh, you poor dear. Of course you are tired. It's late, isn't it? We rarely see folks coming in this time of the night, but I suppose we have to be grateful the train is running again. Are you hungry? I can—"

Quill interrupted. "Just the room. We had food with us on the train." He turned the ledger around and pushed it toward her then set the pen aside.

"Of course, Mr.—" Mrs. Putty absently reset a pin in the collapsing knot at the back of her head while she looked at the ledger. "Yes, I see it here. Mr. McKenna. Very good." She looked up, regarding Quill with more interest than she had shown upon his arrival. When she finished eyeing him, she made an equally thorough examination of Calico.

"Mr. and Mrs. McKenna," she said softly, more to herself than to them. "But no, you haven't been here before, have you?"

Quill and Calico exchanged cautious glances as Mrs. Putty thumbed back a page and ran a forefinger down the entries.

"Here it is," she said triumphantly. She leaned sideways to look around Quill and catch her boys' eyes. "You remember the McKennas, don't you? You carried water for their tub and she gave you good money for your trouble, then later, so did he." When they nodded, she straightened and pointed out the entry to her guests. "Right here. Mr. and Mrs. Israel McKenna. He must be kin of yours, Mr. McKenna. Look. There's a similarity in the way you each penned your surname. Lots of flourish in that 'M' and 'K.'"

Before Quill could reply, Mrs. Putty was going on again. "Strange, or maybe not so strange if you're related, that you have the look of him." Her eyes narrowed fractionally. "Except I'd have to say that he's definitely your darker self."

"Sounds about right," Calico said under her breath. Her comment brought Mrs. Putty's attention back to her and Calico wondered at her scrutiny.

Without any prompting from Calico, Mrs. Putty went on. "It's the oddest thing, dear, that you should be dressed like she was. Dressed in trousers, I mean. Like a man. You don't resemble her in any other regard, what with you having all that red hair and hers being almost as black as her husband's."

Quill finally found his voice. "You're certain they were married?"

"As certain as I can be without asking for proof."

From behind Quill and Calico, one of the boys spoke up, "She was wearing a wedding band, Ma. We saw it when she was leaving."

Mrs. Putty nodded. "Well, there you have it. She was wearing gloves when she came and went, so I didn't see it, but my boys were taken with her. Nothing surprising about them noticing."

Quill had to make a decision about what he could tell Mrs. Putty without her raising more questions than he wanted to answer. Beginning with a compliment seemed the best overture. "You have a very astute eye, Mrs. Putty, and an excellent recollection of detail. As it happens, Israel and I *are* kin. We haven't been in touch for a while, but the last I heard, he was living out this way. My wife and I were going to look him up, and since I'm learning that he's married, it seems we should arrive bearing gifts. I'm confident we'll be able to find something suitable to purchase in Lansing, but I'm wondering now if we'll find Israel and his wife here."

"Oh, I'm sure you won't. He doesn't live in town. Doesn't really live outside of it either. I'm thinking they went back to Pancake Valley." She speared her boys with sharp look. "Is that right, boys? Didn't you tell me she introduced herself to you as Willa Pancake?"

"That's right," the crafty one said, separating himself

from his brother. "I guess she forgot she was married. It seemed like it embarrassed her, 'cause she blushed real pretty like, and told us she was Mrs. McKenna."

Mrs. Putty leaned forward and spoke in confidential tones. "I told you the boys were taken with her. They sure did take their time filling that tub." She straightened and closed the ledger. "You're one stop away from Jupiter. That's the end of the line. Anyone there can tell you how to get to Pancake Valley. I've never been, but I know the Pancakes have a big spread. Make sure you don't get lost and end up at Big Bar looking for them. There is no love lost between those families. You don't have to be from Jupiter to know that."

Jesse Snow was stretched out on his bunk, head cradled in his palms, and considering his options when Buster kicked one bed leg hard enough to shake him out of his trance. "What the hell?"

"Get up," said Buster. "Get your coat and come with me."

Jesse pushed himself to his elbows. "I just got back. Can't it wait?"

"The way I hear it, you just got back from a week of plowing Mary Edith's lower forty."

"Three days."

"Four."

"I wasn't counting. There was nothing else to do in Jupiter." Aware that other men in the bunkhouse were taking note of this exchange, Jesse reluctantly rolled out of bed and got to his feet. "Give me a minute."

"We will talk in the barn." He jabbed a finger in Jesse's thin chest. "There is some shit that needs to be shoveled."

Jesse waited until Buster was gone before he shrugged. The gesture was meant to impress his bunkmates, but he wasn't sure it worked. He got dressed to go out, jammed his hat on his head, and went to meet Buster.

"Who the hell is Sam Easterbrook?"

Jesse blinked as much from the lantern that Buster held up in his face as from the question he put to him. "Hell if I know. Why are you asking me?"

"Because I already asked everyone else."

"And?"

"And I gotta feeling someone's lying to me. My money's on you."

"Well, you're gonna lose. Where did you hear the name, and why is it so important it's got your balls shriveled like raisins?"

Buster told him about Zach's visit.

"So?" asked Jesse. "He got something wrong."

"No." Buster shook his head vehemently. "He didn't. I know Zach. You don't. He was telling me something. He tried to make it seem as if he wasn't, but he was."

"Sounds complicated." Jesse jammed his hands in his pockets. "I don't get what you're saying." He suffered Buster's scrutiny by shifting his weight.

"Forget that for now. Tell me what Eli was up to in Jupiter."

"Wasn't much to get up to, and that's a fact. He picked up the contracts when they finally came in and played some cards. Didn't touch a whore to my knowledge, then again, I was occupied, and we know he prefers to take his girls in Denver."

"That's it? That's all you've got to say?" Buster returned the lantern to its hook, and when he faced Jesse again, his hands were clenched. "Are you sure?"

Jesse frowned. "I don't—"

Buster put one fist squarely in Jesse's gut, and when Jesse doubled over, the other fist connected with his jaw. "Don't lie to me," Buster said, shaking out his hands. "You can have a moment to catch your breath and think about what you want to say."

Jesse required that moment to suck in a breath. He couldn't think at all.

Buster said, "I'll help you. Before Eli dragged your ass to Jupiter on his father's business, he asked me to go with him. He wanted to find out what he could about the man Willa Pancake married. He's obsessed. Does any of that sound familiar?"

Jesse was forced to nod because he couldn't speak.

"So you helped him ask around?" When Jesse nodded

again, Buster said, "You were there a long time. You better have found out something worth knowing."

"Israel," Jesse said on a breath. "Israel McKenna." He rubbed his jaw and then worked it back and forth. He was still dazed by the double blows that Buster had delivered, but not so confused that he missed the other man's slow, satisfied exhale. "What is it? You look relieved."

"Do I? I suppose I am. It's been crossing my mind since I learned that Miss Willa took a husband that maybe she married Buck McKay. Now I know that wouldn't have crossed yours since you were given the task of disappearing that body, and you swore that you had."

"I did. I did just like I was told."

"Uh-huh. I wanted to believe that in the worst way, but you can appreciate that my experience with you got me to wondering. Do you think I don't know that you hide out at Monarch Lake when there's hard work to be done? You want me to tick off the number of things you were supposed to do that didn't get done unless someone was standing over you?"

"You make it sound like it's all the time. I work plenty and I work hard. And I guess what I did for Eli should count for something."

"That's what I figured you'd say. You might want to tread carefully there."

Since Eli had used almost those same words, Jesse recognized they were sincerely meant. He stared back at Buster. "I'm remembering you had a hand it."

"And I'm remembering it was after the fact. My mistake was not thinking Eli was serious when he proposed taking back what he lost. Your mistake was being too drunk to care. If I had gotten to the ridge in time, I would have put a stop to it. Eli knows it, and you damn well know it, too. But I didn't make it in time, and it happened, and that was that. All that was left was for you to clean up the mess you and Eli made of things. Given what was at stake, I didn't think I had to supervise you getting rid of the body, so I made sure Eli got home with his daddy's money. What would have served him right was for him to explain how he lost it all in a rolling poker game. I'd give both of my shriveled balls to never have run into Eli when he was hell-bent on revenge. That's a day you should rue as well. Push is coming to shove, Jesse, just see if it isn't."

Jesse would have thrust his chin out if it wouldn't have hurt so damn bad. "What's that mean?"

"It means that I just had it from Eli that the letter Zach brought over from the valley was an invitation. Seems Happy Pancake is askin' for a sit-down with him and Malcolm. Genuine peace talks about ending the feud, or so it seems. The best part is those talks are going to happen at the Pancake spread. Like I told you, it's a relief knowing Eli isn't going to run into Buck McKay."

Willa refreshed Israel's bath with hot water. Annalea had lingered a little too long in the tub, so the water had cooled considerably from the time Willa tucked her into bed and called to Israel that it was safe to come into the kitchen.

"Hey! Careful with that," he said when hot water from the kettle splashed his uncovered knees.

"Sorry." She proceeded with more caution after that. "When we build that extra bedroom in the spring, I'm thinking we should add a bathing room for privacy."

"I could have bathed in the bunkhouse."

"And where's the fun in that for me?" She managed to get out of his way before he splashed her, then she began to fill the kettle again from the pump. "What you do think about a bathing room? It wouldn't have to be fancy."

"Out of the draft would be good enough for me."

Willa set the kettle on the stove and went to make sure the back door was closed.

"I didn't say that for you to do something about it," he told her when she returned to the tub. "Sit down. Please. You should be in this bath right now, not me. You've got an edge on you so sharp I'm surprised you haven't cut yourself."

Willa sat. She rolled her neck and shoulders and kept her voice low in the event Annalea had crept out of bed and was trying to listen. "I thought I'd be relieved when Zach delivered the letter, but the waiting has been interminable. They could have replied by now, and I think it's intentionally cruel that they haven't. I keep wondering if they will set a date like Happy asked them to do, or if they'll just show up without warning."

"I know you're worried about Annalea."

"And you."

"Forget about me." He soaped his arms and shoulders and then stopped suddenly. "I smell lavender."

"Annalea wanted the scented salts. I'm sorry. I gave in."

"Well, then, as long as it was for Annalea." He grinned when Willa bent toward the tub and flicked water in his face. "What if you send Annalea with Cutter tomorrow morning? That way if the Barbers just show up, she'll be gone. You must have thought of it."

"I have. This feels different than when you and I left her to go to Lansing. She had Happy here, and while that might not have struck me as a good thing before you came here, it turned out fine for both of them. She had Zach and Cutter, too. You know she's sweet on Cutter?"

"I suspected. I don't think he realizes it, though."

"Oh, I know he doesn't. It'll pass and he'll look at her someday when she's full grown and wonder why he never noticed."

"Probably." He wrung out the sponge and tossed it to her. "You're still fidgeting. Come fidget with my back."

Willa threw the sponge at his head. It would have been more satisfying if he hadn't caught it. She made a face at him that was in keeping with her childish mood of the moment. When he merely grinned at her, she sighed and folded a towel, then knelt on it so she could wash his back. "You're going to do this for me."

"That is my current plan." He reached over his shoulder and brushed her hand with his fingertips. "About Annalea . . ." he said, and deliberately did not complete the thought.

"I'll speak to Cutter first thing in the morning. You can tell Annalea."

He groaned softly. "Do you spend time thinking of ways I can atone for past sins, or are you just naturally gifted?"

Chapter Twenty-seven

Malcolm and Eli Barber arrived in the middle of the afternoon the following day. Cutter had not yet returned from escorting Annalea and John Henry to his mother's. Willa's first concern when she saw the Barbers approaching was whether they had crossed paths with her daughter. The timing seemed slightly off for that to have happened, but the fact that she had to worry about it at all was added to her list of grievances against her guests.

Willa was halfway to the barn when she caught sight of the pair in her peripheral vision. She stopped, braced to face them, and called out for Happy, who was in the smokehouse. Her shout brought Zach out of the barn. His brisk stride allowed him to reach her side before her father loped over.

Willa turned her head a quarter to sniff the air around Happy. She did not even try to keep the disappointment out of her voice. "I smell whiskey. Did you have to? Did you?"

Happy shifted his weight unsteadily. "Eau de liquor. I always keep a bottle in the smokehouse. Heard you holler that they're coming, so I splashed myself a little and rinsed out my mouth. Don't you worry about me, Willa. I'm sober as a man at his own funeral, but those two expect something else."

Willa was not entirely sure she could believe him, but it was not a question she could entertain now. The Barbers had closed the distance separating them to fifty yards. "I thought for sure they'd bring Buster with them."

Out of the corner of his mouth, Zach said, "Wouldn't be at all surprised if he's somewhere around. Is Israel in the house?"

"Mm-hmm. He was going to follow me to the barn after he found his gloves. We think Annalea made off with them. She was full of spite and spittle this morning. Wanted no part of leaving."

There was only enough time for Zach to chuckle quietly before the Barbers were upon them.

Malcolm brought his mount to a halt and looked over all three members of the welcoming party before he touched the brim of his silver-banded Stetson and nodded to each of them in turn. His attention lingered on Happy. "Still at the bottle, are you? And here I thought negotiations such as you suggested would require some temperance." He shrugged, tossed his reins to Zach, and dismounted, landing lightly on his feet in spite of the breadth and height of him. "You remember my son?"

Happy listed sideways as he looked up at Eli. "Sure, I do. Been a while, hasn't it?"

Willa surreptitiously caught Happy by the sleeve of his coat and held on in the event he began to topple.

Happy did not wait for Eli to reply. He grinned toothily at Malcolm. "It's not escaped my notice that your boy is a whole lot prettier than you, Mal. That has to be his mother's doing. Or maybe it *is* his father's doing. Us men, we don't ever really know, do we?"

Malcolm glanced up at Eli. "That's the sort of thing I warned you about, Eli. No sense taking any part of it to heart. Better you think on how long it took Happy to work himself up to it, and you'll find it in you to pity him." He shifted his gaze to Willa, green eyes sharply boring into her. "I know this was your idea, Wilhelmina, so let us dispense with any pretense otherwise. We're here at your request. I confess to anticipating a more hospitable welcome."

Willa showed no reaction when Malcolm used her full name, but inside, her stomach roiled. "And I confess to anticipating the pleasure of your reply. We had no reason to expect you'd be here today."

Malcolm's head tilted to the side and he regarded her narrowly as if parsing her words for truth. "We sent a reply." Now he favored Eli with the same look he'd had for Willa.

Eli bore the scrutiny every bit as well but made no reply until Malcolm added, "Well? Didn't we?"

"I gave the reply to Jesse to carry."

"I guess we know what happened to that. It's with him wherever he's got himself off to." He turned to Willa. "Please accept my sincere apologies. Jesse Snow was not the person who should have been charged with delivering my answer, but perhaps you can forgive us for offering a young man the chance of redemption through hard work and a show of loyalty. I have only recently learned from my foreman that Jesse showed poor judgment in the past and may have had skirmishes with the law."

"Then he should have fit right in at Big Bar," Willa said, unmoved. "You're here now, so let's get to it. Eli, you want to get down off your high horse and join us in the front room. We'll get some food together, and Lord knows, you see we have drink, and we will behave in a civil manner just as if being in the same room did not make our skin crawl."

"Well put," said Malcolm. "Eli, give Zach here your reins."

Willa let go of Happy's sleeve and hoped he would not overplay the inebriated fool, if indeed he was playing at all. He hung back, and Malcolm fell into step beside her, asking after Cutter. The question surprised her. She had been expecting a query about her husband. "Cutter's on an errand."

"And your sister?" asked Malcolm. "I fully expected to see her."

"She wanted to go with Cutter."

"Hmm. I don't think I've seen her since I paid my respects when your mama died. What a sad little thing she was then." When Willa said nothing, he went on. "You, too."

Willa stood back and opened the kitchen door for him. "Go on," she said when he hesitated. "No one's there to bite you."

"No one? Where is your husband?"

"With Cutter. This is what happens when we have no reply. We go about our business."

"I suppose Eli and I are fortunate there is anyone around at all, though perhaps we could have depended on seeing Happy."

Inside, Willa took his hat, coat, and gloves, and pointed

out the direction of the front room while she waited for Eli to step inside. She put all of it, including her own outerwear, in Happy's arms when he stumbled in after Eli. "Join us when you've hung it up."

"Maybe I'll just toss it on your bed," he said. "Has to be easier."

"Whatever you like." She nodded to Eli to go ahead of her and managed not to steal a look back at her father. She suspected that he was counting on Israel being in one of the bedrooms and hoped he was right.

Eli passed up the sofa where his father was sitting in favor of the rocking chair. Willa, in an effort to honor her edict regarding civil behavior, did not yank him out of it. She chose the wide armchair instead and left Happy with the option of being the other bookend on the sofa or sitting on the piano bench.

"I'd rather hoped we could do this without guns. You see I am not carrying, but I understand if you want to keep yours."

Malcolm's smile was appreciative. "There's no one in here I want to shoot. Yet. You can have mine. Eli can do what he likes." He stood, removed his gun belt, and handed it to Willa. Eli remained seated.

Shrugging, as though indifferent to the choices they made, Willa placed Malcolm's gun belt on a table out of anyone's easy reach and then returned to her seat. She sat back and rested her forearms on the comfortably wide arms of the chair, her hands curled lightly over the curves. She had actually practiced sitting in just this fashion in anticipation of facing Malcolm and Eli. It was infinitely more difficult now.

"I don't know what is taking Happy so long," she said, "but as you noted earlier, Malcolm, this was my idea, not his. We may as well begin." She spoke directly to Malcolm while carefully watching Eli out of the corner of her eye. "We had a visitor here from Big Bar not long ago. It put the thought in my mind that we should discuss the way things are between us. I prefer that we speak directly as opposed to you sending one of your hands to nose around, whether it's up at Monarch Lake or here." She saw Eli push himself back in the rocker, but it was Malcolm dropping his guard enough for her to glimpse his confusion that interested her more. "Did I misunderstand something?" she asked guilelessly. "My husband and I were not here on the evening your man came by, so perhaps I don't have it quite right. His story was an odd one, full of misdirection and misinformation, but the one thing everyone agreed on was that he was riding a horse with the Big Bar brand." She pointed to her left shoulder. "Right here. Right where you like to brand your working horses."

It was Eli who spoke up. "Did he *say* he worked for us?"

"On the contrary, he said he was doing a favor for a friend. He wanted us to believe he had just come from your place after making the same inquiries of you and Mal that he put to my father, Zach, and Cutter."

"Well, then, the man's a liar," said Malcolm. "The only visitor we've had to Big Bar was your foreman Zach, and Buster headed him off before he reached the house."

Willa's attention was all for Eli now. "So what accounts for the horse he was riding?"

"Stolen," said Eli. "It'd have to be."

"Buster would know," said Malcolm. "It's troubling that he hasn't said a word about it."

"Perhaps because he *doesn't* know. Zach asked him when he delivered our invitation. He said there'd been no trouble with rustlers. All your horses are accounted for. Odd, don't you agree?"

"For God's sake, Wilhelmina, the man must have given you a name. Who the hell did he say he was?"

"Samuel Easterbrook." She watched Malcolm frown deeply and Eli only a little less so. It was difficult to gauge the sincerity of the expressions, as in her opinion, neither man owned an honest emotion. "Are you going to insist you don't know the name?"

Malcolm said, "I heard the name for the first time when I received your letter. I had it from Buster, who had it from Zach. It's clear now that what Zach presented was only a story, and I'm clear, too, on why he presented it, but being familiar with the name doesn't mean I'm familiar with the man. I would not know him if he presented himself here right now."

With impeccable timing and perfect obliviousness, Happy walked in carrying a tray with four cut glass tumblers surrounding a decanter of whiskey. "Everyone stop starin' like you expect me to drop this. I got more respect for good liquor than that. Plus, this was my mother's prized set of glasses from back East." He set the tray on the table beside Malcolm and began to pour. His hands only shook a little. While he passed out the glasses, each filled with two fingers of whiskey, Willa summarized what he had missed.

Happy squeezed himself into the corner of the couch opposite Malcolm. "So we've come to the place where somebody's lyin'. Imagine that. Didn't figure it for happenin' quite this fast. Good thing I decided to bring libation instead of sandwiches or you'd be knee deep in deception by now."

Malcolm grunted softly and raised his glass. He didn't drink immediately, studying Eli over the rim instead. "Tell them, Eli. Tell them what you told me when I asked you."

"I never heard the name 'Samuel Easterbrook' before my father asked me about him. No one by that name works for us. I believe Buster told Zach the same thing."

Willa sighed. "I think we've all figured out by now that he doesn't work for you *by that name*. Let's see if you can't think of another he might go by."

Malcolm's fingertips whitened on his glass. "This isn't what I came for, Wilhelmina, and I don't have the patience for you to get around to where I think you're going. I'm here to discuss water rights. You said you were willing to revisit the terms you laid out for my father a couple of years before he died. That's why I came."

Willa's eyes never wavered from his. She refused to blink. Her mouth curved into the mere suggestion of a knowing smile. "I know exactly why you're here, Malcolm, and it isn't because you want my water."

Happy cleared his throat. It sounded as if he were moving gravel. He moved the conversation back to the point. "What Willa's tryin' to say is that we need to play an open hand here. Put our cards on the table and see what's what. Can't be anything up a sleeve, now can there? Eli? You square with that?"

"Of course." Eli raised one sandy-colored eyebrow a

fraction and kept his green eyes narrowly fixed on Happy's rheumy ones. "I am all for a fair and honest game."

"You sure don't take after your father there."

Malcolm growled at the back of his throat. "Dammit, Shadrach, you won that game. How long are you going to keep holding it over me and acting like you didn't?"

"You call me Shadrach again, and I reckon you won't live long enough to find out."

Willa spared a look for Eli, only to discover he was already looking at her. For the briefest of moments she truly believed they shared secretive, knowing smiles at the foibles of their fathers, and that both of them were transported back to the time when they had first pledged their futures to each other at the barbed wire fence line.

Their gazes slipped away. Willa could not say how Eli would remember that moment, or even if he would, but for her, it was a bittersweet memory of youth and she promised to recall it in just that way. It would not, however, stop her from doing what needed to be done.

She set down her drink and raised both hands, pushing them toward the combatants. "Stop. The pair of you, just stop. Happy, if you cannot manage to keep from speaking out of the side your mouth, you might as well go make those sandwiches. And, Malcolm, if you cannot keep from snapping at the bait, maybe you should go to the kitchen and help him. Eli and I will conduct business on our own."

"Over my dead body," said Happy.

"Over my dead body," said Malcolm.

Willa nodded, her smile perfectly sanguine. "Eli. You heard them. If this takes another turn, shoot them." She ignored the rumblings from the couch and continued. "If we are agreed then that we are playing our cards openly, I want to revisit the identity of Samuel Easterbrook. Happy, why don't you tell them what the man looked like? Maybe that will loosen a thread of memory."

Happy told them what he recalled.

Malcolm shook his head. "That could be anybody."

"No," said Willa. "It couldn't. It couldn't be Buster, for instance. He's too short, too square. Easterbrook is a little rangy, loose-limbed, like our Cutter. Don't you still have a cowboy working for you named Hammond?"

"Sure," said Eli. "But he's a colored fellow."

"That's what I recall, too. See, it can't be him either. You better keep thinking."

Malcolm said, "Well, I guess it fits Jesse Snow better than anyone. He'd be the youngest hand working the ranch. Doesn't make a lick of sense why he'd come to you with any kind of story. I never needed to ask anyone to poke around here when I could find whatever I wanted to know by just asking in town."

"That's you, Malcolm. I don't know if Eli can say the same." She picked up her drink again. "Can you, Eli?"

"This is a little bit ridiculous," he said.

Everyone stared at him.

"Why would I—" He stopped, pushed back in his chair without rocking it, and began again. "Very well. It must have been Jesse. I don't know anything about Samuel Easterbrook or why Jesse felt he had to use a name other than his own, but I sent him here because of you, Willa."

"Me?"

"I heard you finally accepted some man's proposal. I didn't think I would be welcome, so I asked Jesse to come in my stead and relay my best wishes. That was it. He told me that's what he did, although he did say that you and your husband were not here. I figured it for a missed opportunity and didn't think any more of it."

"Hmm. If that's all it was, why not say so right off when I told you we had a visitor?"

Eli shrugged. "A man's embarrassment can tie his tongue, can't it?"

"I suppose. Are you sure that all he was supposed to do was pass on your congratulations?"

"I'm sure."

Still curious, Willa rubbed the hollow behind her ear with the back of her fingers while she continued to frown. "Happy? What was the name of the man Easterbrook said he was looking for?"

"Give me a moment. It'll come to me." He sipped his

drink as if it could supply inspiration. His eyebrows climbed his forehead and he smiled widely. "Buck McKay."

Eli's drink sloshed over the rim of his tumbler as his arm jerked.

Willa pounced. "You know that name, Eli?"

"What is she talking about, son?" asked Malcolm. "Who is Buck McKay? For God's sake, don't tell me he's working for us, too."

"He doesn't," said Willa. She stood and walked to the archway. Israel was waiting patiently in the hall, his shoulder braced against the wall, his arms crossed casually in front of him. Like Eli, he was wearing a gun belt. Unlike their guest, he was grinning. "You heard?"

Israel pulled his spectacles down from where they were resting on top of his head and settled them on his nose. "Everything."

Willa stared at his extraordinarily colored blue-gray eyes through the lenses, shook her head, and said under her breath, "It's indecent how handsome you look in those." She could only shake her head again, helplessly this time, when surprise made him blink. "You better follow me now."

Composed again, Willa stepped back into the front room and then to the side to make space for Israel. Before she began proper introductions, Eli was on his feet. Willa could only imagine what was going through his mind, but at least he retained enough sense to keep his hand away from his gun.

"Sit down, Eli. Please."

Eli took a step backward, retreating in the direction of the fireplace, not the rocking chair. He might have kept on going if Malcolm had not barked at him to sit. As if pierced, Eli deflated from the puffed-up balloon he had been and was fortunate to get the rocker under him before he completely collapsed.

Eli was no sooner down than Malcolm was on his feet. "Someone damn well better tell me what's going on. Is this your husband, Wilhelmina?"

Israel did not wait for her to answer. Pretending that Malcolm coming to his feet was an introductory gesture and not a gauntlet being thrown, he walked over and held out his hand. He waited for Malcolm to take it before he spoke. "You must be Malcolm Barber," he said. "You can imagine I've heard quite a lot about you and Big Bar. I am Israel McKenna." Off to the side, he heard Eli emit a soft, somewhat despairing groan. He released Malcolm's hand but did not step back yet. "As you might suspect, Mr. Barber, your son and I are already acquainted."

Malcolm had a sharp glance for Eli. "Is he speaking the truth, Eli? Do you know him?"

Eli's fingertips whitened where they gripped the arms of the rocker. "The last I saw him, he told me his name was Buck McKay. Jesse knew him by that name, too."

Malcolm's eyes darted between Eli and Israel. His frown folded his broad forehead into deep furrows. When he finally spoke, it was Willa that he addressed. "You told me your husband was with Cutter. Was that a lie?"

"It was," she said unapologetically.

"And that's your idea of putting your cards on the table? You begin with a lie?"

"It was my opening bid, yes. And Israel here is my final one. Eli can tell you everything you want to know, or you can have it from Israel, but you really do need to hear one of them out. Now."

Israel returned to Willa's side and waited for Malcolm to decide who the storyteller would be.

Happy ventured into the heavy silence by rising from the sofa on very steady feet and going to the tray that held the whiskey. With a hand that never trembled, he gave Malcolm a generous pour and splashed some in his own glass before he set the decanter down. He looked sideways at Willa and winked.

"You're not drunk," said Malcolm. His tone was less accusing than it was resigned.

Happy shrugged. "I might lay myself out later once we resolve this business. That'd be a reason to celebrate. But now, I'm itchin' to hear what Eli's got to say for himself."

Willa admired her father's intervention. Prompting Malcolm to take one direction was the surest way to push him in the other.

Malcolm thrust his chin at Israel. "I want to hear from you." He did not return to the sofa but chose the armchair where Willa had previously been sitting. That vantage point gave him a good view of all parties.

Israel said, "I met Eli after the train I was taking from Chicago took on more cars and passengers in Saint Louis. There was a poker game going on in one of the cars, and I stopped to watch even though I only meant to pass through. Eli was doing well. He lost some hands now and again, as I recall, but he always came back. It was hard not to admire that skill, so I stayed around. There were some others that did, too. Some men left the game and others joined. Eli stayed. I observed until I figured out his game, and then I got in."

"What do you mean, you figured out his game?" asked Malcolm.

Israel had no memory of doing any such thing on that train, but he knew his habits on the riverboats and doubted he had deviated from what worked so well in the past. He had also been keeping an eye on Eli's expression as he spoke and while Eli's fine features had finally settled into one of credible calm, he had very little color in his complexion and the faintest tic at the corner of his left eye. Israel was confident that he had not misspoken yet.

"Your son cheats," said Israel. "And not badly. Not badly at all. I'm sure that's the reason no one called him out."

Eli sat forward in the rocker. "That's a goddamn lie."

"Well, I'm not surprised you'd say that, but I had hoped you could appreciate the compliment. You were good."

"You know damn well that you were the one cheating. You're the card sharp."

"I've been called that before, so I've learned not to take offense, but I have to tell you that you're wrong. I don't cheat. Part of learning your game is figuring how I can best you without using tricks like dealing from the bottom or holding back a card or playing with a marked deck. You cheated indiscriminately, taking money from everyone. In my eyes, at least, I played a much fairer game, taking most of my winnings from you."

Israel tracked Eli's every movement from the rise and

fall of his breathing to the subtle contraction of his fingers on the arms of the rocker.

"You remember me telling you that, don't you? Or some version of it. I told you all of it when you demanded your money back, and I think you knew then that I was speaking the truth. You simply didn't want to hear that I'd won fairly, or maybe you couldn't hear it. I don't think I mistook your desperation to have your losses returned."

Malcolm was looking at his son now. "How much did you lose, Eli?"

"Nothing," said Eli.

Israel chuckled flatly. "He's not lying, Mr. Barber. I guess since he stole it all back from me, he didn't lose a penny."

"But he says you cheated. He was in the right."

"See? That is where we have a difference of opinion."

Malcolm asked Israel, "How much did you win?"

"I can't give you a precise figure. I never really had a chance to count it, but it filled a bag about so big. Almost all of it came from your son." He caught the faint narrowing of Eli's eyes and adjusted the spread of his hands to make the bag bigger.

Malcolm clutched his glass but spoke without inflection. "You are mistaken, Mr. McKenna. Eli has never had that kind of money to lose."

Happy slapped his knee. "That's exactly the answer I expected from you, Mal. Can't you disappoint me just once?"

"Happy," Willa said gently. "Allow me, please." When her father offered his reluctant nod, she continued. "No one truly thought you'd say anything else, Mal. How can you when we all know the money Eli was carrying was really yours? It's hard to believe that he didn't accept a check for whatever business he transacted for you in Saint Louis, but that's hubris for you. I'm only supposing here, you understand, but it makes sense to me that Eli would want to put all that money at your feet, so to speak, just to prove he was worthy of your trust. Does that sound about right?"

Malcolm said nothing.

"What about you, Eli? Sound right to you?" Her stare dropped to his twitchy fingers. "Oh, for God's sake, Eli.

Don't go for your gun. That will not end well. We're going to settle this real easy."

Eli was immediately suspicious. "How's that?"

"Well, as long as your father is willing to put up what you stole from Israel, and you agree to the terms, then it'll be cards."

"Now why would I want to play poker with him?" asked Eli. "I already told you he's a sharp. The game will be fixed."

"On behalf of my husband, it's hard not to take offense to that, but I'm going to let it pass because I know what's at stake for you. There will be no poker. High card draw, one draw each. If you draw high, that means your father gets to keep every penny of his that you lost to Israel, and for you it means that we won't tell him exactly what you did to steal it back. You think about that, because there's plenty that hasn't been said and you know it."

"Maybe I want to hear it anyway," said Malcolm.

Happy shook his head. "No. You don't. It's a sorry story."

Malcolm asked Willa, "Why should I put up my money? My son says he took back what he was cheated out of. He should have called your husband out."

"We could debate that until spring and still not have a clear winner, but if you don't put up the money and sign a paper that says you did, then we're going to the sheriff and Eli's going to jail. I'm not promising that it won't happen regardless, but it's a guarantee if you don't stay and play."

Malcolm snorted. He stood and walked over to the fireplace. For a few moments, he toyed with the iron poker and was still holding it when he turned around. "Listen to me, Wilhelmina. Brandywine is not going to put my son in jail for stealing. Your husband's word carries no weight around here, and you weren't with him on that train or I'd have heard about it."

"Put up the money," Eli said suddenly. "I'll play."

"You're still real easy with someone else's money, son, just like you were on that train. I don't like the fact that you had a card sharp at your table, but I like it even less that you played with my money. I'll put up the money, Eli, but I will be drawing the card, not you."

Eli's jaw clenched and unclenched. "Willa mentioned

hubris," he said tautly. "I guess everyone here sees how deeply it's rooted in the Barber tree."

Willa covered her mouth with her hand when Malcolm took a step toward Eli as if he meant to strike him with the poker. She did not know what stopped him where he stood or what stayed his hand, but she was grateful for it until she caught sight of the murderous look in Eli's eyes. That was when comprehension took her breath away. She was staring at a man who could surely kill his father.

Malcolm said, "Where do we do this? Here?"

"Yes." Willa lifted the lid on the piano bench and produced a document and a pen. "I prepared this in anticipation that we would come to an agreement. It only requires that Eli's name be changed to yours as the person who will draw the card, and then both of you will sign it."

Israel took the paper and pen from her and carried them to Malcolm. He waited without speaking as Malcolm read the agreement and then asked for the pen. Laying the document on the mantelpiece, he struck out Eli's name, added his, and then signed it. Israel took it to Eli, gave him the same courtesy of time, and when it was done, he turned it over to Happy for safekeeping.

Happy nodded, satisfied, and stood. "I'll get the cards."

"I'll want to look them over," Malcolm said.

"Fine by me," Happy called back, heading into the hall. "Brand-new deck. Never been opened. Gift from my daughter when she was up Lansing way." He continued to talk but his voice was less clear as he got farther away and then disappeared entirely after the back door opened and closed.

"Where the hell is he going?" asked Malcolm.

Israel shrugged. "The cards must be in the bunkhouse."

Malcolm swore under his breath, more in disbelief than frustration. "You had a document all prepared in spite of the fact that you say you weren't expecting us today, but you didn't think to keep the cards here? Seems a bit shortsighted of you." He thought about it a moment, and before Willa responded, he was chuckling. "Right. You put Happy in charge of making sure the cards were around."

"Why do you think that's funny, Father?" asked Eli.

"You've been laughing at Happy Pancake for years without any good reason that I could ever figure. He bested you at cards once, and you still laugh at him as if he's no account. He bested *you*, yet you always puff up like you got the better of him." He turned sharply to Willa. "And you, arranging all this so you could rub my nose in it in front of *him*." He jerked his head sideways to indicate Malcolm. "You didn't have to bring him. We could have come to terms without him."

Willa remained calm; she spoke quietly. Eli's agitation was palpable and it scraped against her composure like sandpaper. "You were not in a position to play for money once we realized it was always your father's, and frankly, we didn't know the extent of Malcolm's involvement in what happened afterward."

Eli sharpened his look on Israel. "You know damn well he wasn't there."

Israel was tempted to say that he was only one hundred percent sure of it now that Eli had given it away. "True, but that doesn't mean you were not acting at his direction."

Eli came halfway out of his chair at that. "What? You don't believe I can think for myself?"

"Shut up, Eli," said Malcolm. "And sit back down. Even I am wondering if you can think."

Those words did not push Eli back. They brought him to his feet, and rather than turning his malevolent stare on his father, he impaled Willa with it. "This is your fault. You want to shame me. You have for years, always with your high and mighty airs, looking down on me, looking down, in fact, on every man who asked after you. I don't know what I did to deserve your enmity, but I can return the shame you visited on me tenfold, Willa."

Willa realized she was no longer in control of any part of these proceedings and that she wouldn't be as long as Eli was talking out of his head.

"You probably need to stop talking now," said Israel. "Seems as if it would be good for everyone if you did."

But Eli was not finished. "You'll want to hear what I have to say since you took on this family when you wedded and bedded Willa."

"Oh, I know I don't want to hear it," said Israel. He took a half step forward, not to menace Eli, but to protectively shelter Willa with his shoulder.

"Eli," said Malcolm. He tapped the poker against the floor. "Stop."

Eli shook his head. "You'll want to hear this, too. You really will." He raised his hands helplessly as he turned back to Willa. "Not every hour that I spent in Saint Louis was devoted to Big Bar business. I had time to look into something that has always tickled my curiosity. Don't bother pretending you don't know what I'm talking about. That's beneath you. Let me tell you right off that the doors of the Margaret Lowe School are still open, and I guess you know firsthand what kind of schooling goes on there since it was where your parents boarded you. From what I could see, there is still a great need for their charity." He shook his head in a parody of pity. "So many girls, and so many of them hardly more than children themselves. It broke my heart, but then I saw the necessity of a place like that. It struck me as a kind of sanctuary for young women who got themselves in trouble. At the very least, it removed them from their own society for a while."

Willa's stomach curdled and she tasted acid at the back of her throat. Her fingers curled surreptitiously in the sleeve of Israel's shirt. She thought she might throw up.

"That's enough, Eli," said Israel.

Willa tugged on his sleeve and shook her head. "Please, Eli, you have no idea where this is going."

"Don't I? Still believe I can't think a thing through? It's like this, Willa. I *know* I never bedded you. Christ, we hardly knew how to kiss." Without looking at his father, he said, "You hear that, Malcolm? I never bedded her."

"You told me—"

Eli snarled at him. "You beat that confession out of me. I never touched her like that. Never. Tell him, Willa. Tell him!"

Israel answered for her. "It's true. She told me."

"But did she tell you the rest?" Eli asked. "When you realized your bride was no virgin, did she tell you the rest? Did she tell you how her daddy poked her, put his baby inside her, and then sent her away to a home for unwed mothers just like it was a school for fine ladies. Willa had no one sniffing after her skirts back then. It could only have been Happy or one of his ranch hands who stuck her, and my money's on her father."

Willa moaned. It was a pitiful, keening cry of grief for that thing that was dying inside her. She wondered if it were her soul. Her knees buckled. Israel caught her before she dropped to the floor and gently lowered her to the piano bench. He put his hand on her shoulder and held her steady.

Malcolm stared at Willa. His mouth hung open as he sucked in a breath. He shook his head as though to clear it, and then he took a single step toward her. "Is he right about the child? Is Annalea mine?"

Eli's head snapped up and then twisted around. "What?"

But Malcolm was paying no attention to his son. "Is it true, Wilhelmina? Is Annalea my daughter?"

Willa didn't speak, didn't say the words that she wanted him to hear, namely that Annalea would never be his daughter. Her silence, though, was not predicated on the fact that she couldn't find her voice. It was because Eli drew his gun and fired at Malcolm, and the sound of it was deafening.

She would have jumped to her feet then, but Israel was still holding her down with one hand and drawing on Eli with the other. Malcolm was on his knees, blood blossoming high on his chest, wounded but not, it seemed, gravely, while Eli stood with his arm extended, finger on the trigger, and every grim line on his face an indication that he meant to rectify that.

Malcolm put out his hands as though he could ward off the bullet. He had no experience appealing to his son, and his attempt to do so now came to nothing. Eli's finger tightened on the trigger.

Israel shot him.

Eli staggered backward and his shot went over Malcolm's head. He fired again and this bullet lodged in the ceiling. Israel dropped him where he stood.

Willa had no time to make sense of the tableau in front of her. Eli was sprawled on his back on the floor, blood pooling under his thigh and seeping through his jacket at the shoulder.

Was he dead? And then there was Malcolm, still on his knees, clutching his chest and howling, although it was impossible for her to determine what part of his wail was provoked by physical pain and what part was emotional anguish. Finally, there was Israel standing at her side, one hand holstering the Colt, the other still on her shoulder, though whether he was steadying her or himself was no longer clear.

The commotion at the back door effectively closed her mind to every other thing. She heard Happy coming at a run, throwing down curses like they were lighted sticks of dynamite. Zach followed, his heavy tread recognizable for its staccato step. Behind him were two more people whose footfalls were unfamiliar, but one of them spoke, and Willa could have sworn it was a woman's voice that she heard.

Happy barreled into the front room and stopped short of banging into the sofa. Zach held his ground better and moved in far enough to make room for the pair behind him. That couple halted in the archway and stood side by side, taking in the same scene that Willa had moments earlier.

Calico had no difficulty identifying her brother-in-law. The similarity in the brothers' features was remarkable, and only Israel's dark hair immediately distinguished him from Quill. "Is any of this your work?" she asked just as if she had known him for years.

And Israel, with no indication that he was at all surprised to see them, nodded and pointed to Eli.

Calico gently nudged her husband with an elbow. "Damn, Quill. I thought you said your brother couldn't shoot."

Chapter Twenty-eight

Eli Barber did not die. His father did.

When Willa realized there was a chance to save them, she sent Zach for the doctor while she and Israel worked together to stop Eli's bleeding. Happy gathered bandages, tweezers, needles, and thread, and every other item he thought they would need, including the whiskey. The bullet in Eli's thigh had missed the artery and passed through the meat of his leg. The shoulder wound was initially more concerning, but when they were able to examine it closely, they located the bullet and Israel was able to extract it. Eli's bleeding was profuse but not, as it turned out, deadly. No one present thought that Eli would be grateful for it.

Calico and Quill worked feverishly over Malcolm. While Eli's wounds were not catastrophic, the same was not true of his father. Although it was not immediately apparent, Malcolm was dying even as he was in the throes of pain for himself and his son. The angle of the bullet's entry put it on a course grazing Malcolm's shoulder and burying itself beside his heart. His cries stopped when one of his lungs collapsed. His heart kept pumping blood into his chest cavity, and the bruise appearing under his skin was a warning of inevitable death.

They made him as comfortable as possible and then got out of his way so he would have a clear line of sight to his son lying just beyond an arm's length reach. It was Calico, standing off to the side, who had the clearest view of Malcolm in his final moments, and she would tell Quill later that it was not the vision of Eli that Malcolm carried to his grave. It was the image of Willa.

Israel and Quill wrapped Malcolm's body in a sheet and carried him outside at Happy's request. Happy fired his shotgun in the air twice and hollered for Buster Rawlins, who he figured was somewhere around, waiting for Malcolm's direction. Quill was not so sure there would be a response to Happy's overture, but then someone appeared out of a cluster of pines a hundred yards beyond the barn and Quill became a believer.

"It's Malcolm," Happy told Buster, pointing to the shrouded corpse. "His horse is in the barn. You can get it, and one of us will help you with the body. Take him home."

"What about Eli?"

"In the house. We sent for the doc. We'll get him to the bunkhouse later, and he can stay there until he's fit enough to move. Just so you know, there's probably no chance of him going back to Big Bar. His daddy here, well, that's Eli's doing."

Buster nodded, regret etched deeply in his broad features.

Happy set his eyes on the rifle in Buster's scabbard. "Malcolm order you to snipe at Willa's husband? That'd be like him, but it doesn't mean I think it would be like you. So . . . would you have done it, Buster? Would you have made my little girl a widow?"

"Guess we'll never have to find out," said Buster. "I'll get Mr. Barber's horse now."

Inside the house, both women startled at the twin shotgun blasts. Calico was halfway to her feet to investigate the source when Willa shook her head and told her not to bother.

"That's Happy." A moment later they heard him shouting for Buster. Willa explained to her who Buster was and why Happy thought he was around.

Calico eyed Eli. "He's still breathing," she said, and then added in practical tones, "And since we've done all we can for now, come with me into the kitchen and I'll make you a cup of tea if you have any, or coffee if you don't." When Willa didn't move, Calico placed a hand over hers. "Come on. Your hands are shaking. Chamomile will calm that."

Hardly aware that Calico's hand had moved to her elbow

and was gently nudging her, Willa accompanied her sister-in-law into the kitchen. Her contribution to making the tea was to point out the pantry. She sat in a chair that Calico pulled out for her. "I am not usually so discomposed," she said quietly. "You are not meeting me at my best."

Calico's response was to chuckle. "Oh, Willa, it's in the nature of what I do that I rarely meet anyone at their best. True, I mostly tangle with varmints like the one in your front room, and they are a pitiful lot, but I think I can confide in you that my hands shake when I am confronting a quilting circle."

Willa regarded her suspiciously. "I don't believe that, but you're kind to say so." When Calico merely shrugged and began to add kindling to fire up the stove, Willa asked, "Are you really Calico Nash?"

"Calico McKenna now," she said. "I guess Israel didn't tell you."

"No, he didn't. Your name came up once. I don't quite remember the circumstance now, but he could have told me then, and he didn't."

"Your husband and I don't really know each other except through Quill. I never put eyes on him until today. Quill visited him in prison—" She stopped and looked back over her shoulder at Willa, her green eyes as wide as an owl's. "Lord, you know about that, don't you?"

"I know."

Calico blew out a relieved breath. "I couldn't tell from the disjointed explanation your father gave us when we intercepted him in the yard. Of necessity, introductions were brief, but he accepted that Quill was Israel's brother without question."

"I shouldn't wonder. The two of them, they're like kings on opposite sides of a chessboard. One white, one black. In every other way virtually identical."

"Mm." Calico finished filling the kettle from the pump and set it on the stove. "I was saying earlier that Quill visited Israel in prison, and I knew he didn't want me to go, so I didn't ask. My husband says his brother is a charming rascal who can sell wool to sheep."

Willa's slim smile appeared. "My husband says his brother is a saint who would shepherd those sheep to safety."

Calico laughed, shaking her head. "Quill is no saint, but is he right about Israel?"

"Actually, he might have underestimated his brother," said Willa. "Israel could persuade sheep to buy back the very wool he had just sheared from them." She waited for Calico's appreciative chuckle to fade away, and then she added with quiet intensity, "He simply chooses not to do it any longer."

Calico sat down and took one of Willa's hands in both of hers. "I'm glad. Quill will be, too."

Willa said, "It will take Quill some time to believe it. I know that. So does Israel. He was against involving his brother. He wanted to prove himself first, or at least uncover the truth first."

"Uncover it?" asked Calico.

"Yes. Oh, I see. You can't possibly know all of it. He doesn't recall anything about his journey here. We had to piece it together from a lot of different sources."

Willa found that summarizing the chronology of events for Calico helped her as well. As she neared the end, she felt a calm that owed nothing to the chamomile tea that Calico put in front of her and that she sipped from time to time. There was little she left unsaid, and the only detail of importance that she omitted was the exchange of words that goaded Eli to shoot his father. That secret now existed in a closed triangle connecting her and Israel and Eli. She hoped it would remain among them, as Eli would not want to claim Annalea as his sister or reveal to anyone that his father was a rapist.

Willa finished by asking, "How did you find us? Israel wrote to Quill but he did not tell him where he was."

"He wrote? We never received any correspondence from him. I suppose it will be waiting for us once we return to Eden." She was on the verge of saying more when the back door opened and Happy, Quill, and Israel walked in.

Willa smiled to herself as Happy strode in without pausing, while Quill and Israel both stomped snow and dried mud off their boots before they crossed the threshold into the kitchen.

"Buster took him away," said Happy without preamble. "How's Eli, and is there coffee?"

"Still breathing, and you'll have to make it," said Willa. She welcomed Israel's hands on her shoulders after he circled the table to get to her. He stood behind her and worked the knots in the back of her neck and across her shoulders. She nearly moaned aloud. She wasn't sure that she would have been embarrassed for anyone to hear her if she had. She lowered her head to give him better access to her nape.

To no one in particular, she said, "I should have told Zach to bring the sheriff. I wonder if he'll think of it on his own?"

When this was met by complete silence, she looked up and caught an exchange of glances that she could not interpret. Since all of them eventually ended at her husband, she knew he was part of whatever was going on.

"What?" she asked. "What don't I know that all of you do?"

"I only just now found out," Happy said, adding water to the coffeepot. "I guess your husband figured he had his reasons."

Israel's mouth flattened. "Thank you for that spirited defense, Happy."

Willa tipped her head back to look up at Israel. "You probably should tell me before someone else does."

"Yes, well, I did have my reasons. I was thinking . . . that is, it occurred to me that, um, I didn't want, or rather, I didn't know—"

Quill leaned a hip against the sink when Happy moved out of the way. He was grinning, and his eyes, so much like Israel's with their unique blue-gray cast, were thoroughly amused.

"Not such a smooth talker now, are you? 'Tongue-tied' is a word that comes to mind."

Calico shushed her husband. "Let him say it, Quill."

Israel started again, but the words did not come any easier the second time. Finally he gave up and looked at his brother. "Ah, hell, Quill. Just show her."

Willa dropped her head so she could see Quill. "I guess you better show me then." The words were barely out of her mouth when Quill began to unbutton his coat and peel back one side to reveal his jacket and the silver badge pinned to it.

Willa was familiar with Sheriff Brandywine's tin star, but this was different. The five points of this star filled the circumference of a silver circle, and even with the distance separating her from Quill, she could make out the words U.S. MARSHAL stamped in the arc above the star.

Willa ducked under Israel's hands and twisted around in her chair to see him better. "This is what you couldn't tell me about him? You didn't want me to know that your brother *is* the law?"

Israel backed up a step and put up his hands in a protective gesture. "It's embarrassing," he said, his gaze moving to Quill's and then back to Willa. "For both of us. All right. I'll give you that it's more embarrassing for him to be my brother than it is for me to be his, and that's why—"

"Don't say that," said Quill. "I've never been embarrassed to be your brother. Never. Frustrated. Confused. Annoyed. Those come immediately to mind. Now tell me what the hell you're talking about."

Israel lowered his hands to his sides. "I didn't want you here, not when I had no memory of what I'd done. The truth is, I'm tired of disappointing you, and if I had done something that was going to put me back in jail, I preferred that you were not the one taking me."

"Well, you didn't do anything wrong except disappear," said Quill, "and like it or not, I *am* your brother, and I damn well will be around."

"Are you two gonna tussle?" asked Happy. "'Cause I got coffee brewing and there's plenty of ways you can hurt yourselves in here. Better take it outside." He scratched behind his ear. "But wait for me. I'm gonna check on Eli first."

There was silence on his exit.

"Are we gonna tussle?" asked Quill.

Israel shook his head. "It's never come to that, has it? I don't suppose there's a good enough reason to start now." When Quill nodded in agreement, Israel's eyes darted to Willa. "Are *we* gonna tussle?"

"Later. And not outside."

Quill whooped with laughter. "There's no butter melting in that mouth, brother. You are in the kind of trouble that no one can get you out of."

Calico leaned over and swatted at her husband. "Does he look as if he wants help, Quill? Leave him be or we're gonna tussle, and you know I fight dirty."

Willa's attention was instantly arrested. Israel was similarly intrigued.

Quill pointed to them for Calico's sake. "Not in front of the newlyweds."

She chuckled, and then spoke to Israel. "Did Quill tell you how we tracked you down? I've already explained it to Willa."

"He did. Outside. I don't know why I thought I could hide from the two of you."

"It was insulting," said Calico.

"Uh-huh," said Quill. "And we could have been here yesterday if Calico could let a thing go, but she has an uncanny sense when it comes to names and faces that has a way of diverting us."

Willa frowned, puzzled. "What do you mean?"

Quill removed his coat and hung it up before he pulled up a chair beside his wife and sat. "We took the train from Lansing to Jupiter, rented horses at the livery, and got directions. We had ridden about two miles from—"

"Two and a quarter," said Calico.

"As I said, *about* two miles outside of Jupiter when we came across this fellow headed in the direction of town. I noticed Calico slowing her horse as he got closer, so I'm alert to the possibility of trouble. Then she pulls up and asks him for directions to Pancake Valley. Now I already told you that we had those from the livery owner, so there is another reason for me to pay attention. He was pleasant enough, happy to put us on the right path, and about a couple of minutes into the conversation—"

"Three minutes," said Calico.

Quill gave his wife an aggrieved look. "Oh, we *are* gonna tussle." When the ribbing that comment caused quieted, he said, "Three minutes into that conversation, she introduces herself as Calico Nash, which she only does when she forgets her last name is McKenna, or when she's about to take someone into custody. I was fairly sure which instance this was, and when she asked politely if the stranger's name was Jesse Snow and he bolted like his horse had been struck by lightning, I knew I had guessed correctly. Of course, I had to run him to ground because I won't let her ride hell-bent for leather when she's pregnant."

This last news seemed infinitely more important to Willa and Israel than anything about Jesse Snow, but after congratulatory sentiments and embraces were exchanged, the conversation returned to Mr. Snow.

Quill said, "I had to lasso him. His horse, a fine black gelding, ran right out from under him and the snow didn't cushion his fall much. He was no problem after that. We tied him up and put him back on his horse and escorted him to the sheriff's office. Brandywine hadn't been through the pile of wanted notices he had jammed in his desk for a long time, but because Calico insisted, he thumbed through them all. Twice. He found Jesse Snow the second time thanks to Calico's recollection that when he was working riverboats, he called himself—"

"Samuel Easterbrook," Willa and Israel said the name simultaneously.

"Mm-hmm." Quill turned over his hand, gesturing for Calico to finish.

"Jesse Snow is wanted for his part in a mail train robbery three years past in Cheyenne. I suppose he thought it was long enough ago and that he was far enough away from that branch of the U.P. that he could use his name around here. It's only because I was familiar with the poster that I knew about his thieving on the Mississippi. It was all petty crimes, pickpocketing, cutting purses from female patrons on the showboats, lifting jewelry. He was Easterbrook then; that might even be his real name. The connection between his river crimes and his railroad crimes probably came about because an accomplice who did not fare as well struck a deal."

Israel said, "So he really did know me from the riverboats."

"He probably observed you playing cards any number of times," said Willa. "And he's surely the one who tied you with that bowline."

"If I'd known about that," said Quill, "I would have dragged him for a piece behind my horse."

Willa asked Israel, "So do you think Jesse was running away?"

"Sounds right. Who do you suppose the third person was with Eli and Jesse on the ridge?"

"Buster," said Happy, reentering the kitchen. By way of explanation, he said, "I was lurking. Eli's still breathing, if anyone's interested. How's my coffee?" He went straight to the stove and sniffed the pot. "Damn near to burning, that's how it is." He pointed to the china cupboard and gestured to Quill to get him a cup. "It's just my gut telling me it was Buster, but unless Eli or Jesse says something, I don't expect we'll ever know the full story." He poured coffee into the cup Quill handed him and put the pot on the table. "I forgot about you, Israel. You could solve this. You remember anything now?"

"No. Except for knowing what happened to the pot of money I won, I don't care about the details."

"I expect Eli can be persuaded to help with that," said Happy. "If the money's not tucked away on the ranch somewhere, which I suspect it is not, then he can make a withdrawal on the Big Bar's account at the bank. Murderer or not, he's his father's heir."

"Do you have plans for the money, Israel?" asked Calico. "Quill thinks you do. In fact, he thinks he knows what you're going to do with it."

The smile Israel exchanged with his brother was appreciative on both ends. "I would not be at all surprised if he does." He looked at Willa, who was already watching, her dark eyes full of pride and her splendid mouth provocatively slanted as she smiled up at him. He took her hand. "You know?" he asked.

"Of course I know. You're my heart. Go on. You can say it out loud because we are going to make it happen."

"Those winnings . . ." Willa squeezed his hand and he

was able to move his voice past the constriction in his throat. "Those winnings are going to be distributed among every tent church congregation I stole from. It's not enough to pay them back in full, but it is a good beginning. That's what I have now. A good beginning."

Epilogue

It was five days before Eli could be moved from the bunkhouse to a jail cell, and another three days before he was persuaded to transfer the stolen poker winnings from the Big Bar account to one Israel and Willa set up specifically for reparations. Eli had lots of reasons why he did not want to do it, but at Israel's suggestion, Sheriff Brandywine threatened to put him in the same cell with Jesse Snow, and that decided him.

Calico and Quill left for Temptation and their Eden Ranch the next day. Willa and Calico had stood off to the side, watching the brothers say good-bye, and attempting to blink back tears with only marginal success. Looking on at the same exchange, and then at his daughter and Calico, Happy had grimaced. Everyone pretended not to notice that his eyes were damp.

Annalea returned to Pancake Valley after Eli was gone and in time to meet Quill and Calico. She changed her mind about becoming a card sharp and decided she would be a bounty hunter instead. After that, she spent a great many hours trying to sneak up on John Henry. The dog was so pitiful he mostly let her.

Willa sat curled on the sofa next to Israel, resting her head on his shoulder. He was still reading, but her book was lying closed on the floor. She did not look toward the fireplace, choosing to listen to the hiss and crackle of the flames instead. Israel had taught her how to hear the music that made the fire leap and dance, and sometimes she imagined she heard it when she was away from the house, but what she always saw when that music, or any music, wandered through her mind was Israel. She would observe him as if from a distance, sometimes at the piano or reading as he was doing now, or just as likely, sitting astride that beast Galahad as he prepared to ride out to some part of the ranch that required his attention. He drew her to him in those quiet moments, and always she heard the whisper of music in her ear.

"What do you suppose will become of Big Bar?" she asked.

Israel continued to read. "That's what you've been thinking about?"

"No. Not at all. But I'm thinking about it now."

"I suppose what happens depends on a jury finding for Eli's guilt or innocence, and if guilty, on what the judge determines is his punishment. If Eli goes to prison, he could put the ranch in Buster's hands until his release, but that could be a very long time, if ever."

"What if he's sentenced to hang?"

Eli closed the book, marking his place with his index finger. "What are you really concerned about?"

"I worry that he'll leave Big Bar to Annalea. I keep asking myself if he could be that cruel. There'd be talk. You know there would, and suspicion would not fall on Malcolm—I can be thankful for that, at least—but there would be speculation about Eli and me. People who knew my mother, people who can still recall that she gave birth to Annalea when she was visiting me, those people will begin to wonder and then they'll begin to whisper and eventually Annalea will get wind of it. I don't want that, Israel. She does not deserve that."

"Neither do you." He bent his head and kissed the top of hers. "We could buy the spread from him."

"We don't have that kind of money."

"Pancake Valley is your family's free and clear, isn't it?"

"Yes."

"Then I don't know a bank anywhere that wouldn't accept the valley as collateral against a loan for Big Bar. We could manage that, Willa. If Happy agrees, I'll ride in to see Eli tomorrow." Willa's head rose and fell when he shrugged modestly. "I think I can persuade him. Quill says I can sell wool to—"

Willa sat up, threw her arms around him, and kissed him hard on the mouth. "I know what Quill says," she whispered against his lips. "He's mostly right."

"Mostly?"

She repeated what she had told Calico.

Israel chuckled quietly. "Shearing sheep and selling them back their own wool. You think I'm that good?"

"No," she said, and claimed his mouth again. When she lifted her head, there was mischief in her eyes. "I think you can be that bad."

"Oh."

"Mm-hmm. Bad, but in a good way. You are a man of many interesting contradictions."

"Well, then, here's one for you. Do you recall asking what would tempt me to play a serious game of poker here?"

"Yes. And you told me there was nothing."

"I was wrong. There *is* something."

Willa regarded with narrowed eyes and a pucker between her eyebrows. "What is it?"

"Clothes."

Surprise made her blink. "Clothes? I don't understand. If you need clothes, you can buy them. You don't have to play for them."

"I'm not going to play for mine. I want to play for yours."

"That makes no sense."

"It does if you're playing by my rules. Every hand I win, you have to give up something you are wearing. You can start with the ribbon in your hair, if you like."

"And what if I win?"

"I like that you're optimistic." When she wrinkled her nose at him, he said, "I'll tell you what, when I win, you can surrender any piece of yours that you want, and if you win, you can choose the article I have to remove."

"Hmm." She tilted her head to one side as she considered the offer. "I guess you better get those cards then, because the first thing I mean to take from you is that cocky grin."

She did get it . . . eventually . . . but by then she was wearing only a pair of drawers and playing her cards very close to her chest. Still, it was good to see him sober when she won the hand, and even better to hear his breath catch when she tossed the cards in the air and bore him down on the bed. He had to play by her rules then, which meant forfeiting whatever item of clothing struck her fancy no matter what card she pulled from around them.

"I like this game," she said, lying fully on top of him. "I'm still wearing my drawers, and you're wearing me, and I don't even care if you think that makes you the victor."

His devilish chuckle tickled her breasts with its vibration. "You might want to claim your winnings now."

"You think that's important, do you?"

Her grin was a wicked complement to his chuckle. She moved sinuously over him. "It's a little bit important."

Growling softly in her ear, Israel turned Willa over and, in pursuit of their mutual pleasure, proved that loving her was more than a little bit important.

It was everything.

August 1888
Falls Hollow, Colorado

He watched her pause at the head of the stairs and survey the room. Her eyes swept over him and did not return. If she noticed that she had his full attention, she gave no indication. Perhaps she considered it no more than her due. Experience must have taught her that it gave a man a savoring sort of pleasure to look at her. Her pause had been deliberate, had it not? She raised one hand in a graceful, measured arc and placed it on the banister. The gesture drew his gaze away from her face. He doubted that he was alone in following it, but he glanced neither right nor left to confirm his suspicion.

She wore no gloves, no rings. Her hands needed no adornment. Her fingers were long and slender, the nails short but buffed. There was a moment, no more than that, when he could have sworn her hand tightened on the railing, gripping it hard enough for her knuckles to appear in stark, bloodless relief. Curious, his eyes lifted to her face to search for corroborating evidence that she was not quite at her ease. Nothing in her expression gave her away, and when he regarded her hand again, her fingers were merely curved over the rail, pink and perfect, and featherlight in their touch.

Quill McKenna wondered at what price she could be bought.

He had money. He had not planned to spend any of it on a whore, true, but experience had taught him that plans could, and should, change when new facts presented themselves.

She was a new fact, and her presentation damn near took his breath away.

He was not entirely sure why that was so. As a rule, he preferred curves. Round breasts. Rounder bottoms. Soft, warm flesh in the cup of his palms. Also, he was drawn to blondes. Strawberry. Gold. Corn silk. Honey. Ash. Wheat. He liked a woman he could tuck under his chin. There was a certain comfort there, her being just so high that she was tuckable. Blue eyes, of course, liquid, lambent, and promising. He appreciated a woman who made promises, whether or not she intended to honor them. It kept him hopeful.

The woman standing on the lip of the uppermost step had none of the physical features that he typically admired. From face to feet, he counted more angles than curves. High cheekbones and a small pointed chin that was softened by the shadowed hint of a center cleft defined her oval face. Heavily applied lip rouge the color of ripe cherries accented the wide lush line of her mouth. Her eyes were almond shaped. He could not make out their precise color, but he doubted they were blue. Her hair, hanging loose behind her back, evoked the colors of night, not noon. Nothing about this woman was as it should be, and yet he continued to stare, knowing himself to be oddly fascinated.

With the exception of the brothel's madam, who wore an emerald green silk gown and matching green slippers, the whores who worked for her appeared in various states of dress—or undress, as it were. Sleeveless, loose-fitting, white cotton shifts that dipped low at the neckline seemed to be preferred, and fallen straps artfully arranged around plump arms exposed naked shoulders. The women wore the shifts under tightly laced corsets to accentuate hourglass figures. Most of the whores sported ruffled knickers that they tugged above their knees. A few wore black stockings and black ankle boots. Some wore no stockings at all and red or silver kid slippers.

Quill had spent enough time in uniform to recognize one when he saw it. The woman at the top of the stairs wore a variation of the theme. The straps of her shift rested on her shoulders; perhaps because she had not yet resigned herself to the languid, lounging posture of her sisters who occupied overstuffed sofas, wide armchairs, and the laps of contented cowboys and miners.

She apparently had no use for a corset, and the shift hung straight to the middle of her calves. There was no flash of ruffle to indicate that she wore knickers. It was an intriguing notion that she might be naked under the shift, and the notion was supported by the fact that not only was she without stockings, she was also without shoes. Quill had no memory that he had ever found a barefooted woman immediately desirable, and yet . . .

Judging by the stirring in the room as the woman began her descent, he was not alone in his notions.

Quill's gaze returned to her face, and he saw that her eyes—whatever the color—were no longer surveying the room but had found their target. He tracked the direction to the source and discovered a man of considerable height and heft standing in the brothel's open doorway. It occurred to Quill that he might have mistaken the reason for the earlier stir in the room. It was certainly possible the madam, her girls, and her patrons had more interest in the man crossing the threshold than they had in the barefoot whore.

Out of the corner of his eye, Quill saw the madam step away from her place beside the upright piano, where she had been turning pages for one of the girls. She came into his line of vision as she approached her new guest. Quill recalled that he had been greeted warmly when he entered the house, but not by the madam. She had smiled and nodded at him, acknowledging his presence, but she had not left her post. Instead, one of the girls—whose name he never caught—relieved him of his hat and gun belt and escorted him to his present chair. Except to fetch him a whiskey, she had not left his side.

Clearly the madam had decided this customer deserved her special attention, although whether it was because he was a favorite or because of his considerable size and the potential threat it posed, Quill had no way of knowing. It occurred to him to put the question to the girl at his side, but then he became aware that her fingers were curled like talons around his forearm where they had only been resting lightly moments before. Posing the question seemed unnecessary. This man represented someone worth fearing.

The madam smiled brightly if a shade stiffly. She held out her hand for his hat and gun belt, neither of which he gave her. Her extended arm hung awkwardly before she withdrew it. She took a visible breath and then spoke. "We've been expecting you, Mr. Whitfield. I suppose this means you heard about our new girl, the one I found especially for you." She tilted her head ever so slightly toward the stairs.

Quill thought the gesture was unnecessary. Mr. Whitfield's gaze had been riveted on the woman on the staircase since he entered the brothel. Quill was not convinced that Whitfield had even seen the madam's outstretched arm or been aware that she wanted to relieve him of his gun.

"By God, you did, Mrs. Fry," he said under his breath. "I'll be damned."

"You will get no argument from me."

Quill suppressed a grin at the madam's cheek. Mrs. Fry had spoken softly, but she was in no danger of being heard even if she had shouted the retort. Whitfield was paying her no mind.

Whitfield lifted his hat, slicked back his hair with the palm of his hand, and then replaced the black Stetson. He sucked in his lips as he took a deep breath. He had the manner of a man calming himself, a man who did not want to appear too eager or at risk for losing control.

Quill's gaze swiveled back to the stairs. The woman was standing on the lip of the bottom step. He could see that she was not as young as she appeared from a distance. He had taken her for eighteen and no more than twenty when she appeared on the landing. He revised that notion now, adding four, maybe five years to his estimate. There was a certain maturity in her level stare, a composure that would not have been carried so easily by someone younger, or someone inexperienced. If the madam had hoped to present a virgin to Mr. Whitfield, she had very much mistaken the matter. It did not seem Mrs. Fry would have made such an obvious error. That could only mean that something else was afoot.

Quill wished he had resisted giving over his Colt. It would have been a comfort just then to have it at his side.

Whitfield's gaze did not shift to the madam when he asked, "What's her name?"

"Katie. Katie Nash."

Whitfield's lips moved as he repeated the name but there was no accompanying sound. He nodded slightly, as though satisfied it suited her, and it struck Quill that there was something inherently reverent in the small gesture.

Mrs. Fry crooked a finger in Katie's direction. "Over here, girl, and make Mr. Whitfield's acquaintance."

Katie took a step forward, smiled.

Whitfield put out his hand, stopping her approach. "You don't have to listen to her," he said. "I'm paying for your time now. You listen to me, Miss Katie Nash, and you and I will do proper acquaintance-making upstairs."

Katie Nash stayed precisely where she was.

The madam boldly cocked a painted eyebrow at Whitfield and turned over her hand, showing her empty palm. Quill thought Mrs. Fry demonstrated considerable temerity to demand payment up front from this customer, especially when it appeared she had made some effort to please him by recruiting Katie Nash for her house. Again, he was not alone in his thinking; he was aware that the girl at his side was holding her breath.

Whitfield stared at the madam's hand for several long moments. He had the broad shoulders and barrel chest befitting a man of his height. His chest jumped slightly as quiet laughter rumbled through him. Abruptly, it was over. He laid his large palm over Mrs. Fry's, covering hers completely. "You must be very certain of my satisfaction." When she did not respond, he said, "In good time, Mrs. Fry. Allow me to be the judge of how well you've done." He waited for the madam to withdraw her hand before he lowered his. He smiled, but it did not reach his eyes, and no one in the parlor was comforted by it.

It was Katie Nash who eased the tension. She ignored Whitfield's earlier edict and crossed the room to stand directly in front of him. With no hesitation, she laid her palms against his chest and raised her face. Her smile held all the warmth that his had not. "About that acquaintance making . . ."

As though mesmerized, he blinked slowly.

Katie Nash's dark, unbound hair swung softly as she tilted her head in the direction of the stairs. "I have whiskey in my room. Mrs. Fry told me what you most particularly like."

Quill did not doubt that Miss Nash was speaking to something more than Whitfield's taste in liquor. Whitfield seemed to know it, too. Quill almost laughed as the man nodded dumbly.

Katie's palms slid across Whitfield's chest to his upper arms, and after a moment's pause, glided down to his shirt cuffs. Her long fingers were still not long enough to completely circle his wrists. She held them loosely, lifted them a fraction, and then dropped the left one in favor of taking him by the right hand. "Come with me," she said. And when he did not move, she tugged and turned, and led him, docile as a lamb, toward the staircase.

Quill tracked them as they climbed. They were just more than three-quarters of the way up when he was seized by a sudden impulse to follow. He did not realize that he had in some way communicated that urge until he felt his companion's outstretched arm across his chest. He glanced sideways at her, saw the small shake of her head, and released the breath he had not known he was holding. He leaned back the smallest fraction necessary to encourage her to withdraw her restraining arm. When she did, he settled more deeply in his chair, the picture of self-control and containment while every one of his senses was alert to a danger he could not quite identify.

At the top of the stairs Katie Nash and Whitfield turned left and disappeared from view. The moment they were out of sight, there was a subtle, but unmistakable, shift in the mood of the girls, their patrons, and the madam herself. The whore at the piano began playing again, softly at first, and then more loudly as her confidence grew. Someone tittered. A giggle, pitched nervously north of high C, followed. That elicited a chuckle from one of the cowboys, then some deep-throated laughter from another.

Quill did not join in, although the woman beside him did. Without asking if he wanted another drink, she plucked the empty glass from his hand and went to the sideboard to refill it. She returned quickly, a little swing in her nicely rounded hips as she approached. Standing in front of him, she held out the glass. When he took it, she eased herself onto his lap.

"So what about you?" she asked, sliding one arm around Quill's neck as she fit her warm bottom comfortably against his thighs. "What is it I can do for you, Mr.—" She stopped and made a pouty face. "I do not believe you told me your name. I would remember." She leaned in so her lips were close to his ear. Her warm breath tickled. "I remember names. I am very good at it."

"I can't say the same right now," he said. "I don't recall yours."

She sat up, the pout still defining the shape of her mouth. "Honey. They call me Honey on account of my hair." With this, she tilted her head to one side so a fall of curls cascaded over her shoulder. She fingered the tips. "See? You can touch. It feels like honey. Soft, you know. But thick, too."

"Viscous."

"What? Did you say vicious?"

"Viscous. Thick and sticky."

"Oh." Her pout disappeared in place of an uncertain smile. "I suppose." She withdrew her fingers from her hair. A few strands clung stubbornly until she brushed them away. "I don't figure I would mind having your fingers caught in my hair."

"Hmm." Quill's eyes darted toward the top of the stairs.

Honey touched his chin with her fingertip and turned his attention back to her. "Forget about her. You have no cause to worry. Do you see anyone else here showing a lick of concern?"

He did not. There had been interest when she appeared, but it was Whitfield's arrival that aroused apprehension. What he felt in the room now that Whitfield was gone was collective relief.

"Quill McKenna."

"How's that again?"

"My name. Quill McKenna."

She smiled, tapped him on the mouth with the tip of her index finger. "I see. Finally." She removed her finger. "Quill. It's unusual, isn't it? What sort of name is it?"

"Mine." He remained expressionless as Honey regarded him steadily.

"Not much for words, are you?"

"Not much."

His response gave rise to Honey's husky chuckle. "That's all right by me," she said. "I'm thinking there's other things we could be doing. You want to finish that drink, maybe go upstairs, have a poke at me?"

He should have wanted her, he thought. When she first approached him, he was glad of it. Honey hair, in color and texture. An abundance of curves. Lambent, cornflower blue eyes. A nicely rounded bottom that fit snugly in his lap and breasts that looked as if they would overflow the cup of his palms to the perfect degree. Spillage, but no waste. Before he saw Katie Nash, this woman would have satisfied him.

Quill finished his drink, knocking it back in a single gulp, and placed the glass on the side table. He held Honey's eyes and jerked his chin toward the stairs. She grinned, took him by the hand as she wiggled off his lap, and Quill gave her no reason to think he did not enjoy it. She drew him to his feet, letting him bump against her before she coyly turned and led him to the steps. Giving him an over-the-shoulder glance, she released his hand and began to climb.

Quill followed until she reached the top. She went right; he went left.

"My room's this way," she said when she realized he was no longer behind her. Quill ignored her and she hurried after him, looping her arm through his. She tugged hard enough to pull him up. "The other way."

"Show me where her room is." Gaslight flickered in the narrow hallway. Shadows came and went across Honey's troubled face as she shook her head vigorously. Quill was unmoved. "Show me."

"No. It's nothing but trouble for me if I do. You, too."

"I'll knock on every door." He counted them quickly. "All four."

In response, Honey doubled her efforts to hold him back by circling her other arm around his. She squeezed. "You don't understand. You're a stranger here. Let it be."

Quill looked down at her restraining arms and then at her. "I don't want to hurt you, and I will if I have to shake you off. And I *will* shake you off. Let me go." He was used to being taken at his word, but she was right that he was a stranger, and so he allowed her a few extra moments to make a decision about the nature of his character. He held her gaze until he felt her arms relax, unwind, and then fall back to her sides. "Which room?" he asked quietly.

Honey tilted her head in the direction of the room on her right. "You are hell bent on makin' trouble, aren't you?"

Quill had no answer for that, at least not one that he cared to entertain now, so he merely shrugged. He was not surprised when Honey, clearly disappointed by his lack of response, sighed heavily.

"Go," she said, waving him on. "But don't ever say you weren't—" She stopped abruptly, startled by a thud heavy enough to make the door she had pointed out shudder in its frame. A second thud, only a slightly weaker echo of the first, caused the floor to vibrate.

Quill moved quickly, pushing at the door while it was still juddering. He expected some give in it, but there was none. He looked over at Honey. She had turned toward him, hands raised, palms out, a gesture that was meant to absolve her of all responsibility and remind him he was on his own.

Behind the door, Quill could hear scuffling sounds and labored breathing. He examined the door; saw there was no lock plate, and therefore no key. He raised an eyebrow at Honey. This time she was the one who shrugged.

Quill turned the knob again and threw his shoulder into the door. It moved a fraction, but he could feel resistance on the other side. From below stairs, he heard Mrs. Fry calling for Honey. She did not hesitate to desert him to answer the summons. Once he heard Honey offer assurances to the madam, he paid no more attention to their exchange.

When Quill put his shoulder to the door again, it moved just enough for him to insert his fingers between the door and frame and provide additional leverage.

"Good way to get your knuckles crushed."

Quill recognized the voice immediately, and nothing about it was masculine. He withdrew his fingers.

"Very wise."

Katie Nash did not show herself in the narrow opening, but neither did she close it. Quill did not know what to make of that. "Are you all right?" he asked.

"No one's holding a gun to my head, if that's what you mean."

He wondered if that were true. He heard some more scuffling, a husky moan, and then . . . nothing. He glanced down the hallway and saw that Honey was no longer standing at the top of the stairs. He waited several long beats before he pushed at the door a third time.

The response he got for his effort was, "What do you want?"

"In."

"I am with someone."

"I know."

"I do not entertain two men at one time." A brief pause. "Unless they are brothers. I believe I would make an exception for brothers."

"Winfield *is* my brother."

"His name is Whitfield."

"That's his *last* name. Winfield's his first."

"Uh-huh."

Her dry response raised Quill's smile. He was coming around to the notion that she was just fine, but before he quite got there, he heard her swear softly. This was followed by another thud against the door, this one hard enough to shut it in his face. "Oh, for God's sake," he muttered, and twisted the knob and pushed.

This time he was met with little resistance, which made his entrance ungainly as he more or less fell over himself crossing the threshold. He stumbled clumsily past the woman he meant to save.

"That's one way to do it," she said, not sparing him a glance as she pushed the door closed behind him.

Quill straightened, regaining his equilibrium if not his dignity, and turned. He was glad she did not look up as astonishment had momentarily made him slack-jawed. She was kneeling at Mr. Whitfield's side, testing the ropes that trussed that former tree of a man into something more closely resembling a stump. He lay awkwardly and uncomfortably curled on his side by virtue of the fact that his wrists and ankles were now bound behind him. His sweat-stained neckerchief was wadded in his mouth, secured by a piece of linen that Quill recognized as a strip torn from the hem of Katie Nash's shift.

He watched her place a hand on Whitfield's shoulder, shake him hard enough to rattle his teeth if he had not been gagged and unconscious, and then, apparently satisfied, raise herself so she could rock back on her heels and finally turn narrowed eyes on him.

"Well," he said. "So it's true."

She cocked an eyebrow at him. "What's true?"

"The ropes and gag. My brother's proclivities in the bedroom run to the peculiar." He thought she might smile, but she didn't. She continued to stare at him, more suspicious than curious.

"I was concerned about you," he said.

"Can't think of a reason why that should be so."

"Just now, neither can I." Quill's gaze darted to Whitfield and then to the clothes scattered across the floor. His gun belt hung over the headboard. The man certainly had been eager. She had managed to subdue him while he was still wearing his union suit, but even that was unbuttoned to the navel. Whitfield had a chest of hair like a grizzly. His cock was a small bulge pressing weakly against the front flap of his drawers. It occurred to Quill that stumbling through a door was a lesser indignity than being laid low with a cock curled in on itself like a slug.

When Quill's attention returned to her, his eyebrows

beetled as he scratched lightly behind his right ear. "I admit to being a tad perplexed."

She stood, hands at her sides. "A tad?"

"A touch. A mite. A bit."

"I know what 'a tad' means."

"Good. It's better if I don't have to explain."

"Words I live by." She pointed to Whitfield. "You want to give me a hand, you being here and all? Uninvited, for a fact."

"Depends. Are you going to drop him out the window?"

"A temptation, but no. Help me get him on the bed and then tell Mrs. Fry she can send for Joe Pepper. He's the sheriff."

"All right." He observed that his agreement seemed to make her more suspicious, not less. "Did you expect an argument?"

She said nothing for a moment then her cheeks puffed with an expulsion of air. "Not sure what I expect. You're not a bounty hunter, are you?"

"No, ma'am."

"That's no good," she said, more to herself than to him.

"How's that again?"

"I said it's no good. You would lie about it if you were."

"Lying doesn't come naturally to me. I have to work real hard at it."

"Are you working hard now?"

"No, ma'am."

"Katie," she said. "Call me Katie."

"I don't think that's your name." If he had not been watching her closely, he would have missed her almost imperceptible start. It pleased him that he had guessed correctly, though he took pains not to show it.

"You were sitting beside Honey downstairs. I saw you. You heard Mrs. Fry tell Whit my name."

"I heard what she said. I am no longer certain I believe it."

"I can't be responsible for what you believe. Call me Katie or nothing at all. Now, you take his shoulders while I get his feet."

It was no easy task hoisting the man she called Whit, so they dragged and carried and dragged some more, and heaved him onto the bed together. Whit made unintelligible guttural sounds but never woke up.

"He's a big one," Quill said. "What did you use to put him down?" When she did not answer, he surveyed the room again, overlooking the scattered clothes and gun belt this time. His eyes fell on the whiskey bottle on the bedside table and the twin tumblers beside it. Only one of the tumblers still had whiskey in it. "Remind me not to drink from that bottle."

"Suit yourself." She picked up the glass that held a generous finger of liquor and knocked it back. Smiling ever so slightly, she replaced the tumbler on the table.

Eyeing the bottle again, Quill said, "I don't suppose he is worth laying a bottle of good whiskey to waste, not when you can drop chloral hydrate into his drink."

She gave him no direct response, pointing to the door instead. "You are supposed to tell Mrs. Fry about getting Joe Pepper."

"Right. The sheriff." His eyes darted briefly to Whitfield. "He's going to come around soon, a big man like that. Will you be—" He did not finish his sentence because she gave him a withering look. "I am going now."

Quill did not have an opportunity to close the door; she closed it for him. He had not yet taken two steps when he heard the telltale sounds of a chair banging against the door and then being fitted securely under the knob. Shaking his head, he went in search of Mrs. Fry and discovered that the twin parlors on the first floor were largely deserted.

Honey, he saw, had found another lap to warm. He meant to give her a wide berth, but she put out a hand to stop him when he would have walked by. "If you're looking for Mrs. Fry, she's gone for the sheriff herself. I warned you not to interfere."

He frowned. "What are you saying? She's not bringing the sheriff here for me."

"You certain about that?"

"He's coming for Whitfield."

Honey shrugged, dropping her hand. "Two birds. One stone."

Quill looked to Honey's companion for confirmation, but the lanky cowboy had his face in the curve of her neck and was rooting like a piglet to his mama's teat. He regarded Honey's guileless expression and wondered what he could believe. After a moment's consideration, he said, "I'll take my chances."

She merely smiled and ruffled her cowboy's hair. "Upstairs, lover. You can nuzzle at your leisure."

Quill stood back as the pair got to their feet. He watched Honey pull her cowboy along just as she had pulled on him. It was as choreographed a move as any he had seen in a Chicago dance hall, and while he could appreciate, even admire, the practice needed to acquire the skill that made such moments appear spontaneous, he had a deeper regard for those moments between a man and a woman that *were* spontaneous.

He turned away before Honey and her new partner reached the stairs. No one was at the piano. The brothel was as quiet as it had been when Whit came calling. He approached a pair of whores drinking beer in a dark corner of the main parlor. Although they looked up when he came upon them, neither gave an indication they welcomed his attention. Just the opposite was true. Their expressions were identically sullen.

"Mrs. Fry," he said. "Where can I find her?" At first, Quill thought they did not mean to answer him, but then they traded glances, shrugged simultaneously, and pointed to the front door.

"She's really gone for Joe Pepper?" he asked.

They nodded, and the one with a drooping green velvet ribbon in her hair was moved to add, "Had to, what with you causin' such a fuss. The menfolk that took off kicked up dust like stampeding cattle. You cost us some earnings there."

The whore who wore a cameo pendant around her neck said, "The ones who stayed skedaddled to the rooms. I expect they're under the beds, not on them."

Quill frowned, but he said, "All right. I suppose you can tell the sheriff that I am waiting for him upstairs."

"As if we wouldn't," said Droopy Ribbon.

It occurred to Quill to retrieve his hat and gun belt, but then he thought better of it. There was no sense in tempting fate, and Whit was no longer armed. That evened things out if he came around, and the Colt was useless against Katie Nash. Quill had never shot a woman, never pointed a gun at one, and if he were going to start now, he figured he would take aim at Miss Droopy Ribbon or her equally bad-tempered companion, Miss Cameo Pendant.

That thought buoyed him all the way to where Mr. Whitfield was being held, and he was still grinning when he politely knocked on the door.

"Is that you, Joe Pepper?"

"No. Not Sheriff Pepper. But he will be here directly if that eases your mind."

"My mind is not uneasy."

"That's good. A clear conscience is a comfortable companion."

"Who said that?"

"I thought I just did. Why? Did it seem profound?" Quill drew back when he heard the chair being moved aside. A moment later the door opened, although she blocked his entrance with a hand placed on either side of the frame.

"It seemed," she said, "like something a badly behaved schoolboy would have to write repetitively. Probably under his teacher's watchful eye."

A small vertical crease appeared between Quill's eyebrows as he gave her observation full consideration. A few strands of sun-licked hair fell across his forehead when he tipped his head sideways. He raked them back absently, still mulling. When he was done, his face cleared and he regarded her with guileless blue-gray eyes.

"No," he said. "I never put chalk to a slate to write something like that. I think it is an original thought."

"Well, damn. When I woke this morning, I did not anticipate standing in the presence of a man with an original thought, and yet here I am, practically basking in his glow. My day is steadily improving, wouldn't you say?"

Quill grinned. "You think I have a glow?" A chuckle stirred at the back of his throat when her eyes narrowed—green eyes, he noticed, not blue, not soft, but remarkably fine in their own way, sharp and sentient, a shade sly, and framed by a sweep of thick, dark lashes. She surprised him by opening the door wider and gesturing him to enter. Afraid she would change her mind, he did not hesitate to accept the invitation.

Whit was still bound and gagged on the bed, though it was clear from the state of the covers and the angle of his body that he had been restless in Quill's absence. "He woke?" asked Quill.

"Briefly."

Quill did not ask how she subdued him a second time. He suspected that a careful inspection of Whit's skull would reveal a lump or two. The man's revolver was no longer in its holster. Instead, the .36 caliber Remington rested on the windowsill, far outside of Whit's reach should he free himself. He did wonder for a moment if Whit was still alive, but then he observed a breath shudder through the big man and had his answer.

"I wasn't sure you would let me in," he said.

She shrugged. "I wasn't sure I could keep you out."

He nodded, looked her over. She was no longer wearing the cotton shift; or rather she was no longer wearing *only* the cotton shift. He supposed it was under her black-and-white-striped sateen dress, along with a tightly laced corset, a chemise, a flounced petticoat, a wire bustle of only moderate size, white or black stockings, suspenders to hold them up, and knickers. Courtesy of the corset and bustle, there was an illusion of curves, but Quill did not think they suited her.

"You dressed," he said.

"Nothing gets past you."

His grin came and went like quicksilver. "The sheriff should be here soon. Mrs. Fry had already gone to get him when I went downstairs. It appears there is some confusion about her mission. Honey seems to think she's bringing Joe Pepper here for me."

"And?"

Quill pointed to the bed. "He's the one roped like a calf for branding."

"He sure is. You, on the other hand, are still free to go. You probably should."

Quill decided not to pursue it. It would require a conversation with Joe Pepper to make sense of what the women were saying. "Mind if I sit?" he asked.

"Suit yourself."

He ignored the room's only chair and sat on the oak chest at the foot of the bed. That put his back to Whitfield, but he was confident that he would feel the man stir. The room was sparsely furnished but cluttered nonetheless. The surface of the vanity was crowded with pots of creams, perfumes, and a pitcher and basin. One door of the wardrobe was ajar, stuck in that open position by a white froth of petticoats spilling out from the bottom. Hanging over the knobs was an array of limp velvet ribbons in a rainbow of colors, all except for green.

"Huh," he said. Aware that she was watching him, he lifted his head and turned to her. "This is not your room."

"Huh," she said.

"The ribbons," he said, although she did not ask for an explanation. "They belong to one of the women still sitting downstairs. This is her room." When she merely shrugged, he asked, "Do you even work here?"

"Today I do."

"Are you a whore?"

"Whit certainly thinks so."

"What am I supposed to think?"

"Whatever you like."

"Huh." His blue-gray eyes made another head-to-toe assessment, which he observed tested the limits of her patience. Although her placid expression remained firmly in place, Quill detected a flutter at the hem of her gown indicative of a rhythmically tapping foot.

"Well?" she asked. "Are you decided?"

"I am."

"And?"

"It doesn't matter."

"I don't understand."

"Whether you're a whore or not. It doesn't matter."

"Oh."

He smiled because her features finally hinted at the confusion she was feeling. Her foot had stopped tapping, and he supposed that was because she needed to regain her balance. She had no idea what to make of what he said, even less idea what to make of him. That was all right. The confusion should not be solely on his side.

"Who are you?" she asked.

"Are you asking for my name or seeking a broader answer to the nature of my existence?"

She retreated to the straight-backed chair he had ignored and, much like a deflated balloon, abruptly sank. A soft whoosh of air accompanied the movement. She blinked. "Jesus, Mary, and Joseph."

"No," he said. "Quill McKenna." The squinty-eyed look she gave him made him steal a glance at the windowsill. The Remington revolver was still there.

"I would not use the Remington." She turned over her right hand, revealing a bulge at her wrist beneath the long sleeve of her gown. "Derringer."

"Ah. Some things do get past me."

"It happens." She settled her hands in her lap, threading her fingers together. "I am not sufficiently provoked to shoot you. Yet."

"Good to know."

"So, Quill McKenna, what matter of business brings you to Falls Hollow?"

"No business. Passing through."

"On your way to . . ."

"Stonechurch. That's near—"

"Leadville. Yes. I know where it is. Stonechurch Mining. You can't pitch a nickel there without hitting something named after the man himself."

"Ramsey Stonechurch."

She snorted softly. "Ramses is more like it. The pharaoh."

"People call him that?"

"Not to his face. Not that I ever heard."

"You know him?"

"I know *of* him."

"Then he has never sought your . . . um, services."

She smiled thinly. "Um, no."

"Have you been to—" Quill stopped, distracted by footfalls on the stairs. "Company." He cocked his head, listened, and held up two fingers.

"Mrs. Fry and the sheriff," she said. "This is your last chance to leave."

Since the window was his only exit, he shook his head.

Shrugging, she stood, smoothed the front of her gown, and went to greet Joe Pepper and the madam. Her mistake, she reflected immediately, was in not confirming identities before she opened the door. It seemed that Mr. Whitfield had at least two friends, and she was confronting the pair of them across the threshold. She nodded to each in turn, one half a head taller than she, the other at eye level. Black Stetsons shadowed their broad, squared-off faces. The taller of the two had a silver-studded hatband and stubble on his chin. The shorter one's hat sported a sweat-stained leather band. He was clean-shaven. They both carried Remington revolvers, and both guns were still strapped.

"Gentlemen," she said, genial in spite of the fact that they were more interested in looking past her than at her. She might have been insulted if it had not served her purpose.

"He's really here," the taller one said. "Damn me if she wasn't telling the truth."

"I didn't doubt her, not after you knocked her sense in and her teeth out."

"Gentlemen? Who did the knocking? And who was knocked?"

The shorter one jerked his thumb at his compatriot. "Not me. Him."

"Mrs. Goddamn Fry," the compatriot said. "How about you stepping aside?"

She did not move. Her mind whirled. If this pair had intercepted Mrs. Fry on her way to the sheriff's office, that meant Joe Pepper was not coming, and with so much time having already passed, that seemed the likeliest scenario. She lifted her left hand and placed it on the door frame while she shrugged her right shoulder. The movement was as casual as it was calculated. The derringer slipped comfortably into her palm, unnoticed by either of them. She would have one shot. Her chances of making it count, should it prove necessary, were improved by the fact that the guns of both men were still strapped.

"Step aside," the taller one said again.

This time she did, pivoting out of the way before they hurried past her. It did not surprise her that Quill McKenna was not in sight. Although she primarily worked alone, and entered into partnerships with considerable reluctance, she had not forgotten her guest or the reason for his interference in the first place: *I was concerned about you*. Perhaps it was not a lie. Not only had McKenna disappeared, so had Whitfield's gun belt and gun. The chair she had been sitting on was now the resting place for petticoats, shifts, chemises, and a bright scarlet corset.

She did not permit herself to glance at the wardrobe, although she doubted Whit's friends would have noticed. They only had eyes for him.

The short one nudged the bed with his knee so that it shook slightly. Whitfield did not stir. "Is he alive?"

"Would he still be tied if he wasn't? Use your head, Amos." He looked to Katie for an explanation. "Who did this to him?"

So Mrs. Fry had not given her up. "I don't know," she said. "I was told to sit with him until the sheriff came. I did not see what happened."

He watched her closely, looking for the lie. He knuckled his stubble thoughtfully. "This is on account of that whore he tussled with the last time he was in town."

"You must mean Daria. I've only heard things, you

understand. Whispered things. I am new to the house and not long for it what with the goings-on tonight."

Amos leaned forward and began tugging on Whit's gag. His fingers were clumsy on the knot, and after several attempts he gave up and yanked the strip of linen down and removed it. Whit snuffled, sucked in a mouthful of air, and began to snore. Sighing heavily, Amos straightened. "I don't see how we're going to get him to his horse. Whit's not a lightweight in any circumstance, Chick, and in this circumstance, he's a deadweight."

Chick ignored his partner and continued to direct his attention elsewhere. "What do you know about that whore's kin? Did you hear a whisper maybe that one of them was around tonight? Plenty of folks knew Whit was coming back today. Could be someone was waiting for him."

"I never heard anyone say that she had kin. Most of us don't, or we have kin that don't claim us."

Chick's dark eyes narrowed as they settled on her mouth. "You haven't taken a notion in your head to protect someone, have you?" He did not wait for a response. "Because I have to tell you, that would be as foolish a notion as there ever was. I got the sense that you're the sort of woman that Whit would want under him. Hair color's right. He likes it dark. And you're on the bony side of thin. You put me a little in mind of his sister, fragile-like." He elbowed Amos to get his attention. "What do you think? Does she put you in mind of Whit's sister?"

"Not sayin' one way or the other. Hell, I'm not even going to think about it. The way Whit talks about her, it ain't right."

Chick shrugged. "Just an observation. It makes me wonder if you were bait, you being new to Mrs. Fry's establishment, her being a businesswoman who doesn't want her girls roughed so they can't work. You have anything to say to that?"

"No," she said. "I don't."

He grunted softly, skeptically, but then turned his back while he helped Amos tear at the knots at Whit's ankles.

"Would it help if you had a knife?" she asked as she looked on with interest.

"Yeah, it'd help," said Chick. "Do you have one?"

"No, but I can get one from the kitchen." She started to turn, but Chick barked at her to stop. She tried another tack. "Perhaps some cold water in his face would bring him around. Then he could walk out on his own."

"Well, do you have *that* here?"

"Behind you, on the vanity. The pitcher's half full."

"All right. Bring it here."

She did, holding it in her left hand so she could grip it properly without interference from the derringer. When she returned to the bed, she went around to the side opposite Amos and Chick so she was facing Whitfield. His eyes were still closed. Except for the occasional snore shuddering through him, he was quiet. Amos and Chick had been successful at untying the ropes, and Chick was unfolding Whitfield's stiff legs while Amos tried to arrange his arms in what he imagined was a more comfortable position.

Comprehending her time for action was short, she cleared her throat and held up the pitcher. Amos and Chick looked up in unison and, confronted by her genial smile, did not see the shower of water coming at them until they were wet-faced and sputtering. She threw the pitcher, aiming for Chick's head, but he sidestepped it, and it glanced off his shoulder and hit Amos squarely in the jaw. Amos yelped, palming the side of his face while Chick momentarily lost his mind and threw himself across Whit and the bed to get to her.

She raised her right hand and delivered a hard blow to the crown of his head with the derringer still in her palm. He collapsed, arms and legs splayed, pinning his friend under him. She entertained the fleeting thought that she was fortunate the pistol did not discharge because then she would have no defense against the revolver Amos was trying to draw. He fumbled with the strap in the same manner he had fumbled with the knots.

"Leave it," she said. "Leave it or I will shoot."

Amos's fingers stopped twitching. He blinked rapidly; water dripped from his eyes like tears. When he could see clearly, he stared at the derringer and put his hands out.

"Easy now. Go easy. Just tryin' to do a friend a favor. You mind if I look after Chick? You clobbered him pretty hard."

"He's fine."

"Maybe I could just pull him off Whit."

"You can try."

Amos started to reach for Chick's legs and then stopped abruptly. He straightened.

She smiled. "Uh-huh. I'll shoot."

"You ain't right. In the head, I mean. Even for a whore, you ain't right."

She declined to comment, asking instead, "Where did you and Chick leave Mrs. Fry?"

"Behind Sweeney's. We bumped into her when we was leaving the saloon. Since we was coming here anyway on account of what we heard inside, Chick decided we should escort her around back and hear what she had to say for herself. Chick's the one who knocked her around. I told him to pull his punches. You gotta know, I made him stop. We left her alive on account of that."

"All right," she said, believing about half of what he told her. "Take off your gun belt—carefully—put it on the floor and kick it under the bed."

"Aw, Jeez. Don't make me give it up, I—" He stopped. "I know. You'll shoot if I don't."

"No," she said, surprising him. Her eyes darted to the wardrobe, where Quill McKenna was finally stepping out. "But I'm fairly certain he will."

Amos turned his neck so sharply that vertebrae cracked. Wide-eyed, he put a hand to his nape and massaged the crick while he stared at the gun aimed squarely at his chest. "That looks like Whit's gun."

"It should," said Quill. "It *is* his gun." He shook off the ruffled petticoat clinging rather comically to his shoulders, caught it before it reached the floor, and tossed it toward the chair. It spread open, fluttering like angel wings, and mostly covered the scarlet corset when it dropped. He intercepted Katie's amused glance and gave her a much less amused one in exchange.

"I have you to thank for smelling like attar of roses," he told her. "Droopy Ribbon must wash everything she owns in the stuff."

"You could have hidden under the bed."

"You could have shown more caution opening the door. You did when I was doing the knocking."

"I had reason to be suspicious then."

"I wasn't carrying."

"I didn't need your help. Still don't."

"And I didn't want to give it just now. Still don't."

"So why . . ."

"Leg cramp."

"Really?"

"Yes." Quill sneezed. "That, and I don't like the smell of roses."

Amos listened to this exchange, eyes darting back and forth, fascinated in spite of himself. He carefully released the gun strap, and his hand curled around the butt of the Remington. He drew the gun out slowly.

The barrel just cleared his tooled leather holster when they both shot him.

Jo Goodman is the *USA Today* bestselling author of numerous romance novels, including *This Gun for Hire*, *In Want of a Wife*, and *True to the Law*, and is also a fan of the happily ever after. When not writing, she is a licensed professional counselor working with children and families in West Virginia's Northern Panhandle. Visit her online at jogoodman.com or facebook.com/jogoodmanromance.

Also available from
USA Today bestselling author

JO GOODMAN

Boots Under Her Bed

From four acclaimed authors come four all-new novellas featuring the rugged men of the West and the women who want them . . .

FROM JODI THOMAS . . . Callie has done a lot of crazy things, but it'll take one more to prove she isn't nuts: find a husband, fast!

FROM JO GOODMAN . . . Felicity Ravenwood was raised to be independent-minded, but when this runaway bride opposes her father's choices, it is up to Nat Church to bring her around.

FROM KAKI WARNER . . . Two strangers on a train have more in common than they know—both have hidden purposes and ties to a Nebraska bank robbery.

FROM ALISON KENT . . . When runaway New York socialite Maeve Daugherty joins her father's bodyguard Zeb Crow on his personal mission of revenge, what was a slightly scandalous new life as a bookkeeper for an infamous San Antonio brothel becomes downright dangerous.

M1595T1114

ALSO AVAILABLE FROM
USA TODAY BESTSELLING AUTHOR

JO GOODMAN

True to the Law

Private detective Cobb Bridger is on the hunt for a treacherous beauty, who's stolen a priceless artifact from a wealthy man. But the more he investigates Tru Morrow, the less he believes her guilty—and the more he wants to let her in . . .

PRAISE FOR *TRUE TO THE LAW*

"Engrossing . . . Engaging characters and a well-plotted story will captivate the reader all the way to the satisfying conclusion."

—Publishers Weekly

jogoodman.com
facebook.com/jogoodmanromance
facebook.com/LoveAlwaysBooks
penguin.com

M1596T1114